praise for Trici

'A book you can't put down … Stringer's skill is in weaving the experiences of different generations of women together, with sensitivity and familiarity, gently showing how context can shape women's decisions. … A moving, feel-good, warm read about strong, loving women … the exact book we all need right now.'

—*Mamamia*

'a polished family saga … all delivered with intelligence, wit and emotion in equal measures. … Perfection!'

—*Better Reading*

'Tricia Stringer is an intuitive and tender-hearted storyteller who displays a real ability to interrogate issues that affect families and individuals. *The Family Inheritance* is another gratifying read from Tricia Stringer.'

—*Mrs B's Book Reviews*

'Tricia Stringer has written a gorgeous book … The pages are filled with wonderful characters, each with their own well-crafted arc and polished prose. This book is the equivalent of a hot bath or a box of chocolates, it's comforting and an absolute pleasure to immerse yourself in. It's realistically romantic, filled with hope, a tale of second chances. If you enjoy well-written family sagas, look no further. *The Model Wife* is perfect.'

—*Better Reading*

'Tricia Stringer's *The Model Wife* is a beautiful multi-dimensional family saga.'

—*Beauty and Lace*

'[A] heartfelt saga.'

'Tricia Stringer excels at two things: strong, empathetic characters; and finding an experience or emotion shared by many, then spinning that small kernel of commonality into an engaging novel. *The Model Wife* is no exception ... Stringer's prose is warm and friendly. She pulls you in with an easy and flowing writing style that quickly has you absorbed by the action. It's easy to read, but that doesn't mean it's shallow.'

'A well-written, engaging story of the everyday challenges of life and love ... a wise, warm, and wonderful story'

'Delivers a gentle satisfaction that makes it a great choice for a lazy Sunday afternoon read.'

'A witty, warm and wise story of how embracing the new with an open heart can transform your life.'

'... a moving, feel-good read ... a warm and uplifting novel of second chances and love old and new in a story of unlikely dining companions thrown together on a glamorous cruise.'

'A wonderful story of friendships, heartbreak and second chances that may change your life.'

'Stringer's inviting new novel is sprinkled with moments of self reflection, relationship building, friendships and love.'

—*Mrs B's Book Reviews* on *Table for Eight*

'... a really moving tale ... This truly was a delightful read that left me with that feel-good happy sigh ... be enticed by this tale of love and laughter, trauma and tears, reflection and resolution.'

—*The Royal Reviews* on *Table for Eight*

'This winner from Tricia Stringer ... is a light-hearted and easy-to-read novel with twists and turns along the way ... enjoyable and fun.'

—*The Black and White Guide* on *Table for Eight*

'Tricia has no trouble juggling a large cast and ensuring we get to know and connect with them ... captivated me start to finish; if it wasn't the wishing myself on board for a relaxing and pampered break from reality, it was connecting with the characters and hoping they managed to find what they were looking for. Definitely a book I didn't want to put down!'

—*Beauty and Lace* on *Table for Eight*

'A heart-warming novel that celebrates friendships old and new, reminding us that it's never too late to try again ... If you enjoy stories that explore connections between people and pay tribute to the endurance of love and friendship, you will love Stringer's new novel. *Table For Eight* is a beautiful book ... If you're looking for a getaway but don't quite have the time or funds, look no further – this book is your next holiday. Pull up a deck chair and enjoy.'

—*Better Reading* on *Table for Eight*

Tricia Stringer is a bestselling Australian author of contemporary fiction, historical fiction and rural romance.

Tricia grew up on a farm in country South Australia and has spent most of her life in rural communities, as owner of a post office and book shop, as a teacher and librarian, and now as a full-time writer. She lives in the beautiful Copper Coast region with her husband Daryl. From there she travels and explores Australia's diverse communities and landscapes, and shares this passion for the country and its people through her stories.

For further information go to triciastringer.com or connect with Tricia on Facebook, Instagram @triciastringerauthor or Twitter @tricia_stringer

Also by Tricia Stringer

Table for Eight
The Model Wife

Queen of the Road
Right as Rain
Riverboat Point
Between the Vines
A Chance of Stormy Weather
Come Rain or Shine
Something in the Wine

The Flinders Ranges Series
Heart of the Country
Dust on the Horizon
Jewel in the North

TRICIA STRINGER

the family inheritance

FICTION
HQ

First Published 2020
Second Australian Paperback Edition 2021
ISBN 9781867234630

THE FAMILY INHERITANCE
© 2020 by Tricia Stringer
Australian Copyright 2020
New Zealand Copyright 2020

Published by
HQ Fiction
An imprint of Harlequin Enterprises (Australia) Pty Limited (ABN 47 001 180 918), a subsidiary of HarperCollins Publishers Australia Pty Limited (ABN 36 009 913 517)
Level 13, 201 Elizabeth St
SYDNEY NSW 2000
AUSTRALIA

® and TM (apart from those relating to FSC®) are trademarks of Harlequin Enterprises (Australia) Pty Limited or its corporate affiliates. Trademarks indicated with ® are registered in Australia, New Zealand and in other countries.

A catalogue record for this book is available from the National Library of Australia
www.librariesaustralia.nla.gov.au

Printed and bound in Australia by McPherson's Printing Group

For Nerrilee

one

Felicity

Felicity Lewis paused a minute to take it all in.

It was a balmy night in Adelaide; the temperature had dropped just enough after a hot March day for perfect outdoor entertaining. At number seventeen Herbert Street, West Beach, two streets back from the ocean, a party was in progress. Behind Felicity the carefully selected mood music resonated from the curved teak speaker, enough to be heard but not so loud people couldn't hear themselves speak. It had been a birthday gift from Ian and Greta, not a total surprise, not any kind of surprise. She'd dropped several hints, which included leaving shop brochures lying around opened to pages with the desired gift circled.

The speaker sat on the polished shelf below their wall-mounted television in the big open-plan family room that stretched almost the full width of the back of the house. The glass doors to the deck were all thrown open. Around her milled friends and family enjoying the food she'd cooked and the drinks she'd selected.

Light spilled across the freshly oiled deck and out onto the back lawn where strands of festoon lights, hung in precise loops across the garden, added their glow to the glorious spectacle of a million stars twinkling overhead. It was a perfect autumn evening.

An arm slipped around her waist. "Everything looks fabulous, Mum."

"As do you." Felicity beamed at her daughter.

"I've taken lots of photos of the guests." Greta lifted her phone and leaned her head against Felicity's. "Selfie."

Felicity blinked at the flash. "I haven't had a chance to tell you how good you look in that outfit." She adjusted the soft bow pulling Greta's drapey pants in.

Greta batted her hand away and readjusted the bow. "I don't know that cream is a good colour for me."

"It's perfect against your tan."

"I was thinking more that I'm likely to spill something down it." She glanced around. "Where's Suzie? I haven't seen her yet."

"I told you Paul took her to America for her birthday."

"No you didn't." Greta frowned.

"They'll be gone for two months."

"How will you manage not seeing her for that long?"

"Technology."

"Dad should have taken you away, instead of you doing all this work."

"I've enjoyed it—"

"Oh look, there're the Gilberts. Thank goodness there's someone more my age. I'll get a photo of them too." Greta dashed away.

Once more Felicity stood alone. She'd organised this special night to the last detail, a combined celebration for her fiftieth birthday and the completion of the renovations. She'd been planning, styling, cooking for weeks. The only downside was her best friend Suzie couldn't be there.

Suzie and Paul had only been gone for two weeks and were having the best time. Felicity had already seen the photos of their Caribbean cruise and now they were driving themselves up the coast to New York. Suzie had rung this morning via WhatsApp to sing her happy birthday all the way from Jacksonville, Florida. Her brilliant smile and animated words had filled the room. Felicity had sat for a long time after the call had ended trying to swallow her glum mood and lack of enthusiasm for a party without her best friend. Suzie had provided all the energy for both of them during the call.

"Happy birthday, Felicity." Humphrey from next door drew her into a bear hug and planted one of his sloppy kisses on her cheek.

She adjusted her new glasses firmly back in place as his wife Melody also wrapped her in a hug.

"Perfect night for a party," Melody said.

"Thanks for coming. What would you like to drink?" Felicity waved over one of the young uni students Greta had organised to act as waiters for the night.

"Feliciteee, I love what you've done with the house." Pam, her social tennis friend, air kissed her cheeks. "I haven't seen it since you did this back extension, and the deck is fabulous. I can picture us having a few post tennis sessions here." Pam clutched a glass of champagne and as her arm swept out in a dramatic arc it connected with a man just stepping up onto the deck.

"Oh, I'm so sorry." She dabbed at his wet sleeve.

"No problem."

"Pam, I don't think you've met Tony," Felicity said. "He's been overseeing the renovations."

"Has he now?" Pam looked him up and down. "Well, there's a secret you've been keeping to yourself."

"Nice to meet you, Pam." Tony smiled, and offered his hand.

Pam's return look was vampish.

"Let me get you another drink," he said.

The bar was an old table Felicity had scrubbed to create a rustic look, adorned with ice buckets and glasses and one large bowl of flowers in soft pinks and mauves. She'd canned Greta's suggestion of balloons but had allowed the banner, which looped across the sheer curtain she'd hung on the wall behind. In cursive letters cut from sparkly gold it said 'Cheers to fifty years'.

Tony set off towards it. Pam stared after him.

"Did you knock into him on purpose?" Felicity said.

"Moi?"

"He's married." Felicity didn't actually know what Tony's marital status was but he was too nice a man to get tangled up with Pam. Every one of her relationships since her last divorce had ended in drama.

"Really? No ring on his finger."

"You've checked already? He's too young for you."

"Past the age of consent."

"Hi Felicity, Pam." More hugs all round, this time from Tansie, another of their tennis group, and her husband Charles.

"This is Tony," Pam said as he came back with several glasses of sparkling gripped between his two large hands. "He's responsible for Felicity's fabulous renovation."

Tony shrugged. "Felicity was the driving force, I just made sure the structural stuff was legit."

"You're very modest, Tony," Felicity said.

Tansie and Charles were planning a new bathroom and when Felicity could see Tony was safely in a discussion with Charles she edged away.

At the other end of the deck her own husband, Ian, was deep in conversation with their across-the-road neighbours, Sal and Les. Like Ian, they were bike riders. They rode regularly, along with several others from their neighbourhood. Not Felicity, of course. She didn't own a bike and never wanted to. Getting hot and sweaty in lycra had never been her thing. Nor Ian's until they'd moved here. Two years older than her, the approach of his fiftieth birthday had seen him turn into some kind of fitness freak. Not that Felicity minded. She was a homebody and the renovations had kept her busy, first in the planning, then in the construction and the refurbishing. Her workout was her weekly social tennis match and that was more about the company than the exercise.

After they'd moved they'd started taking regular walks to the beach but hadn't gone together in ages. These days Ian power walked everywhere on his own or with his walking group, training for more arduous treks, while she'd been filling her time with colour charts and fabric swatches. Ian had been involved in the renovations when they were deciding on the structural changes to the house but after that he'd been happy to let her make decisions about the finishing touches.

This party was a birthday celebration but also the official end to the whole house renovation, a project that had consumed her since the moment they'd made the decision to buy the fixer-upper more than five years ago. She'd given up her job as practice manager at a doctor's office when they'd moved. Now she'd have to find something else to fill her time. It wasn't until she'd been dressing for the party that she'd realised she had no idea what that would be.

"Have you seen our parents yet?"

Felicity gave her sister a quick look then shook her head. Tall and lanky like their father, June was wearing a grass-green all-in-one jumpsuit. It reminded Felicity of a praying mantis. For two sisters born less than a year apart they were chalk and cheese.

"Not like them to be late," June said.

"Dad's hard to get moving these days."

"We did offer to collect them."

"I'm sure they'll be here soon," Felicity said. It was possible her father had pulled another of his tantrums and they wouldn't turn up at all but she kept that to herself. He could do no wrong in June's eyes but there had been so many times over the years when he'd spoiled celebrations or social occasions.

Her wedding day had been mortifying. Most dads were proud and happy on their daughter's wedding day but not her father. Felicity had caused a ruckus by daring to find a husband before June. Not that June minded but their father did. She was always first in his eyes and Felicity had stolen her position this time.

On the day of the wedding he'd been grumpy, oozing disapproval of the goings-on, as he'd called it, as Felicity and her bridesmaids, were getting ready. Just before they'd been due to leave for the church he'd gone out for a walk – to clear his head, he'd declared. They hadn't been bothered until the photographer was tapping his toes waiting to take the standard father–daughter photos. June had been the one to track him down and drag him home to walk his daughter down the aisle. Their mother had been upset and so had Felicity. They'd arrived fifteen minutes late to the church and for the rest of the day her father had told anyone who'd listen it was because Felicity had been disorganised with her preparations and the household had been carrying on like a bunch of chooks.

"Perhaps I should ring Mum." June cut into her thoughts.

"Let's leave it for a while. They'll turn up."

Hazel Gifford was a saint to have put up with her husband all these years and if her father was in one of his moods Felicity would rather he didn't come.

"Oh, isn't that your old neighbour talking to Derek?" June waved in the direction of her husband and another man, both towering over the crowd. "The one that lived down the road and sold up and bought a caravan."

"Yes."

"Such a lovely couple. Can't see her, what were their names, but then she's so short, isn't she." June set off towards the new arrivals without waiting for an answer.

Instead of following her Felicity stepped down off the deck, fanning her face with her hand. The air was slightly cooler out from under the verandah and she relished it. Hormone replacement tablets ensured the hot flushes of menopause didn't affect her too terribly but just at that moment she felt as if her internal thermostat was ready to boil over. She moved further away and took the path to a corner of the yard that wasn't lit. From her vantage point she had time to let her body cool down, to take a breath and observe. She'd been on her feet since she got out of bed this morning and she needed a few minutes to regroup.

She enjoyed creating special dinners for friends, loved parties and entertaining, but she was far better at the preparation, the cooking and the serving than the conversation. If it wasn't for Ian insisting they go out for dinner, see an exhibition, travel, she'd simply stay home in her comfy clothes and slippers.

It had been more her idea to move than his but he'd gone along with it, liking their proximity to the beach and the walking and bike trails. His income was a good one and even though they'd extended their small mortgage to do the renovations they were comfortable these days. Felicity had been careful to stick to the budget they'd allocated and they hadn't overcapitalised.

She took in the sleek lines of the back of the house, the glass, the deck and the party now in full swing. Someone had turned up the music and the voices carried loudly on the still night. All their neighbours were here so the noise shouldn't bother anyone. They'd been lucky with the people in their small street. Ian had made it his business to get to know them all as soon as they'd moved in and they'd proved to be a friendly lot. She was glad they could all come. Even a few who'd moved away were here.

"What's the birthday girl doing out here on her own?" Ian came towards her, a glass of champagne in each hand. He offered her one, brushed a kiss across her forehead and tapped his glass against hers. "Happy birthday, Lissie." She smiled, took a sip and watched as he did the same.

"Thanks," she said. Ian rarely drank these days so she was pleased by the sentiment and that it was just the two of them.

"I should make a speech soon and you should cut the cake before our friends drink too much more of this champagne."

"One more minute," she said. Butterflies flapped inside her at the thought of being the centre of attention and she took another sip.

"You wanted this party." Ian's words were accusatory and yet his tone gentle.

"I love parties, just not being the main event."

"Remember my fiftieth? I wanted us to go away but you insisted on a big party instead."

"Hiking the Inca trail to Machu Picchu wouldn't have been a holiday."

"But it was what I wanted."

She looked away from the yearning in his eyes back to the party. "We've been so lucky," she said.

His yes was barely more than a whisper.

"I worry one day it's all going to come crashing down."

He took a sip of his drink before he responded. "That's a morbid thought on your birthday."

"We've had a trouble-free life."

"Not always." This time his reply was quick and sharp then he drew in a long breath and let it out again, slowly. "Remember when we first married. We had nothing."

"Everyone started that way. We lived on love." She smiled at him but he was looking at the crowd.

"You were laid up with that broken ankle and we nearly lost the house."

"That was so long ago it's hard to imagine now." They'd not had income insurance in those days – a combination of thinking they were bulletproof and not being able to afford it. She'd asked her father for a loan. He'd refused. Ian came from a big family with not much money to go round but his parents had lent them a bit to get them by. They'd paid them back of course, but it had been a terrible struggle.

"Then the babies we lost." Ian was still staring at the crowd. He was usually a cup-half-full kind of guy. This melancholic side of him was rare.

"I wish I hadn't said anything now." She sipped some champagne then tried a light laugh but the liquid caught in her throat and the laugh came out as a series of clucks.

"There were three little ones we never got to know," he said.

She gripped the stem of her glass. She knew how many babies they'd lost as well as he did. It wasn't something she was ever likely to forget but there was no point bringing it up now. "You really are going down the sad old memory lane. The miscarriages were tough but we've got our beautiful Greta."

"She's a wonderful young woman," he said.

Happy to banish any further maudlin thoughts, Felicity tapped her glass to his. "I'll drink to that."

"We should go back to our guests, get the formalities over then you can relax." He started to walk away, his look distracted. She'd hardly seen him these last few days. She'd been so caught up in party preparations, and now that she thought about it they'd not said more than two words to each other for...she couldn't think how long. Weeks?

"Ian?"

He stopped, turned back. The frown he'd worn changed to a smile but she could tell it was forced. He reached out a hand. "Come on, Lissie. This is your night. Time to face the music and have your friends sing 'Happy Birthday'."

"Mum?" Greta came towards them across the lawn, the brightly lit house glowing behind her. "What are you doing out here? I've been looking everywhere for you." She held her mobile phone towards Felicity. "It's Nan. She sounds upset."

Damn Dad, Felicity thought as she pressed the warm phone to her ear. He's kicked up a fuss and decided not to come. "Hello, Mum."

"Felicity, I tried June's phone."

"She never has it on her."

"Then I tried yours."

"Mum, take a breath. Why aren't you here? Is everything all right?" She hated asking that question knowing everything wouldn't be all right. Not that she really cared but for her mum's sake...

"It's your father."

Felicity pursed her lips. Of course it was her father. "What's he up to this time?" She raised her shoulders and gave a slight shake of her head at Greta and Ian who were both standing by.

"Is June there?" Hazel's voice had an edginess to it. Felicity hoped she wasn't going to have one of her dizzy attacks.

"Not right beside me but she and Derek are here."

Ian began to tap his foot.

"I'll call you back, Mum, we're about to cut the cake."

"Oh, I've ruined your lovely party."

"No, you haven't. I'll bring you some cake and leftovers tomorrow." Damn her dad for his moods. For the zillionth time in her life she wondered how her mother put up with him. Tomorrow there'd be the aftermath of the party to clean up and Felicity would be tired but now she'd be stuck in the car for nearly two hours going to and from her parents when they could have come tonight.

"You'll have to be strong for June," Hazel said.

Ian was tapping his watch now and pointing back to the party.

"Mum, I have to go – can you tell me tomo—"

"Felicity, brace yourself." There was a sharp intake of breath. "Your father's dead."

two

Greta

Greta waved off the last of the partygoers. Not that it had been a party once her father had turned off the music and called for everyone's attention and then instead of a birthday speech he'd announced her grandfather's death. Felicity had ushered June and Derek into her bedroom just beforehand so that she could tell them the terrible news in private. Greta had stayed with them until June's heart-wrenching sobs had been too much. She'd left Derek to support the two women and gone out to fend off the barrage of friends who wanted to offer their condolences.

"It was all so sudden," she'd said. "Mum's with Aunty June. They can't see people now." She'd given robotic reassurances. "They need some time to process it…" and yes of course Greta would pass on their love and sympathy. She swallowed the lump in her own throat. Her eyes remained dry. Perhaps it was the shock. She couldn't comprehend the demanding presence that had been her grandfather was now gone from the world.

"Has everyone left?" Ian came from the back of the house.

"Yes."

"What a terrible way to end a party." He put an arm around her shoulder. "The young ones were great. They've brought in all the food and tidied up the bar. There's no-one outside and I've shut it all up and turned off the lights. We'll deal with the mess tomorrow." He kissed the top of her head. "Where's your mum?"

"In the bedroom with June and Derek. They were going to ring Nan back."

As she spoke, the door behind them opened. Derek came out, his arm around June's shoulders. She was still sobbing into a wad of tissues.

"I'm so sorry, June." Ian reached out and hugged them both. "The guests have all gone. Can I get you something...a drink?"

"Thanks, Ian, but we're going to Franklyn's...to Hazel's place," Derek said. "June doesn't want her mum to be on her own. Felicity says she'll come tomorrow."

The two men nodded at each other, reminding Greta of bobble-headed dogs. Derek ushered June forward. Greta opened the door for them and then shut it once she'd seen them down the path, the gentle glow of the perfectly placed solar lamps lighting their way. She clicked the lock.

"Well, that's the last time he'll do that."

She spun at the harsh tone of Felicity's voice.

Her mother was framed by the bedroom door, her robust presence diminished by shock, the hair that normally swept across her forehead tufted up as if she'd been dragging her fingers through it.

"Do what, Mum?"

"Ruin one of my parties."

"Mum!"

"I can say what I like about him." Felicity's look was defiant then her mouth crumpled. "He could be such a bugger but...

but…he was my dad." She pulled off her glasses as tears began to roll down her cheeks.

"Come on, love." Ian put an arm around her shoulders. "I'll make us all a cup of tea."

"I'll be there in a minute," Greta said. "I'm just going to call Joe." She pointed in the direction of the bedroom she still claimed as her own and had planned to spend the night in, even though she and Joe shared a townhouse now.

Once inside she shut the door and sagged to the bed, relieved to be away from her mother's intense emotion and glad the party was over, even though it had taken her grandad's death to end it. She took her phone from her back pocket and flopped backwards onto the pile of pillows Felicity decorated the beds with. Dolly the family cat lifted her head with a startled expression.

"Sorry, Doll." Greta slid her hand over the cat's fluffy head and down her back. Dolly settled again and closed her eyes. "I wish I could do that."

It was only ten o'clock, she'd hardly had a drink and yet it felt like it was two in the morning after a huge night out. She looked at her phone. There were the usual Facebook and Insta posts from girlfriends out on a Sunday night of the long weekend. The 'have fun tonight' text she'd sent Joe, just before the first of the guests arrived, remained unanswered. He never understood her need for a response.

She'd badly wanted him to come tonight, to keep her company, and now she wished even more that he was here. She could have done with his strong arms around her right now. Instead he was at a dinner for his cousin's twenty-first. The Sunday night of the long weekend had been chosen by both birthday girls. Like Greta's family, Joe's was small and close-knit. She couldn't miss her mother's birthday and he couldn't miss his family dinner, so now they were in separate places.

She looked at the time again. She'd have thought the dinner would be finished by now. Even though it would take him almost two hours, she'd hoped he might leave as soon as was permissible and turn up at Felicity's party. No point now but she needed to tell him about her grandad. Joe was fond of Franklyn and the feeling had been mutual. In fact sometimes she felt as if her grandad had liked her boyfriend – she glanced at the delicate diamond ring on her left hand – fiancé, better than her, his only granddaughter.

She tried Joe's number but it went straight to voicemail. She couldn't leave such sad news for him to hear goodness knows when. She hung up and sent another text. *Need to talk…*Her fingers hovered over the letters then she added *Urgently. Will be up till late.* And pressed send.

In the family room her parents sat at one end of the table that had been partly cleared of party food. The other end was loaded with cheese platters, plates of dainty sandwiches and assorted pastries. All homemade, of course.

"What am I going to do with all this?" Felicity wailed as Ian moved a platter of partly eaten canapes to make room for Greta and passed her a cup of tea.

"Could we freeze it?" Greta cast her eye over the mountains of food. Her mother always over-catered and the party had been halted before people had really had time to eat much. The beautiful white chocolate mud cake, topped with the flowers that Greta and her dad had spent hours deliberating over before they'd ordered it, perched untouched on the end of the kitchen bench surrounded by plates of dainty cream-filled lamingtons, brandy snaps and chocolate profiteroles.

"Some of it, but a lot's already been frozen." Felicity slumped back in her chair. "I've been cooking for weeks."

"I could take what we can't freeze to my work on Tuesday," Greta said. "They'd appreciate it. The guys especially. They love it when we have morning teas."

"Will you go to work?" Felicity looked vaguely surprised.

"I thought I would." In Greta's twenty-four years her only other experience of a death had been a school friend who'd died when she was in her teens. Greta's parents had taken her to the funeral, which had been terribly sad, but this was the first time anyone in her own family had died. Were there protocols to be followed? She glanced at her dad. "Should I stay home?"

"Not unless you want to," he said. "We'll visit Hazel tomorrow and find out what the plan will be for the funeral. There will be other things to organise but I'm sure between your mum and I and June and Derek we'll manage. You might want to take some leave later, around the funeral but for now...well, it's probably best to keep busy."

Greta swallowed her relief with a mouthful of tea. It had been a shock but she didn't feel consumed by grief at her grandad's death and things at work were tricky enough at the moment. The coming week would be full of challenges she had to face if she was to make any headway. She'd only had six months in her role as a service desk analyst with a charter aviation company. While she was beginning to feel like she knew her way around, there'd been a few staff changes and they were currently without anyone in her direct manager's role, which had meant she had taken on more responsibility. She was pleased because it suggested the senior staff thought her capable and the extra money was good but it also stretched both her load and her hours at work.

Felicity gripped her head in her hands. "Poor Mum."

"It will be so hard for her," Greta said. "Grandad managed everything. How long were they married?"

"Fifty-four years."

"A life sentence." Both women looked at Ian. He cleared his throat. "I'm joking."

"I know he'd become almost housebound lately but Greta's right, Mum relied on him so much." Felicity glanced at the clock on the wall. "Perhaps I should have gone over there tonight."

"June's with her and there's nothing that can be done until tomorrow," Ian said. "We'll go first thing in the morning."

"I can come with you if you want," Greta said.

Felicity began to cry.

Ian put an arm around his wife's shoulders.

"Will she be all right?" Greta looked from her mum to her dad.

"Of course," he said.

She retrieved the box of tissues from the bench behind her. Felicity took a handful, mopped at her face and blew her nose.

"Come on," Ian said. "Let's try to get some sleep so we can deal with what tomorrow brings."

"The food…"

"I'll pack it away," Greta said. "Sort what can be saved."

Felicity dragged a plate of half-eaten sandwiches towards her. "I can do it. I can't imagine I'll be able to sleep." She gasped back another sob. "I can't believe I said Dad ruined my party. What a horrible person I am."

"You're not horrible, Lissie but you've had a shock and you're exhausted. You should try to get some sleep."

She looked forlornly at the food-laden table and her shoulders sagged. "Maybe you're right."

"Come on." Ian offered his hand, tugged her gently against his shoulder and guided her to the door where he paused to look back.

"Will you be right with the food, Grets?"

She nodded. Ian's use of her childhood nickname made her feel suddenly vulnerable. "I'll get this tidied up. I don't feel tired yet."

He turned away, talking soothingly to her mum as they walked to their bedroom.

She sat back at the table and contemplated the different models of marriage posed by her parents and her grandparents.

Her grandad had impeccable manners – he'd hold doors open for Nan, carry bags for her, but signs of affection were rare. The occasional guiding hand on Hazel's back, a pat on the shoulder or a brief peck on the cheek were the only signs of intimacy between them that Greta had witnessed. Her dad was polite too but he'd probably carry the bag, hug Felicity close and chat as they walked. Franklyn had been the boss in the marriage and Hazel had always deferred to him. Greta's parents were more likely to have discussions about important things and had often included her in deliberations when she'd still lived at home. Felicity had project managed the renovation but Hazel...How would she manage now? She'd be lost without Franklyn to make decisions for her.

Her phone rang and she was relieved to see Joe's photo light up the screen.

"What's up?" he asked as soon as she accepted the call. "Is the party over already?"

"It is but..." Greta stood and walked around the table, not sure how to break this kind of news. The tears she hadn't formed earlier suddenly brimmed in her eyes. "I've got sad news...Grandad...he...he died tonight."

"Oh, babe, I'm so sorry."

Her tears overflowed. She wished he was there so that she could lean on him like her mum had on her dad.

"What happened?" Joe sucked in a breath. "Not at your mum's party?"

"No, he was at home. He and Nan hadn't turned up and then we got her call…we're not sure…it must have been a heart attack or something. He was lying on the bed, Nan said, and when she went in to check he was…he was dead." A sob shuddered through her chest and then another.

"Are you at your parents' place?"

"Yes, can you come over?"

"I've just got home but I can come—"

"It's okay," she said pathetically, hoping he would.

"I'm feeling really tired." The townhouse they shared was a thirty-minute drive away.

"Don't worry. I've got a bit of cleaning up to do then I'll go to bed. We're going to Nan's first thing tomorrow. Perhaps you could meet me there?"

"Of course. I'll call you in the morning." Joe's tone was reassuring and efficient. He was a project manager working in local government and he liked structure and order. Except in their home, where he was the complete opposite. Not that Greta was so good at housework herself. After living with a tidy freak for a mother housework was overrated.

"Night, babe," he said.

"Love you." Greta sagged to a chair again and contemplated the mountain of food.

three

Alice

The sun sparkled off the brilliant blue water of the bay, which stretched in a long lazy curve at the bottom of the peninsula. At the hook end, a small section of land pointed out to sea providing some protection from the huge swells of the Great Australian Bight and from there a jetty jutted into the ocean. The rugged bush beyond the beach was punctuated by a few rows of houses and then more bush. It was a perfect day in Marion Bay.

Along the front street, nearly to the jetty, Alice Pollard stopped in the shade of a tree and mopped her brow with one of her late husband's big handkerchiefs. Still feeling warm and a little light-headed, she plucked off the floppy hat and fanned her face.

She should have come out earlier but she'd slept in then had a batch of sausage rolls to make for the local cafe. That's where she was heading now and she was late. Phoebe, the owner, liked to get the pastries by eleven for lunchtime customers but when Alice had gone out to the car it wouldn't start. It hadn't made a sound so she suspected a flat battery but had no time to wait for roadside assistance. She'd swapped the trays of sausage rolls from the box she'd packed them in to a flat basket and set off on foot. It wasn't a long walk and one she'd done often but the late morning sun was oppressive and the day bereft of any breeze from the beautiful bay behind her.

She replaced her hat, swapped her basket to her other hand, wriggled her sweaty toes inside her sneakers, adjusted the small backpack on her shoulders and set off again. She hoped Phoebe would be at the shop. Sometimes it was her young stepson, Colin, in charge and Alice found him difficult. She pushed open the door and stepped inside to be greeted by marginally cooler air and – she let out a gentle sigh – Colin's scowling face.

"'Bout time," he snapped.

A couple perusing the shelves of chutneys and jams on sale looked up, glanced at her then each other and turned back to the stand of local produce.

"I had car trouble." Alice crossed the shop floor. "Is Phoebe in?"

"I had people asking already." Colin spoke as if Alice hadn't and jabbed a finger in the direction of the blackboard behind his head that announced homemade sausage rolls.

Alice moved to the counter and lifted her basket upwards. Before she could set it down he snatched it from her grasp and flung back the crisp tea towel that covered the warm pastries. He began to reach in.

"Tongs."

"Ghaa…" Colin hissed and snatched them up. He jabbed at the sausage rolls and tossed them in the warmer.

"They look good." A woman spoke from behind Alice. "And they're homemade?"

The couple who'd been inspecting the local produce had moved closer, the man with a jar of jam and a bottle of sauce in his hands.

Alice nodded. "People seem to like my sausage rolls. And I can vouch for that sauce to go with them." She stepped back to allow Colin to serve. It took him a while and they wanted coffee so Alice sat in one of the seats, closer to the struggling air conditioner. The walk and the heat combined had left her light-headed. At her last check-up the doctor had said it was caused by low blood pressure. Alice had been given a thorough going over, a clean bill of health for a woman of sixty-six and a lecture from the young doctor to be careful when rising, to drink plenty of fluids, get plenty of exercise, and the list had gone on.

The couple smiled as they left, loaded with their purchases including the sausage rolls, and Alice rose to her feet...slowly... and went to the counter where Colin ignored her, his attention on his phone.

She cleared her throat. "It's Thursday."

"Yep." Colin didn't look up.

"Phoebe usually pays me on Thursdays."

"She's not here."

Alice had no idea what was so fascinating on the screen that he couldn't make eye contact when he spoke but then he had such fox-like eyes she was rather glad he didn't.

Finally, he looked up. "You still here."

Behind Alice the door burst open and a woman strode in, a bundle of newspapers clutched under one arm and a box in the crook of her other. Colin lowered the hand that held his phone.

"Hello, Alice. Nice to see you. I hope Col gave you the money I left."

"I was just about to." Colin's pinched-face glare dared her to say otherwise. He opened the till, took out an envelope and tossed it on the counter.

"Thank you." Alice tucked it into her backpack.

Phoebe dropped the bundle of papers she'd been carrying on the stand at the end of the counter. "Be a good lad and bring in the rest of the boxes, will ya, Col?" She went out the back with her box so she didn't see the scowl on his face. He stuffed his phone in his pocket and without a glance at Alice slouched off outside.

"Staying for a cuppa, Al?" Phoebe was back.

Alice flinched at the shortening of her name. Her dear Roy was the only one to ever call her that and it broke her heart to hear his personal endearment used by others.

"No, thank you, Phoebe. I'm late because my car broke down and I had to walk."

"Oh, that's no good."

"I'd best get home and call the roadside assist."

"Do you need a ride? Col could drop you."

"Oh, no, thank you. It's a beautiful day for walking."

"It's bloody hot out there. You take care."

"I will." Alice straightened her shoulders. Phoebe had the knack of making her feel as if she were ninety.

"Don't forget your paper...and your basket." Phoebe held out a copy of the day's *Advertiser* and the now-empty basket.

"Thanks." Alice slid the paper into her backpack then held the door wide as Colin approached from the other side, one small box in his hands.

Neither of them spoke. Shutting the door carefully behind her she passed Phoebe's station wagon. The back was down and still held several boxes, bags of groceries and a zipped-up cooler bag that sat in the full sun. She hoped Colin would get it inside before the contents spoiled in the heat. Once more she adjusted her backpack and set off for home.

It was late afternoon before Alice made herself a cup of tea and sat at the table to read the paper. She'd eaten her lunch and played several games of patience while she'd waited for someone to look at her car. When the mechanic finally arrived he'd confirmed, as she'd thought, the battery was dead. He'd replaced it and Alice had been glad of the credit card she rarely used. She knew it was considered old-fashioned these days but she preferred cash. Once a fortnight she made the two-hour round trip to her nearest bank at Yorketown. Then she'd pay her bills, do her shopping, go to the hairdresser when necessary. The money she got for her sausage rolls, and on weekends her pink jelly cakes, was all she needed to get by the rest of the time but it didn't cover a battery.

An hour passed before she reached the personal notices. She'd skipped over the puzzles, saving them for after dinner. There was so little to watch on television and she'd already devoured her pile of library books. Thankfully it was Friday tomorrow, when she made her weekly trek to the next closest town thirty minutes away to change her books and get fresh bread and veg.

Her gaze swept down the death notices then faltered at the name *Gifford, Franklyn Ernest*. The writing faded and was replaced by the vision of sharp blue eyes, a beak nose, tightly drawn lips and the smell of peppermint breath. She blinked and read the notice below the name. *Passed away suddenly at home. Aged eighty. Dearly loved husband of Hazel. Much loved father and father-in-law of June and Derek, Felicity and Ian and grandpa of Greta, Lachlan and Joshua.* Alice sat back in her chair. He was dead. For all she'd known he could have been dead for years but here was the confirmation in black and white. A glimmer of hope wormed its way down her chest. Her family had been lost to her for so long but now…She leaned in and read the notice again then moved on to the funeral notices. It was to be next Monday.

Alice looked up at the calendar on the wall. Her life was neatly mapped out there. She baked most days for The Bay Cafe but as well as that, Monday was her cleaning, washing and ironing day; Tuesday she cooked meals for herself, stocking her freezer and in the afternoon played cards at the community club; Wednesday and Thursday she did odd jobs for a couple of seniors; and Friday she drove to the next town to do her jobs and every second Friday was the longer trip to Yorketown.

Some weekday afternoons she collected Jessie and Lola, who lived in the house behind hers, from the school bus and looked after them until one of their parents got home. Weekends she tended to her own garden, where she also kept laying hens, and sometimes she drove out to the farm. The property was leased and she rented the house to a young couple but no-one minded her visits, just to look around, feel the dirt beneath her feet, smell the earth.

She'd worked hard to keep occupied after Roy died. Not being on the farm had been difficult at first; there her days had been full, from dawn till dusk. She and Roy had made a good team. The sorrow of his loss was a constant ache she kept at bay by keeping herself busy. She couldn't imagine life without him and yet here she was three years later, alive and trying hard to get on with it.

Her glance fell to the paper again and the names of the family she'd been denied because of Franklyn. She traced her finger over the notice, quelling the rumble of the long-buried anger trying to resurface inside her. Was it possible she could cross the divide now that he was gone? Alice had no idea where they'd been for almost fifty years but at least she knew where they'd be next Monday. She could make contact.

Fear mixed with the hope. Her fingers trembled as she traced the names, reading the notice again. A tear formed at the rim of one eye and then in the other and before she knew it they were rolling down her cheeks and dropping in dark blobs on the paper.

Alice flopped forward, resting her head on her arms and let the tears fall. She mourned the loss of her dear Roy, the babies they'd created that had lived but a short time and then she cried for the family wrenched from her all those years before.

Finally Alice sat up, took out Roy's hanky, wiped her eyes and blew her nose. He'd be shaking his head at her. "Don't waste tears on something that's done, Al," he'd say. He was right. She'd done enough crying in her lifetime.

She retrieved her diary from her handbag and copied the details of the funeral into next Monday's space. There were other jobs she could do in Adelaide. She could spend a few nights there. She had plenty of time to get organised, cook extras for Phoebe to freeze, let her card group know she wouldn't be there, make sure Bec didn't need her for child minding, get someone to feed her hens. Without another glance at the paper she folded it and sat it to one side. Sunday she would set off for Adelaide and the only family she had left in the world.

four

Hazel

There was a shift in the air around her. It was almost imperceptible, but Hazel felt it nonetheless. She'd been holding herself together as Franklyn's funeral had gone on and on. She snuck a peek at her watch. Had she been rigid in this hard pew for only half an hour? It felt like forever. Now she wanted to look around to see who or what had caused the sensation of someone staring at her. No doubt there were plenty of eyes on her. The church was full of Franklyn's family, friends and colleagues, and acquaintances from various groups he'd belonged to, most of whom they hadn't seen in years, but she remained resolutely staring ahead. If she turned, she might break the shell of sorrow she'd built around herself and someone might see, in place of a grieving widow, the reality of a woman who, instead of sorrow, felt release. Her life sentence done.

She fixed her gaze on her husband's coffin as Father Donnelly said the final prayer.

"In peace let us now take our brother, Franklyn Ernest Gifford, to his place of rest."

The people who filled the pews stood. Hazel wobbled on her feet. Her daughters, June, her oldest, sniffing into her hanky on one side, and Felicity, standing stiffly stoic on the other, slipped their arms through hers. Together they turned as June's two sons, Josh and Lachlan, Greta's fiancé, Joe, and three of Franklyn's younger relations from interstate carried the coffin from the church. The small choir began to sing 'The Lord is My Shepherd'. Tears brimmed in Hazel's eyes. She'd been to enough funerals over the years to conjure up some for that hymn.

Jammed between her two daughters as they followed the coffin, Hazel kept her eyes fixed on the sheath of red roses adorning the top so she didn't have to look at anyone. Outside she was grateful for the bright sunlight so she could slip on her sunglasses to hide her now-dry eyes. The crowd that followed them out milled at a polite distance from the family gathered behind the hearse.

"Mum!" June's voice was a harsh whisper in her ear. "Here's a flower." A sprig of rosemary was pushed into Hazel's hand and June gripped her elbow, propelling her forward.

She lifted her hand to drop the sprig, then, aware so many people were watching, she laid it reverently on the casket, allowing her fingers to rest briefly on the polished wood. In her mind she pictured Franklyn as she'd last seen him the day before in the dim lights of the funeral parlour. His face had been relaxed, almost calm in appearance, his eyes gently closed as if he was simply asleep in his best suit.

"Goodbye Frank." It was a soft murmur no-one else would hear. Everyone called him Franklyn – his name was never shortened except by Hazel and never out loud. It was a small rebellion on her part, but one that, after being married to the bully of a man who'd been her husband for fifty-four years, gave her some small sense of pleasure.

She slipped from June's grip and stood to one side as her daughters and grandchildren each added their tribute. Then came other family members, cousins mainly – Franklyn had no siblings – and friends, all dropping sprigs of rosemary, covering the end of the coffin with the tiny branches, some falling to the floor of the hearse.

A warm hand slipped into hers and gave a gentle squeeze.

"Are you all right, Nan?"

Hazel smiled at the tender enquiry and turned to look at the kind face beside her, Felicity's only child, and Hazel's only granddaughter. Such a sweet young woman.

"Yes, thank you, Greta."

One of the funeral attendants murmured in June's ear. She nodded and turned to Hazel. "They'll remove the roses for you to take home."

Hazel opened her mouth to object. Why would she want funeral flowers in her house? Greta gave her hand another squeeze. Hazel nodded her head.

They stepped back together as the hearse was closed and slowly driven away. Hazel despaired that they all had to stand in the street watching. She rolled her shoulders. There was that feeling again, as if someone was trying to communicate with her across the space. This time she did turn but her family surrounded her and she couldn't see the faces beyond them. At that moment the hearse and its sombre cargo turned out of the street.

Father Donnelly stepped back onto the footpath. "The family ask that you join them in the hall for a cup of tea and a chance to reminisce."

Greta turned away to speak to Joe and once again Hazel felt the pressure of June's hand on her elbow guiding her towards the hall.

Hazel resisted the urge to shrug off her daughter's grip. She was in desperate need of a cup of tea.

An hour later she was equally desperate to go home. She'd listened over and over again to Franklyn's friends and work colleagues telling her what a fine man he'd been. Where were they during the last few years when she'd been his sole carer? Her face hurt from keeping the stiff sad look she'd practised in the mirror in the privacy of her bedroom.

Her house had felt crowded. Franklyn's cousin and his wife from Sydney had stayed in the spare room and Felicity and Greta on makeshift beds in the study and the front lounge. The Sydney couple had already said their goodbyes and taken a taxi to the airport to catch their return flight. No doubt Felicity would stay on a day or two and Hazel hoped Greta would too. They could move into the spare room and keep her company a little longer.

There were only a few people left in the hall now, her girls, a couple of Franklyn's ex-colleagues who he'd once played a weekly bridge game with, and a woman who was talking to Father Donnelly. She was neatly dressed, not in black but in a simple navy dress and mid-height heels. She had straight grey hair that reached just below her shoulders. Hazel didn't recognise her but then she hadn't known several of the people who'd come up to offer their condolences.

"Mum, would you like something to eat?" Felicity stood before her with a plate of cakes.

"No, thank you."

"You have to eat, Mum." June held out another plate, this one with sandwiches. "You can't stop just because Dad's gone."

"I had a good breakfast." Hazel sniffed. "Greta cooked me an omelette and I had a sandwich and a piece of cake when we first came in."

"Well, that's just as well but we can't be with you all the time."
Hazel pursed her lips.

"We're worried about you, Mum," Felicity chipped in. "You
know how you get wobbly sometimes."

Hazel swallowed her annoyance. "I'm so lucky to have you both
but I really am okay and I truly don't need anything more to eat."

"You look tired." Felicity put the plate of cakes on the table.
"Would you like me to take you home?"

"Oh yes." Both daughter's eyebrows raised at her quick
response. "At least as soon as we can. I think I've spoken to everyone and thanked them."

"No-one expects you to be the perfect hostess today, Mum,"
Felicity said.

"Would you like me to come too?" June asked.

"There's no need, June." Hazel chose her words carefully this
time. "You've been such a help this last week. I don't know how
I'd have managed without you both..." Greta was walking in
their direction. Hazel smiled at her granddaughter. "And the rest
of the family, of course. It was so good of Lachlan to fly home
from New Zealand and Josh to come from Brisbane."

"Good heavens, Mum, they wouldn't not come to their granddad's funeral." June sniffed into her hanky.

Hazel smiled reassuringly. She wished June had gone with
Derek and Lachlan to drive Josh to the airport. His uni course
began this week and she knew June had been torn between last
goodbyes with her son and staying at her mother's side. Felicity's
ever-dependable Ian had said his goodbyes a few minutes ago,
only after reassuring her that he would come at a moment's notice
if she needed anything. Joe had slipped back to work as soon as
the hearse had driven away. So now it was just the women in her
family left.

"Nevertheless it was good of the boys to travel so far." Hazel had to look up to her eldest daughter. Not that Hazel herself was short but Franklyn was, or at least had been, over six foot and June nearly matched him. She was always awkward with it, so angular and sharp-looking. Today she was dressed all in black, as were Hazel, Felicity and most of the other mourners, but while Felicity wore a knee-length dress with soft ruffles, short sleeves and a v-neckline, June was in black pants and a jacket with a turtleneck blouse. She must be so hot. The air in the hall was oppressive. Hazel was glad of her own simple short-sleeved black dress. It had been her go to for any formal event but perhaps she'd get rid of it now that she'd worn it for Franklyn's funeral, splash out on something new.

"I'll go and bring the car closer," Felicity said.

"Let me," Greta said.

"I'll pack up some of this food then." Felicity gave her mother a firm look. "We might feel like something later, once we've all had a rest."

"The church ladies put on quite a spread, didn't they?" Hazel gazed at the table with little interest.

"Grandad would have approved." Greta smiled and turned away, keys in hand.

The last of Franklyn's ex-colleagues said their farewells and for a moment Hazel stood alone. She badly wanted to slip off her heels. She'd do it as soon as she got in the car.

"Hello, Hazel."

The gentle voice startled her. She spun and the room seemed to spin with her as if everything was suddenly slightly off kilter. She stuck out a hand and gripped the back of a chair. The woman before her had been the one she'd noticed talking to Father Donnelly earlier. Hazel hadn't recognised her from the distance but now, here, right in front of her...those eyes...

"Are you all right?" The woman gripped her arm and edged her to the chair.

"What are you doing here?" Hazel's words came out in a croak.

"I've come to see you and..." The woman stood back a little and glanced around. "Your family."

Hazel looked around too but everyone was busy packing up and taking no notice. She got back to her feet, pushed away the hand that still rested on her arm. She had to end this before her daughters came back.

"You keep away from my family. They've had enough for one day."

The woman hesitated, looked at her pityingly. "He's gone now, Hazel."

"I know that," Hazel hissed, her heart beating faster. "But they don't know about you." She could hear footsteps coming closer across the wooden floor. She didn't dare look around. It was bound to be one of her daughters.

"We can start afresh."

"We cannot."

"Hello?" It was Felicity, who'd stepped up beside her mother.

"Who are you?" June asked.

"My name is Alice Pollard." The woman smiled at each of them.

Hazel's heart beat so fast and her head pounded so hard she thought herself in danger of having a stroke like the one that had killed her husband.

"I've just farewelled my husband...this is not the time."

"For what, Mum?" It was June's sharp voice again. "What's going on?"

Alice fixed her gaze on Hazel. "I'm Alice Pollard nee Jones... your mother's sister."

five

The hall was hot and dots danced before Alice's eyes. She found a seat. Hazel had let out a strangled squawk when Alice had announced herself. Now everyone fussed around her, fanning her and giving her water, sending Alice dagger looks in the case of June and questioning looks in the case of Felicity and Greta, who'd appeared just as Hazel had flopped back to her chair.

Alice's breath had nearly left her when the four women had walked together into the church, Hazel, her daughters, June and Felicity, and granddaughter, Greta. It had been easy to work out who they all were. June had her father's looks – tall, angular, full lips that easily turned down – but Felicity had softer features with an open face, more like Hazel had been in her youth.

Now, as Alice watched the four women together, the concern, the low voices, the solicitous looks and touches, she felt the void of what she'd been denied wrench open again. She recalled her own fragility after Roy had died but then she'd not had family to lean on. Roy's three older brothers had driven over for the funeral but they were no longer close, she'd felt as if she hardly knew them any more. They'd embraced her stiffly and returned to their properties in Victoria as quickly as they'd come.

Greta nodded at something the others had said, straightened and walked towards her. Perhaps Alice should have waited and made contact once some time had passed but with no address or phone number she'd felt that turning up at the funeral had been her only way to connect. She braced herself for the rejection she knew was coming. Greta's look changed from concern to curiosity. The young woman came to a stop in front of her, blocking her view of the three left behind, but Alice knew they would be watching.

"Nan's okay."

Alice gripped the side of the chair. She was still feeling shaky herself. "That's good. I didn't mean to upset her."

"She gets wobbly sometimes. It's been an emotional week for her." Greta's gaze softened a little. "What about you? You look a bit pale yourself, Mrs...Pollard was it?"

Alice flapped her free hand in front of her face. "It's the heat. I have low blood pressure. It makes me light-headed every now and then."

"I'm sorry, Mrs Pollard, but—"

"Alice. I'm your great-aunt."

"Yes, well, that's..." Greta glanced behind her. "You can understand, on top of the funeral, it's all been a bit overwhelming. We need to take Nan home for a rest."

"I do understand. I lost my own husband only a few years ago."

"I'm sorry." Greta took another quick glance over her shoulder. "This has been a surprise. We didn't know Nan had a sister."

"We...lost touch...I saw the death notice in the paper."

"Do you live in Adelaide?"

Alice gave a slight shake of her head. "I'm three-and-a-half hours away. In the country. I rarely come to Adelaide..." She faltered as, beyond Greta, Felicity and June were walking their mother to the door. "I need to talk to Hazel."

"Perhaps another time."

"I have to go home tomorrow. I won't keep her long."

June heard her. "Keep away," she snapped, as she whipped her earlier feeble but now steadily moving mother out the door.

Alice scrambled to her feet but she rose too quickly and the combination of higher heels than she normally wore and the uneven surface of the hall floor conspired against her. Once more the dots danced before her eyes and she flopped back onto the chair.

"Are you all right?"

Alice leaned to look past Greta. "Hazel?"

"June's taking Nan home."

"I have to see her."

Felicity moved up beside Greta, blocking Alice's way.

"Mum doesn't want to see you," she said.

The fight went out of Alice then. What a sorry state of affairs. She'd been stupid to come. Now she'd missed her chance to speak to Hazel. She had no idea where her sister lived and it was unlikely the family would tell her. Her head still felt light. She wondered if she'd had any water since breakfast. "My bag?"

Greta fetched it from the end of the table and Alice took out the full bottle of water she'd placed in the bag that morning. She took several large sips.

"Feeling better?" Greta said.

Alice nodded. The heat in her cheeks was now more about embarrassment than the result of being in the stuffy hall. "I get light-headed in the heat, that's all, and I haven't drunk much water today."

One of the women who'd been helping with the refreshments came across the hall to stand beside them.

"We're nearly done in the kitchen. Is there anything else we can do?" Her question was for Felicity but she was looking at Alice.

"No thanks, Sue." Felicity glanced at the rose-gold watch on her wrist. "We shouldn't be much longer."

Sue wiped her hands on her apron, gave them all an appraising look and walked away.

Felicity scrutinised Alice, her gaze intensified by her cat-eye shaped glasses. Not everyone could pull them off but Alice thought them perfect for her oval face. Beside her, Greta continued to inspect her. She was an attractive young woman like her mother. She had straight fair hair styled neatly at chin length, a ready smile and pearly blue eyes that sparkled despite her concern. Alice liked her already.

"Should we call someone for you?" she asked.

"No."

"I don't see any likeness." Felicity's tone was sharp, her voice echoing in the now-empty hall. The only other sounds were the distant clinks and thuds and murmur of voices from the kitchen.

"Pardon?" Alice said.

"You say you're my mother's sister but I can't see it." Felicity remained stiffly distant, her hands gripped tightly together.

"Mum, not now."

"It's all right, Greta. I understand it's been a shock to discover a close member of the family you'd never heard of before."

Felicity gave a soft snort. "I knew Mum had a sister."

"Did you?" Greta said.

"Your nan had a sister who died in her teens."

"That's so sad."

"And not true."

Both women turned back to Alice. Felicity's eyebrows arched.

Alice's fingers trembled and she gripped them in her lap. So many emotions – sorrow for the past denied her, joy at finding her family, fear of rejection, anticipation for what might be, they all swirled inside her. And with them determination.

She looked up at Felicity and for a moment her resolve faltered. Felicity, Greta and the rest of Hazel's family had grown up knowing nothing of a younger sister. Whatever Alice said would be a shock at worst, a surprise at best. She took a breath. She'd come this far and she couldn't simply walk away. "I'm ten years younger than your mother. Our parents always said I was like our mother and Hazel was like our father."

"Anyone could say that when there's no proof." Felicity was quick to dismiss with her words but her expression showed a hint of curiosity.

"Nan never talks about her past and there are no photos," Greta said.

"With good cause." Felicity stood tall, crossed her arms over her chest. Her look dared Alice to know the reason.

Alice sat straighter in the chair. Perhaps there was still a chance. "In 1967 Hazel moved to Melbourne to work as a secretary. I was at high school, living at home in Hobart with our parents. It was February and we'd had a week of oppressive heat. There were several fires and then a terrible wind that drove the flames to inferno level." She took a steadying breath. "Our parents, our home, everything we had in the world was destroyed in a bushfire."

"How awful," Greta said. "No wonder Nan doesn't talk about it."

"And her sister," Felicity said. "Her young sister died too."

Alice shook her head carefully. "I am that sister. I was staying overnight at a friend's house right in Hobart."

"So you survived but...I don't understand." This time it was Greta shaking her head. "Nan must have thought you were dead."

Alice didn't know how to go on. Hazel should be here. They needed to tell the story together.

"This is ridiculous," Felicity snapped then spun as a throat cleared behind her.

"We've finished cleaning up." It was Sue again, her apron gone now.

"Thank you, Sue. You've all been such a help. We're on our way too." She turned to Alice. "Will you be all right to leave now?"

Alice looked at the three faces watching her. "Yes, but—"

Greta's phone rang. "It's Nan," she mouthed then pressed the phone to her ear. "Hi, Nan." She glanced at Alice. "I can ask her." Greta cradled the phone against her shoulder. "Nan wants to know if you can go to her house. It's not far from here."

This time the heat that flooded Alice was fuelled by hope. "Yes, of course."

Greta lifted the phone again while beside her Felicity's face creased with disbelief.

"We'll be there soon," Greta said.

Felicity opened her mouth and closed it again. Sue was still with them, her gaze full of interest. No doubt the sudden appearance of a sister for Hazel had been the subject of conversation in the kitchen and she was hoping to glean more details.

Felicity huffed out a breath. "We'd better go then."

Greta offered her arm to help Alice up, her smile genuine, and once again Alice felt the deep pang of regret for what she'd been missing.

"Thank you." She stood. No spinning this time but nonetheless she allowed her arm to remain firmly gripped by Greta as they followed Felicity to the door.

six

They were seated in Hazel's formal sitting room. She preferred it to the renovation Franklyn had insisted they needed that extended off the kitchen. It had been done after the girls had left home and while Hazel appreciated the new kitchen, the rest of the space felt cavernous, all glass and exposed brick, wooden beams and a tiled floor that was the devil to keep looking nice.

Hazel and Franklyn had lived in the same house since they'd moved to Adelaide, not long after they'd been married. This room where she now sat facing Alice was the original lounge at the front of the house. It was a small room and when they'd all crowded in it had been a squeeze. Hazel had asked June, Felicity and Greta to leave. She wanted to speak with Alice alone. She'd shut the door on her family's querying looks and sat herself in the middle of the two-seater couch opposite Alice, who sat in one of the twin armchairs. Greta had brought in a jug and poured them both some water but the glasses sat untouched on the tray.

Hazel wasn't sure where to start. June had quizzed her all the way home and she'd known there was no way to stop Felicity and Greta asking the same questions. She'd had no choice but to ask

Alice to come, but she was damned if she could think of a reason-able explanation for the lie she'd told her girls about their aunt's supposed demise.

She blew out a breath. Blast Franklyn. Just when she thought she might get some rest, his death had brought her sister back from the past. A past she didn't want to expose but here they were.

The two women studied each other across the small space between them. Hazel could see the vestiges of the good-looking young woman her sister had been even though her hair was grey and hung limply past her shoulders, ageing her beyond her years. Hazel went regularly to the hairdresser to cover her own grey streaks. Fine wrinkles creased Alice's face but her eyes were still the pretty blue they'd been when she was sixteen.

"It's so good to see you, Hazel."

Alice looked genuinely happy and Hazel couldn't help but remember how close they'd once been. A tiny corner of her resolve crumbled.

"Sad circumstances, of course," Alice added quickly. "I'm sorry for your loss."

The wall around Hazel's heart snapped back into place. The brief curious thought she'd given to the life her little sister had led without her was pushed firmly away. She didn't want to know. "Are you?"

Alice sat back as if Hazel had slapped her.

"Did you think just because my husband is dead I could turn back time – forgive what you did?" Hazel said.

"Hazel, please—"

"You tried to ruin my marriage."

"I didn't..." Alice swallowed, her face a mix of emotion. Hazel watched her struggle to compose herself. "It was a long time ago, Hazel. Can't we put it behind us? We're still sisters."

"You destroyed that bond, Alice. We haven't seen each other for...for fifty years. Why should—"

"I tried to keep in touch. You moved away and I tried to find you."

"Franklyn got a job in Adelaide."

"We've not been that far apart all these years. I live—"

"I don't want to know," Hazel hissed.

"Please, Hazel," Alice said. "My Roy died a few years ago. I have no children...I thought—"

"You thought what?" Hazel gasped. "That you'd have mine?"

"I...you make it sound so...I just want the chance to get to know my nieces and their families. I didn't know you had a second daughter." Alice leaned forward and reached out. "I want the chance to know you again."

Hazel stared at the hand as if it was a snake poised to strike her. She looked up into Alice's imploring gaze. Fifty years ago she'd seen that same look and she'd had to cut all ties. For the sake of her family she had to do it all over again.

"No, Alice. There can be no reconciliation." She stood up. "I'd like you to leave now."

Alice studied her a moment then rose carefully to her feet. "Very well," she said. "I won't beg. But if you ever change your mind—"

"I won't."

Alice took a step towards the door then paused. Hazel turned her back and listened as her sister opened the door, said goodbye to the others, who'd no doubt been hovering nearby, and left.

Hazel watched through her plain white net curtains as Alice walked down the path. She frowned as Greta hurried after her, stopped her at the gate and began to talk.

"What happened, Mum?"

She glanced back at June. "I've asked Alice not to contact me again."

"Are you sure that's the right thing to do?" Felicity asked.

Hazel folded her arms and turned to the window again. Alice was gone and Greta was walking back up the path. "You know nothing of what happened and I'm not raking it up again to appease her conscience."

"She's your sister. Perhaps it's time to forgive her."

"Some things can't ever be put right, Felicity."

"Mum knows best," June said.

Hazel fanned her face with her hand. It took little effort to squeeze tears to her eyes. "I don't want to talk about it. It's enough that your father's gone. My sister has been dead to me all these years and nothing can change that now." She turned away from the window as Greta came back inside.

"She's gone." Greta strode to Hazel's side. "That was a bit intense. Are you okay, Nan?"

Hazel took out her hanky and dabbed at her eyes. "I will be." She made a show of blowing her nose and taking a deep breath.

The landline phone rang. Hazel started at the sound. There'd been so many calls.

"Leave it," June said. "It's probably just a nuisance call. You really don't need to keep a landline these days, Mum. It's not even listed on White Pages. We should get it disconnected."

Hazel stiffened. She sounded so like Franklyn.

"I still get some personal calls on that phone. Several of my friends prefer it." Only to herself would she admit those calls had dwindled over the last year. Franklyn had even begrudged her time chatting to friends.

Greta stepped into the hall and the ringing stopped. They heard her speaking and then she appeared in the doorway, the phone pressed to her chest. "It's Grandad's solicitor. He wants to make a time to read the will."

Hazel sighed and reached for the phone. Kurt Blanchard was very officious, the perfect person to look after Franklyn's affairs. He'd already been in touch to assure her she'd be taken care of and to provide help with the financial side of the funeral.

She put the phone to her ear. "Hello, Kurt."

Once more he offered his condolences and then wanted to come the next day to deal with the will.

Hazel looked at her daughters. "Can you be here tomorrow afternoon at two?"

"Of course."

"Yes."

They both answered at once.

"Do you need me?" Greta asked.

"He wants as many of the family here as possible."

"I'll try," Greta said.

"I'll get Lachlan to come with me," June said. "I'm not sure if Derek will be able to leave work."

"Or Ian," Felicity said.

Hazel returned to her call. "That suits most of us, thank you, Kurt. We'll see you tomorrow." She disconnected and placed the phone on the coffee table.

"Why does he want us all here?"

"Will it matter if I'm not?"

"Shall I put the kettle on?"

All three women spoke at once. Hazel held up a hand. "I don't know anything about your father's will, June. He made it without my input." She sighed. "Greta, I'm sure it won't matter if you can't be here. I know you're busy at work. And put the kettle on by all means, Felicity, if you'd like a hot drink but I can't face one more cup of tea. I'm going to change out of this dress and lie down for a while."

"Are you all right, Mum?" June asked as Hazel crossed the room.

She paused at the door, only Greta between her and the hall and escape. Greta's face mirrored the concern in June's voice. Hazel glanced between them all and her gaze fell on the tall vase of red roses. June had arranged them and placed them on the hall table. Hazel stiffened. "I will be," she said, then crossed the hall to her bedroom and shut the door firmly behind her.

Inside she leaned against the solid wood. Her knees trembled and her head pounded. This was not how she'd expected the afternoon following her husband's funeral would go. She'd been looking forward to the release and now she felt like a tightly wound spring. She shut her eyes and immediately Franklyn's stale man smell engulfed her. She jerked away and looked back, realising she'd rested her head against his dressing gown, still hanging on the hook on the back of the door. She glared at the dark brown fabric then yanked it down and tossed it to the floor in the corner of the room.

It had been on Franklyn's order she'd kept her secret and as the years went by she'd almost forgotten her sister and the trouble she'd caused. Sometimes when Hazel thought back on it she saw herself as weak. If only she'd spoken up, perhaps...She gripped her head in her hands. There was no point in what-ifs, they were all too late. She glared at the crumpled dressing gown, a dark lump on the pale carpet. "Damn you, Franklyn," she hissed.

*

Alice rolled her car to a stop in front of room fifteen, turned off the ignition and rested her head on the wheel. She wasn't sure how she'd made her way back to the motel – her mind had been churning over the events of the day. How naive she'd been, how stupid to think Hazel would welcome her with open arms. And yet a small germ of hope reseeded itself in Alice's chest. When Greta had walked with her down the path she'd asked if Alice minded sharing her mobile number. The young woman had typed it quickly into her phone and said she'd text later so Alice would have her number.

The heat inside the car pressed in on her, forcing her to move. Alice gathered her things and stepped gratefully into the shade of the verandah where she struggled with the key in the lock and then the wobbly door handle. The room had been shut up for most of the day and she could almost taste the warm air and the lingering smell of bleach. She switched on the air conditioner then slid out of her heels, what a relief that was, and stripped off her dress. She hung it on a hanger in the open wardrobe, slipped on a loose casual dress and lay on the bed.

No sooner had her head hit the pillow than she sat up, waited a minute then rose and padded across the carpet to a floral box set on the bench beside her small case. She lifted the lid, took out an old black-and-white photo and went back to the bed. Propped up on pillows this time instead of lying flat, she gazed at the photo she held in her hands. It had been snapped in Melbourne not long after the tragic bushfire that had claimed their parents. Hazel had taken Alice to Melbourne to live with her. They'd both been existing in a bubble of devastation and hadn't given a thought to Alice's looming fourteenth birthday. Hazel's work colleagues had banded together to get them both tickets to see The Seekers at the Sidney Myer Music Bowl.

It had been a hot day with so many bodies pressed together. For a young girl from Hobart the crush of people had been overwhelming but Hazel had held her hand tightly. They'd found a place on the grass, and the man next to her had worn a newspaper hat. He'd smelled of sweat and cigarettes but he'd been kind enough to make hats for her and Hazel. Once The Seekers walked out on the stage and began to sing, Alice had lost herself in the music and for a short time forgot she was an orphan with little but the clothes on her back. The concert had been one of the most magical experiences of her young life and Hazel's flatmate had taken their photo when they came home.

Alice traced their faces with her finger. They both looked dishevelled but they'd clung together and smiled for the camera. She remembered feeling safe in that moment with Hazel's arm holding her close. They'd lost everything that was dear to them but at least they had each other. They both looked so young, so innocent. She shuddered as she recalled how short-lived that simplicity had been.

Her phone played a tune. She looked around in surprise, reached over the side of the bed for her handbag and plucked it out. A text message flashed on the screen. She got so few of those. Her fingers fumbled to open it and there it was, a message from Greta. *Hope you got back to your motel safely. Now you have my number. Greta x*

Alice stared at the screen until it finally faded and went black. Then she jabbed at it to wake it up and began to type. The seed of hope inside her grew a little bigger as she pressed send.

seven

Tuesday was another bright and sunny day and by early afternoon the outside heat was pounding the rooftops of suburbia. Inside Hazel's house, the air conditioner was set at a pleasant twenty-four degrees, a perfectly comfortable temperature, but the group gathered around the dining table looked stiff and uncomfortable.

Hazel sat at one end and Kurt, the solicitor, at the other; June with Lachlan beside her on one side and Felicity with Greta on the other. Greta had rearranged her schedule and taken a late lunch so she could be there. Hazel was glad of her granddaughter's presence. It was reassuring. Felicity was fussing with something in her handbag and June was sitting stiffly upright, her matter-of-fact gaze on Kurt.

He cleared his throat. "If this is everyone?"

Hazel nodded.

"I'll make a start then."

Kurt opened the folder in front of him and lifted out some papers. He glanced up at Hazel and cleared his throat again. She felt a niggle of unease. Surely this was to be straightforward.

The first shock was that Franklyn had an extensive share portfolio. He'd always studied the share market, had a filing cabinet full of company correspondence in the spare room he used as a study, but Hazel hadn't questioned it. When he was doing that he wasn't bothering her.

The second shock was that Hazel would receive a small living allowance but the shares plus the money in Franklyn's bank accounts were to be divided between their three grandchildren. She'd heard both June and Felicity gasp as Kurt had read that. And there was more. The two boys, Lachlan and Joshua, would take control of their endowment on their twenty-fifth birthdays, but Greta's gift horse had a proviso: she also had to be married to Joe to receive her share.

They were still looking at each other, taking that in, when Kurt continued.

"For my daughter, June…"

Hazel was even more confused. Franklyn had always managed their finances but they'd led a modest life, what more could he have to give?

"I leave my house—"

"What?" Felicity had yelped.

"Let me continue, please—" Kurt glared at them over his glasses. "For my daughter, June, I leave my house, which she is to allow her mother to live in for as long as she needs. On Hazel's death, any money remaining that has been set aside for her income passes to June."

"What?" Felicity's voice was only a croak this time.

And there was the third shock, and with it the last bit of Hazel's bravado was sucked away. Her husband was dead and she'd imagined with his passing there'd be freedom. She'd never dreamed he would still be in control of her life from the grave.

"That's it?" Felicity looked from Kurt to Hazel with understandable confusion. She'd not been given a mention. Franklyn was disowning her and she'd want to know why. It was his final volley and it had the power to blow her family apart. Hazel didn't have to summon the wooziness she'd often done over the years to divert a situation, it was consuming her of its own accord.

Felicity lurched forward, glaring at Kurt. "How can Dad leave the house to June? Surely it's in joint names?"

Kurt closed the folder, removed his glasses and rested them on top. He turned to Hazel and she trembled under the brunt of his indifferent look. "The house is in Franklyn's name only."

Hazel could feel the collective surprise in the gazes of her daughters and her grandchildren. She shrivelled a little inside. Franklyn had always done the finances and she'd let him. They'd lived a comfortable life and she'd rarely questioned his decisions. To do so would only cause trouble and she'd spent a good deal of her marriage avoiding that.

"You need to contest it, Mum," Felicity said.

"It's not necessary," June said.

"Of course you'd say that," Felicity snapped.

"You could contest if you wished," Kurt cut in. "But I would advise against it."

"You would," Felicity said. "You're on Dad's side."

"I was your father's lawyer and I strongly encouraged him to make sure your mother was taken care of."

Felicity waved dismissively at the folder sitting benignly on the table. "How is this taking care of her?"

"Hazel will have the house and an allowance as long as she needs it."

Once more Kurt looked steadily at Hazel and the realisation hit. Her hand went to her throat. "He wasn't going to leave me anything, was he?"

"He reviewed his will only recently." Kurt shifted in his chair. "Let's just say we had a lengthy discussion on what would be best for everyone."

"Why would he leave me out?" Felicity asked.

June looked down her pointy nose. "You always defied him."

"I did not."

"I'm sure he loved you, Mum," Greta said.

"Grandad was a man's man," Lachlan said.

Felicity frowned at her nephew. "What does that mean?"

"He thought the man should be the provider and that women were dependent on men so the man should be in charge of the finances."

All four women glared at him. He held up his hands. "Hey, I'm not saying I agreed with him. It's just how he saw things."

"Why should Greta have to marry to get her share?" Felicity looked to Kurt. "Is that even legal?"

Hazel reached for the water glass in front of her and nearly knocked it over. Greta's hand shot out, steadying the glass.

"Are you okay, Nan?"

Hazel managed to sip a mouthful. "There's a lot to take in."

"There is." Kurt said. "I've managed Franklyn's affairs for years. Probate should be straightforward but it will be months before everything's sorted. He left instructions that his cars be sold."

"And leave Mum without a car as well." Felicity glowered at Kurt.

"I meant his two classic cars."

"Darn," Lachlan said. "I was hoping he'd leave them to me or Josh."

"That's rather mercenary, Lachlan," June said.

"I don't see why. Grandad used to take us for drives in them. Loved us to go out and tinker under the bonnet with him."

"And me," Greta said.

"Well, yeah, but you weren't really into them like Josh and I were. They were his first two cars. A 1964 Ford Anglia and a 1971 Holden Kingswood, both in pristine condition. Dad said they're worth a bit."

"I believe they have a combined insured value of seventy thousand dollars," Kurt said.

All four women exclaimed in unison and over the top of them Lachlan said, "I told you so."

"And the money will be put into the estate trust account so that your grandmother will have an income." Kurt turned to Hazel. "You'll receive your fortnightly payment as soon as the cars can be sold but everyone else will have to wait until probate is granted and the final paperwork is done. It could be six to eight months from now." Kurt gave a self-satisfied nod of his head and then bent down to the smart leather bag he'd propped against the leg of the chair when he came in. He rummaged inside and pulled out a bundle of envelopes. "There's one last thing."

Hazel stared at the crisp white envelopes. They were made of good quality paper, something Franklyn had always insisted on. She'd posted enough mail for him over the years to know they were the stationery he preferred.

"I suggested to Franklyn the terms of his will might be confusing for you all so he decided to write each of you a letter."

"What do they say?" June asked.

Kurt arched an eyebrow at her. "I have no idea of the contents. He wrote them, sealed them and delivered them to me. As you are all here, with the exception of your son Joshua, I thought I would bring them myself rather than post them. Will you be seeing Joshua?"

"He's gone back to Brisbane."

"If you provide his address I will forward it to him." Kurt took out a notepad and pen and passed it to June.

As June wrote, Hazel's gaze went to the envelopes resting innocuously on her dining table. Inside, her stomach was churning and her hands trembled. She gripped them tightly in her lap. She didn't know what Franklyn had written but she was certain about one thing: her family was about to implode.

June walked Kurt out and they'd barely left the room before Felicity snatched up the pile of envelopes. "Might as well see what Dad's written," she said with a nervous laugh. "I'm guessing mine won't be a love letter."

"It might be full of cash," Lachlan said with a grin as she handed him his.

Hazel's hands remained firmly in her lap. Felicity paused, the envelope she held out to her hovering like an evil spectre.

"Are you all right, Mum?" she asked.

Greta put an arm around Hazel. "This must all be such a shock, Nan. Would you like to lie down for a while?"

Hazel shook her head. As much as she'd prefer to run away, like she had from most confrontations in her life, she knew there was no escaping this one.

June came back and picked up the envelope Felicity had sat in her place. "Let's see what's inside."

"I'm going to put the kettle on," Felicity said. She got up, taking her envelope and crossed the open-plan space to the kitchen.

Hazel looked from one daughter to the other: June, so like Franklyn in appearance and with his determined steel core. She looked at everything in black and white. Felicity was the opposite. Emotional, full of grey areas, more responsive to others.

Hazel ignored her own envelope, unable to shift her gaze from her youngest daughter. Around her the other three opened theirs.

"No cash," Lachlan said with a fake laugh. "Just a note from Grandad saying how proud he is of my achievements and to make sure I use the money in some kind of investment, real estate or shares."

"And mine says to make sure I ask Derek's advice on looking after the house and managing the money." June gave an indignant snort.

Hazel continued to watch Felicity, who'd filled the kettle and taken out cups before picking up her envelope again. She was propped against the kitchen bench now, sliding a knife under the flap to open it, then slipping out the single piece of paper. The voices of the other three faded as Hazel watched Felicity unfold it and begin to read.

Greta snorted. "He was very old-fashioned. Mine says he's proud of my achievements but it's best to wait until I have the stability of a husband before I get my share. He admires Joe's common sense when it comes to money." There was a pause. "And then he says in light of my mother's history he wants me to be cautious. What hist—"

"Is this a joke?" Felicity looked up from the paper she clutched. Her glare was accentuated by the eye shape of her glasses so that Hazel felt physically pierced.

"What does it say?" June asked.

"Mum?" Felicity's single word carried with it disbelief and fear, and Hazel felt the last glimmer of hope that she could keep her family safe slide away.

"What is it?" Greta stood, began to walk, then stopped as Felicity held up a hand.

"Dad's letter tells me he's left me nothing because…because I'm *adopted*."

There were several gasps but no-one spoke. Behind Felicity the kettle came to the boil and switched off.

"True?" Lachlan was the first to gain his voice.

"That's ridiculous. It must be a joke," June huffed.

The air whooshed from Hazel's chest. Black dots danced before her eyes.

"Mum!" June gripped her hand.

"Oh, that'd be right," Felicity growled. "An attack of the vapours is your answer to anything you don't want to face."

"Felicity, don't be so horrid," June snapped.

"She's always done it," Felicity said. "Whenever anything was too tough to face she'd go all woozy and what do you know, crisis avoided."

"Mum, calm down." Greta said.

"You're not the one who's just been told your life's a lie," Felicity spat. "I can assure you, you're not adopted."

"Please don't get upset," Greta said. "There's an explanation. This can't be true." She sat down again and looked imploringly at Hazel. "Can it, Nan?"

Hazel summoned her last ounce of energy. "Water," she croaked and June held the glass to her lips.

Felicity strode back to the table. "Stop this, Mum, and tell me the truth."

Hazel gripped the glass with both hands, took another sip and, with the communal gaze of her family on her, put the glass carefully back on the table.

She smiled weakly at Felicity. There was no longer anything she could do to protect her. "I love you, Felicity. You are my daughter in every sense of the word."

Felicity gasped. "Except biologically."

Hazel slumped in her chair but there was no escape. She could only speak the truth no matter how desperately she wanted to say otherwise. "Yes, Felicity, you were adopted."

"Bloody hell, and I thought our family was boringly normal," Lachlan said. Then as if he'd had an afterthought he added, "But Mum's not adopted, is she?"

Once again they all stared at Hazel.

"No," she whispered.

Felicity's pallor matched the off-white of Hazel's kitchen cupboards. She gripped the back of the chair. "Why didn't you ever tell me?" she croaked, cleared her throat.

"I...we...your father—"

"Wanted to shock me from his deathbed. One last parting blow." She glared down at her feet. "I hope you bloody rot in hell, Dad."

"Felicity!" June gasped.

"You could do no wrong where he was concerned and nothing I did was ever good enough. Now I know why. I wasn't his and he didn't love me." Felicity snatched her handbag from the floor and strode across the room.

"Mum, where are you going?" Greta started to follow.

"Let me explain," Hazel said, not really knowing how she could.

At the hall door Felicity turned, and Hazel ached at the anguish she saw on her daughter's face. "I want time to digest this."

Greta took another step towards her but Felicity put up her hand. "I'll ring you later," she said then spun away.

Her heels clicked across the tiles, the front door banged and then there was silence. Hazel flopped forward and began to sob.

eight

In the city Alice sat in a cafe overlooking Rundle Mall. She finished her mid-afternoon snack, picked up her phone from the table and swiped the screen. It was clear and silent. She placed it back on the table. It was like a watched pot that would never boil. Normally her phone lived somewhere at the bottom of her bag. She used it infrequently but ever since she'd received Greta's text the afternoon before she'd kept it close, hoping her niece would make further contact. The phone had remained stubbornly silent.

Her gaze shifted to the people walking in the mall below her. A small group had stopped to watch a young man playing a guitar, the case open at his feet. He hadn't been there when she'd come in. The same post had been occupied by a dainty older woman dressed in a beautiful costume who'd swayed to some music, her hips and the pretty fans in her hands moving in unison. Alice had stopped to watch her then put five dollars in her open case, wondering at the woman's history. Was she alone, forced to busk to earn money to live, or perhaps she had a big family and did it for her grandchildren's education or, Alice thought back to the woman's glowing smile, simply because she enjoyed it. Alice hoped that was the reason. She'd learned to love dancing in Roy's arms. He'd been a good dancer and a gentle teacher, guiding her gracefully around the floor until she'd been giddy with enjoyment.

She'd be forever grateful for the day Roy Pollard came into her life; forever heartbroken that he was taken from her too young, but life went on. She missed him terribly and yet had been determined to rebuild her life, no matter how tricky that was proving. She managed quite well living on her own but sometimes it was the aloneness that overwhelmed her. She forced the feeling away now.

She'd ridden a wave of expectation on her trip to Adelaide. For a short few days she'd held a sliver of hope that she'd be able to reconnect with the sister she'd lost, but now it seemed she'd been rejected a second time. Alice wasn't filled with pity, simply resignation; her life had been punctuated with loss.

The first time had been just before her fourteenth birthday when her parents had died in the devastating fires that had claimed many in Tasmania. Hazel had been her rock then. Ten years older and struggling with her own grief, she'd come and collected Alice from the friend's where she'd been staying when the fire had taken her parents and her home. She'd had only the overnight bag with the few items Alice had taken with her when her parents had insisted she stay in Hobart until the fires were over. Hazel had taken her back to Melbourne and they'd shared the small bedroom in the flat Hazel rented with Caroline, a young woman from her work.

Alice remembered little about those first few weeks after the fires. They'd both been in shock and full of grief. Hazel had only been able to take a week off and until the payouts from her parents' house insurance and her father's modest life insurance policy came, they'd lived on very little. Caroline had been so kind – it had been she who had instigated the whip-round at work for the tickets to The Seekers.

After a couple of weeks Alice had been enrolled at a nearby school, second-hand uniforms had been found, she'd made some new friends and gradually life had taken on some kind of rhythm again. Then one Saturday morning, several months later in early November, Hazel had woken her early.

"Come on, sleepyhead," she'd chided. "We're going to my work end-of-year dinner and we both need a new dress."

Alice had thought she was dreaming. Hazel and Caroline had been talking about the dinner for weeks but Alice had assumed she wouldn't be going.

"You're going to be my date." Hazel giggled. "And there's nothing decent in your wardrobe or mine that fits that new bust of yours."

Alice blushed. Mostly she wore her school uniform and she'd been making do with the basic weekend wardrobe she'd accumulated since the fire. Recently her stick figure had begun to fill out and now with the weather warming up, the few summer things she had were too tight. Hazel had adjusted an old dress of hers that was a looser fit. It was the only one she had.

"But we don't have money for dresses," Alice said.

"I've squirrelled some away." Hazel winked at her and for a moment Alice had been whisked back to the days when their parents were still alive. Hazel's words were exactly those their father used when he'd planned a special and unexpected treat. Even the wink had been like his.

Alice had bounced out of bed and they'd done their share of the flat cleaning before Caroline had emerged, her hair in disarray, still piled high on her head from her outing the night before.

"Where are you two off to?" she'd asked as she'd lit up her first cigarette for the day.

"Shopping," they'd chorused then looked at each other, laughed, linked arms and set off. The early morning air in Melbourne was fresh and Alice had clutched her cardigan, one of Hazel's hand-me-downs, tightly around her as they'd boarded the tram for the ride into the city.

Once there, Hazel had taken her hand and led her to Bourke Street and to the grand facade of the Myer Emporium where they'd dawdled along taking in the Christmas window displays. Alice had been amazed at the sight of the intricate fairy tales portrayed in each window. Then Hazel had taken her inside and after much deliberation and trying on of dresses, they'd ended up with one each and several extra items for Alice. The dress she'd chosen seemed so grown up and so short. It was vibrant yellow with white stitching around the white neckline and also around the fake pockets at her chest and the fake belt that circled her hips.

Hazel had chosen a more formal dress. It had a deep round neck with short sleeves and was made from black rayon with a wide white sash that formed a bow just under her bust and showed off her trim figure. Alice had been in awe of her sister, who'd looked as sophisticated and as stylish as Margaret Rohan, crowned Miss Australia only a month before.

By the time they left Myer and headed to the Coles cafeteria, their arms were loaded with parcels. Hazel had also purchased smart patent black shoes for herself, and for Alice new sandals – white with a slight heel – as well as a blouse, a pair of shorts and bathers.

Hazel sat a plate loaded with a pie and chips in front of Alice. "Well, tuck in." She put a similar plate on her side of the table then took the lid from a bottle of lemonade and poured them both a glass.

The bubbles fizzed up Alice's nose and she coughed. It had been a long time since she'd had fizzy drink.

Hazel laughed and took a sip of her own glass. "Isn't this fun?"

"Yes." Alice looked across the table at her big sister. "I know it's not been easy for you, finding enough money for both of us. Thank you, Hazel."

Hazel reached out a hand and gripped Alice's. "My darling Alice, you don't have to thank me. You're my sister and I'd do anything for you." She squeezed Alice's hand tighter. "No matter what, I'll always be there for you."

Alice had looked at the hand gripping hers through eyes brimming with tears. Their lives had been ripped apart by the fire but Alice remembered the strange sensation that had filled her chest that day. It had taken a while for her to recognise it but it was hope; hope for feeling truly happy again, hope for a secure future. Thankfully she couldn't see into the future and the events that would come and suck every last drop of that hope from her and leave only true despair.

"Have you finished here?" The waiter's voice startled Alice back to the present and she was shocked to realise there were tears in her eyes.

She nodded and sat back as he reached down for her plate. "You can take the cup too." The remains of her tea would be cold now. She fished in her bag for a hanky, dabbed gently at her eyes and shook her head. Silly to be reminiscing. She'd survived this life by not dwelling on the past. Seeing Hazel again had brought it all back.

Her phone was still lying on the table. She picked it up, resisted the urge to check the screen and shoved it deep in her bag. Her shopping was complete. This afternoon she had one last appointment and after that there was no reason for her to stay in Adelaide. She'd consign Hazel to memory only once more, then first thing tomorrow she'd set off for her home in Marion Bay and resume her ordered existence.

nine

Felicity adjusted her sunglasses on the bridge of her nose, collected her handbag from the seat beside her and thanked the Uber driver.

"You sure you'll be okay?" He half-turned, studying her with deep brown eyes full of concern. No doubt having a woman sobbing in the back of his car hadn't made his day.

"Yes, thank you." She gave a brief nod of her head. "I'll be fine once I get inside." She climbed out of the car, saw the pile of sodden tissues she'd left behind and shut the door on them.

The car pulled away before she'd taken two steps, the driver's concern obviously evaporating with her evacuation of his vehicle. She fumbled in her bag for her keys. Her hands were still shaky. The first tremors of shock had swept her as she'd backed out of her mum's...correction...her fake mum's driveway, then as she'd driven down the road the tears had formed in her eyes. By the time she'd turned the corner into the next street she was howling. A young woman pushing a pram with a toddler in tow was crossing the road and Felicity had pulled up with a squeal of brakes. The mum had looked at her through the windscreen, terror on her face, before hurrying for the safety of the footpath. Felicity had inched her way to the side of the road and ordered an Uber.

She'd managed to pull herself together in the few minutes it took for the car to arrive but she'd not been aboard long before the tears had started again. The worried driver had offered to stop but she'd told him she just wanted to go home. For most of the thirty-minute journey she'd sobbed into the couple of tissues she'd had. He'd passed her a box from the front and she'd sobbed harder for a while then managed to calm down and stop the tears as she neared her house.

Her relationship with Franklyn hadn't been an easy one. From a young age she'd tried so hard to gain his approval. In her teens she'd been rebellious, testing his patience, and finally she'd given up trying to impress him at all. She'd felt guilty at the almost-relief she'd felt when he'd died. Now she had no idea what to think.

Ian's car was in the drive. She hadn't expected him to be home yet. She hurried up the path to the front door, craving his arms around her, the one person she could rely on to be who she knew him to be. They didn't have secrets and their family wasn't built on a lie.

She flung open the front door and hurried inside. Ian's backpack and overnight bag sat beside their bedroom door as she passed. He worked for a construction company as their engineering loss assessor which meant he was regularly on the road. "Not today," she moaned and fled towards the family room.

Ian stood in front of the large glass doors, hands in pockets, facing the back yard.

"Ian!" She flung off her sunglasses and her tears started again as she hurried across the room.

He turned slowly, concern on his face as she threw herself against him. He placed one arm lightly around her shoulders.

"Oh, Ian," she mumbled. Both he and his shirt smelled fresh. He must have showered when he got home. Perhaps he'd been for a ride. "I'm so glad you're home."

"I gather there's been more drama."

"More?"

"There's always something where your parents are concerned."

She sniffed in a breath. "That's the thing, you see…" She hiccupped a sob.

He patted her back. "You sit down." He pushed her gently towards the table.

Felicity flopped onto a chair and slid her feet out of her strappy sandals. "It's been a terrible day."

"I'll put the kettle on."

"Damn, what time is it?" She retrieved her glasses from her handbag, slipped them on and glanced up at the smart silver-rimmed clock with the white face that had been a gift from June for her birthday. Felicity had picked it, of course, to match the Hamptons style she'd used to furnish her new living space. "Four-thirty's not too early for wine, is it? I've had enough tea today."

He disappeared into the butler's pantry and came back with a bottle. "Pinot gris okay?"

"Anything." She groaned and gripped her head in her hands, nervous about telling him her bombshell news. It wouldn't make any difference to Ian but how do you tell the man you've been married to all these years that you're not the person you thought you were? She got up again, retrieved the box of tissues from the dresser, set it in front of her on the table and sat. "I don't know where to start."

"Here you are." He placed a glass in front of her and sat opposite, the space in front of him empty.

"You're not having one?" She took a sip. The creamy taste rolled over her tongue, ending with a crisp finish. "It's good." She took a bigger mouthful.

"I need to talk to you, Liss."

"Okay." She set the glass back down. Perhaps it would be better if he told her whatever it was he had to say first. Give her a moment to think how you told someone you'd known for so long that you'd just found out you were adopted.

He was looking down at his hands, clasped together so tightly the tips of his fingers where turning red.

"Are you going away again?" she asked.

"What?"

"Your bags were in the bedroom."

"Oh...yes."

"I know it's work, Ian." Felicity took another sip of wine. One of the upsides of Ian's job was that the irregularities of it meant he worked flexible hours but that was also the downside because he could be away from home days at a time. "But I wish you didn't have to—"

"It's not work."

She tried to recall what else had been on the calendar this week.

"In fact it's not anything to do with work."

Deep lines creased his forehead. And then she remembered he'd had a doctor's visit the previous week.

"Oh, no, Ian, you're not sick, are you?" She half rose to her feet.

He held up his hands. "No. I'm healthy. As good as a fifty-two-year-old can be."

"Oh thank goodness." She sank back to the chair.

"It's just that…well, there's no easy way to say this."

"Just say it then." Felicity was thinking that's how she'd have to tell him her news. Just spit it out, no lead-ups or explanations.

"I'm leaving, Felicity."

"But you just said you weren't."

"I said I wasn't going away for work but…I haven't been happy for a long time and I've decided I need some time to find out—"

"Wait!" She sat back, blinked. "You're leaving *me*?"

"I know it's not a good time but—"

"You're leaving *me*?" Had she heard him wrong? Perhaps it was a joke and he was about to smile and say 'just kidding'. She searched his face for a sign to tell her he hadn't meant it but his eyes were pools of sadness.

"Why?" She shook her head as tears began to form again. "I don't understand. We're happy. I…thought…we were…h…ha…appy." Her words came out in ragged lumps between sobs.

His grim look remained. "Liss, I'm so sorry. I've been putting off telling you for months but I can't play the charade any longer."

Her mouth hung open, her body stiff like it had been when Greta was young and they'd played Statues. The air left her throat with a strangulated sound and her chest felt so tight she wondered if she was asphyxiating.

Ian made a dash for the sink and came back with a glass of water. "Breathe, Felicity, then have some water."

She gulped in some breaths then gripped the glass with two hands and lifted it with trembling fingers to her mouth. She managed to take a couple of sips before she put it back on the table, worried it would slip and smash like her life seemed to be doing. Hell, she was acting like Hazel but she couldn't help it.

"Months?" she gasped.

"This is a shock, I know," Ian said. "There hasn't been the right time to tell you. There was Greta's engagement then Christmas and the extensions being finalised, then your birthday–housewarming party and then your dad...there's always something. You've been staying at Hazel's since your dad died and I've had plenty of time to—"

"You've been having an affair." The realisation hit her like a slap to the face. "Who is it?"

"No-one!"

"They say the wife's always the last to know."

"God, no, Felicity!" He leaned across the table, his look imploring now. "It's not about anyone else, it's about me."

"You!" Felicity pushed back her chair and this time she stood right up. She looked at the man who'd been her husband for twenty-nine years and saw a stranger. "What happened to *us*?"

"There hasn't been an us for a long time, Lissie."

Her arm flew up, her finger outstretched, jabbing the air between them.

"Don't you Lissie me in that sad voice. You've no right. How could you do this to us...to me? What about Greta?"

"She's a grown woman."

"Our family...our friends."

"They'll have to deal with it."

"I can't believe you'd be so heartless. You're telling me now, when my father's just died and I find out I'm..." Adopted. She couldn't say it now. "You can't leave me."

"I'm sorry, Felicity." He walked to the hall door then turned back. "I'm staying with a bloke from work until we organise things. He's got a granny flat so I'll have my own space."

"Your own space." Felicity flung out an arm. "What do you call this house?"

"You've made it your house. It's so perfect there's no part of it that feels like mine any more."

"That's ridiculous. The renovations were for us, to make a beautiful home."

"And you've done that, Liss," he said softly. "But it doesn't feel like my home. We want different things...we've drifted apart."

Her knees buckled, she sagged to the chair, the fight gone out of her, replaced with dread.

"I'll call you."

She listened to the soft tread of his shoes on the tiles, the muffled rustles as he collected his things and then the clunk as the front door closed. There was a brief pause and then the sound of Ian's car reversing out and driving away.

She reached for her handbag on the end of the table, took out her phone and pressed his number. He answered, the sound of the car loud beyond his voice.

"Please come back," she whispered.

He didn't reply straight away. She pressed the phone to her ear. "Ian?"

"I can't, Felicity."

She took a breath but there was no sound now. She peered at the screen. The call had ended. She jabbed at his number.

"Felicity, stop calling me," he said before she could speak. "You need time to digest this. We'll talk later."

"I want to talk now," she yelled but once more she was speaking to a silent phone. She pressed Ian's number again and this time it went to voicemail. She screamed at the phone clutched tightly in her hand then tossed it on the table. It landed with a thud on the solid wood.

Felicity stared at it a moment then snatched it back up, turned it off then tossed it aside again. "Two can play at that game." She thudded her fists on the table then sat perfectly still, aware only of the jarring rise and fall of her chest until gradually it slowed back to a normal rhythm.

Beyond the glass of the back door, Dolly miaowed. Felicity moved slowly across the room, opened the door and bent to pick the cat up. She pressed the comforting softness of warm fur under her chin but Dolly struggled in her arms then leaped to the floor and stalked towards the laundry where her food was kept.

Felicity went back to her chair. The tears that had brimmed earlier had dried up and she felt devoid of any emotion. Perhaps this was what it was like to be in shock – the numbness. Inside she was as empty as the carefully placed ceramic bowl in the centre of her brand-new table. Her gaze drifted to the two glasses in front of her, one full of wine and the other water. She reached for the wine.

ten

Greta tapped her fingers on the steering wheel. Up ahead there was a red light and she was so far back in the lane it would take at least two cycles to get through. She tried her mum's phone again while she waited and then her dad's, but both went straight to voicemail. Her breath whistled sharply between her clenched teeth. Worrying about her mother was a new experience.

It had been almost five when she'd finally left her nan's place to go home. She'd only driven a short distance when she'd noticed her mum's car parked at a bit of a weird angle in the next street over. The car was empty and she'd immediately tried to ring Felicity and then Ian. Annoyed but concerned, she'd decided to drive to her parents' place. It had been slow going. A combination of peak-hour traffic and roadworks had her trapped in a stop–start convoy of late-afternoon commuters.

Her head hurt from all the emotion of the day and she longed to be with Joe. She'd been staying at her nan's place on and off since her grandad had died and Joe had also had a big project on which had seen him working late and over the weekend. They'd spent little time together in the past couple of weeks and she wanted nothing more than to curl up with him on the couch and chill in his reassuring presence. Moving in with Joe had given her a freedom that had been lacking in her life. It was as if she was a caged bird set free. At home the focus of both parents had been firmly on her. She'd always lamented being an only child.

Once more she tried Joe's number and once more she got his voicemail. She thumped the steering wheel. Why did no-one answer? Were they all playing let's block Greta or had something more happened? She left Joe a message saying there was another family crisis and she would call him later.

Her stomach growled with hunger as she pulled up in her parents' driveway. She'd worked through lunch so she could get away to be at the will reading and now she was starving. Her dad's car wasn't in the street out the front but he may have put it in the garage seeing her mum's car wasn't there. He'd become very fussy about his car since he'd bought this last sporty-looking vehicle. Before this one he'd driven an ageing Golf and hadn't cared about cleaning it or where it was parked but he'd become very possessive when he'd bought the new Mazda last year.

She put her key in the lock and went inside. Her heels echoed on the tiles as she walked down the hall. The house felt eerily empty.

"Mum?" she called.

A quick glance right and left revealed no signs of life in either the main bedroom or the formal lounge. Ahead of her, the lowering sun streamed golden light through the expanse of glass that faced west, giving the family room an ethereal glow.

"Mum?"

Greta heard a sound, perhaps a groan, then realised it was snoring. She squinted into the light – Felicity would usually have pulled down the block-out blinds by now. There on the large

L-shaped couch that dominated one corner of the living space was her mum. Felicity was sprawled on her back, a disorderly jumble of limbs, her dress ridden up to her thighs, her face matching the off-white of the fabric. Greta had never seen her mum look so untidy. A box of tissues sat by her head and several sodden tissues were dotted around her along with her glasses. The many cushions that usually decorated the couch were scattered on the floor, Felicity's handbag upended among them, and a wine bottle and a glass sat on the wooden tray on the ottoman. The glass was empty and there wasn't much left in the bottle.

Felicity made a choking sound, snorted, groaned and rolled over; one arm flopping over the edge of the couch. Dolly emerged from under a cushion and leaped to the floor. Felicity's answer to her shock news had obviously been to drink herself into oblivion, but should Greta leave her?

She tiptoed out into the hall, and tried ringing her dad again – still voicemail – and then Joe, who answered immediately.

"I was about to call you," he said. "I've got a stir-fry on the go."

"That's lovely, thank you." Joe rarely cooked evening meals and Greta's empty tummy growled in anticipation.

"How did the will reading go? How long till you're home?"

Greta ignored the first question, not wanting to go into the ins and outs of her afternoon over the phone. "I'm at Mum and Dad's place."

"What are you doing there?"

She could hear the disappointment in his voice. It meant she was still at least a half hour away from home.

"Mum's a bit…" Behind Greta came the sound of a groan. "She had some surprising news and it's shaken her up."

"Oh, I see." Once more disappointment oozed from the phone.

"Dad's not home and I can't reach him," she said. "I want to make sure Mum's okay before I leave." There was another groan from beyond the door followed by a cough. "I've got to go. I'll call you as I'm leaving. Love you." She ended the call as the cough began to sound more like retching and dashed back through the door. Felicity was struggling upright.

"Are you okay?"

Felicity let out a curse. "You frightened me." She coughed again.

"I thought you were being sick."

"No." She patted at her throat. "I'm dry," she croaked.

Greta filled a glass with water and came back and sat beside her. Felicity was leaning against the back of the couch, her hand to her forehead.

She took the glass and a sip of water, cleared her throat and sipped again. "Where are my glasses?"

"Here." Greta bent to retrieve them from the floor.

Felicity slid them on. "Ooh, my head hurts," she groaned.

"Drink more water. Do you want some painkillers?"

"I couldn't find any." Felicity waved a hand in the direction of her upturned bag.

"Surely there's some in your medicine kit?" Greta went to the pantry and lifted down a plastic storage basket that contained the makings of a small pharmacy and plucked out a packet of paracetamol. She refilled Felicity's glass and offered it with two tablets.

"Thank you," Felicity said once she'd swallowed them. "I didn't expect you to come tonight."

"I was worried." Greta sat again. "I found your car round the corner from Nan's."

"I decided not to drive after all."

"I tried to call you and I tried Dad but—"

Felicity groaned and gripped her head with her hands.

"Is your headache worse?"

"No…I…oh…" Her words became sobs.

"Oh, Mum." Greta hugged her. It felt strange to be the one offering comfort when it had always been her mother soothing and reassuring her in the past. She'd never seen Felicity like this before. "You've had a few shocks this last week. First Grandad and then to find out you were adopted…"

Felicity lurched back, plucked a tissue from the box beside her and blew her nose. "Yes. It's been…a difficult time but…"

"Nan was so upset after you left. Aunty June's staying tonight with her."

"June's her daughter."

"So are you. In every way except she didn't give birth to you. Nothing's changed."

"And yet I feel as if everything has." Felicity shrugged off Greta's arm. "I don't think you can understand how I feel about this, Greta, but I do appreciate you coming over to check on me."

"Dad's not home yet?"

Felicity collected up the tissues scattered around her. "No… at least…he won't be…he's…he's away for one of his work trips."

"Have you told him about today?"

"No. There wasn't a chance and I didn't want to worry him. It can wait till he gets back."

"Do you want to talk about it?"

Felicity turned away, making for the kitchen. "Not now. I'm still processing it myself."

"Would you like me to stay tonight?" Greta stared at Felicity's back as she dropped the bundle of tissues into the bin. What she really wanted was to be back at her place with Joe.

"No, I'll be fine. You go home." Felicity's lips twisted in a crooked smile. "You've been such a wonderful help this last week but poor Joe's hardly seen you. I'll be glad to be in my own bed tonight and I'm sure you must feel the same."

Greta hoped her concerned look masked her relief. "What about your car?"

"I shouldn't drive tonight. I'll get an Uber over there in the morning."

"Perhaps while you're there you can call on Nan. She really wants to see you."

"I'll see what happens in the morning." Felicity glanced away. "I'm going to run a bath."

"Great idea. I'll ring you tomorrow."

Greta stopped and Felicity almost bumped into her. "You'd better check your phone. It might be flat – I kept getting your voicemail."

"Oh, yes. I'll check." She kissed Greta. "Thanks again for calling in, darling. I'll be fine."

Greta barely had time to respond before she was being bundled outside and the door shut firmly behind her. She wasn't convinced Felicity had it as all together as she was saying but she was glad not to have to stay. She sent Joe a quick text as she made her way to her car. *On my way.*

★

Felicity had no sooner shut the door on Greta than she hurried back to the family room, plucked up her phone and switched it on. After Ian had left she'd swallowed the glass of wine in a short time then taken her glass and the bottle to the couch and settled in. By the end of the second glass she was sobbing hysterically at the indignity and injustice of her situation. Her life had been a lie. Not only was she adopted but evidently her husband no longer loved her. Everything she believed to have been true was not so. She would have rung Suzie. Her dearest friend would have comforted her but Suzie was across the other side of the world enjoying her birthday with her husband – her faithful, loving husband.

Felicity had moved to the couch, sunk into its comfortable embrace and sipped her third glass of wine while she surveyed the stylish yet practical kitchen, dining and living area she'd planned, created and furnished. She'd done it as much for Ian as herself. It was for them. She loved to entertain. She'd been happy to cook for Ian's work dinners and to have guests, not just her friends and family but Ian's too. She thought back to the night of her party and all the people who'd been there. They weren't just her friends, they were their friends, hers and Ian's. How was she going to tell them Ian had left her?

By the time she'd poured her fourth glass of wine she'd made a decision. Ian was obviously playing out some kind of mid-life fantasy and he'd probably come to his senses once he was alone and doing all his own cooking and cleaning. And, if there truly was no other woman as he'd said, surely he'd realise he missed Felicity and come home. It was best if they told no-one he'd gone. He was often away on work trips and sometimes treks or bike rides so she could make excuses for a while.

That thought in place, she'd downed the last of her glass and, feeling a bit woozy, she'd decided against a fifth. She'd put her head back and shut her eyes and the next thing she knew she was sprawled on the couch with a throat as dry as the bottom of a cocky's cage and Greta beside her, scaring her half to death. It hadn't been until Greta had asked where Ian was that Felicity had remembered he'd left her.

The phone screen came to life in her hand. She selected messages and slid onto a dining chair, regretting the fourth glass of wine. Her head was pounding in spite of the painkillers. She chose Ian's name and tapped out her request that he not tell anyone for now and if Greta rang he should tell her he was out bush for a while. Then she pressed send and rested her head on her arms. If Ian wouldn't answer her calls, he might at least read a message.

eleven

Hazel sat on the couch in her family room and stared at the television. The sound was turned down and she couldn't make out what was being said but the show was about a couple who were looking to purchase a place in the country. They wanted to escape city life. Normally Hazel enjoyed seeing the different homes they visited but not tonight. Franklyn's death should have brought her own escape but that door had been slammed in her face. Franklyn had made sure she would live off his charity and that of their daughter for the rest of her life.

A sudden sting in her hand made her look down. A small arc of red oozed in her palm. She'd been clenching her fists so tightly she'd cut herself with her own nail. She pressed her palm to her lips.

Behind her June was busy in the kitchen, washing dishes and tidying up after the basic evening meal they'd just shared. Not that Hazel had felt hungry. There was a hollow emptiness inside her but not hunger. Franklyn had dished out a terrible blow from the grave. She might have been able to deal with him leaving her a pittance but that he'd taken Felicity from her was a despicable thing to do. She'd never forgive him.

Poor Felicity. She'd looked absolutely devastated when she'd left. Hazel had been frightened for her. But she'd agreed with June and Greta that it was best to give Felicity some space. Later she'd been glad of Greta's call, letting her know that Felicity was understandably upset but okay.

Damn Franklyn. Hazel's fingers curled again, this time into the soft leather of the couch. The one he'd insisted they buy when they'd done the extension. It had been a surprise when he'd said he wanted leather and two matching armchairs. He'd always made a show about deliberating but had rarely objected to necessary household purchases as long as she sought his opinion and selected items that were durable but not too expensive. She'd put a lot of thought into what would be practical but also look nice in the extension. When she'd shown him the lovely fabric couch with matching recliners that she'd chosen he'd been vehement with his disapproval.

She glared down at the couch now, thinking if she had a knife in her hand she'd slash it. Then she wondered how much she could get for it if she were to sell it, not much after all these years. Her fists curled tighter. That's if she even owned it. She couldn't remember anything being said about the contents of the house in Franklyn's will.

"Mum?"

June was standing behind her.

"I asked if you'd like a cup of tea?"

Hazel ran a hand along the top of the couch. "Is this mine or yours, do you think?"

"Oh, Mum." June stalked around the couch and sat stiffly beside her. She took both of Hazel's hands in hers and jiggled them up and down. "I told you not to worry about any of it. We'll let the dust settle and we'll be able to work everything out. You know I wouldn't see you without a roof over your head."

"Yes, but I'm wondering which roof? You could sell this place and pack me off to a home somewhere."

"You're to stop that kind of talk at once." June's tone was short, just like Franklyn's. "There's no need for you to leave here. Derek and I wouldn't think of moving you." She gave Hazel's hands a last jiggle then let them go. "Now, what about that cup of tea?"

"Thank you," Hazel said and June bustled off to make it.

They might not put her out just yet but one day the time would come. Her son-in-law was an astute businessman. He and Franklyn had got on very well. They'd spent many a family get-together talking money matters. If only Hazel had realised how important that was, perhaps she would have paid more attention. She wished she'd thought to ask Kurt how much her allowance was going to be.

"Here you are." June put a cup of tea in front of her and another for herself before settling on the couch. "What on earth's this you're watching?" She picked up the remote. "There must be something else on surely." And with no discussion, the channel was changed. Hazel closed her eyes against the tears that trembled there.

*

"It's been the strangest day," Greta said as she settled on the couch with a bowl of stir-fry in her lap and a glass of wine on the little table beside her. Joe sat next to her with his own bowl and glass. "You will never believe it."

"With your family, there's always something."

"What do you mean by that?" Greta looked at Joe over the forkful of food she had halfway to her mouth.

"Your nan can get a bit…" he shrugged, "hysterical sometimes, and your aunty June creates mountains out of molehills."

"Today Nan had every right to get hysterical, although she didn't." She paused. That had been more her mum's reaction. Greta swallowed her food and with it the offence at Joe's comment. He hadn't really said anything that wasn't true. Joe's parents were an older couple, closer in age to her nan than her parents, and he had one older sister, Hannah, who was married with two kids, a boy and a girl. Nothing over the top or extraordinary happened in their family. "Grandad's will was a bombshell. He didn't leave anything to Nan other than a living allowance and Mum got nothing."

"What about you?"

"He left some shares to each of his grandchildren but not until our twenty-fifth birthdays."

"That's this year for you."

"Don't get too excited. I don't imagine it'll be much once it's divided by three." Greta played it down, not wanting to show her own excitement at the prospect of some extra money and she didn't mention the part about her also having to be married to receive her inheritance. She was glad her grandad had liked Joe but the way his letter was worded, it was as if the money was for Joe, rather than her. "I'm more worried for Nan and Mum. Grandad was a bit old-fashioned but I never imagined he could be so unkind. The house was in his name and he left it to June."

"Really? Where will Hazel live?"

"She can stay on there. His will says that, but even if it didn't, I can't imagine June kicking her out."

"You'd hope not."

"There's something else." Greta put her bowl on the table and sat forward. "Grandad wrote each of us a letter. Mine was only a few sentences and I gather the others were too but Mum's...well, he said he didn't leave her anything because she was adopted."

"What? I didn't know she was adopted."

"None of us did, except Nan and Grandad, it seems. Nan said it was true. Mum was in shock."

"I can imagine she would have been. Poor Felicity. Is that why you went over?"

"Yes, but she didn't want me to stay."

"There's no doubt about your family."

"What about them?"

"There's always a drama."

"No, there's not. This is big, I must admit, but up until now I've thought we were pretty normal."

"As long as everyone did what Franklyn said. If ever you didn't there was hell to pay."

"He could be a bit difficult at times."

"A bit! What about his eightieth birthday last year! Hazel had planned a dinner for him at home. She and your mum and June had cooked for ages, then a few days before he says it's too much trouble to have it at home and we should all go to a pub for lunch and that's what we did, but not before Hazel had one of her woozy moments."

"That's not really the same as finding out you're adopted though, is it." Greta knew Joe found her family taxing at times but that was because, in comparison, his were boringly dull. Not that she didn't like them. His family were lovely people and always made her feel welcome. They were all so...nice. "You always got on well with Grandad."

"He was very astute when it came to money. I could always learn something from a chat with Franklyn. Speaking of which, how much will your inheritance be?"

"I don't know."

"Didn't you ask?"

"There were bigger things happening, Joe. Mum was devastated and Nan was upset, and the rest of us were so shocked that no-one talked about money. Grandad's old cars were a bit of a surprise though. Evidently he had them insured for seventy thousand dollars."

Joe let out a long, low whistle. "I thought they were just a couple of old bombs he kept in the back shed because they weren't worth anything. I knew he was smart when it came to money. Your share will be handy."

"I don't imagine it will be much."

"Still, every bit we can put towards a house will bring it closer. And then once we have the house we can plan our wedding and then babies."

She glanced away from his bright smile and picked up her bowl again. Joe had their lives all mapped out and she'd been happy to go along with it but today's events had made her pause. In spite of Joe's assessment, she'd thought they were just an everyday family. Now it turned out they had a skeleton in the closet and that made her wonder if there were more secrets. Franklyn had caused a stir and, if she was being honest, his condition that she had to be married to get her inheritance had stung. It was the twenty-first century, after all, and women had been managing their own assets for a long time.

"It's what you want too, isn't it?"

Joe's question startled her. Was it what she wanted? She hoped the smile she gave him was bright enough to match his own. "Of course." She took the last scoop of stir-fry. "We're not in a rush for babies though, are we?"

"The younger the better for women, they say."

Greta wondered who 'they' were. Men who thought women couldn't be trusted with money of their own and should remain barefoot and pregnant?

"It's just that once we have a house, there won't be money for anything else," she said.

"I'm not letting us have a mortgage that big. The bigger our deposit, the smaller our mortgage. We really have to stay on track with this, Greta."

He looked so earnest she envied him. She wished she was as sure about what she wanted for her future. She reached for his bowl. "Thanks, that was delicious."

She carried the dishes to the sink. Behind her Joe flicked on the TV.

Greta knew she loved him and wanted to spend her life with him but did she want a mortgage and babies? Maybe one day, but there were other things she'd like to do first. Joe had travelled for a year between uni and work but she'd gone straight from one to the other. He was a few years older than her and already forging his way up the chain in his career. Greta enjoyed her work but she wasn't planning on staying as a service desk analyst forever. And now with the upheaval in her family, the secrets and the disclosures since Grandad's death, she questioned what she'd thought of as her grandparents' happy marriage. Surely they were happy once? A dark thought hit her. Joe was very focused on money. What if their marriage ended up like Hazel and Franklyn's?

*

Later that night Hazel sat on the edge of her bed, the stiff white envelope gripped in her hands. Around her the house was silent. June had gone to bed and would no doubt be dreaming by now. She slept like the dead. Hazel envied her. Sleep would be a long time coming to her tonight.

The light from the bedside lamp threw a dull glow that didn't reach the corners of the room. It was when she'd flicked it on she'd rediscovered Franklyn's letter lying beside it. She didn't even remember putting it there. She'd been so distressed after Felicity had left, the rest of the afternoon had been a blur.

Hazel's fingers trembled as she removed the single sheet of paper from the envelope. Franklyn's spidery handwriting spread across the page. She wondered when he'd written the letters. Kurt had given the impression that he'd made his final will in recent times. In the last few months Franklyn's strength had waned considerably and she'd even had to help him shower, though he'd refused any outside help. Not even the family had been privy to how dependant on her he'd become. The only time she'd left him alone for more than an hour was for her monthly visit to the hairdresser. Her appointment was always on a Friday morning. She was usually away from home from nine until twelve, making the most of the freedom. Sometimes she'd fit in a coffee or do some personal shopping. It had been her one reprieve for the month. When she returned home Franklyn was usually where she'd last seen him, in his office, reading in the family room or nutting out a sudoku at the table, waiting for her to make lunch.

Now she stared down at the paper scrunched in her hands as if it might bite her. Once, a couple of months ago, she'd been battling a cough and had only stayed out long enough to have her hair trimmed. Kurt had been getting into his car when she'd returned. Franklyn had brushed off her question about why the lawyer had been at their home. Now that she thought about it, Franklyn could have had anyone visit during her hairdresser outings and she wouldn't have known.

She smoothed out the page in her hand and began to read.

Dear Hazel,

If you're reading this it means I have predeceased you. It wasn't something I thought about until this last year as my health has declined. I've built up a comfortable financial backing which I planned should see us through our final years but then I realised without me to oversee it, you wouldn't know what to do. You've never thought about our long-term needs or had to manage the household accounts. I considered it best to put plans in place so that you didn't waste money on fripperies and trips or a new house as you've mentioned in passing. All these things would soon see you without an income.

Hazel gasped. How dare he suggest she would waste their money? And fripperies! When had she ever wasted money on fripperies? She hadn't wished her husband dead but it had occurred to her on several occasions that if he did go first and she was still fit and healthy that she would do some of the things Franklyn had never allowed. They'd travelled only a little and she was keen to do more. She'd also liked the idea of getting a smaller home in one of those retirement village places where there were other people about and all the facilities one could need. She'd suggested it to Franklyn once when the gardening started to get too much but he'd been adamant he wasn't leaving his home until they carried him out. Well, that had happened and he'd left her high and dry. She looked back at the letter again.

I've decided to put a tight rein on your spending. In fact, I thought the pension would be enough for you but Kurt has suggested you would be more comfortable with a little extra and that perhaps you would try to contest my will if I didn't leave you with a roof over your head. I wanted to ensure June and our grandchildren received something from my hard work. I'm sure you wouldn't want to deny them. Therefore what I have organised should be more than enough for you and I forbid you to waste my money contesting my wishes.

Derek will keep an eye on June's affairs but lately I haven't been so confident of the way Ian manages money. He seems to give Felicity a free hand and as she's not actually our daughter I've decided to keep her out of my will.

I realised questions would be asked and perhaps she might contest so I've nipped that in the bud by letting her know she's not entitled. Felicity has always been the difficult one, perhaps because you've always favoured her over your own daughter – like you used to favour your sister over me. I thought if I'm no longer here it would be best for the truth to be out.

Hazel groaned.

And I've noticed a begrudging support of my poor health recently.

Hazel's mouth fell open. "*Begrudging!*" she snapped. "Felicity helped us far more than June did." She blinked to clear the black dots dancing before her eyes and read on.

Since I've no longer been able to accompany you on our morning walk, you can't wait to skip out the door without me. Flaunting your able body when mine is beginning to let me down.

This time Hazel dropped the letter to her lap and gripped her head in her hands. She'd been a good and faithful wife to Franklyn all their married life. How could he say these things, and yet, even as she thought it, she could see herself setting off each morning for her short walk. After he'd retired they'd walked the three blocks together but his knees had become painful and he'd refused the option of replacements. Hazel had insisted she keep up the walks. She was only gone twenty minutes but she'd seen the frustration on his face as she'd checked to make sure he was fine and had all he'd needed before she left. Some mornings he'd made it hard for her, demanding another cup of tea, a different shirt, a more comfortable cushion. Or he'd accuse her of misplacing some papers, which was ridiculous because she'd so rarely entered his office.

There had been one morning a few months ago when she'd left via the back door and Franklyn had called after her. She'd known he was simply being difficult and had pretended not to hear him. She'd almost skipped across the back patio towards the side path, had stopped to smell the first of the roses then, before she'd continued on down the side of the garage, she'd glanced back. Franklyn had got up from his chair and was standing at the window, watching her with such malevolence she'd whipped her head back pretending she hadn't seen him.

"Hazel," he'd called but she'd kept on.

"I know you heard me," he'd said as soon as she'd returned. "How dare you ignore me."

Hazel had denied it of course, but she'd never been a good liar. It had given her small satisfaction to ignore him but she'd paid for it with his fussing demands for the rest of the day and the next day he'd said he wasn't well enough to get out of bed and she'd had to miss her morning walks after that.

Hazel read the last line.

Now you're rid of me but know that I have always remained your faithful husband, Franklyn

Hazel gasped, the page pressed to her chest. She would never be out from under his bullying grasp. Franklyn's parting blow had been a sledgehammer and so many questions swirled around the shattered pieces of her life. How could she set about rebuilding her relationship with Felicity? Would she ever be able to? How would she manage the house and living on whatever frugal income Franklyn had left her? And then in the background there was Alice. What a shock it had been to see her. Hazel hadn't heard from Alice since she'd sent her packing but her image kept popping into Hazel's thoughts. Seeing her again had stirred up old memories and, in light of her current financial predicament, one in particular plagued her now.

When their parents had died there'd been a life insurance policy, but it had been small. Hazel had kept a tight hold on it. Her wage had been enough for her to live on, but her costs had gone up with another mouth to feed. She'd spent none of the insurance money on herself except for a second-hand sewing machine, which had been worth its weight in gold. The rest had gone to pay for anything Alice had needed; school fees and uniforms, clothes, any extra expenses like electricity and gas. It had taken a long time for the house insurance money to come through, so long that she'd almost given up hope they'd receive anything. By the time they did she'd met Franklyn.

It had been at her end-of-year work dinner. She'd been squirrelling away money so that she and Alice could have new dresses for it. Alice had suddenly blossomed and while Hazel had been adjusting some of her own clothes for Alice, her little sister's new bustline outdid Hazel's. The company who employed Hazel supplied temp workers for the local council and Franklyn was one of the council reps who'd come along. He'd been tall, dark and handsome, and, four years older than her, he'd also seemed terribly wise, so when he'd singled her out for conversation Hazel had been almost mute with amazement. She must have said enough though because before the end of the night he'd asked her if she'd like to go out for dinner the following weekend.

Caroline and Alice had been so excited for her, and Caroline especially had been full of advice, having met him at the dinner herself.

"You don't want to muck about with this one," Caroline had said.

"I don't muck about," Hazel had replied indignantly.

"The only two men you've been out with have been boys and you dithered over a second date so long they gave up." Caroline was going through Hazel's wardrobe as she spoke. "Franklyn's the executive type."

"Didn't you say he was a clerk at the local council?" Alice said.

"Clerk now but you mark my words, he's a man who knows what he wants." Caroline pulled out the new dress Hazel had worn to the dinner. "And he wants you," she said as she held the dress in front of Hazel and eyed her up and down. "It'll have to be this one. It's a quality dress and says extravagance without being flashy."

"But I wore it last week when we met."

"We'll take off the white sash and replace it with a black one. He's a money man. If he even notices you're wearing the same dress he'll admire your prudence."

"How do you know he's a money man?" Hazel looked longingly at the couple of less formal dresses now discarded on the bed. "What if he's just taking me for fish and chips?"

"The name of the place he suggested is not a fish and chip shop. And his suit was a little old-fashioned but excellent quality.

I bet he got it marked down at a good price. He likes class and he knows how to get it on a budget."

Caroline had been right about Franklyn taking her somewhere nice and about him commenting on her outfit. She'd felt a flush of pride that he even noticed the subtle change they'd made to her dress. The next weekend he took her for a drive along the coast. She'd worn the best of her skirts and a simple white blouse that time and they'd had fish and chips. No matter what they did, Franklyn always insisted on paying and Hazel was grateful. Her budget didn't extend to many outings.

When she'd eventually told him about losing her parents and caring for her sister he'd been both concerned and impressed that she'd taken on such a burden.

"It's not a burden," she'd said and she'd meant it.

"Financially, I mean," he said.

And that's when she'd told him with both excitement and trepidation about the house insurance money she'd finally received. Franklyn had advised her on how to invest it so that she got a small return she could use to help with expenses. When they'd finally married, they'd lived in a rented house until they'd moved to Adelaide for Franklyn's new job where they'd bought a house of their own. It was this house Hazel was still living in, and the insurance money had helped purchase it. Franklyn had promised her, when she married him, that she'd never have to worry about money again.

Hazel stopped pacing. "You miserable bum, Frank," she hissed.

twelve

It was a sunny afternoon by the sea – not too hot, with just a soft breeze pushing the air through the open glass doors from Elaine Forrest's front deck to her living room. Elaine had just gone downstairs, her high heels clomping on the wooden steps, to let in more guests. Alice had no idea who the others were nor why she was here but she'd come because she liked Elaine and had accepted her vague invitation to hear some plan she'd come up with and was being very secretive about.

Alice and Roy had moved to their farm on the lower Yorke Peninsula over forty years ago, but she had only moved into Marion Bay and her current home after Roy died and she'd leased out the farm. Elaine had bought her house around the same time. They'd sat next to each other at their first community cards tryout and had become acquaintances. Alice knew Elaine was several years younger, not yet sixty, and she was a divorcee with one son who lived with his dad in Adelaide but that was it really. Alice didn't have many friends in town even though she considered herself a local. Roy had been her best and only close friend. After her lousy couple of days in Adelaide she had made up her mind to make more of an effort with people.

Alice had never been inside Elaine's house before and she took the opportunity to look around the open-plan top floor. It was furnished with minimal but elegant furniture, not Alice's taste but it would be easy to maintain. She crossed to the wall of glass beyond which she glimpsed the ocean over densely vegetated sandhills.

Alice's house was also double storey but there were low dunes and sparse vegetation between her and the view of the ocean. When she and Roy had planned their retirement house, she'd been determined not to have to lug her groceries upstairs. Her kitchen and living area were downstairs and she'd decided to use the one downstairs bedroom rather than the big master bedroom upstairs. The upper floor had a second living room and three bedrooms, silly really for two people but Roy had factored in the resale value for the future.

"Here we are."

Alice turned back as Elaine arrived at the top of the stairs, followed by two men.

"Mac and Errol, this is Alice."

They looked at her and she at them until finally one moved forward, hand outstretched. "Hello, Alice. I'm Mac."

She saw him nearly every day when she walked but she'd never spoken to him. He was always accompanied by three large dogs dragging at their leashes. Alice crossed to the other side of the road when she saw him coming.

"Hello." She shook his hand briefly.

"We meet at last." He grinned.

Alice dipped her head. She never knew how to make conversation with men on her own. Roy had always been her buffer, the outgoing one who could talk to anyone, saving her the trouble.

"Come on in, Errol," Elaine urged.

The other man, who Alice had never met before and who she was guessing was the oldest of the three of them by a few years, hadn't moved further than the top of the stairs. He looked as uncomfortable as she felt.

"What's this about, Elaine?" he said.

"You needn't be terrified. I haven't asked you all here for a sex party." Elaine laughed and Mac joined in. Errol, like Alice, remained silent.

"Truly it's nothing weird." Elaine flapped her hands. "Please sit down. Would anyone like a drink? It's late enough in the day for a wine or I've got beer, or what about gin?"

"I'll have a beer, thanks," Mac said and lowered himself to the couch, arms spread across the back rest.

"Yes, okay…a beer thanks." Errol perched on a chair.

"Water will be fine." Alice opted for a chair too. One that was close to the stairs. Now that there were men present she wanted to make a quick getaway as soon as Elaine had told them her plan. Whatever it was, Alice was sure she wasn't going to like it.

"Now," Elaine said once she'd handed out the drinks and sat on the couch along from Mac. "I've discovered we all have something in common."

"Well, if sex is ruled out…" Mac chuckled and folded his arms.

Alice felt heat in her cheeks. She focused her gaze on the plate of pink cream-filled jelly cakes she'd brought with her. They looked silly next to the cheese platter Elaine had set on the table.

"Recently I was away on a cruise," Elaine said. "And I discovered a new hobby." She pointed her finger at Mac. "No more silly comments, this is serious now."

"I promise I won't say a word."

"I went to dancing lessons."

"Really?" Mac's promise was immediately broken.

"Yes, and I loved it. They ran classes and my sister and I went as often as we could. Of course she had her husband with her and I didn't have a partner, which meant sometimes I was with the instructor. He was a fabulous dancer and a good looker."

"Not better than me surely," Mac said.

"Definitely, and he was younger. He flirted outrageously with everyone."

Mac groaned and put his hand to his heart.

Elaine laughed. "Anyway, when he was dancing with someone else, I partnered with whoever I could. Sometimes it was a man, sometimes a woman, it didn't seem to matter and we had so much fun."

"I told you you'd like dancing," Mac said.

"I know, and you've been trying to get me to go to one of the dance sessions up the peninsula but I wondered about starting our own little group here first." She turned to Errol. "Mac told me you used to go to dances all the time when your wife was alive."

"We did."

"And I remember you mentioned something about the old-time dances a few weeks ago at cards, Alice."

Alice frowned. Had she? Roy had been a good dancer and it was something she missed but…"Oh yes, Gwen had been talking about the deb balls they used to have."

"I invited Gwen and her husband today but they had appointments elsewhere."

"That'd make six of us," Mac said.

"Small group," Errol murmured.

"I'm sure if we got it going more people would join us." Elaine looked at them expectantly.

"How were you imagining this would work?" Mac asked.

"We could meet once a fortnight in the community club."

"The floor there's not much chop for dancing," Errol said.

"But it's a start," Mac said. "I've got a portable CD player."

Errol frowned. "No good without music."

"I've got a speaker for my phone." Elaine clicked her fingers. "I bet I could download something appropriate. What do you think, Alice?"

She was startled by Elaine's question, had felt herself separate from their chatter, as if she was on the outside looking in. It was how she often felt at social gatherings.

"Oh...I don't know." It wasn't as if she hadn't danced with other people before. "It's years since I danced."

"Me too," Errol said.

"Probably some time before my last divorce." Mac wiggled his eyebrows at Elaine. "Hard to find someone to dance with."

"Surely it's like riding a bike," Elaine said. "You soon pick it up again."

She threw Alice a desperate look. Alice shifted in her seat. It wasn't as if she had so many things on her plate she couldn't do it, but did she want to? She thought about the many nights she spent alone. "I've got some CDs. They might be a help for finding the right music."

"Great!"

"I can make some posters," Errol said. "See if anyone else would be interested."

"Wonderful!" Elaine's excitement was over-the-top but Alice could see she badly wanted to give the dance sessions a go.

"When would we start?" she asked.

They decided on Saturday night in a week's time then Mac tossed down the rest of his beer and said he was going fishing. Elaine walked out with him, talking all the way. It was suddenly very quiet.

"These lamingtons are good."

Alice glanced around as Errol popped one of her jelly cakes in his mouth. He'd been the only one to eat cake. It was not the sort of food that usually went with beer.

"They're like the ones I buy on Saturdays at The Bay Cafe," he said.

"I make them for the shop. I enjoy cooking."

"I hate it but I've had to learn."

"How long have you been on your own?"

"Just over a year."

"Oh, I'm sorry. Have you lived here long?"

"Only six months."

"I haven't seen you before."

"We lived in the mid-north. I decided to make a complete change. I mostly keep to myself." He picked up another jelly cake and bit into it, leaving a dob of cream on his chin. "But my family are telling me I should get out more, so maybe the dancing will be good for me."

Alice wanted to tell him about the cream. "Probably good for all of us."

"Probably."

The cream wobbled. He popped the rest of the cake in his mouth then whipped out a large hanky, wiped his chin and lips, and stood. "I should go."

"Why don't you take the rest of the cakes." Alice stood too and collected the disposable container from Elaine's bench.

"Won't you want them?"

"I have plenty more in the freezer."

"Thanks," he said as she passed him the container. "It was nice to meet you. I guess I'll see you at our first dance."

"Yes."

He turned and went down the stairs. Elaine's voice echoed up from below.

Alice picked up the glasses and the empty plate. She was glad Errol had taken the jelly cakes. She'd been making lamingtons since she was fifteen. She and Hazel had practised their cooking skills together, wanting to recreate the cakes their mum had been so proud of. When Alice moved to the Pollards's, Roy's sister-in-law had taught her to make the dainty pink cream-filled cakes they'd called jelly cakes. It had become one of her specialities and Roy had loved them. She wondered if Hazel still made lamingtons then clicked her tongue. Hazel again.

Since she'd returned home, Alice had tried hard to forget about Hazel and her family but the more she tried, the more they kept popping into her mind. Hazel had appeared fragile but not grief-stricken like Alice had been when Roy died. She'd been swallowed up by a numbness that had engulfed her. It hadn't been until her move from the farm to the beach that she'd forced herself to go out into the world again. Alice wondered if Hazel mourned Franklyn's loss as keenly as Alice had Roy's.

She had her daughters and her grandchildren, perhaps that made a difference. Alice hadn't seen much of June but she'd been glad of the small opportunity to know a little more about Felicity and Greta, even if it had been her dizzy spell that had brought it about. Alice could understand June and Felicity's reluctance to accept her but Greta had been much more open to the idea of a long-lost great-aunt. How lucky Hazel was to have her and two grandsons as well. Alice had held a small hope that Greta might at least keep in touch but there'd been no response to the text she'd sent while she'd still been in Adelaide.

Alice kept going over every bit of conversation she'd had with them, her family, the family she now knew existed but which she was still not allowed to see. It was as if she'd ripped a plaster off a wound and then kept doing it again and again. Each time she thought of them it was sharp, raw and unsettling.

"I think that went well," Elaine said as she reached the top of the stairs.

"Yes."

"You'll stay for a wine, won't you? I'd love another glass and I try not to drink on my own."

"Oh...well...yes, thank you."

"Great." Elaine strode to her kitchen and poured the wine. "I think those two men will be fine as dance partners. Mac can be a bit cheeky but he's all right and Errol's quiet but a real gentleman. Did you like them?"

"Oh...yes." Mac made her feel uncomfortable but Errol had been nice enough.

"Here's to dancing." Elaine held her glass out.

Alice tapped hers against it. "To dancing."

They both sat, both took another sip.

"Are you okay, Alice?"

"Yes, fine."

"It's only that I heard you'd been to a funeral and you seem very quiet...more than usual. Did you lose someone close?"

"No." Alice gripped the stem of her glass and the contents wobbled. "My brother-in-law, and we were not close."

"Is your sister still alive?"

"Yes, but I hadn't seen her in a long time either."

"I see."

"Not since I was sixteen. I didn't know where Hazel was or even if she was still alive until I read her husband's funeral notice in the paper."

"And you went to the funeral," Elaine said. "How did that go?"

"Difficult, awkward, emotional, all of the above. It was the only way I could think to contact Hazel, to meet her family. But she didn't want to see me."

"I'm sorry, that must have been tough."

Elaine's compassion was almost Alice's undoing. She took a quick sip of wine. "It did knock me a bit. I suppose I expected... well, hoped that she'd somehow be pleased to see me. We were both hurt when we became estranged. I've forgiven her but she obviously can't forgive me."

"Do you want to talk about it?"

The only person who knew the whole terrible story was Roy. Alice had buried it and moved on but now after seeing Hazel again...Roy wasn't here to talk it through. Perhaps it was the loneliness, or the wine, or some deep need to unburden, whatever it was, the story bubbled up inside Alice and she let it out.

"We were very close once. After our parents died, Hazel took me in. She was more than a sister; she was friend, mother, guardian angel all wrapped into one. It seems odd given we'd lost our parents but we settled into a life together and we were very happy. At least that's how I saw it...and then she met Franklyn."

"Her husband who's just died?"

"Yes." Alice's mouth went dry. She took another sip of wine. "I was a bit in awe of him at first. He seemed so much older than both of us, so wise, and Hazel quickly began to rely on him. She'd taken on a huge responsibility with sole care of me thrust upon her and no other family to support us, so I can understand why Franklyn must have seemed like a rock to her. In no time at all they were engaged and then married. Franklyn rented a small house and we moved in with him. Not many men would take a bride that came with a little sister. Franklyn seemed to accept it but he was quiet when I was around. I had a room to myself at least and I tried to give them space and stay there when he was home, apart from meals and the occasional weekend outing. Hazel's old flatmate, Caroline, used to invite me to stay some Friday nights with her.

"There was only a brief honeymoon so I guess me staying away gave them some time alone. It wasn't long before Hazel was pregnant, but the baby, June, came early and it was touch and go for a while. Hazel stayed at the hospital and Franklyn was beside himself with worry. But then June turned a corner, she put on weight and grew and they both came home but...nothing was the same after that." Alice shivered as a vision of Franklyn's reedy moustache and steely blue eyes came unbidden.

"Are you cold?" Elaine asked "Should I shut the doors?"

"No." Alice rolled her shoulders to dispel the unease that prickled down her back. "It's a lovely day and I don't want to spoil it recalling what was such a bad time in my life. Losing my parents and then my...sister." Alice twisted her glass in her hand. "Anyway, I tried, but nothing came of it."

"Did you leave your phone number? She might change her mind."

Alice thought about the last time she'd seen Hazel and the look of contempt on her face. "I don't think she will."

"Perhaps it's for the best then." Elaine gave her a sympathetic smile. "Would you like more wine?"

Alice looked down at her empty glass. "No, it's time I went home."

"You are happy about the dancing, aren't you?"

Alice smiled. "I think it will be worth a try." It would be something to look forward to and better than rattling around in her big empty house turning over memories.

"It might be the start of something new for both of us." Elaine said.

"Perhaps it will."

thirteen

It was Saturday morning and Felicity wasn't doing very well. Another empty day loomed. She'd spent four nights alone since the tsunami that had swept her life away in its surge and dumped little pieces of it in unrecognisable clumps. She'd kept her daytime thoughts at bay by cleaning her already clean house while she listened to podcasts. The nights were harder. She watched TV, played music, tried to read, even dug out a scarf she'd started knitting several winters ago, but eventually she'd fall wearily into bed and there she'd toss and turn while her mind would go over and over the events of the last week, not letting her rest. Thankfully she had Dolly. Not that she was scintillating company but at least she was another living, breathing presence.

There'd been a brief response from Ian to Felicity's request not to tell anyone he'd left. *OK* was all she'd received and nothing since. Greta had rung but Felicity had kept the calls brief, claiming a headache, a shopping trip, visitors, whatever came to mind. None of it was true of course, except perhaps the headache, but she hadn't left the house since the calamity, not to visit anyone, not for the shops, nor for her social tennis game. She hadn't even been to the letterbox, which she could see from her bedroom window was overflowing with junk mail.

There was no bread or fresh fruit or veg left in the house. She hadn't been that fussed about food but as each mealtime came around she ate whatever she could pull together. Thank goodness for her freezer jammed full of her birthday leftovers. Greta had done a good job of packaging the food, there'd been little waste, but she hadn't labelled anything. Last night Felicity had toasted sandwiches which she thought had looked like waldorf chicken but had turned out to be her classic tuna filling and this morning she'd thought she was defrosting small quiches but they were sweet macaron tarts. She'd eaten two with her coffee.

Now another long day stretched out before her. She wandered the house, taking in each room. She'd been so proud of her efforts, and the icing on the cake had been the redecorating. It hurt to think Ian didn't like it, and apparently hadn't been interested enough to even have an opinion. She'd asked his advice on the major things and he'd always agreed.

She thought back over each decision now: the layout of the family room, the size of the butler's pantry, a formal lounge as well as the family room. That had been the one thing Ian had spoken up about. He'd wanted a double garage instead of a second living space but Felicity had worried it would make the house too poky and she'd insisted.

Then there were the colour schemes, the window furnishings, the kitchen cupboards and the couple of new furniture pieces she'd bought. She knew their budget and she hadn't overspent. Most of their furniture was still in good shape. She'd had their lounge chairs re-covered for the front room and only bought the new couch and dining table and chairs for the family room. Ian had always agreed. She had assumed that meant he'd liked what he saw, been excited by it like she was.

She came to the bedroom, their bedroom, the one she'd decorated with love – for the two of them. Like the rest of the house she'd kept the colours neutral, whites, greys and just some touches of blue; a couple of denim cushions; two shell drawings, blue on a white background, either side of the window; the lightest blue feathery headdress decorating the wall above the bed and clear blue glass lamps on the plain white bedside tables. She ran her hand over the dusky blue throw blanket folded neatly across the bottom of the bed. Surely Ian wouldn't leave this beautiful house...leave her.

She wondered how long it would take him to come to his senses. His work meant that they were used to having small bursts of time apart – occasionally his job took him bush and he might be gone a week or, if he went on a trek with his hiking friends, a weekend. It'd only been four days since he'd walked out on her. Perhaps it still seemed like a work or hiking trip to him.

"I have to be patient," she murmured but the other wound still festered inside, the one caused by her parents' deceit. They'd raised her without a word about her adoption. It certainly explained her father's behaviour towards her. She'd always felt he treated her differently to June but it was her mum, her fake mum, she found hard to forgive. They were close...had been. How could she have lied to Felicity all these years? Hazel had left messages each day begging her to ring but Felicity had ignored them. She had no desire to speak to anyone unless it was Ian declaring he'd made a mistake.

She looked at her walk-in robe. Everything had been taken out when it was painted but she'd put it all back without going through it. There were bound to be things she no longer wore. That would be her job for the day.

She'd just begun to drag out the shoes when she heard a car pull into her drive. She lurched to the window and peered through the sheer white curtains. It was June and Hazel. Felicity stepped back quickly. Her doorbell rang. She looked through the open bedroom door to the hall and saw movement beyond the frosted glass beside the door. She edged back into the walk-in robe, flicked off the light and sank to the floor, jumping as several sharp knocks thumped on the front door.

"Felicity?" It was June's voice.

She shrank further back into the wardrobe, picking up a pair of fluffy slippers and clutching them to her chest. June's call came from closer and once more Felicity jumped at a rapping on the bedroom window. No-one could see in with the curtains across but it was as if June was looking right at her.

"She's not here, Mum." June moved away.

Felicity edged forward then flung herself back among her skirts as another thump sounded on the front door.

"You're still my daughter, Felicity." It was Hazel. There was hurt in her voice and for a brief moment Felicity felt guilty. "I love you." Those last three words carried ever so faintly to where Felicity sat. She sucked her bottom lip tightly over her teeth.

"She's not home, Mum, or she would have answered. I told you it was a waste of time driving over here. It's thoughtless of her shutting you out at a time like this."

Felicity huffed. Thoughtless! That was rich coming from June, who rarely thought beyond the needs of her own family. And she was Hazel's real daughter. Let her do the running around for a change. Ever since Felicity had given up her paid job she'd been the most regular visitor, helping out her parents if needed, and

they weren't even her real parents. June lived much closer and
didn't work full-time but she was always too busy when it came
to helping.

Not that Franklyn and Hazel had asked often but Felicity was
considered to be idle. After all, she was only renovating. None of
them realised the work she'd put into the house. To save money
she'd done whatever she could. Tony had shown her how to chip
off the old tiles in the bathroom and she'd done it all herself and
then the kitchen. She'd made all the new curtains, organised skips,
coordinated tradies, prepped for painting, cleaned up after each
part of the renovation was done. Something had filled her days
ever since they moved into this house and now that it was done…

Car doors shut and then there was the sound of the car backing
away. A fresh wave of self-pity swept over her. Her mother and
sister weren't her mother and sister, Greta lived with Joe, and now
Ian had left. Felicity had a beautiful house and no-one to share it
with.

For the hundredth time she wondered how and why her parents had kept such a secret from her. Then a prickle wriggled
down her spine as she had a recollection of a face from her childhood. The family had been on a short holiday to Victoria. She and
June must have been about seven and eight. Trips away were so
rare it was a big deal although it had been very basic. They stayed
in dingy hotel rooms or on-site caravans that smelled musty and
damp. They followed the Great Ocean Road and June had been
carsick. In hindsight Felicity could see why June had hated the
trip but to a little girl who rarely went anywhere beyond their
neighbourhood it had been a grand adventure. All except the visit
to Franklyn's aunt. Isabelle lived in an old weatherboard cottage
and had seemed as ancient as the house. Felicity had thought she

was at least a hundred but later had discovered she would have been in her early eighties.

Felicity and June wore their Sunday church dresses and had been told to be on their best behaviour. The old lady had inspected them, then they'd been given a glass of lemonade and a biscuit and told to sit. The adults' conversation had been stilted, about weather and then about Franklyn's family. Both his parents were dead, and childless Aunt Isabelle was his only living relative of that generation. After what had seemed like forever the girls had been told they could go outside. June had gone straight to the car, parked in the shade of a tree and opened her book. Felicity had wandered the basic front garden and then the heat and boredom had driven her back inside.

She'd crept in as quietly as could be but as she drew level with the door to the lounge she heard her father's raised voice saying something about no-one knowing. She put her face to the crack of the partly open door as Aunt Isabelle responded in a stern voice. "Take care, Franklyn," she'd said. "It's a tangled web we weave when first we practise to deceive." The old lady had looked towards the door. Felicity had jumped back but she'd been sure Aunt Isabelle had seen her. Her look had been odd, a knowing, triumphant sort of gaze that had haunted Felicity's dreams that night and several more over the years since but Felicity hadn't thought of her in a long time. Now she wondered if Isabelle had known about her adoption.

Pins and needles prickled Felicity's feet and legs. That and mounting anger made her move.

"Stuff them all." She marched across the room and closed the block-out curtains. She did the same in the lounge then went to the kitchen and took her phone from the charger. The message box was pathetically empty — neither Ian nor Greta had sent texts. She swore as it vibrated in her hand. She'd turned off the sound so as not to hear when Hazel rang. She peered at the name on the screen and accepted the call.

"Hello, Melody."

"Are you home?" Her next-door neighbour sounded breathless.

Felicity hesitated. "Yes."

"I wondered because your letterbox hadn't been emptied."

Felicity had seen the brochures spilling out onto the garden the last time she'd peeped outside but she'd done nothing about them. "What's up?"

"I'm rushing around like a mad thing. Humphrey's working in Melbourne all next week and I've decided to go with him. We're going to drive, stop off somewhere on the way over and the way back."

"That sounds nice. Do you want me to do anything while you're away?"

"Could you put the bin out and in…oh, and perhaps check the mail, mostly it's junk these days, and keep the usual eye on the place."

"Of course."

There was a thumping sound and Melody huffed. "Sorry, just dragging my case off the bed. Humphrey wants to get on the road. He's loaded the car already and he's waiting on mine."

"Don't worry. I'll do the bin and keep an eye on things.

"Thanks, Felicity. I feel so bad I haven't been over to see you. How are you managing?"

"Managing?" Had Ian told the neighbours he'd left after all?

"I haven't seen you since your dad's funeral. Is your mum doing okay?"

"Oh…yes…at least she's—"

"Such a shock for you all and what a terrible neighbour I am. It's been a crazy week, we've had the grandchildren and—"

Humphrey's voice echoed in the background.

"I'm coming! Sorry, Felicity. I have to go. You must come over for a meal once we get back."

"Yes."

"Love to Ian."

Felicity ended the call and wandered back to her bedroom, lifted the curtain ever so carefully and watched as Melody and Humphrey's car backed on to the street and drove away. Once more she noticed the pile of catalogues overflowing from her letterbox. She opened her front door a crack, peered out then made a dash down the front path. A couple of leaflets had snagged in the rose bush. She bent down to retrieve them, noticed a couple of weeds and tugged them out while she was there.

"Hello, Felicity."

She lurched upright clutching the armload of papers to her chest. It was Les from across the road.

"Sorry, didn't mean to startle you," he said. "I didn't think you were home then I happened to see you as I opened the garage."

Les was dressed in vibrant orange and black lycra, a helmet dangling from his hand. It was his standard outfit for weekends when he wasn't at work but Felicity found it difficult to look at him. His sixty-year-old body was fit but the tight lycra created bulges that looked as if they were preparing for imminent escape.

"I've been busy inside," Felicity said lamely, glancing down at the papers in her hands.

"Only I rang Ian to see if he'd like to go for a ride."

"Oh...I..."

"He said he's working away for a while and I thought...well, you know you can call on us if you need help with anything."

"Thanks," she gasped then gave a silly little laugh. "I'm used to fending for myself."

"I know you are but it's nice to know there's someone else close by if you need."

"Thank you, Les."

Across the road his front door opened. He turned as Sal came out, strapping on her helmet. Her muted blue and black lycra hugged her small frame. She waved. "Beautiful day," she called.

Felicity nodded, waved and began backing up her front path. Once she made it inside she shut the front door and leaned against it. Damn Ian and his mid-life crisis. At least he'd done as she'd asked and hadn't told anyone he'd left. That was a good sign, surely. But what was she to do while she waited for him to come to his senses? She'd be a nervous wreck with all this subterfuge

She took the brochures through to the kitchen and dumped them in the recycle tub. Back in her bedroom she plugged in her earphones, selected her favourite playlist and strode to the walk-in robe. Keeping busy was the key. Hands on hips, she studied the shelves. Dolly emerged to stand beside her, staring into the robe.

"Clean-out time, Dolly," Felicity said and, taking handfuls of hangers, began pulling everything out.

fourteen

Greta opened her eyes to the smell of bacon and eggs. She took a deep breath, stretched her arms above her head and rolled over into the empty space in the bed. From beyond the bedroom came the sound of whistling. Joe was happy and after this totally indulgent weekend so was she.

It had been a big last few days of the week. She'd had lots to catch up on at work after the odd bits of time off and there was a new project starting, which added more to her load. By the time she'd arrived home Friday night, she'd been exhausted. He'd surprised her by cooking dinner again, spaghetti bolognaise this time.

Joe's second surprise had been to tell her he'd booked them a place by the beach south of Adelaide for Saturday night. It belonged to a friend of his family and they'd got it for nothing. Yesterday had been so blissful, just the two of them with no outside interruptions. They'd taken a long walk along the beach, swum briefly – the water had been cold even though the day had been warm. They'd gone from the shower to the bed, a rare but lovely late-afternoon delight, then gone out for a long leisurely dinner and back to the house again where they'd once more taken to their bed. Now they had a slow Sunday in front of them, perhaps some McLaren Vale wineries and lunch before they headed for home later this afternoon.

She gave a brief thought to her mum. They'd only exchanged texts these last few days. Felicity seemed to be doing okay but, with Ian away, Greta wondered if she should call in on their way home. She wished she didn't have to. She was enjoying Joe-time.

At that moment his head appeared around the door. "Do you want breakfast in bed or are you coming out to join me?"

Greta flung back the covers. "I'll come out."

His face spread to a grin. "You'd better put something on then or the food might go cold before we eat."

She picked up the clothes she'd been wearing yesterday from where they'd been discarded across the floor the night before, dragged them on and wandered out to the living area. She winced at the light streaming through the plate-glass windows facing the ocean across the road.

"What time is it?"

"Nine-thirty. I've been for a run already."

"Well done you," she said and brushed a kiss across the light stubble of his cheek. "I've had plenty of exercise this last twenty-four hours."

He winked, handed her a coffee and turned back to the sizzling pan. She took a sip and wandered over to the huge windows. Other people were ploughing up and down the beach across the road, a small group were performing yoga moves and others ran with dogs on leads. Joe was like her dad, an exercise freak, but apart from her weekly netball game and the occasional Pilates session or a walk, that was it as far as working out went for her.

"Come and eat."

She turned back as he placed plates piled high with bacon, eggs, mushrooms and tomatoes on the table.

"Yum," she said, inhaling the delicious smell as she sat. "We should go away more often."

"Accommodation eats into our budget. We were lucky with this place, getting it for nada."

Greta buttered a thick slice of sourdough toast. She knew their budget as well as he did but money-watching was an obsession with Joe.

"I've been thinking we should revisit our budget," she said. "We both work hard and taking a break like this from time to time is good for us."

"We don't want to change things now when we're so close to our target."

"Our own place, you mean? I thought we were still a long way short of the deposit you wanted."

"We are but sounds like you'll be getting some money later in the year—"

"I'm sure it won't be much and anyway I don't want to think about that…it seems like gold-digging when Grandad's only just died." It was, and yet her real reason for brushing it off was because she was being forced to share it with Joe. If she had an inheritance, she wanted to be free to do with it what she wanted.

"Franklyn was practical. He's given you the money and he'd be happy to see you put it towards bricks and mortar rather than fritter it away."

"I never fritter away money." She frowned at him.

"You're rather partial to new clothes." He said it softly but there was a hint of reprimand in his tone.

Greta's cutlery clattered back to her plate. "I can spend my 'me' money on whatever I like. You do."

His hands went up and he smiled his disarming smile. "Hold up, I know. It's just that I've often got money left over and you're always trying to borrow from next week for a handbag or a pair of fancy jeans."

"Not always." When they'd committed to moving in together they'd both studied the newest finance guru's book on how to manage their money and had agreed it was good advice but sometimes Greta felt annoyed by Joe's ability to often have spending money left over. He was always smug about it.

"All that matters is we're on track." Joe went on eating.

Greta took a big slug of her coffee, swallowing the warm liquid along with the feeling she'd been dismissed.

"I thought we could look at a few houses on our way home today," he said.

"It's too soon to start looking at places we can't afford."

"It's good to get to know the market. See what places are selling for and what you get for your money."

"I couldn't bear to find something I love and know I can't have it. Besides, I thought we'd visit some wineries today."

"But it won't be long until we've got our deposit. I'd like to be prepared."

"I haven't even thought about where."

"Somewhere closer to the airport for you and easy access to the city for me. We'd be closer to your parents too." He slid his phone across the table. "This one could be within our price range."

Greta frowned at the screen. She liked living where they did. It was far enough away from her parents so they didn't call in too often.

Joe jumped up. "If we get going as soon as we're packed up here we can do a winery on the way. We can check out the houses and finish with a visit to your mum. Maybe she'll make us one of her Sunday-night pizzas." He carried his empty plate to the kitchen. "I'll get into the shower and pack up my things then give you a hand. We have to take the sheets and towels with us to wash. Mum will get them back to her friend. Maybe we could buy a bottle at the winery as a thank you."

Greta hadn't even finished her breakfast and her easy start to the day was being swept away. She wondered what Joe would say when she told him her inheritance, however much it was, was dependent on them getting married first. Would he deviate from their plan to buy a house and want to put the wedding first? She loved Joe, and wanted to have a future with him, but her grandad's rider had put a dampener on it.

By the time she'd done the dishes, tidied the rooms, vacuumed and bagged up the sheets and linen she was fed up. Perhaps paying for accommodation was a better option if it meant she didn't have all that work to do. To be fair, Joe had stripped the bed and left the sheets in a bundle on the floor with his wet towel. After that he'd disappeared outside with his bag and only came back just as Greta zipped the last of her things into her overnighter.

"Sorry," he said. "I got talking to the bloke next door. Couldn't get away. Let me take that." He reached for her bag and scooped up the towels and sheets with his other arm. "He recommended a great winery for us to visit. Not far from here and they're open early."

Greta picked up their toiletries bags and followed him out of the bedroom. She glanced around the neat living area and thought about their own place. It looked like a tip in comparison. They hadn't done any housework for weeks. Joe always said he'd help but he'd get sidetracked like he had this morning and the bulk of their cleaning and washing fell to her. If she complained, he'd pitch in straight away but then she felt like a nag.

It was late afternoon by the time they pulled into Felicity's driveway. And while Greta felt weary, beside her Joe was buzzing with excitement after an afternoon spent viewing houses. They'd also called at the winery but it had been too early in the day for Greta to sample wine. Joe had tried a few and selected a red for his mum's friend as a thank you for letting them stay, plus a bottle of white for Felicity. It was to cheer her up, he'd said, and Greta was reminded that while he was prudent with money, he was also thoughtful.

She didn't have her keys so she knocked on the front door. All the curtains were drawn in the lounge and front bedroom and there was no sound of movement beyond.

"Perhaps they're out." Joe said as he came up behind her.

"Maybe." Greta knocked again and called out. "Mum?"

They were just about to turn away when the door opened a crack.

"Greta, I didn't realise it was you." Felicity opened the door wider. "Oh, hello, Joe."

"We've been out and about and ended up this way. Thought we'd call in and see how you were." Greta was gabbling. Her mum was blocking the doorway as if she didn't want them to come inside.

Joe waved the bottle of wine he'd bought. "We come bearing gifts."

"That was thoughtful." Felicity took a small step back. "Did you want to come in?"

Greta stepped inside. The hall was dim, the curtains in the lounge were drawn and the door to her mum's bedroom was closed. The air smelled stale, then she noticed the three full garbage bags lined up along the wall.

"I've been cleaning out my wardrobe," Felicity said as she closed the front door behind them. "They're my 'too good for the rubbish' piles."

She led the way into the big family room at the back of the house, bathed in late-afternoon sunshine. Greta glanced around. Every surface gleamed, there were no empty wine bottles or wads of tissues – in fact nothing was out of place. Once more Greta thought of the mess waiting back at their apartment. Sometimes she wished she'd inherited her mum's knack of keeping everything so tidy.

An image was paused on the TV screen. Felicity picked up the remote and switched it off. "Just watching reruns of *The Block*," she said.

Dolly wound around Joe's feet, miaowing plaintively. He bent to pick her up but she was rigid in his arms and jumped straight back down. "What's up with Dolly?"

"She's hungry." Felicity shrugged her shoulders. "She's always hungry. What have you two been up to?"

"Had a great weekend down south." Joe put the wine on the bench and lowered himself to the couch. "Thought we'd catch up with you on our way home. I'm sorry to hear about your latest news. You've had a run of shocks lately."

"I have?" Felicity's gaze darted between Joe and Greta.

"I told Joe about the surprise we got from Grandad's letters."

"Oh yes, of course." Felicity was still standing in the middle of the room. She flapped her hands. "I'm all right though."

Greta studied her mum. She looked different somehow. Even when she'd been chipping tiles off the bathroom wall Felicity always managed to look stylish. Perhaps it was the lack of make-up – she looked washed out and the oversized mint green t-shirt she was wearing over a pair of baggy linen pants wasn't helping.

"Is that a new top?" Greta asked. She wasn't feeling relaxed enough to sit like Joe.

Felicity glanced down. "Yes and no. I found it in the back of my t-shirt drawer. It must be more than ten years old but I think I've only worn it once before. Do you like it?"

"It's not my favourite colour on you."

"It's fine for around home."

"Have you spoken to Nan?" Greta asked.

"Not yet." Felicity brushed a hand over the end of the pristine benchtop. "Sorry I can't offer you a drink or something to eat. I'm out of everything. Haven't been to the shops since my party."

"Oh, no probs," Joe said.

He smiled but Greta heard the disappointment in his voice.

"Actually, you were lucky to catch me." Felicity plucked her keys from the bowl. "I was heading out to the supermarket."

"You don't want a wine before you go?"

"It's not chilled, Joe," Greta said.

"I'll pop it in the fridge for next time," Felicity said but stayed where she was, holding her keys.

"Okay, well, we'll head off then." Greta gave Joe the let's-go look.

"Right." He rose slowly to his feet.

"It was lovely to see you both." Felicity was already walking towards the door.

"How's Dad?"

Felicity stopped and turned back. "Why?"

"Just asking? I haven't heard from him for a while."

"He's fine. Looks like he'll have a few trips away in a row so you probably won't see him for a while. He'll be dashing home, fresh set of clothes, dashing off again...you know..."

"Take care, Felicity," Joe said. He opened the front door and went ahead.

Greta kissed her mum and noticed the stale smell again. Perhaps the t-shirt needed a wash.

"Talk soon," she said.

Felicity shut the door as soon as Greta stepped through it.

Out over the ocean an airbus A320 lined up with the runway. Greta paused to watch its smooth descent towards land. When she was young and they'd lived on the other side of town, her dad would regularly drive her down to the parking space near the end of the Adelaide airport runway. They'd watch planes come and go for hours. She'd dreamed of piloting planes herself one day, now it seemed the closest she'd get to that was her job at the airport working for a charter aviation company.

"Greta, let's go," Joe called from the car. "We'll pick up a pizza on the way home."

She turned away from the descending aircraft and climbed in beside Joe. He didn't like planes.

fifteen

Felicity leaned against the solid wood of her front door. She stayed there for some time, until the weird sensation of wild horses beating a trail inside her chest subsided, then she went back to the family room and closed the door on the rest of the house. This room had become her haven. Increasingly she was only leaving it to use the bathroom and to go to bed. Last night she hadn't even done that but had dragged her quilt to the couch and slept there.

This morning she'd woken late, eaten the last of the cream cakes in her freezer for breakfast and made coffee with the last of her beans. It had only taken a few minutes to tidy up and she'd spent some time out on the back deck reading then started watching reruns of her favourite home renovation show. She'd been half asleep when she'd heard the knock on the front door. She hadn't been going to open it, but then, when she realised it was Greta, she knew she'd have to. She'd pulled herself together enough to convince her daughter that everything was normal. Thank goodness Greta hadn't dug any deeper about her dad's continued absence.

Felicity felt a stab of despair when she thought of Ian then quickly pushed it away. If she didn't think about his leaving her it wouldn't be true. Before Greta and Joe had arrived she'd been lost in the renovation show on the television. She'd watched three and a half episodes in a row and now that she'd been interrupted she didn't feel like going back to it, but she needed to distract herself from her current situation. Dolly appeared from the laundry and wound around her legs, miaowing pitifully again.

"I know you're hungry." They were also out of cat food and Felicity had fed Dolly the tuna from a couple of sandwiches she'd defrosted the day before. She'd run out of her HRT tablets too.

She looked down at the keys she still clutched in her hand. It had been the truth when she'd said there was little left to eat in the house but she'd been putting off going to the supermarket. It would be unlikely she'd meet anyone she knew but the possibility had deterred her. Now she thought it would be best to go further afield to the IGA that stayed open late on Sundays and maybe she'd pass a late-night chemist for her script.

Twenty minutes later Felicity stepped out of the shower. On counting back she'd realised she hadn't showered since Friday morning. It was so rare for her to miss the daily ritual and she'd been appalled at how easily she'd let herself slide. She flicked the towel around her shoulders and stopped as she caught sight of herself in the mirror. There was a loose roll around her midriff. She knew she'd been putting on some weight for a while. She peered closer. The rolls looked bigger and jiggled when she rubbed them with the towel. When she moved her legs the flab on her inner thighs wobbled along with her breasts, which had still been pert not that long ago. She wrapped herself in the towel and dragged a brush through her hair wishing she'd washed it, then she leaned forward and studied her face in the mirror. She grabbed her glasses from the bench and put a hand to her neck. They said you could always tell a woman's age by her neck. There were the beginnings of fine creping in her skin.

Her hand went to her mouth and she spun away. This is what Ian saw when he looked at her; that flabby woman in the mirror, that fifty-year-old who'd let herself go. No wonder he'd gone looking elsewhere. Felicity was sure there had to be another woman or why would he leave?

She looked at the clean clothes she'd set out on the bed, put on the underwear but took the skirt and slim-fitting blouse back to her wardrobe where she took out another pair of drawstring pants and a loose three-quarter sleeved blouse. She didn't stop to look at her reflection in the mirror again but snatched up her small over-shoulder bag. It had her credit card and a few dollars in it, and she didn't plan to be out long.

The supermarket was surprisingly busy for dinnertime on a Sunday night. Felicity kept her sunglasses on and her head down, and moved quickly, tossing things into her trolley. She hadn't made a list but she was out of nearly every basic item so by the time she reached the checkout her trolley was full.

She put her bags on the counter and began to unload.

"Hello, how was your weekend?" The young man at the register looked at her with a wide smile. He wore a white shirt and black tie skewed sideways and looked to be all of sixteen.

"Fine, thank you." Felicity didn't make eye contact as she unpacked.

"Is it still warm outside?" he persisted.

"Yes."

"I sure wish I was out in it."

"Hmm."

"Would you like to buy more bags?"

She looked up. She'd only brought two with her and they were full. She gave the young man a wan smile. "Yes please, I've got more groceries than I thought."

"I see that a lot," he said with another bright smile.

She glanced at the badge on his chest. "I'm sure you do, Milo." She had a sudden urge to ask him if he liked to drink Milo but no doubt he'd been asked that question before.

She transferred the full bags to her trolley as he continued. Behind her a large man in a singlet top revealing tattoo-covered arms placed some items on the conveyer. She inched further away as Milo announced her total.

"One hundred and seventy-six dollars and thirty-five cents."

Thank goodness she had her credit card. Felicity slipped it into the machine, tapped in her pin and added the last bag to her trolley.

"I'm sorry, that's been declined."

"What?" Felicity whipped around and peered at the screen.

"Do you want to try again or a different card?"

"I don't have...try again." Felicity's brain scrambled for possible scenarios. The credit card had a huge limit. They'd used it a lot during the renovations but the last of it had been paid off. It had to work – she didn't have her other cards with her. When she'd gone to Hazel's for the will reading she'd taken the little shoulder bag that didn't fit her wallet. She'd only tossed in her credit card and some cash just in case, and that was the bag she'd brought with her to the supermarket.

Milo pressed several buttons on his side of the counter and they went through the process again with the same result. Heat built inside her chest and spread up her neck with all the ferociousness of a furnace. She glanced around to see there were now three people waiting in the line behind her.

Felicity turned her back to them and leaned closer to the machine. "I don't understand," she muttered. "That card has a huge limit. You must be doing something wrong."

"It might be a problem with the bank. It happens sometimes. We never know why," Milo said helpfully.

She glowered at him then pulled out her phone and selected her bank app. The heat inside her was overwhelming as she peered at the screen. She fanned her face with her hand, blinked and peered again. Where there should have been three accounts there were only two. She tried to scroll but that was it. There was no credit card listed, just their two debit accounts, one for bills and one for spending. The bill account was showing zero and there was only three hundred in their spending account. Her brain was having difficulty registering what her eyes were seeing.

Behind her there was a cough, a shuffling of feet, the queue was getting restless. "How long does it take to get a couple of things?" came a mutter from the back.

"I can pay," she said. "I have cash." She pulled the notes from her bag.

Milo gave her an encouraging smile. "Do you have more?"

She looked at the money she was waving at him. Two twenties wouldn't cover it. Suddenly she felt sick.

"It's okay," he said. "We'll sort it."

"How much short are you, love? I can lend you ten." The voice came from behind and a large hand with the letters LOVE tattooed across the fingers slid forward and placed a note on the counter.

"What's going on, Milo?" A steely-faced older woman wearing a supervisor's badge came up beside the queue. "I've told you before you have to scan faster if you want to keep your job here."

"Oh…no…it's my fault," Felicity squeaked.

Milo just smiled. "Can you open another checkout please, Trudy? I have to help this lady." He lowered his voice. "Card issue."

Trudy huffed and although Felicity had turned away from her she could feel her burning glare.

"Number three is open," she snapped.

Felicity slid the ten dollar note back along the counter. "Thanks," she said sharply without looking around. "But I can manage. I'll have to leave some and come back tomorrow."

"Just trying to help."

Heat flamed up her neck and over her cheeks and sweat formed on her forehead. "Damn!" She flapped at her face with her hand, which stilled as a large drip of sweat ran down her nose, wobbled for a second and dripped to the counter. Milo's stare met hers.

He turned away to the man behind her.

"Thanks for offering the lady some help, sir," Milo said with the maturity of a forty-year-old. "It might be quicker for you to use checkout three."

Felicity scrabbled to find a tissue, made a quick dab at the drop and mopped her face. She had the sense of the man behind her putting his items back in a basket and moving away.

Milo put out his closed sign and turned back to her. "Now, what would you like to do? You can pick out what you need for forty dollars and I can store the rest till tomorrow."

"That's very kind." Felicity wanted to run and leave all this behind. She had little money and on top of that she'd been rude to both the people who'd tried to help her. There was no way she could ever set foot in this shop again. "I'm not sure I can get back tomorrow," she whispered.

"I'll re-shelve the rest then," Milo said patiently. "You take out what you need and put the rest back here." He patted the end of the counter.

"You won't get into trouble?" Felicity risked a glance in Trudy's direction but she was busy scanning items with practised proficiency.

"No." He shook his head. "Trudy gets a bit irritable but she's okay. And she's right, I'm not very fast. I'd prefer to work out-side with a hammer or a drill in my hand but this is the only job I could get that works with school." He lifted out the first item from the nearest bag. "Keep or return."

It was ice-cream. "Return." She could live without it.

By the time Felicity stumbled out to the car with her two bags of basics she was not only mortified, she was angry. It wasn't poor Milo's fault. He'd been very good to her but she'd barely been able to mutter a thank you.

It was Ian she was angry with. Leaving her to be humiliated like that. He must have done something with the money – their money, not his. It had been their money since the day they'd married. He'd always been the bigger earner. He'd left uni with a degree in mechanical engineering and had worked in that field for several years before joining his current employer where he'd risen up through the ranks to be a senior engineering loss adjuster. Felicity had always had clerical jobs and had taken time off when Greta was young but up until the move to this house she'd con-tributed to their household budget. Her last job had been as an office manager and her final payout had helped with the renova-tion costs. They'd never quibbled over who'd earned what.

She flung the bags in the boot, slid into the driver's seat and took out her phone to check the bank again. Ian's payday was last Thursday. His pay went into his personal account and portions were automatically transferred to their bills, spending and mortgage accounts. She could see where the money had gone into the bills account and then had been withdrawn again. She checked the spending. The same thing but in this account there had been some left behind – three hundred dollars. Was this what Ian expected her to live on? For how long? And what had happened to the credit card? He was the primary cardholder. She clapped her hand to her mouth.

"Bloody hell!" Ian must have cancelled her access.

She yelped at a tap on her window. Milo was peering in, a packet of toilet rolls clutched in his hands. She lowered the window.

"You left these on the counter. They were part of what you paid for."

"Thank you."

"Are you going to be all right?"

"Yes." She wiped moisture from her eyes with the back of her hand. "I'll be okay. It's been a hellish week, that's all." She managed to give him a smile. "Thank you, Milo. You've been very kind."

He gave her a wave and set off back towards the front of the shop. Felicity started her car and then lurched to a halt, as the reversing alert beeped a warning. A car passed behind her. With shaking hands she checked the screen and with the coast clear she left the carpark and managed to get herself home and into the safety of the kitchen before the terror of her situation shattered her control. She had no income, and the house she was living in had a mortgage, albeit a small one, but Ian had to pay it. Would he demand she leave? She had money in super but was far too young to access that yet. She hadn't worked outside the home in five years. Jobs were hard to find. What the hell was she supposed to do? Vice-like pressure built inside her, and heat radiated up her neck. Was this a heart attack? Was she going to collapse? She bent over the bench, her head in her hands, and took long slow breaths.

Dolly interrupted her meltdown, miaowing and rubbing herself around Felicity's legs. Her warm body and soft fur were a reassuring comfort.

"I bought you food." Felicity eased herself upright, sucked in another breath. "It's dry cat biscuits and you have to make it last."

Taking care of the cat's needs helped. The pain eased and the warmth subsided. Once Dolly was happily crunching, Felicity went back to the family room and flung herself onto the couch. She was totally dependent on Ian and he'd humiliated her. She pulled her phone from her bag and the doctor's script she'd slid in beside it fell out.

"Damn!" She hadn't got that filled either. Ian had been the one to encourage her to take the bloody drug. She thought she'd been managing the symptoms of menopause well but he'd suggested HRT might help their love life. Bastard! She tapped his name on the screen. The calm sound of his request to leave a message only infuriated her more.

"Damn you, Ian," she screamed at the phone. "You can't cut me off with no money. Ring me! We need to talk."

She dropped her phone to the couch beside her then shrieked in frustration and punched her fists into the cushions on either side.

Her phone rang and she snatched it up. "What do you think you're playing at?" she yelled.

"Felicity?"

She glanced at her screen. It was Tony, the calm, sensible man who'd overseen her renovations. She pressed the phone back to her ear, grimacing so widely her lips hurt. "Tony…I'm so sorry… I thought you were someone else…I've been getting some nasty nuisance calls."

"That's no good. Have you tried blocking them?"

"No!" She stood up and began to pace. "At least not yet. But I will if they continue. What can I do for you?"

"I wondered if you still had the name and contact details for the place you got your loungeroom wallpaper from?"

"Yes. I've got it all recorded in my book."

"I thought you would have. Can you text it to me please? I've got a client who wants something similar to what you chose."

"Of course." Felicity walked towards the third bedroom they'd converted to a study-come-guest room. "I'll do it as soon as I end the call."

"Thanks." There was a pause.

"Anything else you need?"

"No. I…well, I wondered how you were getting on."

"I'm fine," she snapped. "Why wouldn't I be?"

"It was a shock your dad dying, and I haven't seen you since the party. I hope you and your family are doing okay. I've been thinking of you all."

"That's kind of you, Tony." Felicity sank into the sleek office chair drawn up to the desk with its view of the garden. Like the family room, the study had large glass doors that opened onto the deck. She drew a breath to settle her nerves. She kept forgetting most people only knew about Franklyn's passing. They didn't know she'd discovered she was adopted and that Ian had left her. She stiffened. Bloody Ian.

"Pardon?"

Oh hell, had she said that out loud? "Nothing. I knocked something over. Sorry, I must go." She got up and walked back to the kitchen

"No probs. Say hello to Ian."

"Yes…yes, I will, bye." She tossed her phone onto the bench and glared at it. Tony was a good man and their whole conversation had been studded with lies.

She jumped as her phone began to ring again. This time she checked the screen before she answered. It was Ian.

"How dare you cut off the money and not tell me!" she screamed at the phone. "I've been totally embarrassed at the supermarket."

"I'm sorry, Lissie," he said gently, and with those three words the anger whooshed out of her as if she'd been pricked by a pin. She wanted him to come home, put his arms around her and tell her everything would be okay.

"I've been away."

"Working?"

"Yes."

"Ian, I wish you'd come home."

There was silence on the other end. Then a soft sigh before he continued. "I'm not coming back, Felicity. I'm sorry about the money. I should have told you first but I did have to go away suddenly and—"

"Was your phone not working?" The wave of hurt from his desertion was swamped by a surge of anger, sucking the air from her lungs. How could he do this to her? She took slow deliberate breaths.

"I'd planned to come over…explain the money—"

"But you didn't and I went to the shops and had to suffer the disgrace of standing in front of a queue of people at the checkout to sift through the groceries for what I could afford with the bit of cash I luckily had on me."

"There's money in your debit account."

"I didn't have that card with me, Ian."

"I'm sorry," he said again but this time her anger stayed.

"I've worked as much as you to contribute to our home, our family, our— what I thought was our happy life. You can't leave me with nothing."

"Listen a minute. I'll keep giving you spending money each fortnight until you can find work."

"Three hundred dollars!" Her brain scrambled to do the maths. Hell, her hair cut and colour cost her nearly all of that.

"I'll pay all the household bills and the mortgage until we sort things out."

"Sort things out. What does that mean?"

"And Franklyn has left you something. I don't expect you to share that."

"Share it! He didn't…he isn't…he wasn't…" Felicity put a hand to her head. Nothing was making any sense. She pressed her hand to her chest trying to stop the pain that was building like hooves pounding inside her.

"You'll be calmer when you've had more time to think."

"I will not be calmer. Ian, you can't do this to me. How am I going to live, to face people, to…" Had he said work? How long would it take to find something? Who would want her? She took a breath. The phone at her ear was silent. She looked at the screen. He'd disconnected. She dropped the phone to the bench, let out a scream of frustration, then clamped a hand to her mouth.

"Damn you, Ian," she growled. How was she going to live on three hundred dollars a fortnight? It was less than the dole!

She prowled the room, slamming a hand on the table as she passed, punching a cushion on the couch, stopping to tap her forehead against the glass of the deck doors, then she paced again. Finally, as the last rays of sunlight turned the sky golden, she stopped at the kitchen bench where she'd dumped the two meagre bags of shopping. She realised she was hungry. Maybe it was hunger that was inflaming the radiating pain inside her.

At least the bags contained bread and cheese, she could make herself a toasted sandwich. She unpacked the food and put it away, leaving out what she needed. At the open fridge door she paused. She'd just put in a carton of milk, a few vegetables and some sausages – the rest of the shelves were empty except for condiments, dressings and wine. At least wine was something she had plenty of. The supply they'd bought for her party had been barely dented. She took a bottle, poured herself a glass and picked up the empty hessian shopping bags to fold. One of them clunked against the bench. She was sure she'd emptied both. She peered in and there, lying flat at the bottom, was a block of chocolate. It had been one of the items she'd put aside.

"Now I can add thief to my list of woes." She shook her head. There was no way she'd accidently put the chocolate in the bag. She went to the bin and took out the wad of shopping dockets she'd tossed in. There were several bits of paper besides her grocery tally – a fuel offer, a competition to win a home makeover and…she stared at the docket in her hand with one single item on it. The block of chocolate.

"How the hell?"

She pictured Milo's sympathetic smile. He must have bought it for her. Felicity gripped the bench with her hands and wept. Once she'd stopped blubbering, she wiped her eyes and nose and set about making herself a toasted cheese sandwich. Then with toastie, wine and chocolate, she settled herself on the couch and put on the show she'd been halfway through watching when Greta had called in. Dolly came out of the laundry, sauntered across the room and jumped up beside her, nestling against her leg. Felicity raised a glass to the empty room.

"Thanks, Milo," she said and took a large sip of wine.

sixteen

Hazel pulled in outside Blanchard and Flavel Lawyers. Kurt had rung her the day following the reading of the will to organise the collection of Franklyn's cars. She should have asked him then how much money she'd be entitled to but his call had caught her by surprise. By Friday she'd gone over so many scenarios in her head she'd rung to make an appointment to see him. He'd said he could fit her in first thing Monday morning. His first thing was nine-thirty and it wasn't quite nine but Hazel had been awake since six. She'd had breakfast, done a load of washing, tidied the house, showered and dressed and when by eight o'clock she was pacing the kitchen, she'd decided to set off. She knew the traffic would be heavy heading across town at that hour and there was always roadworks somewhere.

She checked her lipstick in the mirror, made sure she had her handkerchief and her phone in her bag then sat back. Several people walked past, some entering the building, others continuing by. She'd been on her own most of the time since the reading of the will. Not totally alone. June had stayed with her that night and had rung each evening since, which was kind of her but Hazel found their conversations very one-sided. She'd never realised how opinionated June was until now, how like Franklyn she was. There'd been a few visitors, neighbours who'd been in the street in the early days but had since moved away, a couple of friends. Hazel was out of touch with all of them and she'd drunk enough tea since Franklyn died to last her the rest of her life. She'd started drinking coffee to mix it up.

June had collected her on Saturday and they'd gone together to drop Lachlan at the airport – he was returning to New Zealand – then they'd called in at Felicity's but there'd been no response. Hazel had felt strongly that her daughter was at home, just not answering the door to them.

Now she ran through her planned discussion with Kurt again, praying it would work in her favour. She'd done little but worry about money since the reading of Franklyn's will. She could live on the pension but there was nothing for extras.

On the footpath she stopped to take a deep breath and straighten her skirt. She caught sight of her reflection in the glass-walled building. In her younger days she'd enjoyed fashion. She'd invested in a few basic good quality pieces and the rest of her wardrobe had been items she'd made herself. She'd sewn for the girls but once they were in their late teens all that had stopped.

Now she'd describe her wardrobe as frugal and boring. For today's meeting she'd dug deep to come up with the maroon skirt and pink paisley-patterned blouse, some colourful beads and medium heels. She'd even worn stockings. She needed the boost of confidence that dressing smartly brought.

The sun was shining, lifting her spirits with its warmth. Her future depended on this meeting. She was hopeful that after today she could at least begin to plan for a retirement village and holidays. She strode purposefully to the office door and pushed it open. Surely the fact that a considerable sum of her money, the insurance money from her parents' home, had gone towards the house where she now lived should count for something even though her name wasn't on the title.

She didn't have to wait long before Kurt was welcoming her into his large black leather and sparkling glass office. He'd been Franklyn's lawyer for years and she wondered how much of Franklyn's money had gone into this designer space. Hazel tried to keep her composure but both Kurt and his office made her feel insignificant and her smart outfit drab.

"Thank you for giving the car people easy access," Kurt said after he'd sat her down. "I would have been there myself but I couldn't leave the office that day."

"It was no problem. And Derek was able to be there to help oversee." Her son-in-law was a finance manager for a dealership that sold prestige cars.

"Yes, he's been very helpful. Handy to have someone in the industry watching out for you. There's been some keen interest in Franklyn's cars already so there shouldn't be much difficulty in selling them. As soon as that's done we can start your fortnightly allowance."

"Is there money I can access in the meantime?"

"You've applied for bereavement support?"

"Yes, my daughters helped me with that after Franklyn died but after his will was read, well, I'll need to apply for a pension and…" Hazel hated having to ask for money. She'd already put herself through the wringer filling out the Centrelink forms, now she was having to ask Kurt for a top-up.

"You don't have your own savings to tide you over?"

"A little…but…well, you see I was totally reliant on the money Franklyn gave me, the fortnightly housekeeping plus a small amount for spending. He paid all the household bills. I haven't worked outside the home since we were married and I don't have much in reserve."

Kurt tapped the tips of his fingers together and slowly shook his head. "I'm sorry. All Franklyn's money, other than what we'll get for the cars, is tied up until the paperwork is finalised, I'm afraid. Perhaps your daughters can help until the pension is approved?"

"I wanted to make sure all avenues had been covered before I ask them." Hazel swallowed the bitter taste in her mouth. She might have asked Felicity if she was desperate but certainly not June.

"I'm hoping the car sales will go through quickly and once that's done the money will go into your account each fortnight. I thought the opposite week to the pension might be helpful."

He was probably right about that but he hadn't even asked her how she wanted to receive the pittance Franklyn was paying her. She swallowed her annoyance. "That will be fine, thank you."

"Other than that, there's nothing else I can tell you at this stage." He folded his hands on top of his desk and smiled grandly at her. "There's really nothing more for you to worry about. Franklyn set it all up to make everything seamless. All the paperwork is being taken care of – it takes time but as I said, all straightforward." He stood up. "If there's ever anything, though, you give me a call."

Hazel remained seated. "Actually, there is something else."

He was already halfway round his desk ready to show her to the door. He stopped and perched on the corner of his desk, still with that lofty smile in place. "Of course, what is it?"

Hazel clasped her hands together neatly in her lap, drew a breath and fixed Kurt with what she hoped was a resolute look. "When Franklyn and I were first married I came into some money. It was the insurance payout for my family home which had been destroyed in a bushfire, and my parents along with it."

Kurt's smile slipped. "I'm so sorry, Hazel. I didn't know that had happened."

"It was a long time ago. However, the payout was a significant amount and meant we had a very small mortgage when we bought our home. The house I still live in today."

Kurt's smile vanished altogether.

"I believe that entitles me to ownership no matter what my husband's will says."

Kurt studied her a moment, then stood abruptly, turned his back to her and walked around to his seat. "I didn't know about that."

"Franklyn was a proud man. He didn't want anyone to know that he hadn't been the total contributor to providing the family home. We never spoke of it again. There was no need to."

"It has no bearing, I'm afraid."

All of the hope that had been building in Hazel over the last few days left her in a rush, causing her to make a moaning sound as the air left her lungs.

Kurt's mask fell back into place. "I'm so sorry, Hazel. I realise it was probably a shock for you to find Franklyn hadn't left you the house but you will be looked after. It's clear that June must let you live there until you either need to go to a home or…" He coughed. "You pass on. You don't need to worry about keeping a roof over your head."

He stood up again and came right round the desk this time, offering his hand. "I'm sorry to rush you but I've fitted you in between some other clients. Did you drive or take a taxi? The girls in the office can call a taxi and they'll make you a cup of tea before you go."

Hazel rose to her feet without taking his hand but found herself being guided to the door. He opened it then paused as if waiting for something.

"Oh…no, I drove myself and no tea," she said. "Thank you."

"All right then. Well, it was lovely to see you, Hazel, and please give me a call if there's ever anything else."

Before Hazel knew it she was standing outside his door and it was being shut firmly behind her. She felt as empty as the minimally designed passage she stood in. It was a shock, as if Franklyn had died all over again, her hopes for a different future dashed. She walked down the hall in a daze, past the waiting room and the reception area and let herself out into the autumn day. She glanced at her watch. She'd been in Kurt's office barely fifteen minutes. What was she to do now? Felicity would have been the one she turned to but Felicity would have nothing to do with her.

Hazel wandered back towards her car, stopped in front of it and looked up and down the street. She was only a few blocks from Norwood Parade. In her purse she had twenty dollars. It was the spending money she'd allowed herself for the week. Perhaps some window shopping might help her clear her thoughts. Until she had her head around the actual money she would get and how much the bills would be she was on a very tight budget. Even more so now that there was no hope of her selling the house and recouping some of her money.

Up until Franklyn died, her job had been to manage the household and her personal needs with the fortnightly allowance he'd given her. She'd never been extravagant and if she needed extra for birthdays, items for the house, a new outfit for a special occasion, he'd always covered it with little complaint. She knew how to budget but she'd never had to manage all the bills before. Since Franklyn had died she'd received a phone bill, water rates and the car registration. When she got home she would have to work out a proper budget. She took a breath to stop the panic that was rising inside her. Right now she wouldn't think about that. Perhaps she would treat herself to a coffee and some kind of cake to cheer herself up. She'd face what must be faced when she got home.

Deep in thought, she strolled down the street, turned into another and was part way across the road when a car careened around the corner. She hurried to reach the other side, caught her heel on the edge of the gutter and toppled forward. Everything slowed down – she knew she was going to fall, there was nothing she could do. The ground came up to meet her. Her hands and then her knees hit the path. For a brief moment she felt nothing, heard nothing, then pain shot up her arms and legs. There was a scream, her own, and a car door slammed.

"Are you all right?" A young woman's voice came to her as if down a tunnel.

Stars danced before Hazel's eyes then cleared. She stared at a small rock on the footpath. An ant scurried around it, a large crumb in its mouth. Her arms still held her up. She hoped that meant nothing was broken.

A gentle hand rested on her shoulder. "I didn't see you as I came round the corner but I didn't hit you, did I?"

Hazel turned her head sideways. A worried face, young like Greta, filled her vision.

"I caught my heel." She moved one hand and then the other.

"You did take it a bit fast though, young lady." An older male voice spoke above her head. "I saw the whole thing from my front verandah."

"She just stepped out." The young woman spluttered. "I didn't see her."

Hazel's cheeks burned with heat. How many more people had witnessed her humiliation? She could feel her skirt up around her thighs but had no way to reach it. "I'm all right."

"Perhaps if you ease yourself over and sit for a moment," the man said.

Hazel allowed herself to be manoeuvred so that she was sitting on the path and tugged her skirt back down.

"Oh, there's blood all down your legs," the young woman wailed.

Hazel looked down at her shredded stockings and bloodied knees. One of her shoes was off and lay beside her in the gutter.

"Should I call an ambulance?"

"No," Hazel snapped.

The young woman's lip wobbled.

"There's no need. It's just grazes," Hazel said, gently this time. "I'll be all right."

"If you're all right, I'd better go." The young woman stepped away. "I've got a meeting."

"I'll be fine." All Hazel wanted was to be left alone. "Thanks for stopping."

"Perhaps drive a little more carefully," the man said but the young woman was hurrying to her car and either didn't hear or chose to ignore him.

Hazel leaned forward to retrieve her shoe. Stars danced before her eyes again.

"You should sit a little while longer," the man said then he leaned forward and peered at her. "Hazel?"

She'd been so caught up in her embarrassment she hadn't looked at him properly. Now she noticed the easy smile hovering at the edge of his lips. "Jack?" He'd been a member of the bowls club when she and Franklyn used to play.

"It is you." His lips lifted in a proper smile. "I haven't seen you in ages."

"What are you doing here?"

"I live here." He waved over his shoulder. "I was sitting on the front verandah and saw you fall."

She put her hand to her head and groaned.

"Does your head hurt?" He leaned in closer.

"No. It's just that I thought at least it was strangers witnessing my clumsiness."

"That young woman was driving like a maniac. You wouldn't have fallen if she hadn't hurried you by driving too fast."

Hazel groaned again.

"Are you sure you're not hurt more than you're letting on?"

"I'm sure." Everything hurt but nothing too badly. "Just embarrassed. Here I am sitting in the gutter and the witness to my fall is someone I know."

Jack lowered himself to the path and put his feet beside hers. "I always think if you're going to end up in the gutter it might as well be with a friend." He grinned.

A car drove slowly past, the occupants staring at them.

Something burbled inside Hazel and erupted as a laugh. Hands and knees smarting aside, it felt good. She laughed louder, not just at the idiocy of her fall but at the strange turn of life she found herself in.

"Are you sure you're all right?" Jack peered at her.

She stifled her laugh and nodded.

"I assume you're here on your own," he said.

"Yes, I had an appointment down the road."

"If you're feeling up to it, how about you come and sit on my verandah and I'll help you clean up?"

"Oh no, I'll go back to my car."

"If someone else sees you they might call an ambulance. You've got blood all over your face from your hands."

She looked down. Blood still oozed from her palms, which were embedded with bits of dirt, and her knees looked as if she'd taken the grater to them. She could only imagine the state of her face. Another car went past, slowed then kept going.

She swallowed her pride and allowed Jack to help her up. "Thank you."

They walked slowly across the footpath and up the drive to the broad front verandah. Once he'd settled her in an old wicker chair and she assured him she'd be all right, he set off around the side of the house.

From where she sat, she was partly screened from the road by a sprawling hedge but through a gap the scene of her humiliating fall was in clear view.

She peeled a piece of ripped stocking away from her leg where the blood was already beginning to dry. What a mess. June would make a fuss if she found out. Probably want to shuffle Hazel straight off to a home.

She glanced up at the few lazy clouds strung out across the beautiful azure-blue sky and shook her head. Her day had begun with such high hopes.

"Here we are."

Jack placed a bucket of water at her feet then drew a small table close and set out cloths, a towel, some antiseptic cream and a small mirror. The cloudy white water in the bucket sloshed from side to side.

"I'll leave you a moment to clean up."

"Thank you," she said, grateful for some privacy. Her stockings were useless and would only be more difficult to get off if she left them. She eased them past her wounds, slipped them off and shoved them in her handbag, then set about cleaning up the rest of her. When she looked in the mirror she could see why Jack had suggested she wash her face.

She dipped a cloth in the warm water and dabbed gently at her knees. The pungent smell of Dettol took her back to the last time she'd needed to bathe her wounds. That time it had been a tangle with her beautiful golden yellow climbing rose. It had needed pruning and with her arms full of cuttings she'd slipped on the small stepladder and lacerated her skin from her fingers almost to her armpits. She'd picked tiny thorns from her flesh for days afterwards. Franklyn had berated her for being so foolish. Several days later she'd come home from cards to find her beautiful climbing rose gone with some kind of succulent in its place. "Young Charlie from down the road chopped it out," he'd said. "I gave him money for beer. He brought the plant, a cutting from his mum's garden. It will be much easier to look after." And so for the cost of a six pack and the provision of a second-hand plant, the job was done as far as Franklyn was concerned.

Hazel looked in the mirror, wiped away the blood she'd smeared on her cheeks and the tears of self-pity. Perhaps she'd replace the ugly succulent with a new rose.

Jack came back just as she was tidying up the rubbish from the dressing she'd put on her knee. He sat a glass of water beside her and sat on the edge of the verandah, his back braced against a pole.

"You look a lot better without that blood on your face. How do you feel?"

"A bit silly but I'll live." She picked up the glass, surprised at the tremble in her fingers. "Thanks for this."

"No problem."

They were both silent then. Hazel wondered how long she should stay before it was polite to leave.

"Do you still go to night owls?" Jack asked.

"Oh, no. It was always fun but Franklyn's knees got too sore."

"I did read in the paper...I was sorry to hear about Franklyn. How are you doing? Apart from tripping on gutters."

"I'm okay."

"What about family? Do you have children and grandchildren?"

"Yes, I have daughters, June and...and Felicity. They both have children but they're all in their twenties now. No little ones."

"Do they live close, your daughters?"

"Both in Adelaide. June's only a quick drive away. Felicity a bit further."

"It's good that you've got them nearby. I could have done with that support when my wife died."

Hazel couldn't remember seeing him with his wife. "Was that recent?"

"Oh no. My dear Freda's been gone for fifteen years now."

"Oh...I'm sorry."

"We had a wonderful life together and I still miss her but friends have been a big help, and keeping busy."

Hazel sipped her water and watched two little birds that were busy flitting between the bushes in the front yard. Would she say she and Franklyn had had a wonderful life together? Perhaps for a while they were happy, when the girls were young, but as he got older the three st's took over – Franklyn had become sterner, stiffer and starchier.

"I've kept up with bowls and croquet and, until recently, golf, since I moved here and joined the local clubs." Jack went on talking. "I have a shoulder that gives me bother these days. The joys of ageing. So no golf for me any more but there's a strong bowling group here and lots of young ones come for the night owls. Brightens the place up."

There'd been a time when Hazel and Franklyn had been more active in their own local community. Her more so than him, but after he retired he didn't like her to go out without him. This last year his health hadn't been so good and they'd hardly done anything beyond their home and family.

"Perhaps I'll join the local bowls again." It might have been the wistful way she spoke but Jack looked suddenly contrite.

"Sorry, I've been prattling on. You probably can't face anything yet," Jack said. "What's it been, a month since Franklyn died?"

"Two weeks."

"Only two weeks. You must still be feeling like you want to stick your head under a pillow and cry. I know I felt so raw for a long time after Freda died."

Raw was one word for it. Emotionally exhausted was how she'd describe herself. From Franklyn's sudden death and everything that had followed it, Hazel had been existing in a vacuum. She sat up in her chair as the realisation hit her. She missed another presence in the house – but she did not miss Franklyn himself. It was having a purpose, something to do and look forward to that she lacked.

"I'm sorry, I shouldn't have brought it up." Jack's face was full of concern.

"It's all right," she said. "Apart from this." She waved one hand at her knees. "It's been pleasant to be with someone who doesn't know much about me. I feel as if the last two weeks have been a blur of appointments and people dropping in, lots of condolences, well-meaning of course, and then the funeral and all that went with it and, lawyers and paperwork. It's nice to simply sit."

He nodded. Dappled sunlight played across her legs, soothing them with its warmth. All was quiet except for the occasional tweets of the birds and the soft rustle of leaves in the breeze. Hazel felt a sense of peace she hadn't felt in a long, long time.

She wasn't sure how long they both just sat but as she swallowed the last of her water she glanced at her watch.

"I should go." She rose carefully to her feet. "I'm parked in a two-hour spot and it'll be getting close to that by the time I get back." That's all she needed, a parking fine to finish off her day.

"I'll walk you to your car."

"There's no need."

"I'd like to." He stood. "I don't suppose you'd take my arm."

"No." She smiled. "But thank you."

They moved out to the path, Hazel making sure she placed each foot carefully as they crossed the leafy street.

"This is a pretty suburb." She caught glimpses of other lush gardens behind well-maintained fences. "You must like living here."

"It's got everything I need. And this is a quiet street...usually."

Hazel pulled a face. They rounded the corner and she waved towards her car. "It's just there. I'll be fine."

But he insisted on walking with her. She unlocked the door. Jack held it open. She hesitated, not sure what to do. Should she wave goodbye, shake his hand, kiss his cheek?

"Thanks for your help, Jack," she said and decided a smile would cover it. "It was lovely to see you again."

"And you."

She eased carefully into the driver's seat.

"Hazel." He bent his head through the open door. "It might be too soon for you to feel you want to be out with people but I wondered if you might like to go to the movies?"

Her heart sank. Jack had been very kind but she was seventy-six, recently widowed and not ready to go on a date. Not because of any regard for her husband but simply because she couldn't be bothered.

"It's this Thursday," Jack said. "A matinee with morning tea supplied. It's a fundraiser for the bowling club at that lovely old theatre on Kensington Road." He spoke quickly, perhaps noticing the concern on her face. "There'll be lots of people there. I don't know what the movie is, something the ladies committee picked."

"That's a kind thought, Jack, but…" If it was a fundraiser the ticket would cost more than normal. Another thing she'd have to factor into her finances.

"I've purchased two tickets in the hope of giving them to someone rather than go myself. Perhaps you could go with one of your daughters?"

"Oh no, they're busy on weekdays." June worked Thursdays and even if Felicity was talking to her by then, Hazel was pretty sure she would reject the idea outright.

"I'm a bit the same. All the younger ones are at work and the people my age already have their own tickets or are doing other things that day." His shoulders slumped just a little.

Hazel thought a moment. For years she'd been under Franklyn's shadow, only doing what he wanted to do and now here was an opportunity to make her own decisions about what she did and where she went. Most of their friends were his friends and she knew they'd soon stop checking in on her. With June and Greta working and no Felicity, the long empty week stretched out before her. "It's years since I went to the movies."

He straightened, his eyes bright. "I'd be honoured if you'd be my guest. My shout. I'm not sure about the movie but I can guarantee the morning tea will be splendid."

Hazel glanced at her watch. "I do have to go. Shall I meet you at the theatre on Thursday?"

"Yes, nine forty-five for the morning tea and the movie starts at ten thirty."

"I'll see you then."

By the time she reached home her hands were weeping again from clutching the steering wheel and her right knee was throbbing with pain radiating down her leg. She let herself in the front door and stopped at the hall table. The roses were still amazingly bright. She plucked up the vase, carried it through the house to the backyard and tipped the contents into the green bin. Back inside she washed the vase and put it away. Her meeting with Kurt had been futile and, with her injuries, it hadn't been much of a day really. But, on the bright side, falling in the gutter had brought Jack to help her and now she had plans for Thursday.

seventeen

Felicity prowled her kitchen, coffee cup in hand. It was only early but she'd already packed up the bed she'd made for herself on the lounge, eaten some toast with the last scrapings from the honey for breakfast and tidied the room. Every bench had been wiped down, the floor vacuumed, chairs were straight and cushions plumped. She hadn't opened the curtains yet. She wasn't quite ready to let the outside in.

She'd woken early to a WhatsApp message from Suzie and it had left her feeling restless. Suzie had sent several photos of her New York experience. But it had been the photos of the *Sex in the City* tour they'd taken that had really upset Felicity. She and Suzie had watched reruns of the show together on and off for years. Suzie's message had said the tour ticket was wasted on her husband and wished Felicity could have been the one with her when they stopped outside Carrie's house, ate cupcakes at the Magnolia Bakery and even had a cosmopolitan at Onieal's Grand Street Bar. There was a beautiful photo of Suzie, glass to her lips, long dark hair swept back from her face, sporting a wicked smile. She reminded Felicity of Charlotte.

If Suzie was home Felicity could tell her best friend everything, but she wasn't going to spoil Suzie's holiday with her news. None of it seemed appropriate to share via a WhatsApp message. Instead she focused on what Suzie was telling her and sent back excited responses to their adventures and bland messages about her own life like, *all good here* or *great weather nothing else to report*. She hadn't even told Suzie Franklyn had died.

She leaned back against the island bench and took a sip of coffee. She was getting used to instant. The bag of coffee beans she'd selected at the supermarket had been one of the items she'd had to leave behind. Just when she thought she'd have to take up drinking tea, she'd remembered the jar of Nescafé in the back of the pantry.

She glanced at the clock. Each day about now there'd been a regular round of texts, one from Greta, which she always answered, one from June telling her she should contact Hazel, which she sometimes answered, and one from Hazel begging her to ring, which Felicity never answered. As if she'd conjured them up, her phone vibrated and then began to ring. It was June. Felicity let it go. Eventually it stopped and shortly after came the ping of a voicemail. She played it.

"Wherever you are, Felicity, you must ring Mum. You're being very selfish." There was a pause. "It's June, by the way."

"No shit, Sherlock." Felicity giggled. She'd learned some great sayings from the young tradies working around her home.

She deleted June's message and began to circle the room again. At the sideboard she stopped, ran her hand over the clean surface. A week ago it had been decorated with family photos, each one depicting an event in their lives that was a lie. There was one of Franklyn, Hazel, June and Felicity taken at Franklyn's eightieth. For all the connection she felt to the other three now, she may as well have been in a photo with random strangers off the street. There'd been another of Ian and Felicity with Greta at Greta's uni graduation but now Felicity no longer had a husband either. There were more but she'd put them all in the drawer, all except the one of her with Greta taken in the lush green garden of a resort in tropical Queensland.

They'd gone on a holiday together after Greta had finished her university studies. It had been a blissful week of walking and talking, day spas and swimming, shopping and reading, total indulgence, and looking back Felicity realised she was so grateful for that time alone with her daughter. Greta had started dating Joe during uni so understandably she spent most of her free time with him after that. And if Ian had been there he'd have wanted them to go sailboarding, bike riding or hiking up mountains. His idea of a holiday was to always be active. Not that she and Ian had taken a proper holiday together in a long time. Thinking back it had probably been the trip to Noosa, the year before they'd bought this house. She recalled their candlelit dinner on their first night and that they'd argued about what to do with their time. They'd resolved it by agreeing to do their own thing. Felicity had booked a day spa, shopped and enjoyed the Eumundi markets. Ian had spent most of his time trekking the walking trails in the national park. A couple of swims and sunset drinks had been their only together time apart from staying in the same apartment. The sex had been good but she did have to wonder, had that been the beginning of Ian's discontent?

The clip-clopping feeling of horses hooves in her chest started again. She pressed a hand to her mouth, holding back the overwhelming urge to scream. Her heart beat faster. She thought she'd been living a happy life, with a family she loved and who she thought had loved her. Why had she never seen the signs that it was all a mirage?

She adjusted the photo, straightened the chairs at the table then fluffed the already tidy cushions on the couch. A complete circuit of the room brought her back to the kitchen where she stopped and stared at the gleaming bench. The ticking of the wall clock and the hum of the fridge combined to make a lonesome duet. She flicked on the television and the bright voices of morning show hosts flooded the room. She lowered the volume till it was barely there, just enough to mask the sounds of the clock and the fridge.

Her phone rang again, perhaps Greta or Hazel this time, but when she looked at the screen it was Pam. She'd rung Felicity after the terrible night of the party but they hadn't spoken since. "What day is it?" Felicity looked around as if the empty room would answer. She snatched up her phone as the ringing stopped and swiped to check the calendar. It was Wednesday, social tennis day. She hadn't played since Franklyn had died. No doubt Pam was calling to see if she was going today.

Felicity brightened. Perhaps she would. None of the girls there knew about her being adopted or that Ian had left. She could keep it to herself for a little longer. There was a ping. Felicity listened to the message Pam left.

"I hope you're up to coming to tennis today. It's Tansie's birthday and she's said no presents but wants us all to go for lunch after at that lovely new wine bar down near the beach. Charles has even offered to pick us up and drop us off so we don't have to worry about drinks. Let me or Tansie know and he'll pick you up at ten. See you soon, I hope."

Felicity's spirits soared and then the air left her lungs as swiftly as if she'd been laid flat on her back. When the girls got together for lunch it was an all-afternoon affair with fancy food and plenty to drink. The new wine bar was trendy and expensive. Felicity could easily blow a third of her money just on lunch. She could go just for the tennis but even that came at a cost. It was fifteen dollars to play each week and if she didn't then go on to lunch Pam would want to know why. The weight of it pressed down on her. She didn't know whether to grip her spinning head or the ache across her chest, which was now feeling like a pack of horses was thundering around in it.

She gripped the phone and painstakingly typed an excuse one letter at a time. *Sorry have to be with Hazel today.* She pressed send then jumped at the sound of an incoming text. It was from Greta. *Hi Mum*, she'd written. *Hope you're doing okay today. Is Dad home yet? I thought I'd pop in on my way home from work tonight.*

Felicity strangled the groan but couldn't stop the tears that formed and rolled in warm trails down her cheeks. Greta was her only true flesh and blood, and someone who loved her unconditionally. What would she think when she found out her dad had left? Would Greta blame her, take his side? Would Felicity lose her daughter as well as everyone else in her family?

She tapped out a text. Her glasses fogged with tears and it took a few attempts. *All good here. Dad still away. I'm out with tennis girls tonight. Catch you another day? Love Mum xx.*

Felicity staggered to the couch, curled herself into the corner and hugged her knees tightly. Dolly jumped up beside her and bunted her head against Felicity's hand. "What are we going to do, Dolly?" She stroked the soft fur of the cat's back.

She'd planned to go to the supermarket again today, not anywhere near Milo's, but somewhere in the other direction where no-one would know her. Just the thought of going shopping, even to a different supermarket, quickened the sensation of hooves galloping around in her chest, and made her stomach churn.

She gripped her head in her hands and rocked forward. "It's not fair," she groaned. The pain was radiating across her back now.

Perhaps she was dying. She was all alone and not expecting anyone else to call. If she died it could be days before she was found. Her phone pinged again. It was a text from Pam with a sad face for missing the lunch but wishing her well and that they'd catch up next week.

Felicity took a deep breath and sat up. She wasn't going to die, not today, and she'd just had a thought. Pam shopped online for her groceries, said she hated wasting time in the supermarket when someone would do the work for her. Felicity had never done it before, preferring to select her own groceries, but it was the perfect solution.

She leaped up and opened the family room door but hesitated on the edge of the shadowy empty house ahead. She took a quick breath and, ignoring the thudding pain in her chest, hurried into the office and took up the laptop. Back in the family room, she shut the door behind her again. It took a moment for her to settle, for her trembling fingers to move evenly across the keyboard, but she managed to open the browser. Once online she decided on the supermarket she wanted and began to shop. It was quite easy really. It added up as she went so she knew exactly how much it would cost. She was quite pleased with herself until she went to check out. Then she remembered she no longer had a credit card.

"Damn!"

She stared angrily at the screen then relaxed. It was all right. They took debit cards. She retrieved hers from her purse and typed in the numbers. Her next decision was when to get it delivered. She opted for the afternoon, before Sal and Les got home from work just in case she happened to be taking in the groceries and they came across for a chat, then, feeling very satisfied with herself, she sat back and surveyed her room again.

If she opened the curtains the space would fill with light during the day. Once she had the rest of the house shut off, she could leave the big glass doors open if she wanted. Sometimes she could even hear the sea from here. No-one could access her backyard. There was only one side gate and it was high and locked. The yard was bounded on one side by the garage wall of the house that faced the next street over. Her back fence had a trellis, courtesy of her backyard makeover, and there was a high fence between her place and Melody and Humphrey on her other side. She could avoid people, avoid having to explain the mess her life had become. This room and her backyard could be her sanctuary.

She strode across the room, pulled back the curtains and screamed. There was a man standing on the other side of the glass. His back was to her but he spun, phone in hand, a startled look on his face.

"Oh!" She gasped. "Tony." Behind her there was a scrabbling sound as Dolly tried to gain traction on the tiles in her haste to run away. Felicity opened one door, suddenly conscious that she was wearing the clothes she'd discarded yesterday and she hadn't showered or even dragged a brush through her hair. "You frightened me."

"I'm sorry. I did knock at the front door but you didn't answer."

Unbidden, the terrible heat began in her neck and rose up to her face. "I didn't hear you knock."

"I must admit it was just a quick tap. The place didn't look as if you were home. I let myself in the side gate." He looked sheepish. "I still have a key." He dangled one from his hand.

"Oh," she said again.

"I feel like a prowler." Tony gave her the key. "I'm sorry I frightened you."

"Don't be silly, it's fine." If she'd heard Tony at the door she wouldn't have answered but here was a living, breathing person in her house and ... it was okay.

"I was over this way and I thought I'd call in to see if you had those details I asked for."

"Details?"

"The wallpaper."

"Oh yes, of course. I'm so sorry. I forgot all about it. I'll get it for you." When she glanced back from across the room he was still standing just outside the door. "Come in."

"I don't want to hold you up."

"Would you like a coffee? It's only instant. I've run out of beans, I'm afraid. Have to get to the shops."

He glanced at his watch. "I've got time before my nine o'clock appointment and instant's fine."

There was a small grin on his face and she remembered his mild teasing when she'd purchased the gleaming new coffee machine for the kitchen. She'd defended herself at the time – the bloody machine had been Ian's idea. At least Tony wasn't fussy about how he took his coffee. The tension in her chest eased a little.

"I'll get my notebook."

"Do you mind if I take some photos?" He held up the phone he still gripped in his hand. "I have another client who wants a new deck and pergola. I want to show him some photos of work I've already done and realised I didn't have any of the finished products. That was why I let myself into your yard." He screwed up his face.

Felicity blew out the breath she'd been holding.

"Go right ahead. I hope it's tidy – I haven't been out there today." She opened the door and sped to the office. Of course, he wanted pictures of the house, not her. She was panicking at the silliest things.

When she came back he was taking a photo of the family room ceiling. She'd spent many hours deliberating before she settled on the combination of the panelling and exposed beams, all painted white, of course. She set the open notebook down in front of him and made his coffee.

"Shall we sit on the deck?" she asked as she carried the cups across the room. After years of working together on and off she knew how he liked his coffee but she had no snacks in her cupboard to offer him.

She placed the cups on the coffee table and sat on the wicker couch. Tony chose one of the chairs, glancing around as he did.

"This really is a credit to you, Felicity. You've got a real eye for decorating. I didn't get a chance for a proper look with so many here at your party."

She smiled and instead of the ghastly heat and pain, she felt a pleasant, warming sense of worth in her chest. "I spent a lot of time researching." She nestled back against the cushions of the grey wicker couch, no longer bothered about her scruffy clothes and lack of make-up. There had been plenty of times during the renovations when she'd still been in pyjamas and dressing gown when Tony had arrived to start work. He'd seen her at her worst on several occasions.

"How are you all getting on?" Tony asked. "You had quite a shock the night of your party."

"It was, yes." Felicity reached for her coffee and wrapped her hands around the mug to stop it from wobbling in her trembling grip. "It's a cliché but life goes on."

"What about your mum? It must be hard for her suddenly on her own after such a long marriage."

"Yes...June's nearby though so she's got company." Felicity had no idea how Hazel was managing and told herself she didn't care, but here was the builder asking after her. Felicity wasn't surprised by his empathy for Hazel. He'd met her on several occasions and they'd hit it off straight away. Tony had spent so much time at their place he knew a lot about Felicity's family, although she knew little about his. Suddenly she felt as though his kind look could see through her charade, see the secrets she was hiding. Pain started to niggle inside her again. She took a sip of coffee.

"It's your party night that's brought me back this way today."

She looked at him over the top of her cup, still unwilling to hold it with only one hand.

"That couple you introduced me to."

Felicity frowned. So much of that night was a blurry memory now.

"Charles and...Tannie, is it?"

"Oh, Tansie, yes. They're only a few blocks away."

"I'm going there now to look at their bathroom. They want a total makeover."

The mention of her tennis friend reminded her of the fun she'd be missing later today. She pulled her lips up into what she hoped was a happy smile. "That's great, Tony. I'm glad you're getting more work."

"I've got a job to look at this morning, an order to follow up for next week's pergola work and then I have to go back and see this woman about the wallpaper."

"Still using your car as an office?"

"Saves on overheads." He grinned. "Although there's a bricks-and-mortar opportunity I'm looking into and I might need to take on an apprentice, thanks to you."

"Me?"

"Word-of-mouth is often the best advertising in small business and you've been singing my praises, I believe. I've gone from having no work when I first met you, to as busy as I can be on my own. I would like to be able to expand a bit so that I'm not always relying on other tradies to do some of the smaller jobs for me."

"You deserve the success, Tony." When she and Ian had met Tony he'd just moved back to South Australia from interstate. After working for a big building company he was keen to start his own business. They'd invited him to look over their place and their ideas for renovating and it had gone from there. Tony had been excited by the designs that Felicity had come up with and excellent at bringing them to life. "You're very good at your work."

"Thanks, Felicity, and thanks for the coffee." He stood and drained the mug. "I'd better go. Don't want to be late for Charles and..." He screwed up his nose.

"Tansie." She took his empty cup and led the way back through the house. The front hall was gloomy compared to the light and airy section they'd just left and she still hadn't done anything about the bags of clothes that lined one wall. "I'm not using this part of the house much while Ian's away." She opened the front door and stepped back out of view from the street.

He paused beside her. "Take care, Felicity," he said. "Give yourself time to adjust."

Before she could respond he was off and striding down the path. She shut the door, the familiar pounding in her chest returning. Tony had looked at her so closely it was as if he knew what was happening in her life but how could he? She went back to the kitchen and made her third cup of coffee for the day.

She curled up on the couch, clutching the mug as if it was a shield to deflect her troubles. Dolly had recovered from her fright and was curled up beside her. Felicity ran one hand over the cat's soft fur and stared out at the beautiful day. It had been lovely sitting out there on the deck while Tony was here but on her own she preferred to be inside. Suddenly tears welled in her eyes and rolled down her cheeks. Frustrated, she put down her coffee, flung off her glasses and reached for the box of tissues that was never far away.

The tears continued to flow. She stood up and paced. The pain in her middle had left her but now heat spread up her neck to her face again. "If it's not one damn thing it's another," she muttered. She threw herself back onto the couch. Dolly leaped to the floor again and something jabbed at Felicity's hip. She slid her hand down and pulled her glasses out from under her. One arm dangled from the misshapen frame.

"Oh no," she moaned and gave in to more tears.

eighteen

Hazel sat back from the small dining table and let out a sigh.

"I hope that was the sound of contentment." Jack smiled across at her. They were sitting in the hotel not far from the picture theatre and they'd just consumed a roast lunch accompanied by a glass of wine.

"I haven't eaten so much in ages." Hazel pressed a hand to her tight stomach. "The morning tea would have been enough but lunch as well."

"And wine." Jack took the last sip of his. "I don't normally drink in the middle of the day but that's a nice house red."

"Nor me, it makes me sleepy. Thank goodness I caught the bus here."

"So did I."

He waved a finger at Hazel's empty glass. "Seeing we're not driving shall we have another?"

The suggestion startled her. Franklyn wouldn't have approved a second glass. Not that they'd often eaten out for lunch.

"Unless you need to be somewhere in a hurry?" Jack said.

"Oh no…and I won't need to make myself any dinner. As long as I'm home before dark I'll be happy."

"We've plenty of time then." He reached for her empty glass. "My shout this time."

Hazel smiled, feeling very decadent, but she didn't object. She had nobody to report to but herself and she was happy for Jack to pay. She'd paid for their lunch as a thank you for Jack shouting her the movie ticket. She'd discovered the fundraiser had been twenty dollars a head. With their seniors cards, two serves of roast and two glasses of wine had cost her far less than the forty he'd forked out.

She'd also decided it was cheaper to use public transport than to drive her car and have the worry of parking. It had been straightforward catching a bus into the city from her place then out along Kensington Road to the theatre. She'd enjoyed the movie. It had been a live-action remake of *Mulan*. She'd watched an animated version with Greta when she was a little girl and, like the new movie, she'd found it both funny and touching. When Jack had suggested they go for lunch after the movie Hazel had been going to say no, she wasn't in the least bit hungry. Jack had been right about the morning tea, it had been a splendid spread. Hazel had thought about her empty house, June at work and Felicity not answering her calls, and decided she could stay out for lunch if she wanted to. The freedom of making her own decisions gave her some small satisfaction.

"Here we are." Jack sat a glass of white in front of her and a glass of red in his place. "Thanks for coming today, Hazel. I must say I was glad to see you none the worse for that trip last week."

Her cheeks warmed at the memory of her sprawl in the gutter. She glanced down at her knees. She hadn't worn stockings today. Her legs were still scabby.

"I know you must be feeling terribly sad," Jack said.

"Just foolish, tripping over like that."

"No, I meant it's very brave of you to put on your happy face and come out so soon after losing Franklyn." He lifted his glass. "I should make a toast. To a fine man, may he rest in peace."

Hazel stared at the glass he held towards her. A strange feeling began in her feet, a tingling, burning sensation, and it spread up into her torso.

Jack set his wine down again. "I'm sorry. I didn't mean to upset you."

She dragged her gaze from the glass to his face as the strange feeling fizzed and bubbled inside her. She gasped as she realised what it was.

"Are you feeling all right, Hazel?" Jack half rose from his chair.

"Yes." Her response came out in a hiss and she sagged just a little as if the air leaving her mouth had released the pressure inside her. She reached for the wine and took a gulp. It was a pinot gris, sharp and crisp on her tongue, just what she needed.

Jack sat again but still looked worried.

The act of drinking calmed her, stopped her from exploding

"I really am fine, Jack. It's just I feel so...so..."

"Sad. I do understand."

"No."

He blinked.

"I'm not sad, I'm..." The pressure inside her built again. "You'll think I'm terrible."

"I'm sure I won't but you don't have to—"

"Angry!" she snapped. "I feel very angry."

Jack opened his mouth, closed it, then leaned in. "I remember feeling like that too. It's a stage of grief and it's normal. I went through a patch where I was so cross at my wife for dying and leaving me alone."

She shook her head. "I'm a wicked woman but when Franklyn died I didn't feel that sad. I didn't wish him dead but when he died I felt more...relief than sorrow."

Jack's mouth formed a perfect O but he didn't speak.

"I did love Franklyn once, of course. I would never have married a man I didn't love." Even as she said it Hazel questioned that statement. Had it been love or had she confused love with security? With no parents to guide her and a sister who relied on her, the weight of responsibility had been heavy. Along had come Franklyn, dependable, strong, knowledgeable and, yes, good-looking and caring, even loving in those early days. He'd courted her diligently. They were engaged and there'd been times, when he'd held her close and kissed her, pressing himself to her, when she'd felt desire so strong she'd have let him do whatever he wanted but he'd been the strong one. Carefully easing her away, saying they must wait until their wedding night.

Their two-night honeymoon had been at a friend's beach house at Lorne. They'd only eaten when they were hungry and slept when they were tired. Inside the house they'd hardly worn clothes and they'd spent the days lazing on the beach, or in bed. The marriage had been well and truly consummated. Hazel was sure June had been conceived some time over that weekend. Her only regret had been not going to the famous Wild Colonial Club where there were great bands and dancing until late. It was the first time Franklyn had said emphatically no to her and she'd acquiesced, setting the pattern for the rest of their lives together.

Hazel looked at the glass of wine she was twisting in her fingers. It was half gone. She'd been so lost in her thoughts she didn't even remember drinking it. Jack was still sitting patiently watching her across the table as if she was something fragile that might break.

"I'm sorry, I've probably shocked you," she said. "You obviously had a very different marriage to mine."

"One thing I know is that you should never compare someone else's life to your own. We all have things we regret."

For a moment Jack's face fell as if a shadow had swept over it then just as quickly his kind smile returned. "I didn't know Franklyn that well but I thought he was perhaps a rather...austere man."

Hazel almost choked on the sip of wine she'd just taken. "That's one way of describing him. I thought when I met him he was my knight in shining armour but of course that's not a good foundation on which to build a relationship. We did have some things in common at first. He was orphaned like me but raised by an aunt, worked hard, had to be careful with money, enjoyed simple pleasures, but somehow after our first child was born he changed. I was so caught up with June – she was premature – I didn't notice it for a while and then...well, we had a second child, I was busy with them, we moved here away from friends, Franklyn worked long hours and by the time our two girls were at primary school I realised one day that I was married to a bully. There is no nice way to put it. Everything had to be done Franklyn's way or it didn't happen."

"He wasn't violent?" Jack's hand reached halfway across the table, rested there.

"Not physically, but he would make life miserable in other ways; cancelling a holiday, not attending the girls' school events or missing sports." Hazel drew a breath. "He wasn't an easy man to live with."

"I'm sorry."

"No, I am. Pouring out all my troubles and spoiling what's been a lovely day."

"You haven't spoiled anything. Sometimes we have to spit things out. I'm happy to listen."

Hazel smiled at him. Jack was a kind man and she felt lighter admitting to someone her marriage had been a difficult one. "You'll think I'm a stupid woman but Franklyn managed all our finances. The house was in his name so he's left that to our daughter June."

"You could contest."

"It's not worth it. He left the proviso that I live in it for my lifetime and I'm to receive a fortnightly allowance, just enough so that it doesn't cut back my pension."

"Not so bad then."

"Perhaps not but Franklyn made sure it would be difficult even when he was dead. He made money over the years. He bought a couple of apartments and had shares. He didn't tell me much. I assumed we'd have a modest safety net for retirement. Our only big expenses were two overseas holidays after he retired. The last few years we went out less and less. Even things like playing bowls stopped. It wasn't until he divvied out the entitlements in his will that I understood the extent of his finances.

"I thought my reward for sticking by him would at least be a comfortable life. I didn't know he was going to drop dead at eighty but I'm only seventy-six. I'd like to do some more travel, move into a smaller place...I'd thought perhaps closer to Felicity but...anyway, Franklyn's will put the kybosh on anything but a quiet future for me, living on his terms as always."

"I'm sorry, Hazel."

"I sound like an ungrateful woman."

"No you don't."

She sat back and folded the napkin that still lay across her lap. "I mustn't wallow in self-pity. I've a roof over my head and food on the table. There're plenty worse off than me."

"I'm sure there are but you're not wallowing. It's okay to feel your own disappointment. You're a smart woman, you'll find a way forward."

She placed the napkin on the table and met Jack's steady gaze. "You're a generous and wise man, Jack. Thanks for listening." She looked around the empty dining room. "I think it must be nearly time for me to catch my bus."

"We should finish our wine first." He nodded towards their glasses with a sparkle in his eyes. "They're still half full."

She picked hers up, held it towards his. "Yes, they are."

"Much better than—"

"Half empty," she finished the sentence with him. They both laughed and sipped their drinks.

"Thanks again for coming today," Jack said. "I've enjoyed it."

"So have I."

"Would you like to do it again? Movie and lunch?"

She looked at him sideways. "Do you have more fundraiser tickets?"

"No." He chuckled. "I thought we could pick our own movie and have lunch afterwards. Same time next week if it suits you."

"It would. Shall we swap phone numbers so we can keep in touch?"

"Good thinking. I realised after you left last week I had no idea how to contact you if arrangements had changed."

Hazel reached into her handbag and pulled out her phone. It vibrated in her hand. "Goodness," she said as she swiped it and several missed calls registered on her screen. "I forgot to turn my sound back on after the movie. June's tried to ring me five times." She selected her daughter's number. "Sorry, I should ring and see what's happened."

"Go ahead."

Hazel stood and took a few steps from the table. She glanced at her watch. It was nearly three o'clock.

"Mum! Where are you? I've been ringing and ringing then I went round to your place during my lunch break. Are you all right?" June's questions boomed in Hazel's ear. She glanced across at Jack who was watching her, eyebrows raised. No doubt he could hear June's voice from where he sat.

"I'm perfectly fine."

"Where are you?"

June's tone was demanding and Hazel stiffened. She turned her back on Jack and took another step away.

"Out to lunch," she said.

"At this hour?"

"I'm about to head home. What did you need me for?"

"Need you?"

"Why were you ringing?"

"To see how you were, of course. When I rang yesterday you didn't mention going out for lunch."

"I forgot."

"After your fall I was so worried."

Hazel flinched. She hadn't been able to hide her bloodied knees from June and as predicted she'd made a big fuss. "You don't usually ring till after dinner."

"We had a slow day at work and I thought I'd see if you'd like to have lunch with me."

"Oh." Hazel's shoulders slumped. "I'm sorry you were worried but I really am okay."

"You should tell me when you plan things. So I can put them on my calendar."

"I don't think we need go that far."

"I'm the only one who checks on you, Mum."

"I don't need checking on and Greta also keeps in touch, and Josh."

"But someone needs to contact you daily. What if you fell over somewhere on your own?"

"I could have a meteor drop on me too but you can't stop what will be."

"What meteor?"

Hazel swallowed her sigh. "I know you've been worried but we'll sort something out when I see you next. I'm about to catch a bus to head home."

"From where?"

"Kensington."

"Why on earth would you catch a bus all the way over there when you have a car? Are you worried to drive?"

"Of course not. June, I do have to go. I'll ring you tonight. Bye." Hazel whipped the phone away from her ear and pressed end on the sound of June's protests.

Back at the table Jack was studiously studying his own phone.

"I assume you heard all that?"

He slipped his phone back in his pocket. "It's good to have a family who cares."

"There's caring and there's smothering."

"It's a change in relationship for both of you."

Hazel felt suddenly selfish. "I think I've talked all about myself today and I don't know the first thing about you or your family, other than you're a widower, of course."

"Then we'll have something to talk about next week over lunch." He held his arm out to allow her to go first. "We're probably catching the same bus," he said as they walked out of the hotel.

Hazel was happy about that too. She didn't have to wait by herself and once on board they sat together until he got off before the city. He waved to her as the bus pulled away from his stop. She lifted a hand in response then rested back against the soft fabric of the seat. Today had been one of the best she'd had in a long time. Jack was good company, a friend of her own. One who, as Hazel conjured an image of June's shocked face, would be best to keep to herself for now.

nineteen

It was late on Thursday afternoon when Greta pulled up outside Hazel's house. She'd finished work a little earlier today and her plan had been to visit her mum on her way home but when she got there the house was all shut up. She'd used her key to open the front door, called out and got no reply. The house was uncomfortably quiet. She'd sent both her parents a text message to say she'd called in and maybe they could catch up on Sunday then she'd left and decided to surprise Hazel instead.

Greta had spoken to her nan a couple of times but she hadn't seen her since the reading of Franklyn's will. A little hope had grown inside her that Felicity's car would be there when she arrived but the drive and street in front had been empty. Greta had decided it was her duty to be the go-between for Hazel and Felicity and get them back together. Without each other to talk to, she'd become the focus of their attention. The load of that burden irritated her, if she was honest. She loved them both dearly but she didn't like being totally responsible for their wellbeing and tending to their neediness.

Her phone pinged with a message as she got out of her car. She smiled as she saw Ivan's name on the screen. He was a load control officer at her work and the life of every party.

Hey Groovy Greta, I've got a flight Saturday arvo. Want to come?

Ivan was also a pilot and while he wasn't employed as one he had to keep his flying hours up to keep his licence current. Like most amateur pilots, he would try to fill his joy flights with friends so that they would help cover the cost of fuel and he asked her to go with him from time to time. He knew how much she loved to fly and sometimes she even got to take the controls. She thought about the weekend ahead. They didn't have anything planned except housework and dinner with Joe's parents on Saturday night. Greta longed to say yes but if she went she might be back late for dinner and Joe wouldn't like that.

A few years ago Ivan had taken them both on a flight and Joe hadn't enjoyed it. Once they were firmly back on the ground he had declared he would fly in nothing smaller than a commercial jet in the future. They'd hit a bit of turbulence during the flight and Greta had to admit it had made them uncomfortable for a few minutes but she'd been kept busy focusing on what Ivan was doing at the controls. Now Joe wasn't keen on her flying either.

She typed *Can't this time but thanks for the offer* and pressed send.

A car cruised along the street and pulled into the driveway beside her. It was the distinctive yellow Audi hatchback that was June's current mode of transport. Derek's work in prestige car sales meant they both changed cars regularly.

"Hello, Greta," June said as she unfolded herself from the driver's seat. "What are you doing here?"

"Just calling in to see Nan." Greta knew her aunt didn't mean to sound brusque but her questions were often more like complaints.

"I've come to see she's made it home all right."

Greta followed June to the front door. "From where? What's happened?"

At the same time June opened the screen door the wooden door swung in and Hazel smiled from one to the other. "Hello, what a nice surprise to see you both."

"I had to check you were all right." June strode inside.

A flicker of irritation crossed Hazel's face before she leaned in to kiss Greta. "Nice to see you, dear." She shut the door and they both followed June to the kitchen.

"I've had a terrible day," June said. "I've been so worried about you, Mum. Do you have any wine?" June opened the fridge and peered in. "Good grief, your fridge is almost empty. You are eating, aren't you?"

Hazel sighed. "Of course." She tugged the door from June's grip and shut it. "And no, I don't have any wine but I can make you a cup of tea."

"That'll have to do." June sat at the table.

Hazel moved a pile of folded clothes to a chair and cleared away the scissors and pins and the pile of magazines that had been beside them. "What about you, Greta?"

"Tea would be lovely, thanks, Nan." She gave Hazel an encouraging smile. "I'll get the cups out."

"So where have you been, Mum?" June asked.

"I told you I was out for lunch."

"Via bus, all the way to Kensington?"

"It's not that far and the buses run very regularly along both routes."

"Are you having car trouble?" Greta asked.

"No." Hazel plopped tea bags into the cups perched on the matching saucers Greta had set out. "I used to catch buses a lot before your grandad retired. We never had two cars at this house." Hazel looked from Greta to June as if making an accusation. "Not useful ones anyway."

"Good grief," June said. "I'd never get to work on time if I had to catch buses."

"That's because you don't live on a direct route." Hazel poured water into the cups and Greta carried hers and June's to the table.

"Do you have any biscuits?" June said just as Hazel sat.

"In the pantry cupboard."

"I'll get them." Greta jumped up. There seemed to be an undercurrent here she wasn't clued up on. She took Hazel's battered biscuit tin from the shelf and put it on the table.

June lifted the lid. "Not homemade," she said but took one of the offending biscuits out and bit into it regardless.

"I'm not the slightest bit hungry," Hazel said.

"Did you have a big lunch?" Greta asked.

"Yes and morning tea."

"Morning tea as well." June sprayed little biscuit crumbs as she spoke. "What have you been up to?"

"I went to a movie." Hazel smoothed the edge of the tablecloth with her fingers. "It was a fundraiser for the bowling club."

"That sounds nice,' Greta said. "What did you see?"

"It was one of your old favourites. *Mulan*, except the new version."

"Oh, I'd love to see that."

"It's a kids' movie isn't it?" June said.

"I thought it had something for all ages." Hazel picked up her cup and took a sip of tea.

"And you went on for lunch by yourself?" June finished her biscuit and wasn't looking at Hazel. Only Greta noticed the flash of guilt that flitted across her nan's face before it was replaced by a smile again.

"I had a lovely meal of roast pork and veg. I'll only need a sandwich for dinner tonight."

"What are you going to make it with?" June snorted. "Perhaps I should whiz you to the shops."

"I have bread, cheese and gherkin. It's one of my favourite sandwich fillings. And there are apples and bananas. I can take myself to the shops tomorrow, which was my plan."

"If you're sure."

"Very." Hazel gave an emphatic nod of her head.

"So tomorrow you're going shopping," June said. "Do you have anything else planned I should know about?"

"June, you really are making a big fuss over nothing." Hazel set her cup back on its saucer. "You know, before your father died you never checked up on me like this."

"That's just it. You're on your own now, Mum, and you had that fall."

"What fall?" Greta asked.

"She fell in the gutter. Could have broken an arm or a leg... or both."

"I tripped. And no great harm done."

"If I don't check on you, who will?" June turned her sharp glare on Greta. "Felicity certainly hasn't bothered."

Greta sucked in a breath.

"She's upset," Hazel said. "I'm sure she'll call on me when she's ready."

"So selfish," June muttered.

"I don't think that's fair," Greta said.

"I do understand it was a shock for Felicity to find out she was adopted but she's had time to get over it," June said. "It's not as if she's had a cancer diagnosis, and Mum needs her. She's got more spare time than me."

"I don't need anyone looking after me," Hazel snapped.

"Don't get your knickers in a knot." June took another biscuit from the tin. "I must admit I can't believe you've kept such a secret from us and I don't understand why."

Greta had hoped to make a quick getaway but her nan was looking like she needed an ally. "There must have been a good reason," she said. She'd like to know all about it too but not by hounding Hazel.

Hazel's lips tightened.

June sniffed and shot to her feet. "I'd better be off then. We're having something more substantial than a cheese sandwich for dinner tonight and it won't happen unless I do it. Derek is good at many things but cooking isn't one of them."

"Good night, dear," Hazel said. "Oh, wait. I have the water rates here." Hazel took an envelope from the dresser. "They're not due for a while but I assume you will be paying anything that pertains to the house from now on."

June huffed and took the envelope then pointed to the bench. "What are you doing with the bags of mints?"

"I found then in the back of the pantry. Your dad liked them but I don't eat them."

"I love mints."

"Take them. I was only going to throw them out."

June scooped up the packets and moved towards the door. "I'll come back over the weekend and make sure you're okay."

Hazel pulled a face. "It will be lovely to see you…if I'm home."

June spun back.

"Where are you going this time?"

"I don't know yet."

Greta pressed her fingers to her lips to hide her smile.

June huffed again and strode off towards the front door. It thudded shut behind her. Just a for a moment there was silence then they both laughed. When they stopped Hazel's eyes sparkled.

"I'm glad you're feeling brighter today, Nan."

"I've had an enjoyable day out. Nothing like it to lift the spirits." She smoothed the tablecloth again. "I know you loved your grandad, but...well, he wasn't an easy man to live with and... while it's quiet being on my own..." She paused, drew a breath, blew it out again. "I am managing and I'm quite capable of looking after myself."

Greta rushed around the table and gave Hazel a hug. "Of course you are. I guess Aunty June's being protective."

Hazel gripped her hand and gave it a squeeze. "I know. I don't want to be ungrateful but I've been reporting my whereabouts to your grandad for over fifty years and since he died...well, I've quite enjoyed not having to answer to anybody."

Greta stepped back. "I see."

"I hope you do. Make sure you don't let others push you around."

"Is that how you've felt? Pushed around?"

Hazel took a moment to answer. "Sometimes."

"By Grandad?"

"I shouldn't talk ill of the dead, I know, but he could be such a charming man and then other times...well, as I said, he could be difficult to be with."

"I never realised it bothered you. I thought that was just the way you two were."

"It was exactly the way we were. I suppose I should have stood up to him more but...it wasn't the way back then. And now he's gone..." Tears brimmed in Hazel's eyes. "But I'm not truly sad."

"Oh, Nan." Greta hugged her close again, tears pooling in her own eyes.

"I shouldn't have said anything. He did love you."

"I know." Greta had loved him too. He was her grandfather after all. Their time together had often been spent on serious discussions or pursuits. He always asked her what she was doing at school or uni and then work. He listened and asked questions. He'd been the one to teach her to play chess and they'd had many games, which she'd enjoyed but now that she thought about it, being with her grandad was never what she'd call fun.

When she was a little girl her dad's dad had always bounced her on his knee and played silly games. He'd had lollies hidden in his pockets and a swing in the backyard which he'd happily push as long as she called for more. He loved telling jokes and always had a few for her when they caught up. Franklyn was the complete opposite.

Hazel sat back, took a hanky from her pocket and dabbed at her eyes. "Please don't say anything to your mother."

"I won't." Greta didn't need to. She was quite sure, from Felicity's comments the night Franklyn had died, she may well be feeling the same way. Greta was beginning to think she hadn't really known Franklyn that well at all. She got up, took a tissue from the box on the bench and wiped her eyes. "I wish she'd talk to you. I think you need each other."

"We do, but I've tried and she won't respond. It's up to her now. How is she?"

"I haven't seen her since Sunday. Dad's been away for work. She's keeping herself busy, I think."

Hazel sighed.

Greta needed to get going but she didn't like to leave her nan on a low note. "What have you been doing with your time? Besides mysterious lunches?" She wriggled her eyebrows and was relieved to see Hazel smile.

"I've decided to revamp my wardrobe. I took a good look at myself and my clothes and decided I've become quite dowdy."

"I wouldn't call you that."

Hazel cupped Greta's cheek in her hand. "You're too kind. Anyway, I started by cleaning out your grandad's wardrobe. He had suits he'd not worn for twenty years. Then I realised I've kept many things too. Dresses and skirts I'll never wear again and others that might be all right with a smarten-up."

"You were always good at sewing. I loved the outfits you made me when I was young, and you made my formal dress. I wish I'd learned to sew."

"I used to enjoy sewing. People don't seem to these days but I've decided it will be my project." Hazel gave a firm nod of her head.

"Good on you, Nan." Greta's phone pinged with a message. "I guess I'd better get going. Unlike Aunty June I'm not sure what we're going to eat tonight."

"I could have cooked you something. You're so busy and I've got lots of time on my hands."

Greta gave a brief thought to how wonderful it would be to have someone cook their meals. She hugged Hazel. "You can sew and go out for lunch, not run around after me. And I'm not that busy that I can't help you. Please call me if you ever need anything."

"I will, darling girl, thank you."

Hazel walked her to her car and waved her off. Around the corner Greta's phone pinged. She pulled over and checked the messages. There was one from Joe saying he would be late. She sighed and tried to remember if there was anything in the fridge she could turn into a meal. And there was a second message, this one from her dad. *Hi Grets. Not sure of our movements Sunday. Will get your mum to call. Love Dad.*

She tossed her phone on the seat and set off again, pondering the things Hazel had revealed about her relationship with Franklyn. Greta was surprised, yet not. Her nan had always appeared strong to her, not a pushover. Greta had assumed her subservience to her husband was out of love and the way life worked for them. To discover her nan hadn't been happy about it and yet had accepted it had been a revelation.

twenty

Felicity rolled over, taking a tangle of sheet and blanket with her to the edge of the couch. Something had woken her, a sound…

"Felicity?"

She reared back as a shape formed in the dimly lit room. Dolly jumped up from her spot at the end of the couch and disappeared under the table.

"Why are you sleeping out here? Aren't you well?" It was Ian.

"I…I was watching TV till late." She sat up and pulled the sheet over her lightly clad body as if it was a stranger standing in her family room instead of her husband of nearly thirty years. "What are you doing here?"

"You're not answering my calls or texts so I thought I'd come over."

Felicity reached for her glasses and pushed them onto her face. "What's the time?" She'd drunk a lot of wine last night and slept heavily. She couldn't even think what day it was.

"Nine o'clock."

"Why aren't you at work?"

"It's Saturday."

Ian opened the curtains and one of the glass doors. "It's warm in here."

Felicity slid her hands up her face and rubbed at her eyes beneath her glasses, blinking at the brightness.

"What's going on?" Ian came back to stand in front of her. "And what's happened to your glasses?"

"I sat on them." She pushed them firmly against the bridge of her nose. The wad of tape she'd wound around to hold them together tugged against some strands of hair.

"You usually have several pairs."

He was right and she had searched but she knew it was futile. "My prescription changed last time and I only bought one pair and sunglasses. I got rid of all the old ones."

"Surely they'd fix them for you."

"Of course. It only happened yesterday," she lied. "I haven't had a chance to go to the optometrist yet." She sat forward and grabbed the loose long-sleeved t-shirt she'd discarded last night. She pulled it on over her nightie and dropped the sheet over the pile of clothes beside the couch. Like she'd done on previous nights, she'd stripped off here before sliding into her couch bed.

She stood up and crossed to the kitchen, flicked on the kettle, then leaned back on the bench and studied her husband. The pain built again, as if there were horses trotting in her chest.

"What are you doing here, Ian?"

"We need to talk." He bent down and picked up Dolly, who'd recovered from her fright. She snuggled into him.

Traitor. Felicity folded her arms. "Now you want to talk."

"It was best to give each other space...to have time to adjust... but we have to make some decisions."

She glared at this man who she'd loved all these years and had thought had loved her. He already looked different. "You've had your hair cut." He was also growing a beard.

He ran his hand over his closely cropped scalp. "I like it short."

Ian had luxuriously thick hair with soft waves that Felicity loved and many men his age envied. Back around his fiftieth birthday he'd had it cut short and started growing a beard. It had turned him into a different man, and she'd begged him not to do it again and he'd complied. The kettle flicked off and she turned to make a coffee. "Do you want one?" she asked over her shoulder as she made her own. "I only have instant." She turned back to look at him. "I can't afford beans."

He put Dolly back on the floor. "Black tea's fine."

She tossed a tea bag into a mug and poured water on it. She'd always been happy with pod coffee. Ian was the coffee snob. He'd wanted them to buy the fancy machine that now sat idle in their kitchen. She set his mug on the island bench, took her cup to the table and sat.

He picked his up and put the teabag in the bin. At the table he hesitated then took a seat opposite.

Felicity took a sip of her coffee, tried not to gasp at the heat of it and set her cup down. She drew in a casual cooling breath and rubbed her tongue around her lips. "Why have you come, Ian?"

"I've been avoiding Greta but...I want to see her."

"She's an adult. Surely you're not asking for custody rights."

"Don't muck me about, Felicity. You asked me to keep our separation quiet."

"No, Ian. I asked you not to tell anyone you'd left me until I could come to terms with it."

"It's been nearly two weeks. I can't keep putting her off, she'll wonder what's up. And Mum called. She and Dad were planning to visit us in April."

The horses picked up speed and she pressed a hand to her chest. She hadn't even thought about Ian's parents. They lived on the New South Wales coast so they didn't see them often but Felicity was fond of them. They were always bright and fun. The polar opposite to her...to Hazel and Franklyn. They'd rung her for her birthday and sent a lovely flower arrangement when Franklyn died.

"You haven't told them."

Ian sighed. "I haven't told anyone. The bloke I'm staying with thinks you're away and we're still renovating."

"I'm not ready."

"The sooner we tell people the sooner life can move on."

Felicity's brain was a mush of scrambling thoughts. What would everyone think? How could she face people? The neighbours, her tennis friends, Greta? "Please, Ian," she begged. "You've got to give me one more week."

"We could just start with Greta."

Felicity shook her head so hard her wonky glasses slipped down her face. She pushed them back. "No."

"I want to see her, to explain."

"What are you going to say? Hi darling, sorry about this but I woke up the other week and decided I no longer love you and your mother."

Pain etched his face. "That's not what happened, Felicity. And I'll never stop loving our daughter."

"Phfft!" Felicity pressed her back against the chair, pushing against the thudding pain gripping her chest. "It's just me you don't love."

"I don't want to fight with you. I simply want us to work this out so we can both move on."

"Well, I'm sorry, Ian, but I'm having trouble with that. You might have been planning this for a while but it's all new to me." Heat rose inside her, molten anger. "One day I'm turning fifty and the next my husband leaves me, my father dies and I'm an orphan."

"That's being a little melodramatic. You're not an orphan. Hazel's still alive and well."

Felicity chewed her lip. She hadn't meant to say the orphan bit. She changed the subject. "And what about the house?"

"We have to split what it's worth."

"What?" She jumped up, pressed her hands to the table, glared at him. "You are not selling this house, Ian Lewis. Not after all my work. You might not like it but I love it."

"Where am I going to live?"

"Wherever you like but I'm not leaving here."

"Calm down." Ian waved his hands in a placating gesture. "Please, Felicity. I didn't mean you had to leave. We can work this out but we both need somewhere to live and all our money is tied up in this house."

She glared at him a moment then, as if someone had pricked her with a pin, the fight left her and she slumped back onto her chair. She put her head in her hands. "You really are leaving me," she groaned.

"Yes, Felicity."

She curled forward, holding her elbows against her sides, trying to stop the pain. How had it all gone so wrong?

"Yoo-hoo!" There was a rattle of a key in the lock at the front door.

Felicity looked up. "Greta," she hissed.

"Hello?" Greta's cheery call came closer.

Ian stood.

"Oh good, you're home." Greta went straight to him and they hugged. "I didn't see your car."

"Hello, Grets," he said. "I parked further down the street."

She moved on to Felicity. "Did you sleep in?" Greta leaned forward to kiss her then stopped. "What's wrong with your glasses?"

"I sat on them."

"Bad luck." Greta glanced at the cups on the table. "I've been at the sportsgrounds down the road with Joe and I decided to call in. Catching you both has been hard lately so I thought I'd surprise you." She went round the bench into the kitchen while Ian and Felicity remained where they were, rigid, staring at each other across the table. "I'd kill for a good coffee. They only had instant at the carnival. Joe's helping with a football clinic his nephews are in. It's all a bit boring, to be honest. Oh, there aren't any beans. Are there more in the pantry?"

"No," Felicity's voice was barely more than a whisper. She cleared her throat. "I've run out."

"Oh...oh well, another cup of instant it is then." Greta set the kettle going and made herself a coffee, all the while chatting, her voice the only bright sparkle in the room. "It was quite nippy first thing at the footy but it's a beautiful day now. We should be out on the deck."

As she walked back towards the table she stopped. "Who's been on the couch? Is someone not well?" She looked from Ian to Felicity. "Mum?"

"Come and sit down, Greta." Ian moved at last. "We want to talk to you."

Felicity glowered at him. She didn't want to talk to anyone.

Greta did as he bid, sitting herself next to Felicity. "You don't look so good. Are you sick?"

"I'm well." Felicity turned her gaze back to Ian who sat opposite again, sending him one last pleading look not to do this.

"You see, Grets," he said. "Your mum and I…"

"No, Ian," Felicity snapped. "Just you." There was no way she was involved in this.

"Your mum and I have separated," he said.

The air left Felicity's lungs in a gasp. This really was how it was going to be. He wasn't joking, he wasn't having a short-term brain fade, he truly was leaving her.

"What?"

"I moved out over a week ago."

"But…you're joking." Greta looked from one to the other of them and then her surprised look turned into a frown. "Are one of you having an affair?"

"Of course not." Ian's voice was sharp

"No!" Felicity was appalled at the idea of intimacy with another man.

"I don't understand." Greta shook her head.

"There's no-one else," Ian said. "Your mum and I have drifted apart. We still love you, of course, just not each other."

"That's not true," Felicity snapped, the anger building inside her again, and with it the pain intensified and heat surged up her neck. Double whammy! Felicity fanned her face with her hand. Greta peered at her with eyes round as saucers.

"At least the loving you is, of course," Felicity said quickly. "But I had no idea your dad…I thought we were happy."

Greta swung back to Ian. "How can you suddenly not love Mum any more?"

He sighed. "It hasn't been a sudden thing. We've been drifting apart for years."

"Apparently," Felicity muttered.

Greta shook her head. "I don't understand. How can you stop loving Mum?"

"I'm sorry but I've been feeling this way for a long time now."

"How, without us knowing? You're always happy, doing things together…" Tears brimmed in Greta's eyes. "I don't believe it."

"We haven't done much together except share a house for more than a year."

Felicity's mouth fell open. "That's not true."

"You have dinners," Greta said. "Parties and theatre tickets."

"There's more to life." Ian looked fixedly at Felicity.

Heat rose up her neck again. Was he referring to their love life? She had to admit it had waned with the onset of menopause but it was a two-way street. She'd taken the bloody HRT for him. When was the last time he'd initiated intimacy? She held her breath trying to recall when they'd last made love and was appalled that she couldn't remember. Was that it? Was that why he left? No sex. She stared at Ian. Had he found someone else to warm his bed?

"Have you tried counselling?" Greta asked.

"No."

"I'm not doing that."

Ian and Felicity both spoke at once.

"We could try it, I suppose," Ian said.

"Not with that attitude," Felicity snapped. "I'm not airing our private lives to a stranger if your heart's not in it and I know mine wouldn't be."

"There you have it," Ian said sadly.

"When you first told me I would have been willing to do anything," Felicity said. "But not now."

Ian stood up. "I think I should go."

"Have you already moved out?" Greta asked.

"Yes."

"How long—"

"Your father was all packed up and ready to go the afternoon of the will reading."

"But that was—"

"Yes." Felicity cut her off.

Ian picked up his mug and walked to the kitchen. The dishwasher swished open and cups chinked.

"That's been...nearly two weeks." Greta gaped at her. "So you've been on your own since then?"

Felicity nodded.

"Did you tell Dad about—"

"No." Felicity had felt enough humiliation without telling Ian she was adopted.

He came back to stand opposite her. "What?"

"Franklyn didn't leave me anything, that's all," Felicity said with a sharp look at Greta.

"Damn!" Ian sat on the chair again.

"He didn't even leave Nan the house," Greta said. "It was in his name and Nan can live in it but it belongs to Aunty June now."

"The old bugger."

"We can agree on that at least."

"He's leaving everything else split between Josh, Lachie and me," Greta said.

"So he redeemed himself a little," Ian said. "I thought you were going to say he'd donated it all to some obscure charity."

"I don't suppose it will be much," Greta said.

"Your grandad was worth a bit."

"Was he?" Felicity frowned. Her parents had lived a simple existence, they'd had a couple of holidays overseas and Franklyn bought a new car regularly but otherwise she would have said they were almost frugal.

"Franklyn invested money in property and shares all his life," Ian said.

"I know but I thought that was just a small nest egg."

"A nest egg all right but not small. He talked to Derek about it more than me. I never showed enough interest, I suppose, but I did see a list of his shares a while back. I can tell you he wouldn't have been getting a pension in his retirement." Ian rubbed at his forehead. "It's a shame he didn't leave you something, Felicity. I'd hoped you could buy me out of the house and then you could stay here."

"I am staying here." She pushed back in her chair and folded her arms across her chest.

"Not unless you've got at least half a million dollars."

"What?"

"You're the real estate expert. You can surely estimate the value of this house and I'll need half of it."

"Over my dead body," Felicity shrieked.

"Stop, please." Greta reached out and put a steadying hand on her arm. "I can't believe this. It happens to other people. Not my parents."

"I know it's not easy, Grets, but it doesn't change my feelings for you," Ian said. "And I'd hoped we could remain friends, Lissie—"

"Get out." Felicity flung off Greta's hand and thumped the table. "Get out, Ian. Go off and find yourself but it won't be with money from this house."

Ian looked imploringly at Greta. "I really am sorry, Grets."

"Mum's right, you should go."

Felicity stared through the open door at the bright day outside. She sensed Ian moving away. As soon as she heard the front door close, she turned. "Thank you."

"For what, Mum? How could you let this happen?"

Felicity's cheeks prickled with heat. "I didn't let anything happen. This was your dad's idea."

"A relationship takes two. I can't believe my parents are getting divorced." Greta paced the floor. "What will I tell Joe's family?" She gasped and stopped in front of Felicity. "And how can we have a wedding?"

Greta's words fuelled the terrified horses inside Felicity. They were at full gallop again now. Her head pounded too. How could she face people? Tell them her marriage had been a sham. "I don't know," she whispered.

Greta snatched up her bag and thrust it over her shoulder. "I have to go."

"Greta?"

"I'll call you later. When I've thought this through."

Felicity remained still until the house settled to silence around her again then she sagged to the couch and curled into a ball, rocking herself against the pain.

twenty-one

Hazel jumped at the sound of tapping on the window. June waved through the glass and moved towards the sliding doors. Hazel sighed and scooped up the papers she'd been poring over, stacking them beside the clothes pile on the table. Another thing about living on her own was she could leave whatever she liked wherever she liked. She kept her front living room tidy in case of visitors but this room at the back of the house was slowly turning into her workspace and comfort zone. She left her knee rug over the back of the couch, her supper tray beside her chair, her books on the coffee table and her library DVDs next to the player. The room felt more like hers. It never had before.

The security screen rattled. "Why have you got all the screens locked?" June called from outside. "I would have come in the front door but I don't have keys for the screen."

"I didn't hear you knock," Hazel said as she unlatched the screen.

"I didn't knock. I just thought you must be out the back so I came round the side." June pecked her on the cheek. "How are you today?"

"I'm fine, thanks."

June glanced around. "I can't stay. I'm on my way to get my hair cut, just thought I'd call in as I was going past."

Hazel inspected June's hair. She kept it short and spiky and Hazel couldn't imagine where there was enough length that required cutting. "Oh, well, it's nice to see you."

"I won't ring tonight now. Derek and I are going to a play. I would have asked you to go with us but it's amateur theatre. Someone from his work's in it and I don't imagine it'll be very good."

"That's all right. I'm going out myself."

June's sharp gaze snapped back to Hazel.

"And before you say I hadn't told you about it." Hazel held up a hand. "I only had the invite about an hour ago. The women I used to play cards with have asked me to join them for a meal tonight. It's Min's birthday."

"Oh...that'll be nice for you. It's ages since you played cards."

"I'm hoping I can take it up again if they'll have me back. I used to enjoy our card afternoons."

"Is it far?"

"A suburb away."

"You're not planning to catch a bus?"

"No, June. I'm driving."

"Good. I don't like the idea of you walking the streets at night on your own."

Hazel opened her mouth to say she could do what she wanted then thought better of it. June wouldn't listen anyway.

"Oh, I almost forgot." June plonked her large handbag on the table and rummaged through it. She pulled out an envelope and a pamphlet. "These are for you."

"What's this?" The envelope was addressed to Hazel and the pamphlet was labelled 'Activities for Seniors'.

"I picked up that pamphlet at the shopping centre and the other is a summary from Derek and I. We've been discussing the house, this house. It's a bit of an unusual situation you living in a house that will belong to us. You won't be paying rent but we will assume responsibility for its upkeep. We thought you could pay the various rates and a little extra for any wear and tear. We'll need to do a proper inspection, of course. This is just an interim until probate is finalised and the house is officially ours."

Hazel lifted her gaze from the envelope and stared blankly at June.

"That's an itemised list of what we thought was fair for you to pay. Now I really have to dash or I'll be late for my appointment." On the other side of the screen door June paused. "I think it's very sensible to keep the front screen locked but you'd better find me a key." And with a wave she was gone.

Hazel wandered back to her chair and sat. When had she gone from being parent to child? Was it when Franklyn died or had it been a gradual process Hazel hadn't noticed until now? She tossed the pamphlet aside, opened the envelope and withdrew the sheets of paper. One was the water rates she'd given June and the other a brief note typed and signed by both June and Derek. Hazel began to read it, murmuring the words as she went.

"We believe the best way to approach the situation of you living in a house that will soon become ours is to clearly outline who's responsible for what so that there's no confusion. We do not expect you to pay rent and in return we ask that you pay all regular costs associated with the house – council rates, water rates, electricity, insurance – and keep the gardens maintained.

"We will of course take responsibility for general upkeep of the house, repairs if needed, and to that end would ask you to pay us a hundred dollars a fortnight—" Hazel gasped, put a hand to her throat and read on. "As we're not asking rent we think this a fair amount. We can of course review each year."

Beneath the words their names had been printed and beneath that they'd both signed and dated. Then there was her name and a place for her to sign.

Hazel dropped the paper to the table and stared across the room to the sunny day outside. She wasn't sure which of the emotions surging inside her was the strongest, anger at their audacity or fear at how she would manage to pay everything. Was this what she got for being relieved that her husband was dead; some kind of payback that had turned one of her daughters into an authoritarian money-grabbing monster and the other into a stranger?

She looked at the pile of papers she'd been working on when June had arrived, picked up the pages June had brought, added them to it then put the newspaper on top so she couldn't see them. She'd planned to ask June to help her map out a budget but now, well, there was no way she was going to allow June to stick her nose in her financial details. Hazel would have asked Felicity, of course, but she was still not answering her calls. The two people she'd always felt she could turn to for help were not an option. What was she to do?

She glanced at the activities pamphlet. At the top of the list was 'Meals for One' and she was welcome to join chef Mason Jones, demonstrating how to prepare and cook delicious, interesting meals on a budget.

"Humph!" As if she couldn't manage that for herself.

She moved on to the next. It was titled 'Scones and Songs' and said she'd enjoy a wonderfully entertaining afternoon with a talented local who would be singing operatic classics followed by a delicious Devonshire tea. She shuddered. Franklyn had played opera music when he worked in his office. Those CDs were among the first things she'd thrown out.

At the bottom of the list was a 'Beyond 60s Dance Class' which urged her to dance to her favourite tunes of yesteryear. She'd learn dance steps, stretch her body and enjoy the mental, physical and social benefits of dancing.

She sighed. She enjoyed watching dance programs but she'd rarely danced herself. Franklyn had never wanted to, so anywhere there'd been dancing they either sat it out or she had the occasional dance with someone else. Dancing was another thing Franklyn had frowned on.

She tossed the pamphlet aside. After the financial paperwork she'd planned to tackle the first of her sewing projects but revamping a skirt held no appeal now. She thought of dinner with the cards girls and even that no longer excited her like it had when Mary had rung to invite her. She wandered the room, stopping to straighten a stack of magazines, adjust a cushion. The anticipation she'd felt for the day ahead leached away and was replaced by a terrible ache. She felt sad, anxious, lonely – the full gamut of emotion that had only briefly touched her after Franklyn had died now settled on her like a grey cloak she couldn't shake.

Her roaming feet took her to the bedroom. She cast her gaze around the neatly organised space – bed made, not a thing out of place. It was easy to keep it that way living alone. Not that Franklyn had been messy, far from it, but this room was especially tidy now as she'd emptied the wardrobes and drawers of his clothes and sorted through her own.

She'd discovered items she'd forgotten she still had, among them some lovely tartan skirts. They're what had inspired her to look at current fashion. She'd borrowed magazines from the library but they were full of styles for younger women. Then she'd got out the tablet the family had given them a couple of Christmases ago. Franklyn hadn't been interested in it but she'd used it to send and receive emails and play a few word games. She'd started searching for fashion ideas for women in their seventies but there hadn't been a lot to inspire her.

Hazel wandered out again and past the second bedroom, which she'd also tidied. The wardrobe in there contained all the items she no longer wore but wasn't sure what to do with; a dress she'd worn on special occasions before her marriage to Franklyn, her modest wedding dress, the outfit she'd worn for Felicity's wedding and another for June's. She was being sentimental keeping them but they'd all been worn at happy times and she'd sewn the wedding dress herself.

She found herself hesitating outside the door of the third bedroom. Franklyn had used it as his study. She pushed the door open. The blind was down, giving the room a gloomy feel. She didn't switch on the light or step further into the room. She'd cleaned in here too, got rid of general rubbish, which had included his CD collection, and cleared the desk of everything except the computer. She had imagined it as a good space for her sewing but Franklyn's presence was strong here and she hadn't had the strength to tackle it properly yet. He had shelves of books, folders of papers, a filing cabinet full of stuff, and it was all too daunting for now. She pulled the door shut and went back to the family room.

Her mobile rang and it took her a moment to find it stuck between the pile of papers and the stack of clothes.

"Hello, Hazel, it's Mary again."

"Hello, Mary." Maybe the dinner was off. Hazel would be relieved. She didn't feel the least bit like going now.

"I didn't offer to pick you up when I rang."

"You didn't have—"

"I was just so delighted you'd agreed to come I didn't think." Mary took only a brief breath. "I remember what it was like when I was widowed. It's not easy to start going out on your own."

"Oh, yes…" It didn't bother Hazel in the least to drive but now that Mary mentioned it, meeting the six or so other women in the card group was adding to her worry. She'd been delighted when Mary had first asked her but she hadn't played cards for over a year and had only run into people like Mary on the odd occasion and when she'd come to Franklyn's funeral. They had nothing else in common but the regular card games.

"I go almost past your door," Mary said. "It's no trouble and we can arrive together."

"Are you sure?" Perhaps it would be easier the first time if she went with someone.

"Of course. When I let Min know you were coming she was thrilled and we both said we hoped you might play cards again now…now that you're no longer a full-time carer."

That's how Hazel had begged off the cards, by telling them Franklyn needed full-time care. He didn't, of course, he simply wanted her at his beck and call. And the last time she'd had the card game at her house he'd made such a fuss afterwards about giggling women and noise and, as she so often had, she'd simply given in and stopped going to cards just to keep the peace.

"Anyway, we can talk about it tonight," Mary said. "I'll pick you up at five-thirty. And you don't have to bring anything. Min's got it all under control. We're both so pleased you're coming and the others will be too when they see you."

"Thank you, Mary."

Hazel had to sink to a chair after she'd ended the call. It had left her feeling breathless. A couple of the women, Mary especially, had tried to keep in contact once she stopped cards but she'd been evasive and gradually they'd lost touch. What would the others think of her now? She swallowed the anxiety that threatened to consume her and stood up.

"Enough." Her voice sounded so loud she decided to put the radio on for background noise then went to the pantry. She'd go to dinner at Min's but she couldn't go empty handed. Franklyn had been a sweet tooth and she still had a stash of chocolates and lollies in the back of the pantry. There was bound to be something she could wrap and take as a happy birthday and thank you for Min.

Several hours later she was relaxing in one of Min's lounge chairs, replete from the delicious dinner, chatting happily over a cup of tea with the five other women present and so glad she'd come. They'd all welcomed her warmly, brought her up to date with their comings and goings: Min and her husband's latest overseas adventure; Mary with photos of a brand-new grandson, her fifteenth grandchild; and each of the others with whatever was happening in their lives.

No-one had pressed Hazel. Given she was recently widowed, no doubt asking her what was new in her life wasn't socially correct. As they'd talked she'd gradually slipped back in with their conversation and now, sitting over a late cuppa, it was as if she'd not been apart from them for more than a week. They were talking about clean-outs. Peg was holding a garage sale, which had prompted Mary to tell them all about cleaning out her sewing cupboard and the fabric she'd found that she'd had since her children were still at home.

"I don't sew any more," Mary said. "One of my grand-daughters wants to learn to sew so I've given her the sewing machine and a few pieces of fabric and I bundled the rest of the material up for the local op shop."

"Do they take that kind of thing?" Hazel asked.

"My local takes anything clean and useful."

"I did donate most of Franklyn's clothing to St Vinnies," Hazel said. "I hadn't thought of other things though. Do they take books and CDs?"

"Mine does," Mary said.

"And mine," Min agreed.

"I haven't tackled Franklyn's office yet."

"There's no rush." Peg, who'd been sitting next to her, patted her leg.

"I know." Once again Hazel felt guilty that the others were being so kind, thinking she was grieving for her husband when really she was grieving for the daughter she'd lost and the future she thought she might have had.

"Don't be in a rush to toss things out either until you know their value," Min said. "My neighbour had a clear-out after his wife died. He'd always hated the glassware she'd collected over the years and donated it all to charity. It wasn't until his daughter came to visit from interstate and wanted to know where it all was that he discovered it was worth a lot of money."

"I can relate to that," Hazel said. "Franklyn still had his first two cars in our backyard shed. He loved to tinker with them and take them for a drive every so often but with his declining health, I'd almost forgotten he had them. His lawyer knew about them, thank goodness, and expects them to fetch quite a lot of money. If I'd had to get rid of them I probably would have called a scrap dealer to tow them away."

"There's nothing that valuable at my house," Peg said.

"People are more important than things," Min said. "And I'm so glad you could all come tonight."

"Happy eighty-first," Mary said and raised her teacup in the air. Everyone joined in.

"I didn't know you were in your eighties, Min," Hazel said. "I always thought you were younger than me and I'm seventy-six."

"That's very flattering, Hazel dear, thank you. Don't you remember the big do for my eightieth last year? The party at the sailing club?"

Hazel's cup rattled on its saucer as she set it on the delicate occasional table beside her. "I missed that one, I'm sorry. It must have been very special."

"Oh dear," Min said. "I'm sure I sent you an invitation but I forgot you've hardly been out much this last year." Her cheeks coloured pink. "Being full-time carer…it must have been…"

"Difficult," Hazel said and four faces looked back at her in surprise. The fifth face belonged to Mary and she simply nodded sagely. Of all the women present she was the one who'd tried hardest to keep in touch.

Hazel sat forward and pulled at the hem of her dress, which had scrunched under her. These women were the closest friends she'd had, and like anyone she'd got close to over the years, Franklyn in his insidious way had separated her from them. And now in death he'd smashed the closeness she'd had with her daughters.

Tonight she'd been reminded how good it was to relax with people she knew, forget about her cares, chat and share stories, laugh – some of Min's travel stories had been especially hilarious – and even shed a tear together. That had been on Peg's part when Hazel had first arrived and they'd all offered condolences. Hazel needed friends. She took a deep breath and looked up.

"My husband was not an easy man to live with," she said. "He made it difficult for me to keep in touch."

The other women remained silent, except for Peg, who said "Oh," and patted her leg again. Hazel saw Mary and Min exchange glances.

"We did wonder," Mary said.

Hazel nodded. "Now that he's gone I'd like to get on with my life and do some things for me for a change."

Peg cleared her throat, a teacup clinked against a saucer and a foot shuffled.

Min was the one to break the silence. "Starting with cards next Wednesday afternoon at Mary's. We've had the devil of a job finding someone to fill your card-sharp shoes."

A huge weight shifted from Hazel's shoulders. She had friends back in her life, and another thought had come to her over dinner. There was someone else she could ask for help with sorting out her budget.

She smiled at Min. "I'm looking forward to coming back."

twenty-two

Alice closed her eyes and imagined the arms that guided her around the floor were Roy's. Engelbert Humperdinck's crooning rendition of 'The Last Waltz' had made her think of her husband and the evenings when they'd pushed aside the table and chairs and danced around the dining room. She hadn't realised including the old song on the playlist would stir up such strong memories.

She opened her eyes as she twirled beneath Errol's outstretched hand. Elaine and Mac were slightly out of step in front of them but Phil and Gwen, in their eighties, were giving a flawless demonstration of a modern waltz. It had been just the six of them and they'd mixed up the partners all evening. Alice preferred dancing with Errol or Phil, who were both fabulous dancers. Mac was a little erratic and too chatty for her liking but they'd made a good job of the Military Two Step earlier.

Alice's full skirt rippled out as she and Errol fell easily into step for the final part of the waltz. Mac had commented on her outfit, winked and called her a dark horse. Alice had averted her gaze, knowing her warm cheeks glowed with embarrassment. The other two women had worn pants and flat shoes but Alice liked to dance in heels, even if her legs were complaining now.

The last notes of the music faded. Errol and Phil bowed but Mac dipped Elaine backwards and pretended to kiss her. Alice was relieved she hadn't been his partner for the last dance of the night but Elaine just laughed and gave Mac a telling off for nearly breaking her back. Then they all clapped hands and immediately made a date for their next get-together.

Elaine and Alice were in charge of returning the key so were the last to leave.

"What a great night," Elaine said as they carried their supper containers out to the car.

"Most enjoyable," Alice said and she meant it.

Elaine opened the car door to the sound of her phone ringing. She snatched it up. "It's Hugh and he's tried before. Sorry, Alice, I should answer."

"Go ahead. I'll go back and lock up the hall."

By the time Alice returned Elaine was finishing her call.

"Is everything all right?"

"Hugh's not coming for Easter."

"That's your son?"

"Yes. A school friend made him a better offer. Skiing up the river somewhere."

"Oh, I'm sorry."

"Don't be. He's fifteen. I didn't know what I was going to do to keep him occupied for four days anyway. And his father reneged on driving him part of the way so I would've had to make two round trips to Adelaide." Elaine dropped her phone back into her bag. "Is everything done?"

"Yes. All tidy and locked up. I'll return the key to the service station in the morning."

"Sorry to leave the last to you but Hugh usually leaves messages when he can't get me. I thought something must have happened when I saw all the missed calls. Kids, they're always a worry. I'm glad he's with his father most of the time and we'll all be happier if Hugh goes with his friend for the Easter break."

"Mmm."

"You think I'm the world's worst mother."

"No, I don't."

Elaine gave a soft snort. "I can see it written all over your face."

Alice closed her car door and the light was extinguished. Roy used to say he could tell what she was thinking by the look on her face.

Elaine started the car. "I could have made a fuss and insisted Hugh come to me and then what? I would have had one grumpy teenager for four days who would have shut himself in his room with his phone and I'd hardly have seen him anyway. This way he has fun, he'll send me lots of photos, so I'll see what he's up to, and I can enjoy the holiday weekend without having to be in the traffic up and back from Adelaide. I'm still his mum, he knows I love him and I'll catch up with him again soon."

"Of course." Alice found her friend's indifference to motherhood difficult to understand.

Elaine turned the car in the empty carpark. "You don't have children, do you?"

"No."

"It's just that Gwen mentioned you'd had two little boys but... they'd died."

"That's right." Alice kept her gaze forward as the headlights illuminated the road. It was such a long time ago but her life would always be defined by it. And, it seemed, it would always be a source of gossip for others.

"That must have been terrible."

"It was."

"You can tell me to back off for being nosey but...what happened to them?"

"They had cystic fibrosis." Alice could say it now with as little emotion as if she were talking of strangers but it had taken many years to get over the loss.

"Oh. I've heard of that but I didn't realise it could kill."

"These days babies can be diagnosed at birth and there's treatment, not a cure, but a much longer life expectancy."

"So that's why you sell those pens and mints and things. I thought you were just doing good deeds."

"It's not much but my small contribution to fundraising might help someone else have a better future. People in this community have been very generous over the years." Alice had collected a new merchandise kit while she was in Adelaide and had taken it to cards. She also continued to make regular donations to the CF organisation.

"I'll buy the mints. They're always handy for my purse."

They pulled into Alice's driveway and Elaine switched off her car. "I can see why you must think I'm a bad mother."

"I don't think that." Alice really would prefer they didn't discuss motherhood at all. Except for the occasional mention of Hugh, up until now they'd never discussed children, grandchildren or family in general. It was one of the reasons she'd made friends so easily with Elaine.

"I might do things differently but I do love my son."

"I'm sure you do."

"I was forty-five and in a demanding job when I had Hugh. He was my change-of-life baby in more ways than one. He was a wonderful surprise, then menopause kicked in and my husband took up with another woman just before Hugh started kindy."

"Oh."

"Yes, oh. Bloody fickle man. I was so busy adjusting to our new life I didn't see it coming." She shrugged. "But I've ended up here and I'm very content. Hugh lived week-on, week-off between us until his teens when I was forced to make some healthy life decisions. My job was becoming increasingly stressful and I opted for a sea change. Hugh stayed in Adelaide with his dad. It made perfect sense but I only see him if I go to Adelaide or if he comes to stay in the school holidays. Other than that we speak regularly via phone or Skype."

"That's good."

"It wasn't easy to leave him in Adelaide but I was on a downhill spiral and I wouldn't have been any good to Hugh if I'd collapsed from exhaustion or even had a breakdown." The light thrown from Alice's verandah highlighted Elaine's pale face and emphasized her dark eye make-up, smudged at the edges now. "It wasn't an easy decision but my doctor told me I had to make a change. It was best for Hugh he stayed with his dad."

"I'm not judging you," Alice said quickly. She'd had no intention of upsetting Elaine. "I can imagine it was a difficult choice but better for Hugh he has a happy healthy mum he sees sometimes than a sick mother—"

"Or a dead one."

"Oh."

"That's the path I was going down. Since I left my job and the city, I'm fitter, I've lost weight and the last time I saw my doctor, my tests showed I no longer have pre-diabetes and my blood pressure is normal without medication."

"That's good news."

"Very. I was determined to make changes. It's my sixtieth birthday present to myself."

"We'll have to do something special for your birthday." Alice was glad to change the subject.

"I'm already planning it. A cruise around Hawaii in late November. My sisters are in." Elaine grabbed Alice's arm. "You could come too. We could dance together."

"Perhaps."

"You're not keen?"

"Roy and I cruised once to New Zealand. It was so rough we couldn't get off at some ports and half the ship, including us, came home with a dreadful cold. We vowed we'd never go again."

"This will be different. We'll fly to Honolulu. Have a few nights there, take the eleven-night cruise then a few more days in Honolulu before we come home. It will be fabulous."

"I'll let you know."

"Living where we do is perfect to be out of the rat race, Alice, but we need to spice it up sometimes, explore beyond the peninsula."

"I enjoy travel." It was true but she'd done none since Roy died and it wasn't as if she didn't have the means. "I prefer exploring places by land, that's all."

"Once I get the full itinerary from the travel agent I'll give you a copy."

"Thanks."

"And we'll be able to dance every night."

"I will think about it." Alice stepped out of the car and collected her things. "Thanks for the ride, Elaine."

"Good night." Elaine waved over the steering wheel. "See you at cards."

Alice let herself inside. Usually her conversations with Elaine were on what was happening in their community or politics or world events, music, movies, the arts, anything but family. Tonight they'd talked about children and sisters, both topics Alice would prefer not to think about let alone discuss. It reopened a deep ache inside her for the lost opportunity to share confidences with her sister.

Since the dreadful day of Franklyn's funeral, she'd resigned herself once more to never seeing her sister again. If Hazel was going to have a change of heart and make contact she would have done it by now. Not that she'd know how to get in touch but Alice had hoped Greta might have been some help with that. Two weeks had passed and she'd not heard from Hazel or had a response to the text she'd sent Greta. She'd told herself to forget about them but a tiny part of her still held onto a glimmer of hope.

Alice rinsed the supper container and smiled at the recollection of Errol's shy grin as she'd popped the last few jelly cakes on his plate. He was pleasant company. Her initial reluctance about their dance get-togethers was gone after tonight.

She glanced around her tidy kitchen and flicked off the light. There was no point holding her breath waiting for the family she never had to come back into her life. Dancing and even Elaine's sixtieth birthday celebrations were much better options to focus on.

twenty-three

The sound of her phone ringing pierced Greta's sleep-fuddled brain. She sat up quickly. Bright sunlight filtered around the edge of the curtains and beside her Joe was still fast asleep. She slid from the bed and her stomach roiled. She'd drunk more than she'd eaten at Joe's parents' the previous night, her mind full of her own parents' break-up, the happy chatter around the table only making her grief stronger.

She made it to the lounge before the phone stopped and was surprised to see the picture on the screen was Hazel's.

"Hi, Nan, is everything okay?"

"Perfectly, thank you. You sound sleepy, did I wake you?"

Greta sank onto the couch to give her head and stomach a moment to settle. "It was time I was up." She had no idea what the time was.

"I thought I'd be safe ringing you at ten."

Greta rubbed her eyes. They really had slept in. "What's happening?"

"I wondered if…well, you and Joe seem to manage your money efficiently."

"I think so."

"You know how much is coming in and how much is going out?"

"Yes."

"You do it together?"

"We do. What's up, Nan? This is a bit of an odd conversation for ten o'clock on a Sunday morning."

"Oh, yes, I'll just get straight to the point...I don't want you to commit if you've already made plans today."

"Nothing yet, just tell me what you want."

There was no reply.

"Nan?"

"I wondered if you might help me plan my budget."

"Oh." That was the last thing Greta had expected to hear. "I... well, you've been doing it much longer than me. I don't see—"

"Only the basics...your grandad paid all the household bills. I've mapped it all out and I'd like a second opinion to make sure I've covered everything."

"Wouldn't Aunty June be the one to ask?"

"I'd prefer it was you. Would you mind popping over?"

Joe walked into the lounge and wrapped Greta in a hug.

"Can I check with Joe?" She pressed her lips to the strong arm that enveloped her.

"Of course."

"I'll get back to you."

Joe stepped away, eyebrows raised, and ambled into the kitchen.

"It can be another time if today doesn't suit."

"It should be fine. I'll ring you back."

"Was that Felicity?" Joe asked as she ended the call. He'd been devastated to hear about her parents' split when she'd told him the previous night.

Greta shook her head. "Nan."

"Does she know about your mum and dad?"

"I don't think so."

Joe sat next to her on the couch, throwing an arm around her shoulders. She nestled into his comforting warmth and rested her head on his chest.

"I still can't believe Dad doesn't love Mum any more."

"I didn't see it coming, that's for sure."

"How does that happen?" Greta could make no sense of it. She'd thought her parents' marriage rock solid. She'd replayed every visit she could remember over the last year, every important event, and they'd seemed as happy together as always.

"I don't know." He kissed the top of her head. "It's a total shock."

"Dad seems so calm about it all."

"Perhaps it's relief."

"What?"

"I'm guessing Ian didn't suddenly wake up one day and decide this. He's probably been thinking on it for a long time. Your dad's not the kind of bloke who makes decisions lightly. It must have been very stressful."

Greta lurched up. "How do you think I'm feeling? My family's falling apart. I didn't ever think I'd come from a broken home."

"Does that term apply when you're a twenty-four-year-old who's left home?"

"I'm the daughter of an adoptee. I don't know my genetic make-up."

"Your parents both have good health. I think that's what counts most."

"What if I've come from a terrible gene pool?"

"Your dad's family are all a sturdy bunch."

"Grandad died."

Joe stared blankly at her.

"Different gene pool but you just don't know."

"Don't get in a flap about this." He drew her gently back to his chest. "Franklyn hadn't been in good health for a while and he was eighty-one."

"Perhaps you were right about my family."

"You know I'm right about most things," he teased. "But what exactly?"

"When you said there's always some drama or another."

"I didn't mean for something as serious as your parents separating though."

"I know. All we'd need now is for June and Derek to do something crazy and the picture would be complete."

"I can't imagine that."

"I couldn't imagine my dad not loving my mum but that's what's happened."

"June and Derek have their relationship worked out."

"Do you think? Uncle Derek always seems to have the final say about everything. Aunty June's bossy but he's even more so."

"That's how June's so clever. She lets him think he's in charge, puts the thought in his head and the decisions come out of his mouth just as she'd planned."

"I'd never thought about it but...you could be right."

"Like I said—"

"You're always right." Greta laughed then lifted her head to kiss him before snuggling back against him again.

"We're rock solid," Joe said.

"Yep." Greta's response was instant but how could she be truly sure? She'd believed her parents were rock solid and they were separating. And even though she hadn't thought of her grandparents' marriage as truly harmonious, she hadn't realised how difficult it had been for her nan.

"Why did Hazel ring?" Joe asked, as if he'd been following her train of thought.

"She wants my help with some paperwork but I had planned on a quiet day here."

"You go. I'll probably do some gardening."

They had cement and stones with a couple of pots in their tiny front yard and a small square of lawn, an ornamental tree and a few assorted native plants in the back. She raised her eyebrows. "That should take you five minutes."

"I'm going for a run first and there's a footy game on the TV this arvo. I've got a full day."

"Uh huh." Greta sat up and stretched. "Well, I shouldn't be gone too long. Perhaps when I get home we can go down to the lake for a walk."

"Sure. Let's just see how I'm situated when you get home."

She laughed. "Probably situated right where you are now, I'd be thinking."

He made a lunge for her but he wasn't quick enough. She strode towards the bathroom. "I'll have a shower then head off."

He waved his fingers at her but stayed where he was, grinning lazily from the couch.

An hour later Greta was sitting beside Hazel at her dining table. It had been cleared of everything except several piles of papers. Greta had been studying a summary of Hazel's bills. If she was honest she was feeling overwhelmed.

"I'm not really an expert, Nan," Greta said. "But Joe and I made a similar list of everything we could think of that came under the heading of bills, added it all up and divided it by twenty-six.

We've set that against our combined fortnightly income, savings and spending money. Once you add the incoming you'll be able to work out how much you have to divvy out between the bills, spending and saving."

"That's a problem at the moment. They've told me how much the pension will be and Kurt seems to think I'll be getting a bit extra on top of that from Franklyn's money."

Greta clicked her tongue. "It doesn't seem fair to me that you're worried about money. Grandad should have left more for you."

Hazel cupped Greta's cheek in her warm hand. "You're such a thoughtful person. It is what it is and even if he had left me more I would still have to work all this out." She waved a hand over the papers.

"I guess you're right." Greta looked back at the summary. If her inheritance was large as the others had assumed, it would have made a difference to Hazel's future, but that was out of her hands. "Have you still got your computer?"

"Yes, in Franklyn's office. Why?"

"I could make you a spreadsheet and enter all your finances. It would help you see the bigger picture."

"Franklyn was the only one to use the computer after we got the tablet. I was going to get rid of it."

"The computer has a big screen and a keyboard. It makes a spreadsheet layout very simple. I'm sure you'd soon get the hang of it."

"It hasn't been switched on since…."

Greta stood up. "Shall I give it a go?"

"If you like."

Hazel followed her into the office and rolled up the blind. "It's always dull in here."

Greta glanced around. This room had been her grandad's domain most of the time. It was dominated by a large colonial desk with a leather computer chair. There was a filing cabinet in one corner that matched the dark cherry desk and had two sets of two drawers side by side. On top of that sat a compact printer and a wireless modem. On one long wall were bookshelves in matching wood, from floor to ceiling. Some of the higher shelves were behind glass and the bottom bays had wooden doors but every visible shelf was crammed with books.

The desk was inlaid with leatherette and usually there were books and papers stacked up all over it but now it was clear of everything except the computer. Greta switched it on and it whirred to life. Hazel stood in front of the bookshelves looking them up and down. "I started clearing out in here. I thought it would make a good sewing room." She straightened some books that were tilted to one side. "It seems rather daunting though."

"You've got time to make changes, even if it's only one shelf at a time. Perhaps I could come and help you."

"I'd like that."

Greta looked away from the hopeful spark in Hazel's eyes. Since the funeral she'd hardly called in and she was sure her mum hadn't been in touch since the will had been read.

The screen flashed.

"Shall I bring you a coffee?"

"Yes, thanks." Greta sat in the comfortable chair and opened a new spreadsheet. "And I'll need your accounts pile as well."

By the time Hazel returned with the papers and a coffee Greta had already started on the spreadsheet. "This won't take long."

"I've got some mending to do. I'll let you get on."

"Once I finish I'll give you a lesson."

Hazel grimaced and left her to it.

It was only half an hour later when Greta went to find Hazel. She was seated in a chair by the window in the sunshine, her head bent over her sewing.

"Ready to take a look?"

"Ready as I'll ever be."

Greta took one of the dining chairs with her and once Hazel was settled beside her at the computer she stepped through the process, making notes as she went so that Hazel could follow them when Greta wasn't there.

"It's not so difficult," Hazel said with a hint of surprise, once they'd worked their way through it. She'd added a couple of notes to Greta's instructions. "It reminds me of the ledgers I used to keep at work."

"I guess that's what it is, but computerised. I've put in all the amounts you gave me but if they ever change or you want to add or delete one, it's quite simple."

"Yes, I see that. Thank you, dear."

Greta glanced back at the screen and located the one figure she'd entered that had puzzled her. "Nan, I hope you don't think I'm being too nosey but…I wondered why you're making fortnightly payments to Aunty June."

Hazel looked down at her lap, her hands twisting together. "I haven't yet. It's something she and Derek suggested."

"Why?"

Hazel continued to wring her hands. "Upkeep of the house."

"Your house?"

"Soon to be theirs, I'm afraid."

"I don't understand why Grandad wouldn't at least leave you the house."

"I did see Kurt about it. There doesn't seem much I can do. And as your neat spreadsheet sets out, there won't be much change between what I will get in from the pension plus the top-up payment and what will be paid out."

"This seems so unfair." Greta closed the spreadsheet. Perhaps her idea to set it all out so clearly hadn't been a good one. Her hand hovered over the mouse. She wasn't sure if she should mention the shortcut she'd seen on the screen.

"Don't you worry about me." Hazel stopped gripping her hands together and patted Greta's cheek. "Now, it's too nice a day to be stuck in this dull room. You should get off back to Joe, or would you like another cuppa before you go?"

Greta wanted nothing more than to be home with Joe but she couldn't forget the shortcut. "Nan, there's something else I'm curious about."

Hazel looked at her expectantly.

"There's a shortcut saved here on the computer." Greta moved the mouse to hover over the link saved as 'My Watchlist'. "I think this could be about Grandad's shares."

"Really?" Hazel sat up straighter, her gaze on the screen.

"We did a unit on shares at school. We had fake portfolios and a competition to see who could make the most profit. I'm wondering if this link might take us to a list of shares."

"Can you check?"

Greta didn't need further prompting. She clicked the link. A screen opened with the heading *My Dashboard* and *Welcome Franklyn*.

Hazel gasped. Greta clicked again and there it was, a list of Franklyn's shares and their current market value, just short of one million dollars. This time it was Greta who sucked in a sharp breath.

"Is that what they're worth?" Hazel pointed a trembling finger towards the total figure.

"It's current market value but I don't know if the list itself is up to date. He may have sold some or all of these shares and not updated his watchlist."

"Why would he keep a list of shares he'd sold?"

"I don't know." Greta was still grappling with the worth of Franklyn's shares. If it was an up-to-date list, her inheritance would be much more than she'd imagined.

"I feel so foolish not knowing anything about this but Franklyn never discussed it with me. I felt I had enough money. There was always some for little extras and I never questioned it."

Greta thought about the conversations she and Joe had about money, right from the day they planned to move in together, and their mutual understanding of their finances. "I suppose it was different when you married. Did you have to give up work?"

Hazel nodded. "I worked for a private company and my employer would have kept me on but government jobs were stricter about employing married women and Franklyn worked in local government. He felt we should set the example, so I didn't go back to work after the wedding." Hazel rubbed her hand over the polished wood edge of the desk. "I missed it terribly but then I found out I was expecting and being a mother filled my days."

"How did you manage without your own income?"

"I suppose you young ones would say I was a kept woman but it wasn't so unusual then. Men went out to work, women stayed home and managed the household. Franklyn asked me to work out how much our weekly groceries were and what other items I might need to spend money on. He gave me an allowance for my personal expenses."

"Sounds a bit controlling to me."

"It was how it was. If there were items we needed for the house we planned for them and saved or used lay-by. Not like the buy-now pay-later world of today. Franklyn only got a credit card just before he retired but I've never had one."

Greta pulled a face. "I can't imagine living without one."

"I was never extravagant but nor did I feel I was hard done by. If I had a reasonable need for extra, Franklyn usually came up with it."

"I'm glad. I'd hate to think he was using all the money for his investments while you got little."

"I've never realised until now how little I did live on."

"I still don't understand why he didn't leave the house and his money to you."

Hazel sighed. "He made it clear he wanted June and his grand-children to have it."

"Well, it doesn't seem fair to me."

Hazel rolled her chair back and stood. "I think I've had enough for one day."

"Of course." Greta closed the share screen and rolled the mouse over another icon. "I've created a shortcut for your spreadsheet so all you have to do is click here when you want to open it."

"Thank you." Hazel tucked the chair back at the computer and squeezed behind Greta. "I think I need a cup of tea."

Greta tidied up and followed Hazel out to the kitchen. "I don't suppose you've heard from Mum?"

Hazel shook her head. "How is she?"

"Not so good."

"I wish she'd talk to me."

Greta felt the weight of her mum's neediness. "So do I, especially now."

Hazel's gaze sharpened. "Why especially now?"

Greta hesitated, chewed her lip. "Dad's left Mum," she blurted.

"What?" Hazel's face crumpled. "When?"

"I think it was the day we were here for the reading of the will."

"I don't believe it." Hazel began to rock gently as if soothing a child. "Oh my poor girl. What on earth has got into Ian? I always thought him such a kind and sensible man."

Greta shrugged her shoulders. That's how she thought of her dad too, still did really. "I didn't see it coming. I don't know what to do."

"I have to go over there."

"I don't think she'll talk to you." Greta felt a swell of emotion solidify to a lump within her chest. She wished one of the other adults in her life would take charge. "Everything's a bit of a mess at the moment."

Hazel wrapped her in a hug and the lump softened. "Don't you worry. Your mum's tough. She's had a few shocks but she'll get through it."

"It's not just Mum, it's you."

"Me?"

"You're on your own and all this money stuff." Greta waved her hands towards the office.

Hazel stepped back and held her at arm's length. "You mustn't worry about me either. I'll be perfectly fine. I've got an income and a roof over my head, which is more than some have. Now you get off back to Joe."

Within minutes Greta had been bundled out the door, with a kiss on the cheek and an encouraging wave from Hazel. It was a relief to leave and she hoped Hazel would manage to get through to Felicity so that Greta didn't have that burden as well. It was bad enough feeling like she was stealing from her nan by inheriting some of her grandad's money.

twenty-four

At ten o'clock on Wednesday morning Hazel parked down the street a little way from Felicity's front door. It had taken her a day to think up a reason Felicity would have to answer the door to her and another day to find the courage. This afternoon she was going back to cards for the first time in two years. She was looking forward to it and the anticipation of that had made her brave enough to try another visit to her daughter.

Hazel hoped this time Felicity would let her in, even if it was only to hand over the sewing machine. That was Hazel's excuse to get her to open the door. On Monday morning when she'd organised herself to start sewing she'd gone to get her machine from the hall cupboard but it wasn't there. It was then that she'd remembered lending it to Felicity late the previous year. Hazel hadn't used it in ages and Felicity, who'd never been a sewer, had decided to teach herself to sew curtains for her renovated house. They'd had an enjoyable few days together while Hazel had helped her get started. Felicity was a quick learner when she had a project in mind and she'd soon got the hang of it. Hazel hadn't needed the machine and hadn't given it a thought until now.

She was worried about Felicity. She hadn't let on to Greta how much. The news that Ian had moved out was a shock and Hazel could only imagine that blow, on top of Franklyn's death and the admission that Felicity was adopted, would be crushing her sometimes fragile daughter. Felicity had suffered a few setbacks in her life. Several miscarriages one after the other until Greta came along had laid her very low in the early years of her marriage. Hazel had spent a lot of time with her during those days while Franklyn and Ian were at work. Some mornings she'd had to drag Felicity from her bed and force her to shower, encourage her to eat, coax her into the garden for some fresh air. Even when Greta was born and they had the joy of a baby, Felicity had hardly left the house for the first few months of Greta's life.

Felicity had become more resilient over the years but perhaps not enough to deal with what was happening in her life now. If only the adoption thing hadn't been mentioned, Hazel would have been Felicity's support instead of cowering in her car wondering how she'd be received.

"Wondering gets you nowhere," Hazel said to herself in the rear-view mirror. She got out of her car, tugged her blouse down to sit neatly over her skirt then took a moment to compose herself.

The door of the house she'd parked in front of opened and a woman came out, carrying a flat basket and secateurs.

"Hello, Hazel."

Hazel lowered the foot she'd lifted to stride forward. "Oh, Melody, hello."

"Are you going to see Felicity? I don't think she's home. I popped over earlier and there was no answer and then I rang and she didn't answer."

"She was probably at the shops," Hazel said quickly. Felicity could well be out but Hazel suspected not.

"Anyway, it's her tennis morning, isn't it?" Melody glanced at her watch. "She'd definitely be out by now."

"Yes…normally…but not today because I was coming… I've popped over to collect some things." Now Hazel wished she hadn't parked here. She'd look silly if she was back in five minutes.

Melody came up to her front gate, leaned over it. "How are you doing, Hazel? We were so sorry to hear about Franklyn."

"Thank you. It's been a difficult time. I'm lucky to have such a supportive family." Hazel could almost feel the pimple that should be growing on her tongue for all the fibs she was telling. "Anyway, I won't hold you up."

"Please tell Felicity I called. I left her a message, it was just about a dinner to catch up."

"Yes." Hazel nodded and strode off along the footpath. Once she stepped inside Felicity's front gate she was blocked from Melody's view by their garage.

Hazel tiptoed up the front path, stopped to take a breath then rapped sharply on the door. She remained still. Not a sound came from the house and all the front curtains were drawn like they had been the last time she'd been here with June. Perhaps Felicity had gone to tennis and Hazel was worrying needlessly. She waited a few minutes, watching the frosted glass panel beside the door, then knocked again.

Beyond the glass she noticed a change in light, as if a door had been opened from another room and let light into the hall. She tapped more gently on the door this time and leaned in.

"Felicity, it's me, your mum," she called softly. "Please let me in."

There was no movement – perhaps she'd imagined it – then she saw something, a slight change, a shadow as if someone had passed by the glass.

"Felicity, if you don't want to talk that's fine but I need my sewing machine back. I'll leave you alone then if you want but please let me in for a moment."

Not a sound came from beyond the door. Hazel fixed her gaze on the glass but there was no movement. She tapped on the door again. "Felicity, I'm not going until you let me in."

Hazel glanced around, thankful there was no-one in the street behind her. She sounded like the big bad wolf at the little pig's door. She put her face to the frosted glass but it was impossible to see anything. She wished she still had a key, but the renovation had included a new front door and Felicity hadn't got around to giving her one.

She tapped on the door again. "Felicity," she hissed. "I know you're in there."

But what if Felicity really was simply at tennis? Hazel suddenly remembered the side gate. She followed the path across the front of the house and walked down between the garage and the side fence. Thankfully the fence was new and high and Melody wouldn't be able to see her if she happened to be in her side yard. Hazel stopped abruptly in front of the new gate, the new keyed gate. She didn't have one for that either and there was no point trying the other side of the house. That had a fence part way down with a small fernery beyond it. She huffed out a breath. Felicity had created a fortress.

Hazel made her way slowly back to the front of the house. She'd knock one more time and then admit defeat, but only for today. She was determined to see Felicity and she'd try again tomorrow and the next day and the next, until her daughter let her in.

★

Felicity paced the length of her gloomy lounge room. There was silence from beyond the front door now but she couldn't be sure Hazel was gone. There'd been a few pauses between her knocks. Felicity approached the front door on silent feet and stopped to listen. She couldn't hear anything but it was a solid door. She closed her eyes, drew in a deep breath and let it out slowly, as the galloping horses in her chest slowed to a trot.

The day had started badly. Someone had knocked on the front door first thing, waking her from her cosy nest on the couch where she was still spending each night. She hadn't answered. Perhaps it had been Hazel too, but it was a couple of hours ago now. Not long after that she'd had two phone calls, both of which she'd let go to voicemail. The first had been from her next-door neighbour Melody, saying they were home, thanking her for keeping an eye on the place and would Felicity and Ian like to come for dinner on Friday night? Felicity had felt a little guilty over that. She'd not really kept an eye on the place at all. Twice she'd snuck out after dark, once to bring in the bin and another time to clear the junk mail when she did her own.

The second call had been from Pam, asking her if she'd like a ride to tennis this morning. Felicity was not going to take up either invitation and she hadn't been sure what excuse she could make to avoid them until she'd caught a glimpse of herself in the bathroom mirror. Her skin was pale, there were dark shadows under her bloodshot eyes and her hair was in need of a wash. She could say she had the flu. That could last for weeks and would keep people away. She'd sent them texts and felt much calmer as she ate breakfast and packed away her bed.

She'd been about to leave her sanctuary to have a shower when Hazel had knocked. It had frightened the life out of her. Finally, when Hazel didn't let up, she'd carefully opened the internal door and tiptoed along the hall. She'd stood on the other side of the front door listening to Hazel's pleas to let her in. Felicity nearly had then. For a brief moment she'd longed for the security of her mother's arms, for someone she could pour out her heartache over Ian too, but then she remembered Hazel wasn't her mother and the hurt returned. How could someone who professed to love you keep such a big secret?

Anger had fizzed and she'd paced the lounge. Now here she was, holding her breath, anticipating another knock but all was quiet. She rested her forehead against the door. Damn Hazel for coming here. Felicity had forgotten she still had the sewing machine. No doubt it was just an excuse.

A knock thudded on the other side of the door. She jerked back and let out a strangled scream. Felicity was fed up. Heart thumping, she flung open the door. "All right, you can come in," she shouted.

Tony stood on her doorstep, a very surprised look on his face.

"Oh...I'm sorry." She peered over his shoulder. His four-wheel drive was parked out the front but there was no sign of Hazel. "I thought you were..." She flapped a hand. "Never mind."

"Is everything all right?" he asked, his face creased in concern.

Felicity glanced down at her rumpled appearance. She knew what she looked like from her earlier inspection and she still hadn't made it to the shower. "I'm not well."

Someone walked along the street, not anyone Felicity knew but she pushed the door forward a little and stepped behind it. "Nothing to worry about."

"I was at Tansie's earlier. She said you weren't going to tennis today."

"Oh...yes." Damn. No doubt Pam had spread the word. "I've caught something, probably the flu. I'm feeling a bit off."

She pushed the door further. He leaned into the gap.

"I don't mean to pester you but I wondered if I could take a few bathroom pictures. Talking with Tansie reminded me of the ledge we included in the shower of your second bathroom and I couldn't find an example online to show her. I'd be really quick."

"Oh," Felicity said again.

"It's not fair of me to turn up without warning but…I was worried about you."

"Why?"

"It was the tennis?"

"Tennis?"

"Last week you missed tennis too and then when Tansie said you weren't well I thought…" He lowered his voice. "Is everything okay, Felicity? Even when you were in the thick of renovating you rarely missed your tennis. We sometimes had to work around it."

To Felicity's mortification tears sprang from nowhere and rolled down her cheeks.

"Hell, I didn't mean to upset you."

She pressed a hand to her mouth. "I'm sorry," she moaned through her fingers and began to close the door with her other hand.

"Wait." Tony stepped forward. "I can't leave you like this. Can I make you a cup of…something…coffee?"

Felicity dug in her pockets for a tissue as liquid dripped from her nose. There was no tissue. She left the door and fled to the kitchen. The pain inside her deepened again, constricting and pounding at the same time. She snatched tissues from the box, bent over the kitchen bench, flung off her glasses and wiped her face.

"Felicity?"

Beneath the crook of her arm she caught a glimpse of Tony standing awkwardly in the doorway.

"Perhaps you should sit down," he said.

She didn't have the strength to argue.

"Let me make you a coffee." Tony came all the way in and crossed to the kitchen. "It will have to be instant though. I don't know how to work your fancy machine."

"Instant's fine." Today she had to place another online food order or she'd be out of the basics again.

Tony made two coffees and carried them to the couch along with her glasses.

"What happened to your glasses?" he asked as he passed them to her.

"I sat on them." Felicity slid the wobbly frames on, struggling to get the broken wing to sit properly. She needed to redo the tape. She dabbed the last of the moisture from her cheeks, blew her nose and sat back with the mug of coffee in her hand.

Tony lowered his tall frame to the other end of the couch. "I've missed catching up with you and Ian and Greta. How are they?"

"Greta's good." Felicity hadn't heard from her daughter other than brief replies to her texts since Ian had broken the news.

"No wedding date yet?"

She sucked in a breath. Greta was right. How could they hold a wedding? Everyone would know Ian had left her by then. How would she face them? She'd be front and centre as mother of the bride. There'd be nowhere to hide. Heat radiated up her neck and the horses picked up speed.

"Felicity?"

Tony was studying her, his face creased with worry again.

"No, no date yet," she managed and flapped a hand at her face.

He placed his cup firmly back on the coffee table and turned to her. "I'm sorry. I can tell something's wrong and I understand I'm probably not the right person for you to talk to. Can I get someone for you? Your mum? Or could Ian come home?"

"No!"

Tony blinked at her vehement response.

"At least...I don't...ohh!" She leaned forward and gripped her head in her hands. "Ian's left me." The words came out sharply and she held her breath, couldn't bear to look at Tony. What would he think of her now?

"Felicity, I'm so sorry. Here I am blundering in wanting to talk and take photos and you must be feeling terrible."

She risked a glance in his direction. His look had changed from worry to compassion.

He stood up. "I should leave."

She blew out a breath and with it the pain eased, just a little. Tony had become a friend but one quite separate to the rest of her life. Telling him had almost felt like relief. "You don't have to. I promise not to cry any more. Please finish your coffee."

He perched awkwardly on the end of the couch. "Do you want to talk about it?"

Felicity was sure hearing her woes was the last thing he needed. She shook her head. The sound of her heart thumped loudly in her ears. It was the only sound for a while then Tony spoke, his voice low.

"It's hard telling people, isn't it?"

She nodded.

"You wonder what they will think, how they'll react. Whether you'll ever be able to face the future."

She risked a glance at him. He was talking as if he understood exactly how she felt.

"My wife left me," he said. "It was the worst time of my life."

"Oh, Tony, I didn't know."

"I didn't want you to. Coming to South Australia was a new start for me."

"Do you have children?" Felicity was appalled to think she knew so little about this man who'd been in and out of their home for so long.

"Thankfully, no. Just a dog, and my ex got custody of her. Trixie was more hers than mine anyway, although I was very fond of the crazy little mutt. I'd like to get a lab or a border collie but I live in a small place with hardly any yard and I'm gone long hours."

"Cats are easier." Felicity nodded at Dolly who was sitting in a twisted pose on the mat in the sunshine licking her rear end. "They don't really care if you're here or not as long as you feed them." Would Ian want to take Dolly? She'd been Greta's cat but had stayed when Greta moved out. Felicity was glad of her company during the day and Dolly had taken to sleeping by her feet on the end of the couch each night. It would be a terrible blow to lose her.

"We had a cat when I was a kid."

"They don't take much looking after."

Dolly rolled over and stretched out in the sun close to Tony's feet. He reached down to pat her. She curled around his hand purring loudly then jumped up and with a flick of her tail stalked away.

"Perhaps I'm not a cat person."

Felicity smiled.

"Thanks for the coffee. I'm sorry I intruded."

"You're a friend, not an intruder, and I'm sorry you were subjected to my tears. I feel better after telling you."

"It will get easier." He rose to his feet.

"Did you want to take those photos before you go?"

"Would you mind?'

"Of course not." Felicity led the way to the main bathroom where she'd decided to keep the original bath and extend the boxed-in end of it inside the shower to create a ledge. It could be a toiletries shelf, a footrest or even a seat if necessary. She hung back and let Tony take photos from several angles. Bathrooms were expensive to renovate and Felicity had been proud of her success at keeping this room to budget without compromising on functionality and style.

Tony peered at his phone. "That should be enough."

"Phone screens are so small. You should build a portfolio on your tablet."

He shook his head. "No time to fiddle."

"If you saved the portfolio to the cloud you could access it from any of your devices."

He glanced her way, a look of defeat on his face.

"Have you created any kind of online presence yet?"

He shook his head. "I'm getting plenty of work."

"At the moment, and word-of-mouth is good, but people search for everything online these days. You don't even have to leave the house."

He opened his mouth to speak but she hurried on. "I can take pictures of my place. Why don't I start a portfolio for you? See what you think."

"I don't want to make work for you."

"I'd enjoy it and it would give me something else to focus on." Felicity was feeling much brighter already. The vice had lessened its grip on her chest. She had a project to work on, something to fill the lonely hours of her day and she wouldn't have to leave home to do it.

twenty-five

It was Thursday afternoon and Hazel and Jack were strolling through the Botanic Gardens enjoying the April sunshine. They'd met in the city this time, had lunch and gone to a small theatre in the east end to see a movie.

"What a beautiful day," Jack said. "I always prefer to be out than in, especially after a show like that."

Hazel laughed. "Next time you can pick the movie." It had been a dark and brooding story, not really her thing either. An art-house film that had sounded interesting in the write-ups but not so in reality.

"It will have to be after Easter. I'm going away, leaving next Thursday."

"That will be nice for you." Hazel was disappointed, both at not having something to look forward to next Thursday and at the thought of having nothing planned for Easter. She and Franklyn had been regular attendees at their local church but she hadn't been to a service since his funeral. Father Donnelly had called on her and she'd been grateful but she hadn't been ready to attend services again. Perhaps she'd go this weekend for Palm Sunday.

"Some of these statues are intriguing, aren't they?" Jack stopped to read a plaque. Hazel moved on a little, staring up at a tree towering above.

"I told you we went the wrong way."

The deep belligerent voice startled her. For a second it had sounded like Franklyn. A man and woman were hurrying along the path – at least the woman was hurrying, the man was tall and she was having trouble keeping up with his long strides.

"I thought it would be quicker," the woman said as she passed, a harried look on her face.

"Thought! You don't think, Helen, that's your trouble," the man snapped.

"It should be just ahead." Her voice had a whining edge to it as they disappeared around a bend.

Hazel's back prickled. How often had Franklyn spoken in that tone? She'd never snapped back, had always placated, kept the peace. Standing up to Franklyn only caused trouble, mostly for her. She could see his bullying so clearly now but when he was alive it had crept up on her, wormed around her, stripped her of her independence and become the norm. Divorce was out of the question, not that she'd considered it, but it would never have happened, not in the Catholic church. And not to people like Franklyn.

"I'm sorry I won't be here," Jack said.

He was standing back beside her. She looked at him, puzzled.

"For Easter. It's a blokes' weekend away. We catch up every year."

"Oh…yes…of course." Hazel rolled her shoulders to banish the prickling down her back. "I don't expect you to dedicate every Thursday to me. We both have others in our lives."

"Will you spend time with your daughters?"

"We haven't made plans. In the past we've gone to each other's places for meals. Sometimes the girls go away on a holiday but Easter has crept up on us this year. I don't know what they've got planned."

"Surely to look after their recently widowed mother."

Jack's look was so kind it pierced Hazel's resolve to keep her family business to herself. Her annoyance at both her daughters bubbled inside her and before she knew it she found herself telling him about Franklyn's letter to Felicity announcing she was adopted and the fallout from that, Felicity not speaking to her, and June inheriting the house and how she made Hazel feel like an interloper in her home. Jack hadn't interrupted, he'd let her talk, and when she'd finished they'd come to a stop close to a bench overlooking a lake.

Jack sat and patted the seat beside him. "What an extra terrible time you've had of it, Hazel. I'm so sorry."

Hazel blew her nose firmly to avert the build-up of tears and sat. "I should be apologising," she said. "You don't need to listen to my complaints again."

"That's what friends are for," he said. "And anyway, they're hardly complaints. I think you've been very poorly treated. I hope you don't think I'm interfering but I don't see how your house can be given away even if it isn't in your name. Have you had legal advice?"

"Kurt Blanchard has been managing Franklyn's affairs for years. He didn't seem to think I could do much."

"That sounds very unfair. I'm sorry, Hazel."

"Nothing for you to be sorry about."

"It's horrible for you though. You see, I had a similar situation."

"Did you?"

"When I met my wife we were in our forties and she'd been married before. Her children had all left home but they were never keen on me. We lived in her house. Her mortgage had been paid off by her late husband's life insurance but I paid my share of the bills, and I maintained it. When she got sick I gave up work to look after her, paid for her care and medication. At the same time I lost the rest of my savings in an investment company collapse. When my wife died, her children gave me a month to pack up and get out of the house."

"Oh, Jack, that's so cruel."

He gave a wry smile. "It's done now. No point dwelling on it. I used to rent a place out your way. That's how I met you at bowls, but when the rent went up I had to move."

"The house you're in now looks lovely."

"Hmm, yes." He gave a sheepish grin. "It's not mine. It belongs to a couple who work away a lot. There's a flat out the back. I live there for low rent in exchange for keeping an eye on the place and looking after the garden and maintenance."

"I see."

"I count myself lucky to live in such a nice place in a nice suburb after all that happened."

"I'm sorry."

"Thank you but I didn't tell you to gain sympathy. I didn't have a leg to stand on. I was at the mercy of my wife's children and they showed none. But I reckon you have more of a case."

"I don't think I have but thank you for caring." Hazel glanced at her watch. "Goodness, look at the time. I'd better head off to the bus."

They began the walk back towards North Terrace.

"Shall we wait until after Easter to decide on the next movie?" Jack said.

"Yes, ring me once you're back and you can choose what we see."

He chuckled and offered his arm. She accepted, enjoying the comfort it gave her as they walked side by side.

"Thank you for coming," he said. "I really do enjoy our movie days."

"As do I."

"There's something different about you today."

"Is there?"

"You look..." They both stopped at the red pedestrian light and he smiled at her. "Perhaps...I know this is risky but...you look younger."

"Do I? Maybe it's because I imposed on your good company and unburdened my woes. That can make people look younger."

The light changed and they began to walk again. "I think it's your dress. It's the right colour for you. You look very smart."

Hazel glanced down at the blue linen frock she'd restyled. It had been loose on her before and she'd tapered it in with darts, by hand, of course, because she didn't have her machine. And she'd matched it with a three-quarter sleeve navy-and-white floral jacket that she'd changed the buttons on to give it a more modern look. She'd been pleased with what she'd seen in the mirror but she'd done it for herself and she hadn't expected Jack to notice.

"That's very nice of you, Jack, thank you." They came to a halt by her bus stop. "And thanks again for today," she said.

He hesitated then leaned forward and gave her the briefest kiss on the cheek. It surprised her. They'd only ever shaken hands before.

"Take care, Hazel and please...if you ever feel you need to chat, I'm only a phone call away."

"That's very kind. I truly do have some other friends, you know, so I'm not totally Lonesome Hazel."

"I'm sure you're not but sometimes...well, I might just ring you, if that would be all right."

"Of course." Her bus pulled in beside them. "Enjoy your holiday, Jack, and I'll see you again soon."

His hand was in the air waving her farewell as the bus moved away.

She thought about their time together all the way home. They'd had an early lunch at a small eatery part way along Rundle Street. It had been more expensive than a pub but she'd been interested by the menu. They'd both had a glass of wine and had enjoyed the food. Jack had been surprised. She gathered he wasn't usually very adventurous when it came to food. She wasn't when she was at home either, but when she was out she liked to try something she wouldn't cook for herself.

Hazel got off the bus at her stop and felt her cheeks go hot as she recalled pouring out her heart about her daughters to Jack. He'd been very kind to listen as she'd babbled on. It had been cathartic but she was no wiser as to how to tackle Felicity although she was determined to drive over there again tomorrow and try to get her daughter to open the door to her. That'd be a start – even if Felicity yelled at her, at least they'd be communicating.

When Hazel was almost to her house she nearly turned around and walked away again. June's car was in her driveway. If it had been Felicity's car, Hazel would have run the rest of the way but now her steps slowed. She'd had a delightful day out and she wasn't in the mood to have it spoiled by June.

With a deep sigh she slid her key into the lock and let herself in her front door.

"Is that you, Mum?"

Hazel dragged her feet over the tiles. "It is." Hazel wondered who else was likely to be letting themselves into her house.

The family room was empty. She put her bag on the island bench and turned as June appeared from the side passage which led to the second bedroom and office.

"Did you enjoy the movie?" June had a pile of books in her hands. She set them down beside Hazel's bag and kissed her on the cheek.

"It was quite good," Hazel said. "What are you doing with those?" She waved a hand at the books.

"Derek asked me to have a look at Dad's books. There were a few that he liked and…what on earth are you wearing?" June was staring at Hazel's dress and frowning. "That looks a bit fancy for the movies."

Hazel bristled. She was enjoying playing with her wardrobe, giving her clothes a more up-to-date look.

"Jack thought it made me look younger."

"Who's Jack?"

Hazel turned away from June's sharp gaze and slipped off the jacket, annoyed with herself for mentioning him but June had been so dismissive. "A friend of mine. Do you want a cup of tea?"

"Is that who you go to the movies with? A man?" The last two words were said with such incredulity Hazel might as well have said Jack was an elephant.

"He's an old bowls friend of your father's and mine," Hazel said. "I bumped into him a while back and…"

"And you've been seeing a man when Dad's only been gone a few weeks."

Hazel plonked two mugs on the bench. "Do you want tea?"

"No. I can't believe you're seeing a man."

Hazel turned to her daughter and squared her shoulders. "I am not 'seeing' a man. He's a friend who enjoys the movies and a meal."

"A meal?"

"We make a day of it and there's no need for that face. If he was a woman you wouldn't question it."

"There are men who prey on vulnerable women, you know."

"I'm not vulnerable."

"You're recently widowed – he might think you've got money."

Hazel snorted. "Well, he'd be wrong about that, wouldn't he."

"Oh, Mum. Don't start. You're being well taken care of."

"Am I?"

"Of course. You're not destitute."

Hazel had had enough. She was tired and lacked the energy to stand up to June. "Why are you here?"

"To see you, of course."

"You knew I was going to the movies today."

"I didn't realise you'd be so late home."

"You don't need to check on me all the time. I've had a big day and I want to take off my shoes and sit down with a cuppa. If you're not having one perhaps you can leave me to it."

"You get so huffy about nothing." June swiped up the pile of books. "I'll call you tomorrow."

"You can leave those books. Your father might have left you the house but I believe the contents are mine."

June faltered. "I'm not stealing them."

"I didn't say you were but you can leave them here. If Derek would like to look at them he's welcome to visit…when I'm home."

Hazel almost shivered as June's steely eyes, so like Franklyn's, glared back at her.

June opened her mouth, closed it then put the books back on the bench. She huffed out a breath. "I'll call you tomorrow when you've calmed down," she said and let herself out.

No sooner had she left than Hazel locked both screen doors. She had no idea what had come over her. She really didn't care a fig about Franklyn's books but she'd lost everything else and she was damned if she was giving up anything more unless she decided to do so.

*

For the first time in weeks Felicity was opening a bottle of wine to celebrate her day rather than to commiserate it. She drew the curtains to block the darkening sky and lifted her glass in a mock toast to herself. Since Tony's visit the day before she'd been working on his photo portfolio and she was happy with the results. For a while she'd forgotten her husband had left her, forgotten the man she'd thought of as her father was dead and forgotten she was adopted. She'd simply been Felicity, throwing herself into a task she'd enjoyed.

She'd spent ages taking photos around her own home – styling, getting the light and the angle just right. She'd even baked a batch of biscuits for a few of the kitchen shots. She'd asked Tony to email her some of his photos of other jobs he'd done and now she'd created what she thought was an impressive portfolio for him to share with prospective clients. In the case of her own home she'd been able to set up a group of before and after shots as well. She'd also messaged Greta to send her some of the photos she'd taken of the back deck set up for the party but she'd had no response. Her daughter's silence was the only blip in her day.

Felicity took another sip of wine and sat back on the couch. Immediately Dolly appeared, jumped up and settled onto her lap. Felicity began to stroke her fur.

"Just you and me, Dolly. We don't need anyone else, do we?"

Dolly tucked her head under one paw and Felicity had a little pang of angst at the thought of Ian taking the cat. She'd had a text from him earlier that day, which she'd read and ignored. He wanted to make a time to have the house evaluated. She'd been busy working on Tony's portfolio and hadn't responded but now the message wormed uneasily back to her mind. There was no way Ian was selling this house.

She jumped at a sound beyond the closed door to the hall.

"Mum?"

"In the family room."

Greta came in rubbing her hands together. "It's nicer in here. It's quite chilly in the front of the house." She came towards Felicity but instead of kissing her mother she leaned down to rub Dolly's head. The cat stretched and resettled herself on Felicity's lap.

Greta glanced around. "You on your own?"

"Of course."

"Oh." Greta flopped to the couch. "You look a bit brighter today."

"I've been busy. Would you like some wine?"

"No thanks. I wondered if I could eat with you. Joe's out with some mates tonight and I was at work until late so thought I'd call in."

"I haven't thought about dinner yet. I'm not sure what I've got." What she was sure about was the fridge was all but empty – she'd been so busy with Tony's portfolio she'd forgotten to place her online food order.

"Let's go out for a meal then."

The horses that had left Felicity alone all day began to trot. "I'd have to change."

"No, you wouldn't. You look perfectly fine as you are."

Felicity glanced down at her shirt and tailored skirt. This morning she'd made an effort when she'd dressed. She'd set her laptop up in the study and pretended she was going to work and had dressed accordingly. "I don't really feel like going out."

"You need a change of scene." Greta stood up. "We'll go to that little Thai place you like. It's not far."

Felicity usually went there with Ian and the owners were a delightful couple and knew them well. Always made a fuss of the two of them. What would they think when they heard Ian had left her? What if she saw someone else she knew? The horses picked up speed. "I can't."

"Of course you can." Greta's tone was brusque. She shot up from the couch. "I feel like Thai, come on."

Dolly stretched, gave Felicity an aggrieved look and jumped to the floor. Felicity adjusted her wonky glasses on her nose.

"And we have to drive past your optometrist to get there," Greta said. "It's Thursday so they'll be open late. You can get your glasses fixed."

Felicity shook her head and the glasses slid down her nose. She pushed them back on.

"Come on." Greta headed towards the door. "Just cause Dad's not here you don't have to hide at home. He's probably eating out every night."

Was that what Ian was doing? Giving her a meagre three hundred dollars to live on and splurging on himself? She placed a hand against her chest and took a long slow breath. She did love Thai food. Perhaps having Greta with her would make it easier. Greta could do the ordering and any other talking necessary. Felicity rose to her feet.

Greta turned back. "All you need is some lipstick and you'll be good to go."

Felicity made her way to the main bathroom. Her brush and make-up were there. She tried to avoid her bedroom and the en suite as much as possible. It made her think of Ian and how lonely she was.

"Why is the sewing machine by the front door?" Greta asked when Felicity came out.

"It's Hazel's. She wants it back."

"Have you spoken to her?"

"Not exactly – she called in one day and yelled through the door. And don't look at me like that, Greta. I've got enough to deal with."

"Would you like me to take it? I can drop it in to her over the weekend."

"Thanks."

Greta picked up the old metal carry case that housed the machine and opened the front door. Felicity hesitated behind her. It was twilight outside. Almost dark but in the light from the hall she felt exposed. She flicked it off, shut the door behind her and hurried to Greta's car. She hoped none of her neighbours were outside or looking through windows.

Once in the car she slid low in the seat, pressed her aching back against the softness of the seat cover and closed her eyes.

"Hello, Mrs Lewis. What's happened to your glasses?"

They'd made it to the optometrist and got a park right out the front, and she'd managed to walk inside. Now the woman behind the counter, whose name Felicity never remembered but who always remembered hers, was watching her closely.

"I…" Felicity's mouth went dry.

"She sat on them." Greta had followed her in.

"That's a regular occurrence for some people." The woman chuckled. "How's Mr Lewis getting on with his reading glasses, no accidents there?"

Felicity stared at the woman. Ian didn't wear glasses. Always prided himself on his twenty-twenty vision.

"Let me take a look for you."

"Mum." Greta gave her a nudge.

Felicity realised the woman was holding out her hand. The horses were thundering so hard in her chest it was difficult to hear over the noise in her ears. She reached up and slid the glasses from her face. Her fingers trembled as she handed them over.

"Take a seat. I won't be long."

Greta tugged her towards the row of chairs. The door opened and two people came in, glanced in Felicity's direction and moved to the counter.

Felicity pulled up abruptly. She took quick short breaths to combat the steady pressure in her chest. "I can't. I want to go home."

"But we're going out for dinner."

Felicity began to tremble. "Please…Greta…take me home."

Greta frowned at her. "All right, but we can't go without your glasses."

"I need…to get…to the car."

"Okay, okay." Greta handed over her keys. "I'll wait for your glasses."

Felicity locked herself in and pressed her back against the seat. The pain in her chest deepened, radiating through to her back, and pins and needles prickled her fingers and toes. The strange tingling sensation crept up her neck to her head. She jumped as Greta tapped on her window. She lowered it a short way.

"The lady wants you to try them on. She can tweak them for you if they're not right."

Felicity took the glasses Greta passed through the gap and put them on. "They're fine."

"Are you sure because—"

"They're fine," she gasped. "Please, Greta, take me home. I'm feeling light-headed."

Greta hurried around to the driver's side, flicked on the internal light and studied Felicity. "What's the matter?"

"I don't feel well." Felicity pressed her hands to her chest. "I just want to go home."

"Are you in pain?"

"Yes," Felicity hissed through clenched teeth.

"Where?"

"Here." She kept her hands at her chest. "I can't...can't breathe properly." She looked at Greta in terror.

"Take slow breaths." Greta started the car.

Felicity leaned back and closed her eyes, trying not to take short sharp breaths but it was hard when her body seemed to want more oxygen than she could pull in.

When the car stopped and Felicity opened her eyes they were in the brightly lit exterior of a hospital emergency department.

"What...?" Felicity gasped. She felt as if she was about to faint.

"I couldn't just take you home," Greta said. "You're getting checked over, Mum."

With absolute dread, Felicity surrendered herself to the ministrations of the admitting and then medical staff, quite certain she was about to die.

★

"Hi, Dad."

"Greta! Hello."

She was relieved to hear his voice. She'd tried him earlier and he hadn't answered.

"Is everything all right? It's late."

"Sorry, did I wake you?" Greta looked at the sign in front of her. She was in the hospital carpark trying to find her car.

"No, no, I'm watching TV. What's up?"

"I've just left Mum at the hospital."

"What's happened?"

"Nothing life threatening but she isn't in a good way. They've done lots of tests and they're keeping her overnight. They think she's had a panic attack."

"Okay."

Greta stopped walking. That wasn't the response she'd expected. "I thought you might want to see her."

"At eleven o'clock at night?"

"I…"

"She's getting the right care, I'm assuming."

"I guess…they'll discharge her in the morning. I was hoping you could pick her up."

"No Greta, I can't."

Greta gripped her phone tighter. "Can't or won't?"

"Both really. I have to be on the road early and it won't help for me to be the one to pick her up. She's got to face up to life without me."

At last Greta recognised her car up ahead. She started walking again

"I'm sorry, Grets, but you're an adult. You must realise I'm not coming back."

"That's not what I was thinking at all."

"It won't help for me to get involved."

"I'll pick Mum up. I'm sorry I bothered you."

"Don't be upset. You must see it will only make it harder for her if I come."

Greta reached her car and fossicked in her bag for her keys.

"Grets? Are you still there?"

"Yes."

"If you ever needed me," he said. "I'd be there in a heartbeat. I'm still your dad."

She sighed. Maybe he was right. She was exhausted from her evening in emergency, the emotion of sitting with her mum through all the tests. She'd had to be the strong one and she'd hoped her dad would pick up that baton.

"Night, Dad."

"I love you, Grets."

She ended the call. How silly she'd been. Of course he wouldn't come but she'd asked him more for herself than her mum. He'd promised he'd still be her father and she'd wanted his support. She understood he had work but so did she. Felicity needed help. Greta couldn't understand how he could shut her out and switch off years of marriage so easily. If she married Joe would he feel that way one day?

The sparkle of the ring on her finger caught her eye as she unlocked her car. It wasn't 'if' she married Joe. They hadn't set a date yet but she'd accepted his ring and she'd said she would. She believed they had a future together but her parents' situation had shaken her faith in her own relationship. She'd been angry with her parents for breaking up their family but tonight, seeing her mum in such distress and now her dad saying he wouldn't come, she simply felt sad.

She was about to start the car when she received a text. It was from Joe asking how her mum was and did Greta want him to come to the hospital. She gazed at the words through watery eyes. Joe wasn't like her dad. She sent him a quick response saying her mum was okay and that she was on her way home. She tossed the phone back in her bag and set off, wishing she could simply transport herself into his arms.

twenty-six

Felicity let herself into the house, shut the door and leaned against it with a sigh. She was safe, back inside her haven. After the hospital she felt some relief. She wasn't having a heart attack or some other physical breakdown of her body but she was suffering from anxiety: panic attacks, which the doctor had said were giving her the symptoms she was experiencing. He'd given her some mild temporary medication and wanted her to follow up with her GP, and that's where she'd just come from.

Her phone began to ring. She was relieved to see Greta's cheery face on the screen. Felicity had insisted Greta go to work and that she would taxi home from the hospital. She'd done that and then taken Ubers to and from the GP. It was hard enough being out and about – she knew she was in no state to drive herself yet.

"Hello, Greta, I'm home again."

She'd been texting her daughter, letting her know her movements.

"How did you get on at the doctors?"

"She was very thorough. She's ordered more tests, made several suggestions and wants me to see a counsellor."

"That's sounds good. How are you feeling now?"

"A bit shaky but much better. I'm fine when I'm at home."

"Are you sure? I'll be finished work in an hour. I could come over."

"No. I really will be okay. You go home to Joe."

"Have you got plenty to eat?"

Felicity felt like the child instead of the mother. "Yes, Greta. I truly can look after myself."

"I know, Mum. I wish…" Her voice trailed away. "I wish you'd talk to Nan."

Felicity's insides tightened like threads being wound around a reel. She remembered the doctor's instructions, took a deep breath in through her nose and blew it out slowly.

"Mum?"

"I can't, Greta. Maybe one day but not yet."

"Okay, well, I can't come tomorrow, I'm flying, but I'll come over on Sunday."

"You really don't have to but if you have time it will be lovely to see you. Are you flying with Ivan?"

"Yes. He's wants to get a few more hours up. We'll be gone most of the day."

"You have a wonderful time and I'll talk to you on Sunday."

Felicity finished the call and jumped at a knock on her front door. She closed her eyes, wondering who it was and why people couldn't just leave her alone.

"Felicity? It's Melody."

"Damn," Felicity muttered. She'd sent Melody a text earlier in the week saying she had the flu and couldn't come to dinner tonight.

The knock came again, a bit louder this time.

Felicity opened the door a crack.

"Hello, you poor thing," Melody said. "I haven't called in because I didn't want to disturb you but I saw you getting out of a car and thought I'd bring you over some of my chicken soup." Melody held out a container with a paper bag perched on top.

Felicity had to open the door a little further. "That's very kind, thanks." Her voice came out in a convenient croak. "I've just been to the doctor." Which was true.

"How are you feeling?"

"Still not so good." It wasn't a lie. She took the container then managed a cough.

Melody took a small step back. "There's enough there for Ian as well and a couple of fresh bread rolls."

"Thanks, Melody."

"You send me a message if there's anything I can do. The flu can really knock you around."

"Mmm," Felicity murmured and gave another small cough into the crook of her arm.

Melody backed further away. "Make sure Ian takes good care of you," she said and with a wave of her fingers she turned and strode back across the yard.

Felicity closed the door and blew out a breath. Melody was a stickler for healthy living and staying home if you were sick. She'd keep away for a while now and at least Felicity wouldn't have to cook dinner for herself tonight.

★

Hazel closed the doors on the glassed-in bookcase, stepped back and looked around the office. She'd gone through the filing cabinets and had emptied all but one drawer, which was set up with folders for the different household accounts. That at least would be useful. The rest had been about shares and investments, mainly historical from what she could tell. And she'd found more packets of mints. Franklyn had stashed the damn things everywhere.

She'd piled everything into boxes, which she planned to store in the shed in case there was anything important among them. She hadn't even bothered to look at half of it. In a file aptly titled 'Books' she'd found a small notebook, a bit like a ledger, where Franklyn had written pages and pages of titles. She realised they must relate to the books on the shelves because there was a complete list of Biggles books and it had been Biggles books that June had been trying to take home with her.

Next to each title there was the name of the place it was purchased from, the date and the cost. Franklyn had paid a high price for some of the books and others had been purchased for very little. She wasn't quite sure what it all meant but she thought back to the conversation at Min's house over dinner and Peg saying how someone had thrown out the glassware that had been worth quite a lot. Now she wondered about the shelves of books and the amount of money that might be sitting there. She put the notebook on one of the open shelves and thought about the time she'd wanted to buy a set of Scarlett O'Hara replicas. *Gone with the Wind* had been one of her favourite books and she'd loved the movie too. She'd seen the small ceramic dolls dressed as Scarlett advertised in a magazine and she'd adored them.

Hazel left the study and went to the front lounge where she had a glass cabinet of special items. She opened the door and lifted out one of the dolls. It was a perfect replica of Scarlett in her forest green outfit. Named 'Scarlett's Deception', the figure was only ten centimetres tall and it stood on a small dais enclosed in a glass dome. Next to it on the shelf was Scarlett in her pretty white dress with its full skirt and layers of frills. Hazel had bought them with the fortnightly allowance Franklyn had given her and she remembered how angry he'd become when she showed him. He'd said if she was going to waste money on dolls he'd cut her allowance. She hadn't bought the rest of the set.

She replaced the figure, locked the glass door and returned to the office. One wall was lined with books and, judging by the number of entries in the ledger and the dates, Franklyn had been purchasing them since the girls were in primary school. She stared at the shelves wondering how she'd not known. He certainly didn't get that many parcels at home. Perhaps they'd been delivered to him at work. She sagged back against the desk. She'd never questioned the money he'd spent or the money tied up in what she'd thought were two old cars in the shed. With these things and the shares she wondered what else he'd collected over the years. It made his denial of her few ornamental dolls seem even more despicable.

Hazel strode out of the room, pulling the door shut with a satisfying bang. She flicked on the television but wasn't one for game shows and endless news reports. That too reminded her of Franklyn. The house had to be in silence for the seven o'clock news on the ABC. She hadn't minded that once upon a time but more recently, as Franklyn had done less outside, the all-day news channel was often going in the background with its continual loop of stories playing over and over again. Thankfully Hazel had had her front lounge to retreat to.

She looked around her tidy living space. With cards and movies done for the week it suddenly seemed a long time until her next outing. She'd planned to drive to Felicity's again today but had lacked the resolve to be rejected again, and she certainly wasn't calling on June. Her three grandchildren emailed or texted her regularly. Thank goodness for them but the boys were too far away to call in and she couldn't expect Greta to come very often. She had her own life to live.

Hazel had never been one for self-pity but what was she going to do with her time?

A tap on the sliding door startled her. Greta was waving at her through the glass. A halo shone around her head, thrown from the golden light of the setting sun.

Hazel unlocked the door. "Hello."

"I come bearing gifts."

Hazel recognised her sewing machine. "Oh!" she gasped.

"Nan. What's the matter?" Greta put down the carry case and wrapped Hazel in a hug.

Hazel sniffed in a breath and eased herself from Greta's arms. "Nothing much," she said. "I'm just feeling a bit sorry for myself."

"I thought you'd be happy to see your machine again."

"I am." Hazel picked up the case and put it on the table. "It's lovely to see you too, but I had hoped your mum might have…oh well, it doesn't matter."

"Mum's not been good."

"What's happened?"

"I took her to hospital because she was having chest pain but the doctors think it's caused by anxiety."

"Are they sure?"

"They kept her in overnight, did a lot of tests and she's been to her GP today. They're trying some medication to see if that helps with the anxiety."

Hazel plopped on to a chair. "I do wish she'd let me visit."

"You might need to give her a bit more time. I promise I'll keep you posted with her progress." Greta placed a gentle hand on her shoulder. "We've all had a lot to deal with this last month.

I wondered if you'd given any more thought to talking with your sister."

Hazel sat back sharply as if Greta had poked her with a pin. "I never plan to see her again."

"But why, Nan? Surely everything that happened between you was so long ago."

Hazel shook her head. There was no way she was going to open that can of worms. Her only hope of mending the bridge with Felicity and keeping what remained of her family safe was to keep Alice shut out. She fanned her face – not that she was hot but it gave the impression. "I need some water." Hazel made sure there was just enough shakiness in her voice.

Greta dashed to the sink. "Don't get upset," she said as she handed over a glass. "It's just that we're not a big family and I thought you might enjoy getting to know your sister again."

"No, please Greta, I can't begin to tell you how bad that would be."

"All right." Greta squeezed her hand.

Hazel hated making her granddaughter think she was frail but she had no other way to distract her. Greta's phone buzzed and she checked the screen.

"Joe's going to be late," she said. "What are you doing for the next hour?"

"I might need to check my diary," Hazel said, glad to change the subject. "Why?"

"I was wondering if I could help you set up your sewing machine in the office. If you don't plan to use the computer much, I could move it to one end of the desk then you'd have plenty of space to do your sewing."

Greta was so enthusiastic Hazel shook off her own poor mood and smiled back. "I actually made a start in there today and emptied out the filing cabinet."

"Is that why you have these books out?" Greta indicated the pile stacked on the end of the kitchen bench.

"I didn't get them out, June did. I got cross because she was in the house while I was still out on Thursday and she'd helped herself to the books. I made her leave them behind."

"Why would Aunty June be in your house when you're not here?"

"She was expecting me to be home. I was out later than I'd planned. She's decided she has to keep a close eye on me, and the house. I wouldn't care if she took all the books. I could put a few of my own things on the office shelves."

Greta picked up the top book then put it down again as if it had burned her. "These are Grandad's Biggles books."

"We both enjoyed reading them when we were first married. I bought him some of them for birthdays. I couldn't give two hoots about them now."

"I think you should, Nan."

"Why?" Hazel had thought she'd box up most of the books to make some space for a few of her own she had stashed around the house. She had quite an extensive recipe book collection that was too big for the shelf in the kitchen. She could put the less used ones in the office.

"Years ago, when the family were all here for a meal, Josh and Lachie and I went into the office to play a board game. I think it was Lach who noticed the Biggles books and took them out of the cupboard. Grandad came in later and saw them lying on the desk and got really cross but in that quiet way of his when you know you've done something terrible. He told us in no uncertain terms that we shouldn't touch his books and that he had almost the complete set of Biggles books. They were precious and not to be played with. I can't believe I'd forgotten about it. He really scared me at the time, he was so angry. I felt terrible about it and I never told Mum and Dad."

"I'm sorry, Greta. What an awful memory." Hazel had plenty of her own similar experiences. Franklyn could be stern with the children at times but she hadn't known about the book incident. Perhaps these books were worth something and if they were, she'd be damned if June was getting them. She scooped them up. "I'll put these back and perhaps you'd have a look at something for me."

Greta's face was creased in puzzlement.

"I found a ledger in your grandad's filing cabinet. I think it's a list of all the books on the shelves, how much he paid for them and when."

"I don't know anything about old books."

"But you're good with technology and research. Surely we could find out." Hazel set off towards the office.

Greta followed her as far as the office door. She stared at the bookshelves as if they were something to be afraid of.

"Your grandad's gone now, Greta, and he denied me the benefit of income that would have made my life so much easier. If these books are worth anything I want to know."

"If they were, surely Kurt would know. Grandad listed the cars in his estate."

Hazel chuckled. "Old books aren't the same. I don't expect they'll be worth much more than he paid for them, but I might be able to get something for them and clear out the space."

"I guess I can do some research."

Hazel took the ledger containing the lists of titles and handed it to Greta. "I think they're all recorded in here. There's no rush. Just when you've got time to look."

Greta took the book from her, still with a face that said she'd rather not.

"We'll keep it as our little secret." Hazel tapped a finger to her lips. "Now what about this desk? I'm quite excited at the idea of having a sewing room of my own."

Greta set down the book and picked up the keyboard. "The computer doesn't need to be spread across the centre."

Hazel felt the delicious warmth of anticipation, both at the thought of turning the office into her own space and that perhaps she might one day end up with a small amount of money from Franklyn. She didn't care that it wouldn't be much, just that she'd be able to get something extra out of him that Kurt and June didn't know about.

twenty-seven

Alice paced the floor of her tidy living area and glanced at the clock on the wall again. It was only ten o'clock, too early to pick up Elaine for their special trip to Yorketown and Alice had run out of things to do to keep her mind occupied and her excitement at bay. Last night she'd had a text message from Greta and she'd been on tenterhooks ever since. Greta was flying with a pilot friend and they were landing at the Yorketown airstrip. The pilot was meeting a friend and they'd be on the ground for about an hour. Greta's message was to ask if Alice was close enough to come and say hello.

Alice wasn't fond of texting and her fingers had fumbled on the keys, so she'd taken the plunge and rung Greta back instead. Greta's enthusiasm had sounded genuine – another reason Alice preferred talking to texting. It was easier to gauge the other person's tone and mood rather than from a few words on a screen. They'd arranged that Alice would meet Greta at the airstrip and drive her into town where they'd have a coffee and a chat.

Alice had barely been able to sit still since and she'd certainly not slept well. This morning she'd been up before the sun to make her pink jelly cakes for The Bay Cafe. She'd made extra, planning to give Greta a small package to take home with her. Then she'd cleaned up and as soon as the shop had opened she'd dropped the cakes in to Phoebe. Now she watched the clock and wondered what they'd talk about. She hoped Greta wouldn't find her too nosey but Alice wanted to know as much about her family as she could.

Elaine was coming with her to Yorketown. The plan was for her to visit a friend while Alice and Greta caught up and then Alice and Elaine were going to travel on up the coast to a Saturday night dance. They'd seen it advertised in the local paper. None of the others from their group could go but they decided they'd try it, expecting they'd dance together.

Alice checked her overnight bag. Of course it hadn't shifted from its position by the back door. She went back to the kitchen and looked at the clock again. Five minutes had passed since she'd looked last.

There was a knock on her front door and, glad of a distraction, she crossed the room to answer. The entry was at the side of her house rather than the front to avoid the strong winds that could howl directly off the ocean. She hadn't noticed anyone coming into the yard but from the sound of the excited chatter beyond the door she knew who it was.

"Who's that knocking on my door?" Alice called in a squeaky voice.

There were more giggles from Jessie and Lola then an attempt at a growled reply. "Let us in, let us in, little pig," followed by more giggles.

Alice opened the door to find the two little girls with a handful of flowers each and their mum Bec standing behind them.

"What funny-looking wolves," Alice said as the girls did their best imitations of growling roars.

Bec laughed. "We've been gardening and the girls wanted to bring you some flowers." She drew out the last word.

"How lovely." Alice accepted the assorted posies, which appeared to be more weeds than garden flowers but she would happily put them in a vase. Bec rarely came to her house. She usually rang to ask if Alice could look after the girls.

"And I've got some fish." Bec held out a foam tray with fillets encased in a plastic bag.

"Thank you." When Alice had agreed to look after the girls, Bec had wanted to pay her but she'd refused. In the end they'd agreed Alice would accept the occasional pack of fish. She enjoyed spending time with the girls and she never needed to buy fish, so for Alice it was a win-win. "Would you like to come in? I've got some fresh jelly cakes."

The girls squealed in delight.

"I'd love a tea." Bec pulled a face. "Darren's away all weekend and I'm already running out of patience."

Alice stepped back to let her past. Jessie and Lola had zoomed around her legs and were climbing up onto the bar stools at the kitchen bench. She sometimes brought them to her house if she was having them for longer than an hour.

"Wash your hands first, girls," Alice said. The little fingers that had handed over the flowers had looked very grubby. The girls shot off to the bathroom.

"How do you do that?" Bec said. "If I'd asked them there'd have been an argument."

Alice chuckled. "Sit down and I'll put the kettle on." There were dark shadows under Bec's eyes. She'd been working long hours and Darren had been away fishing. Alice had looked after the girls on several occasions before and after school over the last couple of weeks.

The girls were back in a flash and after Alice made a show of inspecting their hands she offered them a jelly cake each and a glass of water. She made a pot of tea for her and Bec and they retreated to the living area.

"I love that you still make tea in a pot," Bec said as Alice poured some into her mug.

"I don't when it's just me but I like the difference fresh tea leaves make to a good cup of tea."

"Have you finished the jigsaw yet?" Lola had sidled up beside Alice and slipped a warm hand around her neck.

"No, and I was wondering how I was going to manage," Alice said. "Would you girls like to do some more while you're here?"

"Okay." Lola nodded thoughtfully as if she were doing Alice a giant favour and moved to the dining table where the current jigsaw was taking up one end. Jessie finished her cake and joined her sister and they were soon heads down, absorbed in the puzzle.

Bec watched her daughters a moment. "Thanks, Alice."

"What for?"

"We're so grateful to you for looking after them. Darren often says it was our lucky day when you moved in. There are holiday homes either side of us with only the occasional occupants. We know them but it's not like they're proper neighbours." Bec glanced around. "Your house is lovely."

"Thank you. It has everything I need."

"It's tidy." Bec groaned. "You must think a mob of pigs has invaded our place when you come over."

"You lead busy lives." Bec and Darren's house was compact with one living area and three small bedrooms. It seemed ridiculous that Alice had all this space to herself and they were squeezed into their tiny house. "And there's no-one but me to pick up after here."

They chatted pleasantly until the girls tired of the puzzle and started to bicker.

"That doesn't go there," Lola said in a condescending tone to her younger sister.

"I want it to," Jessie moaned. "Don't push."

"Time to go, I think." Bec stood up. "Thanks for the cuppa, Alice. And the cakes. What do you say, girls?"

"Thank you, Alice," they chorused.

"I think young ladies with such beautiful manners probably need a cake to take home for afternoon tea."

The girls clapped their hands and Alice drew herself up and eyed them with mock sternness. "Only to be had if their mum thinks they've been helpful at home and done all the jobs she's asked."

"We will," they giggled.

Alice put four cakes in a container and handed it to Bec. "Make sure you save one for your dad," she said to the girls. She wouldn't have many left to give to Greta now but it didn't matter.

"Thanks, Alice," Bec said. "You're so good to us."

Alice opened the door and bent her head as the two girls brushed kisses across her cheek.

"Oh, and I forgot to say you'll be free from the girls over Easter. It's the start of the school holidays. I swapped a couple of shifts and took a few extra days leave and we're going to Melbourne to see my folks. Not Darren of course, the fishing's too busy."

"Your parents will be pleased to see you."

"Not as pleased as I'll be to see them. I'm planning on letting them spoil me too. And you'll get nearly two weeks without us asking babysitting favours."

"You know I love having them." Alice meant it and she was disappointed there'd be no children to create an egg hunt for this year. "I'll save their choc until they get back, shall I?"

"That might be best." Bec chuckled. "Or perhaps keep them till mid-year. Mum and Dad will ply them with so much sugar they'll still be high as kites when we get home."

Alice waved them off. Back inside she looked at the clock again. Only another hour until she could pick up Elaine and make the trip to Yorketown.

*

Greta's stomach tingled, partly from the tight turn Ivan was making in the plane and partly because in a few moments she'd be meeting Alice again. If the truth be told, the flight had also been shadowed by the memory of her departure from home earlier in the day. Joe hadn't said much but she knew from his body language he didn't want her to go flying. She didn't know how to make him understand the adrenaline rush as the plane zoomed along the runway, the exhilaration of being airborne. It was an addiction that only left her wanting to do it again at the end of each flight. She'd put the strength of her love for it on the same level as her feelings for Joe but she couldn't tell him that.

Beside her Ivan was going through his landing procedures as they lined up with the runway.

"Runway is clear," he said then glanced at Greta. "They've sealed this strip since the last time I landed here. Should make for an even smoother landing."

Greta grinned and nodded. She'd teased him about their bumpy landing on a gravel strip earlier in the day. She kept watch, switching between the looming runway and what Ivan was doing, and then, with only a small lurch, they were on the ground and taxiing towards a parking area. Two vehicles waited nearby. Ivan was going with a mate to look at a place he wanted to buy at Coobowie and Alice had said she'd take Greta to a cafe in Yorketown.

Introductions were made and then they went their separate ways. Ivan had warned her they only had an hour. There was some stormy weather forming in the north and he wanted to be back on the ground in Adelaide well before it arrived.

It was strange once Greta was in the car with Alice. They knew so little about each other and yet they were related. Alice drove them along a road bordered by paddocks and the occasional house and sheds.

"How was your flight?"

"Wonderful," Greta said. "It's been the best day for flying. Great visibility and you can see so much from a light plane."

"I've never been in anything that small."

"I love it."

"Do you have a licence?"

"Unfortunately, no. I have to rely on friends wanting company to get my flying fix."

"Excuse my ignorance but why don't you learn to fly yourself if you love it so much? I assume it's an expensive thing to do?"

"It is, and Joe and I are saving for a house and a wedding so that's our goal at the moment."

"But surely once you're qualified, work as a pilot would be well paid."

Greta stared at Alice. For her it was all about the flying. She was still buzzing from her morning in the air with Ivan. Under his guidance, she'd taken over the controls and all that mattered was when would she do it again? She'd never thought beyond to actually being employed as a pilot.

"I'm sorry," Alice said. "You hardly know me and I'm sticking my nose in your business."

"It's all right."

"Does Joe know how you feel about flying?"

"Yes and no. I love it, he hates it. I know he worries when I fly."

"None of us want to see our loved ones in danger."

"Statistically I'm safer in that plane with Ivan than I am in this car with you."

Alice raised her eyebrows.

"No offence intended, just stating the facts."

"None taken," Alice said but she took an extra-long pause at the corner before they turned onto the main road and drove at a sedate pace through the outskirts of town.

Greta pushed away thoughts of flying and took in her surroundings. "You don't live in Yorketown?" Greta asked.

"No. I'd take you to my place but it's over an hour's drive from here."

"I didn't realise. That's made a big trip for you."

"I was so pleased when you contacted me I would have walked over hot coals to meet you." Alice glanced at Greta. "That sounded a bit needy, didn't it? It's just that my husband Roy's family live in Victoria and we hardly saw them once we moved here so we're not close and I haven't had family for so long. I'm sorry your granddad died but if he hadn't I'd still not know where my only sister lived. How is Hazel?"

"She's doing okay." Greta wasn't sure how much Alice would really want to know about the family that seemed to be collapsing in on itself since Franklyn's death. "I have tried to get her to make contact with you again."

"Thank you." Alice smiled. "Hazel always had a determined streak. She taught herself to sew on an old treadle machine our mother gave her. She'd design her own clothes and create patterns and spend hours bent over that clunky machine. Often she unpicked things several times before she was happy."

"She made my formal dress but she hasn't done much since. I helped her set up the office in her house as a sewing room just last night. She wants to get back into sewing."

"She was good at it."

"I think she's finding life a bit lonely but she's doing things to keep busy."

"I know what that's like."

"Do you have children?"

"No." Alice's face was turned away as she manoeuvred around a corner and pulled up in front of an old cottage. "Here we are," she said. "It's a tea and cake shop and they also make good coffee."

"Which do you prefer?"

Alice shot her a puzzled look.

"Tea or coffee?"

"Tea. At least at this hour of the day. I have one cup of coffee in the morning and that's it for me. Roy was a coffee drinker. I liked to have one with him over breakfast. Now it's a habit."

"How long since he died?"

"Three years. But like Hazel I've kept myself busy." Alice released her seat belt and twisted to look at Greta. "That's another reason why it was no trouble to meet you here. My friend, Elaine, and I are heading off later today to a dance further north." She reached for the door handle. "We'd better get in and place our order or we'll run out of time. Your friend Ivan sounded pretty keen to stick to his schedule."

Greta followed Alice up the path to the front door of the cottage and Alice ushered her inside.

It amazed Greta to think Alice and Hazel had been apart for fifty years and yet something about the way Alice ordered their afternoon tea, insisted on paying and suggested the best seats were in the small room off to the right reminded Greta of her nan. They didn't look much alike but some of their mannerisms were the same and when Alice studied at her it was with the same tender gaze Hazel had.

Alice asked Greta where she worked and then Greta heard about Alice's move from the farm after Roy died.

"Nan would like to move to one of those retirement villages."

"That's probably a good idea. Roy wanted us to have a big house by the sea but I find I rattle around in it on my own most of the time. I've got a whole upstairs section I rarely use."

"I'm not sure that she'll be able to move."

"Why not?"

Greta chewed her lip then found herself telling Alice about Franklyn's will.

"It doesn't surprise me," Alice said. "He was a..." Alice looked down and pressed her fingers to her lips. After a brief pause she went on. "He was a difficult man."

"That's what Nan said."

"Did she?"

"I didn't realise you even knew Grandad."

"Oh yes. I knew him."

Greta was surprised by the bitterness in Alice's voice.

"Hazel started dating him not that long after our parents died in the fire."

"That must have been so terrible."

Alice glanced up, surprise on her face this time.

"Losing your parents like that."

"Oh, yes. It was. But luckily for me I had Hazel."

"But then something happened to drive you apart?"

"It was just after June was born. I suppose you know she was very early."

Greta nodded. June loved to announce how small she'd been at birth, as if it was some badge of honour Greta didn't understand.

"She was so tiny and Hazel had a terrible time with the birth. They were both in hospital for months. I was amazed to find out Hazel had another child, to be honest. I was only sixteen but I remember overhearing the nurses say she'd be lucky to give birth again."

"Were you living with Nan and Grandad when June was born?"

"Yes."

"You were young to be an aunt."

"Mmm," Alice's gaze fell to the table where she fidgeted with the handle of her cup then lifted it to her lips and sipped. "You haven't touched your food yet. I don't want to have to whisk you back to the airstrip without having finished your afternoon tea."

Greta took a bite of cake, wishing her new-found aunt would keep talking about her early life but it seemed the subject had been changed.

Alice told Greta about her neighbours and the two little girls she looked after sometimes. "Do you still live at home?" she asked Greta.

"No. I moved in with my fiancé, Joe, last year."

"I did notice you had a pretty ring on your finger. I presume Joe is the tall, good-looking man who had his arm around you during the funeral."

Greta nodded. The same man she'd hardly seen for several days. He'd been caught up at work and with mates, she'd been dashing between her mum and her nan. Then this morning Joe had been very grumpy when she'd reminded him she was going flying with Ivan.

"And you're an only child?" Alice asked.

"Yes. Mum and Dad wanted a bigger family but I'm it."

"I'm sure they feel blessed to have you." Alice's smile was so kind Greta's face crumpled.

"Oh dear. Did I say something wrong?" Alice took a small packet of tissues from her handbag and passed them over.

"No." Greta dabbed at her eyes and took a deep breath. She'd been caught up with her mum and her nan for weeks now, trying to help them cope with the changes in their lives and a few sympathetic words from Alice had set her emotions in free fall. "I've been so worried about them, that's all."

"Your parents?"

Greta nodded again. "Nan too. She's being brave but she seems so lost." Alice was studying her with such kindness that Greta felt the need to unburden. Suddenly she was divulging everything about her dad walking out, how upset and torn Greta felt, how worried she was for her mum who didn't want to leave the house and the diagnosis of panic attacks. Finally, she stopped and sat back.

"You must feel a little better for getting that off your chest," Alice said.

"I'm sorry." Greta took a fresh tissue from the pack and blew her nose. "I don't know why I blurted all that out."

"Don't underestimate the pressure you've been under. Everyone needs a release."

"But you're almost a stranger."

A sharp look crossed Alice's face.

"I'm sorry…I didn't mean…"

"I am a stranger but one who also happens to be your great-aunt and I'm pleased you felt you could talk to me about what's upsetting you. You lost your grandad and now your parents' marriage. It's as if your very being has been ripped away."

"Yes, that's exactly what it's like." Greta wished they were sitting closer. She would like to put her head on Alice's shoulder and feel the comfort of her arm around her.

"You're grieving, Greta. I've experienced that a few times in my life. You have to look after yourself." Alice leaned across and covered one of Greta's hands in her soft warm clasp. "If only we were closer. I might have been able to help. I understand what it's like to be a widow and perhaps I could even help your mum. But at least she has Hazel. They seemed close the day of the funeral. The two of them should be able to help each other."

If only that were true. Greta hadn't mentioned the fact that Felicity had just discovered she was adopted.

"I don't mean this in a condescending way, Greta, but even though you're an adult you are still the child in the family. You're not responsible for your parents' or Hazel's happiness." She gave Greta's hand a firm squeeze then sat back. "Perhaps you should step away a little or they might get too reliant on you."

So many thoughts whirred in Greta's brain she wasn't sure what to say, but in spite of her turmoil Alice was making sense. A strange noise made her look down. Her phone was vibrating on the wooden table and Ivan's name was on the screen.

"Oh no." She snatched up the phone. "I haven't been watching the time."

She put the phone to her ear.

"Greta, where are you? We need to go."

Alice stood up. Ivan's voice was so loud no doubt she could hear. "We're only five minutes away," she said.

Greta repeated that for Ivan and they scrambled to collect their things.

At the airstrip, Alice hugged Greta goodbye and pressed a small plastic container of coconut-covered pink cakes into her hands.

"I made jelly cakes for you and Joe," she said. "Please keep in touch."

"I will," Greta promised.

Once safely inside the plane, they were soon speeding back along the runway. Greta remained twisted in her seat staring out the window until the figure of Alice, leaning against the bonnet of her car, disappeared from sight and only then did she look ahead at the distant grey skyline. Thankfully Ivan was so focused on getting them airborne he wasn't making conversation. He pointed the nose of the plane towards the gulf, and she only half listened as he gave Adelaide air traffic control their location and requested airways clearance. Normally she'd be taking it all in, imagining herself following the flight instructions the controller radioed back but now there was a small ache inside her, distracting her, as if she'd lost something and she couldn't work out what.

*

Alice waited until the plane had become a small dot swallowed by the sky before she got back in her car. They'd had such an enjoyable afternoon and then Greta's hurried departure had brought an abrupt end to it. Alice should have invited her to come back, perhaps drive over and bring her fiancé. There was plenty of room at her house and Marion Bay was a beautiful place for a holiday.

She'd wanted to ask Greta to keep her updated about Hazel and to let her know if there was ever anything she thought Alice could do but all there'd been time for was a quick hug and to hand over the food. Now Alice felt hollow inside.

At least there was tonight's dance and some sightseeing with Elaine to fill the rest of weekend. She was about to start the car when her phone rang. It was Elaine.

"I'm just heading in to pick you up," Alice said when she answered.

"I'm sorry, Alice, I've got to go home and then drive to Adelaide. Hugh has broken his leg, playing football. They're not sure how bad. He might need surgery."

"Oh, I'm sorry."

"I want to be with him."

"Of course. I'm leaving the airstrip now and I'll come straight to pick you up."

Alice set off for town as soon as she'd disconnected. Disappointment filled the void that had been left by Greta's departure. It was selfish of her but she'd been looking forward to the dance and staying away overnight. She could go on her own but, Alice sighed, she didn't really feel like it. She'd go home, maybe get something from the tavern for dinner and watch the couple of movies she had on loan from the library. That'd be better than feeling sorry for herself like she was now.

twenty-eight

Hazel hadn't been home for very long when June and Derek made their way across the back patio towards the glass door. They were the last people she felt like seeing today. She was still annoyed with June and she wasn't keen on seeing Derek either after reading his suggested financial arrangements. June had said they'd done it together but Hazel recognised his style.

She'd had a miserable husband and now it turned out both of her sons-in-law were a disappointment. And she was worried about Greta's relationship with Joe. It sounded as if he was making all the decisions. Thank goodness for her new friend Jack or she'd be despairing of all the men in her life.

June called out 'yoo-hoo' and waved. Hazel couldn't escape their visit.

"You look very smart for a Sunday morning." June strode into the room as soon as Hazel slid open the door.

"Hello, Hazel." Derek followed behind.

June looked around the room as if inspecting it. No doubt wondering what else she could take. Her gaze came back to Hazel and narrowed. "Is that a new outfit?"

"No," Hazel said. "It's something from my wardrobe I've remodelled." The black shirt with large white swirls had been a shapeless design she used to wear over slacks. But it was made of silk shantung, too good to discard and working on it had given her several pleasurable afternoons. She'd adjusted the darts so it was more fitted and remodelled the collar in a mandarin style. Today she wore it over a plain black skirt.

"Have you been out with Jack again?" June sounded incredulous.

Hazel wanted to say she'd stayed the night with him and had only just got home wearing her outfit from the night before but she didn't have the courage.

"I've been to church, June."

"Oh…oh…" June opened and closed her mouth like a giant goldfish. "That's good you're going back again. You've got some nice friends there."

"Suited to a recently widowed woman," Hazel snapped.

June did her goldfish impression again.

Derek cleared his throat. "Shall I put the kettle on?"

"I've just got home," Hazel said. "And I don't need a tea. I was about to change and go for a walk." She hadn't been going to do that at all but she just might.

"There's no rush is there? We won't be staying long anyway. We're going to a fundraiser lunch at the golf club later. We came this way specially to see you." June opened the cupboard and took out the mugs – three mugs. Evidently Hazel was having a tea whether she wanted one or not.

She sat at her table while Derek and June took over her kitchen. Once they were all seated, a mug of tea each, silence settled. Hazel glanced at her daughter as June blew on the hot tea. The act of blowing sharpened her features, made her even more like

Franklyn. She'd been the apple of his eye from the day she was born. He'd been the one to insist she be named June after his mother. Hazel had thought it such an old-fashioned name at the time but now she saw how well it suited her daughter's austere looks and often outdated choice of clothing. June looked up, met Hazel's stare. A prickle trickled down Hazel's spine. That look made her feel as if Franklyn was still here but in female form.

Hazel shifted in her seat. "I had an email from Josh yesterday. He seems to be taking to Brisbane and uni life."

"Yes, he sounds like he's settling in well," Derek said.

"We thought we might fly up and see him in a couple of months," June said. "You'd be welcome to come with us."

"That's kind of you, June, but I'm not sure if I can afford flights to Brisbane on my income. I'll have to see."

"We'd pay for your flight," Derek said.

Hazel nearly choked on the biscuit she'd just bitten into. She gave a little cough. "That's kind of you." It truly was but it made her feel even more beholden to June and Derek.

"I told June if you need any help sorting your finances to let me know." Derek drew himself up. "Finance is what I do for a living, after all."

June nodded sagely beside him.

"The list of expenses we made up for this house was just a guide to get us started," he said. "I'm happy to discuss it with you."

"Not today though," June said. "We've got the lunch to go to. Perhaps over Easter. We'll have plenty of time to catch up then."

Once more Hazel had an awful sinking feeling. The Easter holiday loomed with no-one but Derek and June to help pass the time.

"June also mentioned you'd taken up with a man."

"What?"

"I didn't say 'taken up with'," June snapped at Derek. "Going out with."

"What's the difference?" Derek said then turned back to Hazel. "Just be wary, Hazel, that's all. In my line of work, I sometimes see women—"

"Being taken for a ride." Hazel stood up. She'd had quite enough. "You do sell cars, Derek." She glared at June. "And who I see and what I do is really none of your business."

"We're just watching out for you, Mum." June stood too and collected the cups. "I'll wash these up."

"And once Franklyn's affairs are settled I'm sure we'll work something out about the house so I don't want you to worry," Derek said.

Hazel pressed her lips together and nodded, not trusting herself to speak.

"Before we go I wondered if I could have a look at Franklyn's books?" Derek began to move across the room. "He was very proud of his Biggles collection and showed it to me on several occasions when he added to it. I suspect he's probably got a full set now."

Hazel stepped in front of the passage door. "The books aren't here!"

Derek's jaw dropped. June stopped wiping cups and looked around.

"At least, they're not on the shelves," Hazel said quickly. "I wanted the space and I've packed the books into boxes for safe-keeping." She hoped they didn't insist. The books were all still on the shelves but she'd planned to pack some of them away so that she could put her sewing gear in their place.

"Derek can look in the box then," June said.

Derek took another step towards Hazel. She stood her ground.

"I didn't think to put them in series so they could be spread between the boxes."

She'd never thought of herself as a liar but the words had come easily. Perhaps because her life since she'd married Franklyn had been peppered with lies, even though she'd only recently realised the extent of it.

"I hope you packed them carefully, Hazel."

"I did." She nodded emphatically and held Derek's gaze until he turned away.

"Derek could sort them for you, repack them," June said. "If they're in your way we could store some at our house."

"Greta said she'd help me with them over the Easter break." Hazel had no idea of Greta's plans for Easter but she felt confident June wouldn't either. "So there'll be no need for you to do it, and I've got a few plans for Easter – the card girls are having a get-together and there are several things on at church. Perhaps I can come your way one evening for dinner."

"I'm glad you're keeping busy, Hazel," Derek said.

June wiped down the bench. "Is there anything else we can do?" She spoke in a tone that suggested they'd just done a host of jobs for Hazel.

"As I said, I'm going for a walk." Hazel's shoulders relaxed as Derek turned away from the passage door. "Didn't you say you were going out for lunch?"

"Yes." Derek looked at his watch. "We should get going, June."

Hazel ushered them to the door, waved them off and leaned her back against the glass. Her Easter arrangements had all been made up, except for the church services, of course, but she had no other activities planned. She wouldn't be able to avoid June and Derek the whole holiday. What the hell was she going to do?

★

Felicity ignored the knock on the front door. It wouldn't be Greta. She'd already rung to say she wasn't coming over and that she and Joe were having a catch-up day at home. There was certainly no-one else Felicity wanted to see.

The front door opened. Perhaps Greta had come after all. She got up from the couch and went to the hall door.

"Ian!"

"Hello, Felicity."

She regarded her husband closely as she shut the front door behind him. He was tidily dressed as always, and the beard he was growing had thickened and was neatly trimmed. He returned her gaze with an equally frank analysis and she was acutely aware she was wearing the same clothes she'd worn to the doctor's on Friday afternoon. She hadn't bothered with make-up, and even though it was mid-afternoon neither had she brushed her hair or cleaned her teeth.

"What are you doing here?" she said.

"This is still my house, Felicity, and if you won't answer the door, I have to let myself in."

She turned her back on him and wondered how much it cost to get locks changed. He followed her into the family room.

"How are you?"

"I'm fine." Which was mostly true. Since her meltdown, and her trips to the ED and then her GP she was feeling much calmer. Of course she hadn't left the house since and the tablets were probably helping. Her GP had also suggested she continue with the HRT.

"Greta said you hadn't been well."

Felicity frowned at that and hoped Greta hadn't told anyone else about her mini crisis.

"What do you want, Ian?"

"To talk. You haven't answered my calls and messages. We need to move forward, make arrangements—"

"What arrangements?"

"Practical things like finances. I don't plan to keep giving you money and paying your bills forever."

"That's not fair. I gave up my job to save us money by managing the renovations."

"The renovations have finished."

Her hands went to her hips. "I'm fifty and haven't been employed for five years. How easy do you think it will be for me to find a job?"

"Have you tried?"

Finding a job was the last thing on her mind at the moment. She'd have to leave the house and she wasn't ready to do that yet. She swung away from him and looked out the back window and up at the sky. The storm clouds that had gathered last night were still hanging around and the day looked grey.

"We have to put the house on the market."

She flinched as if he'd hit her. "Why?" she said. She studied his reflection in the glass. He didn't move.

"We both need money to get places of our own."

"We have somewhere. This house. You chose to leave it…leave me." She spun back. "You made that decision, Ian. Why should I suffer because of it?"

He sighed, sat at the dining table.

"Don't make yourself comfortable. I've nothing to say to you."

"We can do this civilly or through lawyers. Either way we have to sort things out. The first step is to get the house valued. I've organised for someone to come on Wednesday morning."

Felicity folded her arms and didn't answer.

"Will that be all right with you?"

"It's my tennis morning." She had no more planned to go to tennis than take up bike riding but she wasn't telling Ian that.

"I'll give the agent my key then."

"I'm not having strangers in the house when I'm not here."

Ian took a breath. She could see she was testing his patience. He wasn't easy to rile but on the few occasions he got his back up he could explode.

"I can change it to another time."

"Good."

"Tell me when you're available."

She shrugged. "Anytime. You know I play tennis on Wednesdays."

Ian stood up. "Thank you, Felicity. At least the agent can give us an idea of what the house is worth and how quickly it might sell."

The pain that had faded over the last few days deepened again in her chest. She pressed her arms to her sides. "Why, Ian?" she whispered.

"I told you, we have to sell—"

"No, I mean why did you leave? What happened to us?"

He blew out a sigh, shook his head. "We want different things."

"A home and family, you mean?"

"No. It's just…we're just…I like being outside, being active, meeting new people—"

"So do I."

He gave her a sceptical look. "There's your life and mine, and we've been living side by side for a long time now. This house has consumed you."

"You could have tried to get more involved."

"So could you in my interests."

"Bike riding!"

"Anything. We stopped going for walks along the beach and that was one of the reasons we moved here. To be out and get more active."

"The renovations were full on. You could have helped more and then I'd have had more time for walks."

"You didn't need me."

"What?"

"You made all the decisions."

"I asked your opinion."

"No, you didn't. You just wanted me to rubber stamp what you'd already decided."

Felicity opened her mouth, closed it again. Is that what she'd done?

"It's not just the house. You have to control everything down to what we eat for dinner. I've tried to make some changes, experiment with food, and you howl me down."

"Are you talking about that gluggy quinoa salad? And the tofu? You didn't like that either."

"I know but I like to at least have some input. To have a go at some meals."

"By having a go do you mean making such a mess in the kitchen it took me half a day to get the muck off the pans?"

He sighed. "I can't even be allowed to choose you a birthday present."

Felicity thought about the catalogues she left lying around leading up to each birthday. "I was saving you the hassle." He'd bought her sessions with a personal trainer several years ago and she'd made sure that wasn't going to happen again.

"We're different people now. It doesn't work for us any more."

He was right. She could see it now but she wasn't taking all the blame. "The personal trainer was something you'd like, Ian. If you'd truly understood me you would never have bought me such a hideous gift."

They stared at each other across the kitchen. Felicity was determined she wasn't going to cry.

He jiggled his keys. "I'll message you with a new time for the agent. If it's out of hours I can come too."

She nodded sharply.

"Things will work out eventually, Lissie."

She flung her hands in the air. "Don't Lissie me, Ian. I think we're past terms of endearment."

Once more he sighed. "Okay. I'll go. I'll be in touch when I know the new time."

She stood rigid and still until she heard the door close then she let her hands fall to her sides and took some slow steady breaths. In spite of her best efforts, tears began to roll down her cheeks. She rested her chin in her hands, slid her fingers beneath her glasses and pressed them into her eyes. Her shoulders shook with her sobs.

Dolly miaowed. Felicity sobbed harder. At least Ian hadn't said he'd wanted the cat.

"Felicity?"

The voice was so soft she thought she'd imagined it. She took her hands from her face and blinked at the blurry shape across the room. She blinked again. "Hazel?"

"Ian let me in. I'm sorry about…that he's moved out." Hazel took a tentative step towards her. "Please don't make me go. I want to be here for you."

Felicity let out a groan and sank to her knees. The pulsing pain, still not completely gone, built again in her chest. So much for feeling better. Perhaps she'd never be truly well again. The thought terrified her and she groaned.

Hazel's legs and feet appeared beside her, then she was kneeling down, her face full of concern. "Felicity?" she said gently and opened her arms.

With a giant howl Felicity fell into them.

*

It took several minutes for Felicity's sobbing to ease and in that time Hazel lost all feeling in her lower legs. As soon as she felt able, she suggested they move to the couch. It was a struggle for both of them but finally they were seated side by side, Felicity's hand firmly gripped in Hazel's.

"I'm so sorry, Felicity."

"What for? Your husband dying and leaving us nothing, my husband leaving me, or perhaps that you never bothered to tell me I was adopted?"

The words were harsh but said in a tone of defeat.

"All of it. I'm so sorry for all of it." After all that had happened, she needed to tell Felicity the truth, at least, her version of the truth.

"Why?"

Hazel shook her head. "Why were you adopted?"

Felicity shrugged and drew her hand away. "That's as good a place to start as any."

"We'd always planned to have two children." Hazel gave a soft snort, it was something she and Franklyn had agreed on easily. "I had a difficult time during June's birth. It was a long labour. June was pre-term and in distress. The doctors had to intervene and I tore very badly. It took me a long time to recover and…well, things down below weren't good for a long time. It wasn't impossible but they advised it would be best for me not to have more children. Then we heard about you, being abandoned and—"

"Abandoned?"

"Yes. I took one look at you and my heart melted. June wasn't even a year old but I knew you'd be the perfect little sister and make our family complete."

"You said I." Felicity's voice wavered. "Franklyn didn't want me, did he?"

"He wanted another child but I was terrified of giving birth again. I think even he was worried about it. I suppose it was me who convinced him to adopt you, but you know what he was like. I could never have persuaded him if he hadn't fallen for you as well."

"Why keep it a secret?"

"It wasn't unusual back then. Your original birth certificate was sealed and a new one issued with our names and…" Hazel hesitated. Felicity was studying her with such shock she was worried how much more to say.

"And what?" Felicity said. "You have to tell me all of it now."

"It was Franklyn's condition that if we adopted you, you were to be raised as our own and never told about your adoption."

"Why?"

"He was a proud man. He didn't want people to know you were adopted."

"Surely your family and friends would have known. You can't just suddenly turn up with a baby."

Hazel drew a breath. This is where it got tricky. "I told you I wasn't well for a long time after June's birth. I ended up in the country. I stayed with Franklyn's aunt for a while."

"Aunt Isabelle?"

"Yes. She was very good to me."

"That's not how I remember her."

"You hardly ever saw her. She was a stern woman and not used to children. There was a home not far from her for unmarried mothers and when I found out about you, not only was I feeling much better physically but we were also about to move to Adelaide. Isabelle was the only one who knew you were adopted."

"I don't understand what happened then – why did Franklyn hate me?"

"He was a good father to you. Treated you the same as June."

"That's not how it was."

"You did push his buttons when you were in your teens but up until then he was a good father."

"Good!" Felicity pushed away. "I don't know how you can defend him. He shot us both down with his will and follow-up letters." Felicity grabbed her arm. "You got a letter too. Did he tell you why he decided to spill all from his grave?"

Hazel thought about the letter that she'd ripped to little shreds and tossed in the compost bin. Franklyn hadn't trusted Ian. He'd been right not to but for the wrong reason. She had no doubt Ian was as capable with money as Felicity was, he just didn't want to be married to her.

"He didn't trust Ian to manage your money."

"Ha! Well, he'd be laughing from his grave now. Ian's got all the money."

"Your house is in joint names, surely."

"Yes, but that's it. All my savings went into the renovations. I'm dependent on the measly amount Ian gives me to live on. And now you're saying because Franklyn didn't trust Ian to manage money he cut me out?"

"And in case you decided to contest…"

"He decided to tell the world I wasn't his child."

Hazel's shoulders sagged. "Yes."

"He must have known he'd be hurting us both. Didn't he love you either?"

"In his way, I believe he did."

"A very strange way."

And there it was. Hazel couldn't deny it. She'd thought she'd loved Franklyn in those early days but as the girls grew and changed, he did too. Her married life had been like a seesaw dependent on Franklyn's mood. Everything was done his way or it wasn't done at all – and yet they'd had some good times.

"Why did you stay with him?" Felicity's question startled her.

"He was my husband and…even if I could have left him, the Catholic church didn't allow divorce and I was totally dependent on him for everything. I had no-one to turn to so I had to make the best of it."

"Times have certainly changed, haven't they?" Felicity sniffed and rubbed at her eyes. "My husband didn't have any qualms about leaving me and I thought our marriage was a happy one."

"I'm sorry you thought you had to keep it to yourself."

Felicity turned a panic-stricken face to Hazel. "That's why you didn't leave Franklyn. Everyone offers sympathy to a widow but a divorcee, well, they're all wondering what you did to make your husband want to leave, aren't they?"

Hazel grasped both of Felicity's hands in her own. "You have to stop thinking like that. There's nothing for you to be ashamed of. You loved your husband, raised a gorgeous daughter, created a beautiful home."

"Ian wants to sell the house," Felicity wailed.

"Oh dear. That will be tough." Hazel gave the warm hands in hers a gentle squeeze. "What an odd pair we are. You've got a beautiful home you don't want to give up and I'd love to sell mine for something smaller."

Felicity's lip trembled but her eyes remained dry. "What am I going to do?"

"You've got lots of friends who'd support you through this—"

"I can't tell them. I'm so embarrassed. Ian left me. We were the perfect couple, with a healthy happy daughter and a beautiful home but it's all a lie. How can I face people?"

"You've still got a healthy happy daughter and you've got me." Hazel gripped Felicity's hands tighter. "It was a mistake not to tell you that you were adopted but as time went by I honestly didn't even think of it any more. We were a family and you one of my daughters."

Felicity let out a big sigh and dropped her head to Hazel's shoulder. Hazel rested a hand on Felicity's head. "We can face the future together." She slid her hand down her daughter's back and pulled her in closer. They sat a moment, huddled together on the giant couch not saying anything. Then Hazel became aware of Felicity's body odour. She patted her shoulder. "Why don't you have a shower and freshen up and I'll put the kettle on. Would you like tea or coffee?"

Felicity sat up, dug out a tissue and blew her nose. "Neither." She glanced across at the gleaming wall clock. "It's four o'clock, I'm having wine."

"Is there some in your fridge?"

"Plenty. We hardly touched the party wine."

Felicity dragged herself from the couch and left the room. Hazel didn't say that perhaps it was a bit early, and she didn't ask how much or how often Felicity was drinking. For the moment she was content her daughter had opened up to her and she would leave it at that.

*

Felicity watched from behind the partly open front door as Hazel got into her car. She felt a small pang of guilt. Hazel had made them dinner and they'd shared a bottle of wine. Well, Felicity had consumed most of it. Hazel had only had one glass and now it was dark and she had a long drive to get home.

Felicity shut the door and pressed her forehead to the cool solid wood. Hazel had suggested they meet at her house next time and Felicity had intimated she might but hadn't committed. Her trip to the hospital and then the doctor had been enough stress for a while.

To begin with Felicity hadn't wanted to know anything about her adoption but once Hazel had started telling her there was so much more she wanted to know. Mostly they were questions Hazel didn't have the answers for; how old was her mum, what did she look like and was Felicity the result of a one-night stand or had her parents been young lovers torn apart by an unplanned pregnancy? Suddenly those details seemed important. Hazel knew little though and they'd moved on to other topics, matters that were new to them; managing on a budget, food for one, tricks for getting back to sleep when you were wide awake in the middle of the night.

It had been as close to an enjoyable afternoon with Hazel as Felicity could recall in quite a while, apart from the time Hazel had taught her to sew curtains. And even that had been punctuated by Franklyn's demands. In the last year or so of his life he'd become more possessive of Hazel's time and there'd been only rare opportunities for mother–daughter chats.

She lifted her head as her phone pinged in her pocket. It was a message from Ian saying the agent could come at four on Wednesday afternoon if that suited her.

"No, it doesn't suit me, Ian," she shouted at the silent screen. "Damn you."

She shoved the phone back in her pocket. She wasn't going to rush to answer. She thumped her fist against the door, then flattened out her hand and pressed it to the wooden surface.

Moving with a speed she'd lacked for weeks she retreated back through the house, through the laundry and into to the garage where she pulled some plastic boxes from a shelf and rummaged inside.

"Yes!" She held a small package in the air triumphantly. It contained a brass door bolt with security chain. They'd been going to put one on the front door but it was such beautiful wood Felicity hadn't wanted to spoil it.

She took the cordless drill and marched back into the house, glad she'd got one of the young carpenters to show her how to use a drill properly. During the course of the renovations she'd put up all her own art, clocks and hangings. She stopped in front of the door and took the pieces from the packet. Ten minutes later she slid the bolt across and stood back to admire her handiwork. The chain dangled securely below it. No-one would come into her house unless she let them in.

twenty-nine

"They were amazing," Joe mumbled through a mouthful of the last of Alice's jelly cakes. There'd been four in the container and Greta had only eaten one. "Do you think she'd part with the recipe?"

"Maybe," Greta murmured.

It was Sunday evening and they were curled up on the couch together. Joe was watching football on the TV and Greta was so comfortable and sleepy she didn't care what was on.

They'd had a busy day that had ended magically and she was sated, with both love for Joe and delicious food in her belly. This morning after they'd slept late she'd decided to take Alice's advice and leave Hazel and Felicity to their own devices. Joe needed her attention. He'd been worried about her flying yesterday, especially when the day turned stormy, but Ivan had them safely back on the ground before the worst of the weather came through.

Last night when she'd returned home Joe had been a bit prickly. She knew it was his way when he was worried and she'd worked hard to restore his usual good humour. She hadn't thought it was the right time to tell him Ivan had asked her to fly with him again over Easter.

This morning Joe had cooked brunch while she'd stripped the bed and started the washing. While he was out for his run she'd cleaned the bathroom and when he'd returned he'd found her soaking in the freshly washed bath. He'd joined her, and they'd ended up in the bed she'd only just remade. Was there anything more sensual than clean sheets?

When they'd eventually dragged themselves from the bedroom Joe had cooked pasta and she'd made a carbonara sauce and they'd retired to the couch where they were still ensconced, the remains of their pasta congealing on the plates with the now-empty container of Alice's cakes and the remains of a bottle of wine.

She twisted her head from where it had been resting on his chest to look up at him. A few crumbs of coconut clung to his lips. She brushed them off with her finger. She needed to talk to Joe about something she'd been pondering since her last visit to Hazel's.

"I've been thinking about seeing a lawyer," she said.

"If you're doing a pre-nup I get possession of any future jelly cakes." He brushed a hand over her hair without taking his gaze from the screen.

"This is serious, Joe. It's about the money Grandad's leaving me. I've decided I want Nan to have it."

He shifted his gaze from the TV to her. "Steady on, that money could make a real difference to our future."

"And it could make a difference to Nan's. I feel as if I'm stealing what should be hers."

"Is that why she rang earlier? About the money."

"No. Nan would never ask me to do it. It was my idea. She rang to tell me she'd been to Mum's and they've talked. Things are still a bit tense but they've broken the ice."

"Like *Days of Our Lives*, your lot."

"I didn't know you watched it," she dug back. "Anyway, we've got two good incomes and our lives ahead of us. It's not right that Nan's struggling for money at this stage of hers."

He frowned, then nodded. "I guess you're right. What about your cousins? If you give up your inheritance they should too."

"I haven't spoken to them yet. I thought I'd find out about the legalities first. I can't make them give it up but I hope they'll feel the same way as me."

He took the wine glass from the table near his hand, drained it and set it down again. "Easy come, easy go."

"We weren't expecting money anyway so we're still on track with our savings."

"Would you consider just giving back half?"

"Joe!"

He held up his hands. "Okay, okay. It'll take us a bit longer to get our own place, that's all." The crowd roared on the TV and his attention turned to the footy.

She put her head back on his chest and rested there a moment while Joe told the TV the point was clearly a goal. Once he'd settled again, she asked what he had planned for the week.

"It'll be a busy one. It's a short week and our current project's behind schedule."

"Then we get a four-day break."

"Yeah." Once more his hand stroked her head. "I wanted to talk to you about that."

She eased away from him and sat up. "Are you planning something?" She recalled their weekend down south; it seemed an age ago now. The coming Easter break had snuck up on them with one thing and another, but she wouldn't say no to getting away for a few days.

He screwed up his face and Greta had the feeling she wasn't going to like what he was about to say.

"Hannah's asked if I can help paint their house."

"Oh." Greta flopped back against the couch. Joe's sister and brother-in-law had moved into the foothills late last year. They'd bought a large block with fruit trees and veggie gardens and an old house that needed work. Joe's parents, Joe and sometimes Greta had been helping them ever since.

"You don't have to paint," he said quickly. "Dad's going to help too. We thought you and mum could be on food and kids duty."

"Did you?"

"It'll only be for two days, maybe three depending on how quick it dries. There'd be four of us painting...five if you did want to help."

Greta gaped at him. "How much are they doing?"

"The four main rooms and the hall."

"Bloody hell, what about all the furniture?"

"We'll shift out what we can on Friday and stack the rest up and cover it."

"So a day to shift furniture and three days of painting." Greta threw her hands in the air. "And there goes Easter."

Normally she wouldn't mind but with her own family needing so much from her lately she didn't want to spend her entire break working for Joe's. Not that she didn't get on with his family but her mum had put her off renovating for life. Greta had been happy to move in with Joe when he'd suggested it because she loved him and it had felt right but it'd also meant she could leave behind the constant round of sawing, hammering, dust-covered surfaces and the smell of plaster and paint that had been part of her home life since her parents had moved house.

"When we buy a house it will have everything done," she said.

"Wouldn't you want to put our stamp on it? Maybe paint some walls, revamp cupboards?"

"It will need nothing more than our furniture," she said emphatically. "And if you're going to be busy all weekend I might as well go for another flight with Ivan."

"What's Ivan got that I haven't got?" Joe pouted.

"A pilot's licence."

"And more money than we've got, obviously, if he can afford that."

"I think his parents helped pay for it. His aim is to be a commercial pilot one day." Greta recalled Alice's suggestion that she could do the same but kept it to herself. The last time she and Joe had talked about it was after they'd watched her favourite movie about Amelia Earhart, the famous American aviator. Greta had said she wanted to be a pilot and Joe had said their life wasn't a Hollywood film and he'd made a joke of it. Besides, he was right about the money. It was beyond her reach.

A serious look settled on his face. "I wish you'd take up running or some kind of sport that kept you on the ground."

"And I wish we were having at least some of Easter to ourselves." She knew it sounded petty but she couldn't help herself.

Joe draped his arm around her and drew her back towards him.

"The weekend after Easter we'll do something special, I promise."

One of their phones began to vibrate on the table. Greta groaned as Joe leaned forward.

"It's yours," he said. "Alice."

She slipped out of his embrace and picked up her phone. If it had been anyone else she might have ignored it but she wondered why Alice would be ringing her.

"And tell her thanks for the cakes," Joe said.

"Hello, Alice." Greta stood up and moved away from the football, resting her butt against the kitchen bench.

"Oh, Greta. I hope you don't mind me calling you. Is it too late?"

"Of course not. What's up?"

"Nothing really. Only you had to rush off in such a hurry yesterday and I didn't get a chance to say…"

Greta heard Alice take a deep breath.

"If you ever wanted a weekend away, or anytime really, perhaps you and Joe, or you and your mum or just you." There was another brief pause. "Sorry, I'm sounding desperate but I wanted you to know you'd be welcome here."

Joe picked up the nearly empty wine bottle and waved it at her. Greta nodded and he poured the last of it evenly between them.

"Thank you, Alice," Greta said. "That's a lovely thought and I might take you up on it."

"Really? I'd truly love it if you could come. You'd only need to bring yourselves. I have plenty of beds and I enjoy the opportunity to cook for others or we have a tavern here with a great menu if you'd prefer to eat out." Alice paused for a breath. "There I go again."

"It's fine, Alice, really." Greta chuckled. A weekend at Marion Bay sounded the perfect place for Joe's promised escape.

"Anyway, I'll let you go," Alice said. "You've got my number. Ring when you can come, or message if you prefer, and it would be lovely to see you again."

Joe looked up and pointed to the empty cake box.

"Oh and we both enjoyed the cakes you sent home with me," Greta said. "Joe sends his thanks."

"You tell Joe I'll make him a fresh batch or two when he comes."

"I will." Greta smiled as Joe's eyes lit up. He could obviously hear Alice's response. "Bye, Alice."

He swooped on Greta as soon as she ended the call. "So the gist of that is that we've got a place for a free holiday and it comes with a never ending supply of pink jelly cakes. I like the sound of this Alice."

"She's lovely but I don't know about the free part. We'd have to offer something."

"Maybe we can take her some wine or shout her a meal out."

"I'm sure she won't expect anything but I would like to do something to say thank you."

"Of course." He kissed her on the nose.

Greta extricated herself from his arms and picked up the empty plates. Sometimes it annoyed her that Joe was often on the look-out to get something for nothing.

"What's this book for?"

He was leafing through Franklyn's notebook.

"It was Grandad's. Nan gave it to me. She thought I might be able to find out if any of the books he collected would be worth anything."

"I assumed his book collection would all be part of his estate. He showed me a few he'd bought. He reckoned they were worth a bit."

"I hope they are, for Nan's sake." Greta shrugged, her hands full of plates and cutlery. "But I don't know when I'll do it."

"Do you want me to do a bit of checking?"

"If you like." She stacked the dishes in the dishwasher and ran water in the sink. "Josh and Lach and I were looking at them once when we were kids. Grandad went off at us for daring to touch them. I don't remember him being so cross with us ever. He frightened me. I've never been near the damn books since."

"He was very particular about them. That's why there are some behind glass and the blind is often down. He didn't want to let light or dust settle on them. I can do some searching." Joe put the book on their bookshelf. "I've got an early start in the morning. I'll get my clothes ready. And then we might turn in, hey?" He raised his eyebrows.

"I'll be there soon." Greta turned back to the dishes.

"Leave them." Joe grabbed her by the hand. "I'll do them tomorrow."

She glanced around the lounge. His running shoes and a pair of thongs lay by the front door with two pairs of her shoes, a sweat towel and t-shirt were draped across a chair and the coffee table was covered with empty food packets, some water glasses, his tablet, wallet and keys and a pair of his socks. On the floor beside it was the empty wine bottle and his work satchel.

She sighed. "I'll just do these pans, the rest can go in the dishwasher."

"Okay." He wandered towards the bedroom.

It only took half an hour to finish in the kitchen. She'd ended up doing a quick tidy of the lounge as well and was feeling quite pleased with herself. By the time she'd cleaned her teeth Joe was fast asleep, his sport magazine rising and falling on his chest with his breathing. She slid it out from under his hands and he snuffled and rolled over, his back to her. Greta switched out the light, and curled into him.

If she went with Joe to his sister's next weekend she'd be roped into painting for sure. She could organise some girlfriends to come round or they could go to the movies, but her closest friends were all heading off for the four-day break. If she remained home on her own she could stay in her pjs, read books, watch movies or a whole series of something on TV, but she also knew their place was turning into a tip. She wasn't too fussed by mess but they hadn't done a proper clean in ages. Joe would be too tired to do anything all weekend, he'd probably stay over at Hannah's one night, maybe two, and Greta would end up doing the washing and housework on her own.

She sighed, rolled over and stared up at the ceiling. Maybe she could go by herself to visit Alice. Even if it was just an overnight trip it'd be a change. The weather was looking promising still. It'd be great to walk on the beach, maybe even swim. She'd ask Felicity to go with her but she didn't like her chances of getting her mum to go that far from home and she could ask her nan but she knew Hazel wouldn't go.

Greta rolled to her other side and stared into the dark. She'd been tired earlier but now she was wide awake, restless, as if she was expecting something to happen but she didn't know what.

thirty

Hazel had just finished her evening meal and cleaned up when her phone rang. She glanced at the clock. June usually rang at this hour so it was a surprise to see Felicity's name on the screen.

"Bloody Ian," her daughter yelled before she could even say hello.

"What's he done?"

"He's told the neighbours he's left me."

"Well, I suppose—"

"At least, he's told Les and Sal from across the road. I don't know about the rest of the street. I've just had Les over here saying how sorry he was and if there's anything he could do to let him know."

"That was kind of him," Hazel spoke quickly to get a word in.

"Kind! He was wearing his lycra, Mum!"

Hazel smiled. It was the first time Felicity had called her 'mum' since the revelation of her adoption.

"I wouldn't have even opened the door but he must have seen me put the bin out. It's mortifying. I didn't know what to say. I've not noticed before but he's got the strangest smile. Said to call him any time of the day *or night*. Gave me the creeps. Why would he come over on his own? You'd think Sal would be the one to come, not Les."

"Perhaps she wasn't home. I'm sure he was just being friendly."

"Too friendly. Ian's only just left me." There was a pause and the sound of Felicity sipping something. "I had to talk to someone and Greta…well, she wouldn't understand and I think she's avoiding me. Ian's probably poisoning her against me."

"I'm sure he isn—"

"Have you had men calling since Dad died?"

"Oh yes, hundreds of them. Some are lined up outside as we speak."

There was a brief silence then Felicity huffed. "All right, I get it, you think I'm overreacting but you didn't see him. Prancing on my doorstep in his tight clothes. I never know where to look. At least Ian's lycra protects his modesty. Not that I give a damn."

"How did you get on today? Did you go outside besides to get the bin?"

"I walked around the backyard. Pulled out some weeds."

"It was a lovely day. I did some gardening as well."

"Did you?" Once more there was silence and the sound of sipping.

"Have you had dinner?"

"Yes, leftovers. You?"

Hazel glanced towards her kitchen. She hadn't felt like cooking after her afternoon in the garden. She'd heated some baked beans and had them on toast. "Leftovers like you." Once again it wasn't a real lie. She'd had a few spoonsful from the can with her egg for breakfast.

"We should eat together again."

Hazel sucked in a breath. "I'd like that."

"I think you'll have to come here though. I'm not sure I can... well, the drive..."

Hazel wanted to howl. She'd missed Felicity so much and even though her daughter wasn't in a good state right now at least they were talking and, by the sound of it, continuing to see each other.

"What are you doing for Easter?" she asked.

"When's Easter?"

"This coming weekend."

"Oh." There was a forced laugh. "I don't have any plans."

"Perhaps we could spend it together."

Felicity didn't answer. There was another sipping sound. "Maybe."

Hazel's optimism ebbed at the lack of commitment in Felicity's response but she didn't press her. They'd come a long way in a short time.

"Thanks for listening, Mum. Sorry I raved on. I'm feeling calmer now."

Hazel hoped it was because of their chat and not the wine she assumed her daughter was drinking. "Anytime you want to let off steam you can call me."

"Thanks. Goodnight."

Hazel had just put down the phone and turned on the television when it rang again. It had to be June. But this time when Hazel picked up her phone it was Greta's name on the screen.

"Hello, darling," she said.

"Hi, Nan. I hear we're catching up over Easter."

"Are we?"

"I've just had Aunty June chewing my ear."

"Oh." Hazel winced.

"Yes, oh! Evidently we're sorting Grandad's books."

"I was going to talk to you about that."

"Don't worry. I didn't blow your story."

Hazel let out a breath. "June was pushing me to sort the books and I'm tired of her bossing me about."

"I don't blame you but do you really want to spend Easter looking through old books?"

"No, I—"

"Joe's going to be busy helping his family all weekend. How about coming on a little holiday with me?"

Hazel's spirits lifted immediately. "I'd love to but where would we go?"

"Don't worry, I know a place. I'm wondering though if you might be able to help me think of a way to get Mum to join us."

"Oh, Greta, wouldn't that be wonderful."

"It's about a three-and-a-half-hour drive to where I'm taking you. We could set off early Friday morning. Your job is to work out how to get Mum to come with us."

"All right."

"Great. I'll talk to you again soon."

Hazel hugged the phone to her chest. She didn't have to spend her long weekend avoiding June and Derek. She was going on a holiday. The only problem was Felicity. She'd hardly left the house since Ian had moved out. But maybe a holiday would enthuse her. The phone in her hand rang again and this time June's name lit up the screen. She could ignore it but then June would probably be around knocking on her door.

She drew in a breath and accepted the call.

"Hello, Mum, I've been talking to Greta," June said. "Seeing she's going to help you with the books over the weekend I thought we could all meet at your place. Saturday suits us. I can

bring a quiche for lunch. Do you think you could make something for sweets? It'll give you something to do before Saturday
and everyone loves your cake and biscuits."

Hazel was gripping her phone so tightly her wrist ached.

"You and Derek don't need to come," she said with all the
authority she could muster. "It won't take four of us to sort
through a few old books."

"Derek says they need to be treated with care, Mum. He was
worried when you said you'd tossed them in boxes."

"I didn't toss them." She hadn't done anything with them
yet, not that June knew that. "I don't think Saturday suits me
either. I'll let you know what day does. Thanks for ringing, June.
Goodnight."

Hazel jabbed at the end call button. Derek and June were very
interested in those blasted books. Perhaps they were worth more
than she'd imagined. And if they were, June and Derek wouldn't
be getting whatever money they'd fetch.

Her phone pinged again, this time with a voice message. She
was surprised to see it was from Jack, and even more surprised
when she listened to his message.

"Hello Hazel. It's Jack, err...you know...I'm your movie and
lunch friend. Sorry to leave a message. Can't reach you. Make sure
you hold off making any further financial decisions until I speak
to you next week."

Hazel listened a second time, both perplexed and intrigued by
his message. What on earth did it mean? Had he won the lotto
and was going to share it with her? If only. She put her phone
down.

It was the thought of money that sent her into the office. With
the light of a higher watt bulb the room was much brighter. The
curtains she'd made from some royal blue plush fabric she'd found

at Spotlight had helped give the room some colour and warmth and she'd taken down Franklyn's ghastly old gilt-framed pictures of English countryside and put up one she liked. It was a large floral abstract print with beautiful hues of pink and blue and yellow. Felicity had been going to throw it out when she'd moved house, said it wouldn't suit the new place, and Hazel had kept it. Franklyn didn't like it, of course, so she'd hung it in the spare bedroom but now it was opposite the desk, so when she looked up from her sewing machine she could enjoy it. The room felt so much more like hers now.

She sat behind the desk, switched on the computer then studied the bookshelves while she waited for it to start up. She hoped Greta might be able to throw some light on the potential value of the books Franklyn had collected.

*

Alice was vacuuming the spare bedrooms. It was a silly thing to be doing at eight o'clock at night but she'd been so excited after Greta's call, she couldn't settle to watching TV. When Greta had asked if she could come to stay for a few days over Easter, Alice had immediately given her an emphatic yes. Then Greta had said she'd planned to bring both Hazel and Felicity with her but she'd warned Alice she wasn't sure how it was all going to work. Greta hadn't told Hazel it was Alice's place they were taking a holiday in and she'd said Felicity wasn't even aware of their plans yet but she was determined to make it happen. She'd said something about enough secrets in the family and how it was time to clear them out.

The word family was the one Alice had clung to. If their visit worked out, perhaps they'd come on a regular basis. How she'd love that and it would be wonderful to use the space her home offered. There were three bedrooms upstairs and two bathrooms, and the living area at the front had a beautiful view over the bay. So did the main bedroom beside it. The curtains were drawn but in the daylight, when they were open, you could see the bay from the bed. She'd offer this room to Hazel…her sister.

On top of the chest of drawers she'd put two framed photos. The first was of Hazel and Alice at the Seekers concert. After her return from Adelaide she'd dug out a couple of old frames and slipped the photos inside, placing them side by side, thinking it might truly be the last time they'd be together. Now a glimmer of hope buzzed inside her.

She picked up the second frame, which held a photo taken of the two of them on Hazel's wedding day. It wasn't one of the official photos, there weren't many of those, but this one of the two sisters smiling demurely at the camera had been snapped by Hazel's flatmate. Thank goodness for Caroline or Alice would have no photos of the two of them together. She studied their young faces, so excited for the future.

Alice had been in awe of her new brother-in-law. In her eyes he'd been Prince Charming – tall, dark and handsome, so solicitous in his manner with Hazel and even Alice then. After the wedding it had all changed. It was as if Franklyn had come back from the honeymoon a different man – in his manner towards Alice, at least. With Hazel he still acted in a considerate and loving manner but he became authoritarian with Alice, always wanting to know who she talked to at school, where she went, what she did. Not that she was ever anywhere much other than school or home unless she was with Hazel.

Once Hazel was going to be out in the afternoon after school and she'd given Alice the money to buy a milkshake. Alice had stopped at a milk bar on the way home with her schoolfriends.

When she got home Franklyn was there and he'd questioned her at length as to her whereabouts, intimated that she'd been doing something bad. He'd frightened her with his angry tirade and she'd cried, which seemed to give him some satisfaction. Then he'd banned her from going outside the house the following weekend, except to church.

Hazel had come home, seen Alice's distress and explained to Franklyn she'd given her permission but he was having none of it. Alice had been sent to her room. Through the crack in the door she'd heard him tell Hazel that as her husband, Franklyn was Alice's guardian and had a duty to make sure she was not led astray. It was Hazel's duty to support his wishes. Later that night, when Franklyn had been taking a bath, Hazel had slipped into her room with some food. "He just wants what's best for you," she'd said and hugged Alice tight. "Everything will be all right."

But it hadn't. That had been the start of the end, as Alice remembered it. The next night after dinner, Franklyn had told Alice to clear up and wash the dishes – not that she minded, she'd always helped Hazel but he sent her to do it alone. It was that way every night from then on. He and Hazel would sit in the lounge and read, listen to music or watch TV together and after Alice was done she had to spend the evening alone in her room.

Hazel deferred to Franklyn from then on but the highlights of Alice's life after that were when she and Hazel were home together. They'd cook, go for walks, sunbake in the backyard or play their favourite records on Franklyn's player and dance around the lounge. That was the sister she had kept locked in her heart.

Alice gazed again at the photo, took a cloth from her cleaning basket and polished the already gleaming glass then replaced it on top of the chest. She looked from one photo to the other, moved away then came back, picked them up and decided to put them away. She didn't want to overwhelm Hazel with old memories too soon. It might be better to save the photos until after they'd settled in.

Alice wondered if Hazel had told her family why they'd become estranged. It would be her version and not the truth but that wasn't Hazel's fault. She'd been deceived by Franklyn just as Alice had been. A shiver ran down her spine. It was cooler in the upstairs rooms. Even though April days were often sunny and warm, the overnight temperatures were beginning to require extra layers. But it wasn't just the cooler air that made her skin prickle. She badly wanted to reunite with her sister but even though Franklyn was dead Alice knew it wouldn't be easy. There were still some awful truths that needed to be exposed and rather than the reconciliation she prayed for, they might instead be blown apart once more.

thirty-one

The knock on the front door came again. "Mrs Lewis?" The man's voice was deep and commanding. Felicity pressed herself to the wall in the hallway. Those jolly horses had been quiet for days but they thudded in her chest now. She was being perverse but there was no way she was letting the real estate agent in. She jumped as he tapped on the bedroom window and called again. All the curtains were closed so there was no way he could see in but she felt exposed all the same.

She began to inch her way towards the back of the house then froze at the sound of her phone ringing. It was faint, coming from somewhere under the jumble of cushions and books on the couch in the family room. She didn't think the man outside would be able to hear it but she held her breath all the same then flinched when she heard him talking and then mention her name. It must have been her number he was calling, he was leaving her a message. Damn Ian, he must have given the agent her number.

Dolly strolled along the hall towards her and let out a plaintive miaow. Felicity scooped her up and pressed against the wall again as another knock thumped on the door.

"I know you're home, Mrs Lewis. I will have to come back at some stage so you might as well let me in now."

Felicity pressed her face to Dolly. "Not by the hair on my chinny chin chin," she whispered.

Dolly struggled in her arms, jumped down and stalked back towards the kitchen.

Only when she saw a shadow cross the glass beside the door did Felicity move. She scurried into the bedroom. By pressing her cheek to the wall and lining up one eye with the thin space between the curtain and the window, she had a good view of her driveway. She'd practised it many times and could see quite a lot without moving the curtains at all. A man in a suit was climbing into a sleek black Mercedes. She watched him sit in the driver's seat with the window down, looking at the house and talking, obviously making another call. Her phone wasn't ringing so he wasn't leaving her another message. She'd barely thought it when she heard the faint ring tone of her phone again. Or perhaps he was. She pulled away from the wall and listened till it stopped. When she lined her eye up with the gap again she saw the black car backing out the driveway.

She blew out a long breath, went back to the family room, shut the door to the hall behind her and rummaged for her phone. It was under the plate she'd eaten a snack from as she'd read her book waiting for the agent's arrival. There was a missed call and a message from an unknown number and then a few minutes later one from Ian. The bloody agent must have rung him.

"Tattletale," she said and deleted both messages without listening to them.

She looked at the clock. It was only four. She shouldn't start drinking this early but she felt like celebrating her victory, even if it was a small one. As the agent had said, he'd be back, but at least she hadn't made it easy for him.

She went to the fridge and took out the wine bottle she'd opened the night before. It was still half full so she was cutting back and today she felt she'd turned a small corner in her...what would she call it? Her new way of life. She took a glass from the cupboard and poured in the wine.

"Here's to a good day."

Dolly stopped licking her leg and stared at her.

"It has been a good day, hasn't it, Doll?"

Felicity hadn't got as far as sleeping in her bed again but she had used the en suite this morning and had showered as soon as she'd eaten breakfast. That was partly because she'd been woken by a Skype call at seven o'clock from Suzie who was in Sacramento, California. Suzie had been full of excitement, babbling with news of their road trip across America and giggling every time she said Salt Lake City in a staccato voice; they'd seen *The Book of Mormon* together the previous year. Suzie looked vibrant and fresh on the small screen while Felicity tried to hold her own phone at arm's length so her friend wouldn't get a clear look at her. She'd done her best to be upbeat in return, telling Suzie she hadn't done much because she'd been laid low with the flu, which explained away her dishevelled appearance.

She'd only just had time to make herself some breakfast when Tony had rung and asked if she'd come with him to look at the building he wanted to put an offer on. It had a shop front, a flat and a yard with a lock-up shed. Evidently the shed was the best part of it. The building was a mess but the structure was sound and he planned to renovate it as his office and live in the flat. He'd wanted her opinion and it was only a suburb away. She was flattered but she'd said no, of course. It would've meant going out and she still wasn't ready for that but she'd been interested in the project. She'd told Tony about the photo portfolio she'd made for him and he'd said he'd drop in to check it out later this evening.

Apart from that she'd fobbed off another call from Melody and lied to Pam again that she still wasn't up to tennis – it wasn't really a lie, she wasn't at all able to resume tennis, it was the reason why that wasn't the truth. She was still using the getting-over-the-flu excuse but it was fast approaching its use-by date.

She sat her glass back on the coffee table and got up. The glass was nearly empty, she needed to slow it down.

*

Hazel sat back from the computer with a sigh. It didn't matter which way she shifted the figures around in Greta's spreadsheet, the bottom line was always the same. After she'd accounted for all her regular outgoing expenses there was very little left from the incoming. She'd had to dip into her meagre savings a couple of times to pay bills already and she didn't want to deplete what was her only bit of emergency money any further. At least the first of the allowance payments after the sale of Franklyn's cars had been transferred and that, with the bereavement allowance, meant she could cover her expenses but only just. She'd have to economise further. She could see from her spreadsheet that the private health insurance would have to go, perhaps even the car.

Greta's offer of a holiday and Hazel's visit to Felicity had been the catalyst for the revisit to the spreadsheet. After spending the previous Sunday afternoon with Felicity, she had realised her daughter was in a much worse place financially than Hazel was. She had no income and no job and Ian wanted to sell the house out from under her. If he did, Felicity would end up with half the money, of course, but it could take a while and then she'd have to find somewhere else to live. Whatever her share of the sale of the house, it wouldn't last her long once she found another place to live.

Hazel wished she could offer her some financial assistance but there was little she could do, in fact nothing when she looked at the red numbers at the bottom of the spreadsheet.

And then there was Greta's holiday. Hazel hadn't worked out how to broach that subject with Felicity yet. If they went, Hazel wasn't going to allow Greta to pay for everything. There'd be fuel and accommodation, meals. Hazel was determined to pay her share but there was still time to back out if it looked like the cost would be too much.

★

Two hours later Felicity was pouring her second glass of wine when she got a text from Tony to say he was out the front and coming in.

She giggled. He made it sound as if he was on a police raid. She got to the door just as he knocked.

"I've brought Thai takeaway," he said and lifted a bag into the air. "I hope you're hungry because I think I've over-catered."

"I am, thank you."

"I haven't eaten since breakfast." He followed her to the kitchen. "I thought we could eat while I show you the photos I took of the place I'm interested in."

Felicity set placemats and cutlery on the table and then some plates while Tony took the lids off the containers.

"Would you like some wine?" She waved a hand at her glass.

He wrinkled his nose. "I didn't think to stop for beer."

"I have beer." She went into the pantry where there was a second fridge and brought out three different types. "Party leftovers," she said holding them in the air.

He pointed to the bottle of pale ale. She put the other bottles on the bench, picked up her glass of wine and joined him at the table.

Her mouth watered at the delicate aromas wafting from the open containers. "I love Thai food."

"That's good. This restaurant was near my last job for the day. I haven't bought from them before. I hope it's okay."

"Delicious," Felicity mumbled through her first mouthful of chicken larb. There was silence for a while as they ate.

Finally she asked him how the property inspection had gone. Tony took his tablet from his battered backpack. Several papers drifted to the floor. He scooped them up and pushed them back into the bag.

"I see your filing system hasn't improved." Felicity couldn't remember how many times he'd sorted through that backpack for an invoice or a list during the renovations.

Tony shrugged. "I can't afford a secretary *and* a new office."

"You won't have either if these photos are anything to go by." Felicity had started to scroll through his images. The building had been derelict for a long time by the look of it. There was rubbish as if someone had used it as an overnight shelter, graffiti on the walls and the windows had been boarded up.

"It's going for a fire-sale price."

"I'm not surprised," Felicity said as she took in what had possibly once been a set of stairs but was now barely more than a few rails dangling from parts of a plaster wall with large chunks missing.

"I was sure you'd see the potential. You're so good at that."

"I've renovated one house and this place was at least habitable." Felicity looked at another picture of a large room, empty but for the rubbish in a corner. She zoomed in on the cement floor. "Has someone had a fire in it?"

"I think just to keep warm and not for ages. It's been boarded up so no-one can get in now. The front and back doors are original and very solid. It's in a good location."

"So you said." She smiled at the concern on his face as he studied her.

"If you'd go with me to have a look…"

Felicity put the tablet back on the table and poured herself more wine.

He watched her, fiddled with his bottle then cleared his throat. "I know it's not my business but you can't stay inside forever. The sooner you try to get back into life the easier it will be. Trust me, I know." He drained the last of his beer.

Felicity plucked up his empty bottle. "Would you like another?"

"Thanks."

She got it for him then, anxious to steer the conversation away from her, she opened up the portfolio of photos she'd created. "I want you to look at this. I've used pictures from your various jobs. I've set it up by rooms, so some don't have many photos, depending on the job, but you've got quite a few bathroom shots. I also set up a section that shows before and after. That's only got photos of this house because I had the before photos, but in the future you could take them before you start. It gives people some vision for the possibilities." She'd begun to babble. She pressed her lips shut, watching Tony's reaction as he scrolled through the various sections.

Finally he shook his head. "This is amazing. You make it look so easy."

"It is for me but I also enjoy it. Years of practice manager experience has helped – I had to be the IT guru too. It was sink or swim and I decided to swim." Felicity wondered how she'd done it now. She'd been much younger, of course, had still thought anything was possible. How had she lost that optimism?

"We could add before and after shots of my new office and apartment."

Felicity nearly choked on her wine. "How many years till the after shots?"

"It won't take me that long and I haven't got anything else to do with my weekends. I'm going to borrow a caravan from my mate and put it in the backyard so I can live on-site as soon as I get the back bathroom done." Passion blazed in his eyes.

Just because her dreams had been shattered she had no right to dampen his.

"Good on you."

"Maybe you'll help me with decorating ideas."

"I'd love to." Felicity didn't have to fake enthusiasm for that. And now that her house was finished, and she recalled the determined real estate agent's visit, in more ways than one it would be good to have another project to work on.

"I would pay you, of course."

"Don't be ridiculous, I'm not a trained interior designer."

"I trust your taste and I'd have to pay someone."

"We'll see." She glanced at the dog-eared pages sticking out of his bag. "You'd be better to spend the money on some account-keeping software. Your backpack and a spreadsheet aren't enough to cope with all the things you have to juggle."

Tony groaned. "Perhaps you could do that for me too."

"Don't be silly, it's easy to set up then it's easy to keep track of."

"For you, maybe."

"I could recommend something. Perhaps set it up for you."

She jumped at the sound of the front door being flung open.

"Felicity!"

"Damn!" She'd forgotten to slide the safety chain across after she'd let Tony in. She didn't even have time to get up from the table before Ian burst into the room. His face was distorted with anger.

"Why didn't you let—" He stopped as soon as he saw Tony. "What are you doing here?"

Tony stood up. "Hello, Ian." He held out his hand. "Haven't seen you in a while."

"No. I've moved out, in case Felicity hasn't told you." Ian's scowl deepened and he ignored Tony's hand as he looked over the table with the takeaway food containers, the wine and the beer. "Or maybe she has."

"What do you mean by that comment?" Felicity snapped.

"Thanks for your help, Felicity." Tony gathered up his things. "I'll get going."

"Ian, that was very rude," Felicity said.

His shoulders drooped. "I'm sorry, Tony. I...there's no need to rush off. I'm not staying."

"That's okay." Tony slung his bag over his shoulder. "You two need to talk and I have some work to do."

Felicity glared at Ian as she walked Tony to the door.

"I'm sorry, Tony," she said.

"Don't be." His lips turned up in a tiny smile. "I do understand what you're going through. It's an emotional time but please think about what I said. You need to face the world sometime. If it helps to do that with a friend, I can be there."

Her heart nearly broke at his kindness. She'd never really thought of Tony as a friend. He was the bloke who'd been in charge of the renovations but that had taken time and she supposed he had become a friend.

"Thanks. You don't need to worry about me." She waved him off but instead of shutting the door she stood and waited.

Eventually Ian came to see where she was. "What are you doing?"

"Waiting for you to leave."

"This is my house too, Felicity."

"In name only." She folded her arms across her chest. "You made it quite clear you didn't like it and that you were leaving it and me."

"I've made another time for the agent," he said. "The afternoon of Good Friday. I'll be with him so you don't have to be here."

Her insides turned to molten lava but she gritted her teeth tightly and said nothing.

"I've found a flat to rent and I'm going to move in over Easter so I'll get the rest of my clothes while I'm here. And some sheets and towels."

Felicity was pressing her arms so firmly around her chest she was having difficulty breathing. Across the road she saw the front curtains move.

"Your friend Les was over here offering his assistance." The words hissed out between her clenched teeth.

"I know you asked me not to say anything yet but he kept ringing me to go for a ride. I had to tell him."

She flung out her arms. "Just leave, Ian."

He nodded. "Friday afternoon. Please yourself if you're here or not."

He'd barely moved across the threshold when she slammed the door shut with such force her new chain lock swung out and put a dent in the paintwork.

"Bastard!" she yelled then pressed her hand to her mouth as the pressure inside her released itself as large salty tears streaming down her cheeks.

thirty-two

It was seven o'clock on Thursday night when Greta pulled into her mum's driveway, Hazel already beside her in the passenger seat. The front light was on but went off as soon as Greta stopped the car.

"This was a good idea of yours," Hazel said. "Coming in the dark."

"Hmm." Greta still wasn't convinced Felicity would actually leave the house. She'd had several chats with Hazel about it and Alice as well. It had been Alice's suggestion they travel at night. They'd leave Adelaide in the dark and arrive at Marion Bay in the dark. Felicity was leaving one safe house for another. Alice had also thought the worst of the long weekend traffic would be over.

Not that Greta had told either of the other women that it had been Alice's idea nor that they were staying at her house. They wouldn't discover that until tomorrow morning. Greta hoped she was doing the right thing. Joe had been sceptical and he was the only other person who knew, besides Alice. He'd thought the whole thing could blow up in her face and then it would be a long, painful drive back to Adelaide.

This morning there'd been a frantic phone call from Felicity saying she wouldn't go if Hazel was going. She'd said it was too much for her to manage, leaving the house and being with Hazel. She could only cope with one if she didn't have to deal with the other. Greta had talked her down from that precipice but goodness knows what she'd face when she went inside.

"Don't worry so much." Hazel ran a hand across Greta's brow. It was warm and soothing. "I think once Felicity does this it will be the start of her getting back to normal."

Greta opened her door then reached up and flicked off the interior light.

"Good idea." Hazel turned to get out.

"Why don't you wait here, Nan." Greta could feel Hazel's penetrating look even though she couldn't see her eyes in the gloom. "We won't be long."

"All right." Hazel sat back and shut her door.

When Greta stepped up to the front door she found it ajar and beyond it the house was in darkness. She glanced over her shoulder, she couldn't see Hazel in the dark car but knew she'd be watching. She pushed the door open slowly. It made a low creaking noise as it swung, making her feel like she was in a spy movie. There was a bag beside the door and an esky but no sign of her mother.

"Mum," she whispered then cleared her throat and called louder, "Mum!"

"I'm here," came a muffled reply.

Greta's eyes adjusted to the half-light in the house, thrown from the streetlights and the almost full moon. Felicity came forward, her face pressed to the cat she held in her arms. Greta's confidence ebbed a little more. Felicity had used Dolly as one of her excuses not to leave.

She reached out to pat the cat. "Did you organise Melody to feed her?" Dolly wasn't an outside cat, making only brief forays into the backyard.

"Yes," Felicity said. "She doesn't like dealing with the litter tray but Ian can do that tomorrow and then we'll be back Monday, won't we?"

Greta nodded. So far so good – her dad bringing the real estate agent to look at the house had been another card Greta had played to get her mum out. Ian had rung asking for help to make sure Felicity didn't make a fuss when he brought the agent over. Greta had thought her mum not being there at all would be better for everyone.

"You be good while I'm gone and remember our agreement." Felicity kissed the top of the cat's head and turned to put her back through the family room door.

"What agreement?" Greta eyed Dolly as she strolled off.

"She's promised to bite the agent when he comes."

Greta shook her head.

"I suppose you've brought Hazel," Felicity said.

"Yes. I really hope you're going to try to connect again, Mum."

"We've talked but for now I don't think there's much else we can say."

"You have to make an effort."

Felicity sighed. "I'll try."

"Good." Greta gave her a quick hug.

"Can you take my things to the car? I'll shut the door behind you and come round the back way. I want to make sure it's all secure before I go."

"Is everything all right?" Hazel called through the door.

"Yes, we're coming," Greta said.

They all met at the front door.

"Hello, Felicity," Hazel said.

"I was just giving Dolly a farewell."

"Right, well, time's a-wasting." Hazel spoke in a nasal drawl.

"Yes, we should hit the road, Jack," Felicity shot back.

Greta looked from one to the other thinking she'd swapped her spy movie for some kind of American road-trip adventure.

Felicity put one hand on the front door while Greta bent to pick up the esky.

"Hell, what have you got in here? It weighs a ton."

"Supplies," Felicity said.

"You do know Nan's already packed a pile of food and we're only going for a few days."

Hazel picked up the overnight bag and Felicity waved. "I'll be out the side gate in a minute."

Greta was still playing Tetris with all the bags and eskies in the boot when Felicity shot from the side of the house and into the back of the car, slamming the door quickly behind her. Greta shut the boot and opened the other passenger door. Felicity was sunk down in the seat on the opposite side, her eyes closed.

"The light's not on," Greta said. "And this bag will have to go on the seat beside you, I can't fit it in."

Felicity peeled one eye open and then the other. "It'll be fine."

"My car has a bigger boot." Hazel turned from the front seat. "We could go back that way and swap."

"No," Greta said. She was already feeling tired after a busy day at work and anxious with anticipation at how this holiday was going to work out. There was no way she wanted to make the journey stretch out any longer. "Mum's got plenty of room."

"I'm fine." Felicity said. A car drove past in the street and she hunched down further.

Greta shut the door and climbed into the driver's seat. She couldn't believe they were actually doing this.

"We're just like Thelma and Louise but with an extra," Hazel said, and pulled out a bag of FruChocs.

"As long as we don't have the police chase and the bleak ending," Felicity said in a muffled voice.

Greta had no idea what they were going on about but at least her mum was talking to Hazel. As she backed down the drive Greta caught a glimpse of Felicity in the rear-view mirror. She'd wound her scarf over her head and part of her face so that only her eyes were showing. She took one of the chocolates Hazel offered and slipped her hand under the scarf to put it in her mouth.

Greta also accepted one of the chocolate-coated fruit balls, put the car into drive and moved off down the street. They were on their way without the drama she'd thought Felicity might create but she was still worried about what she'd got herself into.

Her concern resurfaced as they approached Port Wakefield. Hazel had packed a thermos and all the makings for tea or coffee along with some chocolate-chip biscuits – the FruChocs had gone before they left Adelaide. The plan had been to pull into a parking bay so Greta could stretch her legs and they'd have a cup of tea but Felicity announced she needed a toilet stop and a proper coffee. Greta drove around to the back of the service station. Felicity slunk from the car and made a dash for their outside loos while Greta went inside and bought the coffee. She decided to get one for herself so it was only Hazel who had the tea.

Once they were all settled in the car again, Hazel chatted to Greta until Felicity said she had a headache and would they just be quiet. Not long after that Felicity went to sleep and then eventually Hazel did too. Greta was left to navigate the last of the journey on her own.

It was almost midnight when she pulled into the long narrow driveway beside the large two-storey house. She'd missed the turn-off to Marion Bay in the dark and then had taken a few wrong turns before she found the address she hoped was Alice's. There was a light on over a door on the side that looked like it was the main entrance. She could see the number matched with the one Alice had given her. If this was Alice's place it was certainly much newer and bigger than she'd imagined.

Hazel stirred in the seat beside her but there was only silence from the back seat.

"We're here," Greta said softly.

Hazel took a deep breath and stretched. Greta got out of the car and shivered. After the cocoon of the warm car, the night air was chilly. Alice had said she'd leave a key under the mat. Greta stepped up onto the deck that appeared to stretch across the front of the house and then down the side to the door. There was indeed a key under the mat. She unlocked the door and stuck her head in. No sign of anyone. Alice had said she'd be in her downstairs bedroom out of the way and to take everyone straight upstairs. They'd both thought it best to wait until morning to tell Hazel and Felicity where they were.

There was one light on over the stairs, enough to see the large open-plan living area across the front of the house with a well set-out kitchen overlooking it.

Hazel followed her inside. "What a beautiful holiday house. Are you sure your friend said you could have it for no cost?"

"I'll leave her a thank you gift."

Hazel yawned.

"You go straight upstairs and pick a room. Al…my friend thought you might like the front one. Evidently it has a view over the bay," Greta said.

"You should have it then."

Greta was too tired to haggle over bedrooms. "You decide which room you'd like and I'll bring up the bags."

"I can help."

"No!" Greta smiled to cover her sharp reaction. "It won't take me long and I don't want you carrying bags up those stairs."

"I'm not an invalid," Hazel huffed but she headed for the stairs anyway.

By the time Greta had unloaded and made two trips up and down the stairs she was wishing she was in her bed already. She opened the back door of her car to retrieve the last bag. Felicity was sitting up, her eyes wide, peering towards the house.

"We're here," Greta said.

"There's so much glass."

"It's a beach house, Mum, with views of the bay. You'll be able to see it in the light tomorrow."

"It's like a goldfish bowl, people can see in."

Greta forced a smile and held out her hand. "Come on. I'll take you in and whip you upstairs. You can hop straight into bed and under the covers. The bedroom Nan has picked for you is at the back of the house and only has one small window up high."

"That's odd, isn't it?"

Greta sighed. "I don't think so, Mum. I guess it's so you don't peer down on your backdoor neighbours. It's late. Let's go inside and go to bed. Everything will be fine in the morning."

Felicity gave Greta a sceptical look but she got out of the car all the same and slipped her hand through Greta's arm.

Once both the older women were safely tucked up in the back bedrooms – Hazel had insisted Greta have the front one – she went back to the car for the eskies, locked up and switched off the stair light. She would love to have seen Alice, garnered some quick reassurance that they were doing the right thing, but it was very late and the morning would come soon enough.

At the top of the stairs Felicity beckoned her from around her partly open door. With a sigh Greta went to her mother's room.

"What's up?" she tried to keep her voice casual.

"I can't do it, Greta. I have to go home."

Greta's patience was wearing thin. "Mum, I need to get some sleep and so do you. We can talk about it in the morning. I'm sure the windows have blinds we can pull down and—"

"It's not just the house, it's Hazel. It was a mistake thinking I could spend a weekend with her."

"But Mum, you've reconciled with her."

"I wouldn't say that. She caught me at a vulnerable time, after your dad…I was at a very low point. Anyone with some compassion would have got me through that moment."

"But you talked and she told you about the adoption."

"That doesn't suddenly make fifty years of lying right," Felicity hissed.

Greta sighed. "It's the middle of the night. Can't we just get some sleep and see what tomorrow brings?"

Felicity sagged to the bed and put her head in her hands. "I'm sorry, Greta. It's all such a mess."

Greta sat beside her and put and arm around her. "Life will improve, Mum. You said yourself you were feeling much better."

"I am but then something comes over me. All I want to do is curl up in a ball and hide. I've no power to stop it, Greta." Tears brimmed in her eyes. "What if I never go back to being the person I was?"

"Oh, Mum, you will. When we go home you'll start seeing the counsellor."

"What if she can't help me?"

"What if she can?" Greta hugged her mum tighter and stifled a yawn.

"I'm so sorry. You must be exhausted. You're right – I'm sure things will look brighter in the morning."

Felicity kissed Greta's cheek and bundled her through the door.

In her room a bedside lamp gave a welcoming glow, as had been the case in the other two bedrooms. Greta barely had the energy to strip off her clothes and into her pjs. She didn't wash her face or even clean her teeth but slid straight between the sheets. Immediately her eyes grew heavy as she sank into the luxury of the most comfortable bed. She gave another brief thought to her mum and her nan and what lay ahead in the morning. She'd either created the perfect holiday or the perfect storm.

★

Felicity paced the space around the modest queen bed. The room wasn't large – ten steps took her from one bedside table to the other. There was a small chest of drawers against the wall at the foot end of the bed, a hatstand with hangers and the only other furniture was a single chair where she'd piled the clothes she'd taken off. Her bag was on the floor, open but not unpacked – she'd only pulled out her nightie – and the remaining floor space was the walking path she was taking around the bed.

She stopped at the end of the bed and sat, staring at the door. Greta had left it ajar but Felicity had shut it. With the blind pulled on the high window above the bed the room felt cell-like and pressed in on her but she didn't have the courage to go beyond it. Greta had shown her the bathroom just outside the door and Felicity knew Hazel was in the room that shared a wall with hers but the rest of the house had been a blur to her groggy eyes and frantic brain.

Why had she let Hazel and Greta talk her into this? She began her circuit of the bed again. She could only imagine the horror of the next morning. She'd seen a few beach houses like this one before. The whole front of the house was glass and during the day it was so open and filled with light you'd need your sunglasses.

"Damn!" she muttered and grabbed up her handbag from beside the bed.

She tipped the contents onto the vibrantly coloured doona and spread everything out with her fingers. There were no sunglasses. She thought back over her last few hours at home. She'd packed her bag before she'd set to work on her surprise for Ian – what had she done with her sunglasses? They were usually in her handbag but she'd not needed her handbag these last few weeks. She'd used the glasses though, when she went out into the backyard. In her mind she pictured her kitchen and the bowl where the keys went. She'd got into the habit of putting her sunglasses in there.

"Damn," she said again. Staying in this glass house was a big mistake and without sunglasses it would be unbearable. She began to pace the room again. Greta would be rested in the morning; she'd have to take her home.

*

Hazel was curled up in one of the two single beds, staring into the darkness. After falling asleep in the car, she was now wide awake. The bed was very comfortable and the room sparsely furnished as she'd have expected for holiday accommodation.

Greta had been vague about who the place belonged to. Even though there'd only been the light from the stairs, Hazel had got a bit of a look at the bottom floor. It was well fitted out and homey for a holiday house. There were indoor plants and a shelf

of well-used recipe books with one propped open and some uten-
sils beside it as if someone was about to cook. Further into the
gloom of the sitting area she'd seen a partly done jigsaw, a vase
of flowers and some framed photographs, all things that could be
there to welcome guests or because an owner was not far away.
Had Greta's friends vacated just for them?

Hazel imagined accommodation here, wherever here was,
would be at a premium over Easter and school holidays. Greta
hadn't named the town, just that they would get a lovely surprise
when they woke up and saw the sea. Hazel knew they were somewhere in the southern part of Yorke Peninsula; she'd been awake
when they'd gone through Minlaton but must have dozed off
soon after because the next thing she'd known was the car stopping in the driveway.

She thought back over her conversations with Greta since the
holiday had been suggested. It had all happened quickly. Hazel
had jumped at the chance to escape Adelaide for a few days and
also to spend time with Felicity who she hoped would enjoy the
break too.

But Felicity's behaviour towards her ran hot and cold and Hazel
couldn't help but hear the murmured conversation between Greta
and Felicity from the room next door. Felicity had made it clear
she wasn't keen on spending so much time with Hazel either. The
anger she'd heard in Felicity's voice had pierced Hazel all over
again and, just like the day of the will reading, she felt a terrible
sense of loss. She rolled onto her back, staring up at the ceiling,
overwhelmed by a sense of foreboding that she couldn't shake.

thirty-three

Greta woke to bright sunlight streaming around the edges of the curtains. She squinted, trying to think where she was, then shot bolt upright. Alice's house. She flung herself out of the bed looking for her phone to check the time. It was in the back pocket of the jeans lying in a jumble of clothes on the floor. Eight o'clock. Damn, she'd slept in. She'd hoped to be up before Hazel and Felicity so that she could talk to Alice alone. She paused to listen. There were no sounds from within the house or beyond. Either the room was soundproof or no-one else was up either.

She dressed quickly and peered out her bedroom door. Felicity's door was shut and Hazel's slightly ajar. Once more she paused to listen. There was no sound from upstairs but she could hear movement from the floor below and as she reached the stairs the most delicious smell wafted to greet her. It was warm and spicy like…Greta reached the bottom of the stairs just as Alice put a tray of buns onto the kitchen bench.

She smiled at Greta. "Good morning. You're just in time. I hope you like hot cross buns."

Greta nodded. She feared if she opened her mouth the moisture from her salivating would run down her chin. She swallowed. "Love them."

"Have a seat." Alice waved a hand towards the table which was covered in a yellow gingham tablecloth and had been set with cutlery and plates for four, a cheery jar of daisies and lavender sitting in the middle. "I was going to set up out on the front deck but I thought it might be better if...well, your mum might prefer to be inside and it is a bit chilly out there this morning. Would you like coffee or tea?" Alice asked as Greta sat.

"Coffee, please."

Alice put a basket of buns on the table. "I have instant or a pod machine."

"Pod, please," Greta answered in a stupor. She felt like she'd woken up in another world being waited on and treated to food that smelled so good.

"How did you sleep?" Alice asked as she prepared the coffee.

"Like a log. It was the best sleep I've had in ages."

Alice chuckled. "Roy insisted we spent money on buying decent beds. I think it's a combination of that, the quiet and the fresh sea air. Visitors usually say they sleep well."

She moved with ease around her kitchen, obviously more comfortable here than the previous times they'd met. She wore an apron over jeans and t-shirt and Greta realised the white splodges on her apron and face were flour. She looked back at the buns as Alice placed a cup of coffee in front of her.

"Did you make these?"

"Yes. I hope you don't mind homemade but I've always baked my own. On the farm I made all our bread and rolls. It was the only way to have it fresh in the early days."

"They smell divine."

"Do have one." Alice sat opposite Greta. "I'm keeping the rest warm for the others."

The thought of Felicity and Hazel joining them put a small dampener on Greta's delight.

"You got in quite late," Alice said. "Did the drive go okay?"

"Yes, it took me a bit longer than I'd anticipated. I took a few wrong turns in the dark." Greta slathered butter on the warm bun and took a bite. "Mmm, this is divine, Alice."

"I'm glad you like them." The oven timer binged and Alice got up. "I've got to drop some off at the local shop in a while."

Greta watched in amazement as Alice lined up three more trays of freshly cooked buns then turned off the oven, tidied the bench and rubbed her hands down her apron. This time her movements were twitchy, her earlier ease replaced by a dose of nerves.

Greta opened her mouth to reassure her aunt but was stopped by a sound from the stairs and then Hazel appeared.

"You found the hot cross buns I packed," she said as she crossed to the table.

"I…"

Hazel stilled as she sensed another presence. Behind her, Alice was standing rigidly at the kitchen bench.

Hazel turned and gasped. Her hands shot out to grip the back of the chair.

"Alice," she hissed then cast a disbelieving glance at Greta. "What have you done?"

"We're having a holiday, Nan." Greta's mouth had gone dry. She was glad she'd already swallowed the last piece of her bun. "Alice offered and—"

"I can't believe you'd be so deceitful." Hazel didn't look in Alice's direction again but spun on her heel and marched back up the stairs, then there was the clunk of a door closing.

"That went well," Greta said. She looked to Alice who was still staring towards the stairs, her face drooping with sorrow. "I'm sorry, Alice, but I'm sure she won't stay up there all weekend." She gave an encouraging smile. "Don't worry."

Alice came back to the table. "She's a strong-minded woman."

"I'm starting to see that," Greta said and reached for another bun. "She was always very quiet when grandad was alive but now…"

"She was determined as a young woman. Franklyn changed her."

Greta wanted to know more about that but they were interrupted by a harsh whisper.

"Greta?"

Felicity's legs appeared on the stairs.

Greta gave Alice a hopeful smile and got up. "I'm here, Mum."

Felicity moved slowly down the stairs until she was at the bottom, wincing as if she were in pain.

"Are you all right?" Alice stood too.

Surprise and then recognition crossed her face. "Alice?"

"Hello, Felicity."

"Come and sit down, Mum. Alice has made us hot cross buns for breakfast."

Felicity winced again as Greta turned towards the windows. She'd been so focused on Alice and the buns she'd hardly taken in the rest of the room. The front and part of the driveway side of the house was all glass, the blinds were up and the morning sun was streaming through. "Do you mind if we close the blinds, Alice? Mum's been a bit…she's not…" Greta didn't need to say any more; Alice was already moving towards the windows.

"Of course. I can close them altogether or we can just put down the privacy screens. They don't block the light but people can't see in."

Greta looked to her mum who was still standing on the bottom step.

"Altogether," Felicity said.

As the room darkened, she slunk across the room and onto a chair. "I could smell baking."

Greta lifted the cloth from the basket. "Alice makes her own hot cross buns."

Felicity lifted one out and put it on her plate.

"Would you like tea or coffee with it, Felicity?"

"Coffee."

Greta waited for her mum to say thank you, like you did for a child, but Felicity was busy buttering her bun.

"Mum likes pod coffee too, thank you, Alice."

Felicity looked up then as if she'd remembered something.

"Yes, thank you. Are you staying here too, Alice?"

"I live here."

Felicity turned a puzzled look to Greta. "You said we were staying somewhere that belonged to a friend."

"Since I've got to know Alice a little better, I think she is my friend."

Alice put a coffee in front of Felicity and gave Greta the warmest of smiles.

Felicity glanced around. "Where's Hazel?"

"Up in her room," Greta said.

Felicity sniffed then tucked into her breakfast. Alice packed the last three trays of buns into a large foam food container then joined them at the table again.

"So, you knew my...you knew Franklyn?" Felicity said as soon as Alice sat.

The smile slipped from Alice's face. "Yes, and your sister June, although she was only a baby when I—"

"Did you also know that I was adopted?"

The surprise on Alice's face mirrored Greta's. She had not expected her mum to blurt that out.

"No," Alice said. "I knew nothing about you. When I lost contact with Hazel there was only June."

Felicity sighed and took a mouthful of bun.

"I'm sorry I didn't get to meet you back then, Felicity, but I'm glad I have now."

"Do you have children?"

"I bore three babies, none of them survived."

"I'm sorry. Were they full term?"

"Yes. Two died soon after birth and Toby lived to eighteen months."

Greta studied Alice's face but she gave no sign of sorrow. It was as if she were just stating some facts.

"Something we almost have in common. I had three miscarriages before I had Greta."

Greta whipped her gaze from Alice to Felicity. "I didn't know that," she said.

Felicity shrugged. "We were so happy to have you I never wanted to think back on those sad times."

Greta couldn't believe there was this whole part of her mum's life she didn't know about.

"It would have been much worse for you, Alice," Felicity said. "You would have held your babies in your arms and then to lose them…"

Alice's face fell then. "My husband, Roy was my rock. We got past it together. Life goes on, you find another purpose."

"Ian, my husband, was wonderful too. He was so positive through it all. In spite of the sorrow with each loss he helped me to have hope." Felicity turned to Alice. "And now he's left me.

Says he doesn't love me any more. I don't understand what I did for that to happen and I feel as if there's nothing in my future to look forward to."

Alice reached a hand across the table and lay it on Felicity's. "Give yourself time."

Greta pressed her fingers to her mouth. The two women were talking as if she wasn't there. At that moment she felt so angry at her dad. She didn't understand it either. To her he seemed just the same as he'd always been.

"We don't always understand why but people change," Alice said gently.

"Yes, they *do*."

Everyone was startled by Hazel's sharp retort. She stood at the bottom of the stairs glaring at Alice. There'd been no sound of feet on the wooden steps.

"Have you been eavesdropping?" Felicity said.

Hazel ignored her, her gaze still locked on Alice. "Lots of things happen that are best left buried."

"Like adopting a child," Felicity snapped. "I've got a headache again. I'm going to my room." She pushed back from the table, plucked another bun from the basket, took her cup and stalked across the room.

"Would you like some paracetamol?" Hazel asked.

"No thank you." Felicity stepped around Hazel and clomped up the stairs.

There was silence until they heard her door close.

"You can see she's fragile." Hazel was glaring at Alice and once more Greta had the feeling she was invisible. "There's no point in stirring things up that are best left alone."

A phone began to ring. Alice rose and glanced from Greta to Hazel. The persistent sound of the phone dragged her attention to the kitchen. Greta noticed the old-style landline phone attached to the wall.

Alice answered it. Greta shot Hazel a pleading look but her nan simply folded her arms and stood her ground.

"I've got visitors," Alice said into the phone. "I didn't realise the time. I'll be there in five minutes." Alice hung up and turned back to them. "The local cafe sells my hot cross buns and they've got a customer waiting. I have to drop them off now." She picked up the large container she'd packed with buns. "Can you move your car please, Greta?"

"Let me drive you."

"All right, thank you. It's not far."

"Would you like to come, Nan?"

Hazel shook her head, turned and retreated back up the stairs.

Greta gave Alice an awkward smile. "I'll get my keys."

★

Hazel crossed the upstairs living space and peered through the sheer blind. Greta's car backed out and drove off. Hazel let her arms fall to her sides then. The anger and fear inside her combined with an empty stomach left her feeling sick. She lifted her gaze from the road and took in the low sandhills, the curve of beach and the sparkling blue bay. Outside it was a beautiful day but even that couldn't lift her mood.

She couldn't believe Greta had done this to her. She'd obviously kept in touch with Alice and Alice had managed to beguile her enough to help her plan this ridiculous surprise holiday. Hazel wished they'd brought her car. She would have bundled Felicity into it and driven straight home, left Greta to make her own way. There had to be a bus. Hazel thought about that. She could google it. Maybe she could catch it back home but then she'd have to leave Felicity. She couldn't imagine her daughter was up to travelling on a bus.

Hazel turned her back on the view and went to Felicity's door. She tapped softly.

"Who is it?" Felicity croaked.

Hazel opened the door and peered round it. "Me."

Felicity was in bed, propped up on pillows, a mug on the bed-side table and a book lying flat across her legs. "What do you want, Mum?"

"To check you're okay. I can't believe Greta thought this would be a good idea."

"She's a sweet, kind girl." Felicity's tone was defensive. "She would have thought she was being helpful."

"I know but—"

"I don't want to talk." Felicity picked up her book. "I'm staying in bed. Please shut the door."

Hazel did so and went back to her own room. She'd made the bed, and the bag she'd packed with such excitement for a beach holiday sat neatly repacked by the door. She hadn't thought to bring a book like Felicity. She couldn't bear to be downstairs with Alice and yet every minute she left that woman alone with Greta was dangerous. Felicity was still so fragile. Hazel sank to the bed. She was in danger of losing what family she had left. What the hell was she going to do?

thirty-four

They'd dropped off the buns and been gone for about thirty minutes when Alice directed Greta back to her house.

"Thanks for the guided tour," Greta said as she turned off the car. "Marion Bay's such a pretty place, I can see why you like living here."

"I loved the house on the farm and living there but without Roy I couldn't stay. It was too big a job. We built this place together for our retirement so it was the next step for me and I'm happy."

"You seem to know half the town. Everywhere we stopped someone said hello."

Alice chuckled. "That's the best and the worst thing about a small town. Everyone knows you and your business whether you want them to or not. Although at this time of the year the population doubles with all the tourists and I don't know any of them except perhaps a few regulars. That last couple walking the two little dogs have a holiday place just down the road."

They lapsed into silence, neither of them reaching for door handles. Alice had introduced Greta to Phoebe in the shop and they'd stopped to chat a while until Phoebe had got busy with customers then they'd done a quick tour of the town. Greta had asked questions about the town, and Alice had shown her the entrance to the nearby national park, which was popular with locals and visitors alike. They'd both avoided any mention of Hazel or Felicity.

"It's not going—"

"I'm sorry, Alice."

They smiled as they both spoke at once.

"It was always going to be a gamble bringing them here." Alice looked towards her house. "You can't force people to interact."

"I thought they'd have to," Greta said. "I didn't imagine they'd take to their rooms and not come out."

Alice sighed. "Would you like to see some photos from Hazel and my younger days?"

"I thought they'd all been destroyed in the fire."

"Yes, everything pre sixty-seven has gone but I have a few from the time I lived with Hazel."

Greta pulled her keys from the ignition. "I'd love to see them."

*

Felicity paused at the top of the stairs. Hazel had been quiet in the room next door for about half an hour and then Felicity had heard her go into the bathroom and now there was the sound of the shower running. Felicity was badly in need of another cup of coffee and she was planning on another hot cross bun too if there were any left.

She'd just reached the bottom of the stairs when the front door opened.

"Hello, again." Alice smiled and went into the kitchen.

"Are you feeling a bit better?" Greta followed Alice in and shut the door behind her.

"We were just going to have another cuppa if you'd like one," Alice said.

"Yes, thanks." Felicity stepped down to the floor. "Are there any buns left?"

"Plenty."

"They're rather nice. Much better than the bought ones."

"Thank you, Felicity. I do love to bake."

"Alice was going to show me some photos from her younger days." Greta patted the chair next to her. "Why don't you sit at the table with us?"

Felicity had been planning to slip back to her room but she was getting used to Alice's bright house. To her surprise the wild horses hadn't returned to thunder around in her chest. Perhaps the medication was kicking in. Her GP had said it would take a while to work. Whatever the reason, she felt comfortable here, no-one knew her and Greta had gone to a lot of trouble to create a nice holiday. She sat at the table.

Alice brought over a fresh round of coffee mugs then disappeared to the back of the house where Felicity assumed she had a bedroom.

When she returned she was carrying a floral box, the kind that was popular in cheap shops. Alice sat at the head of the table with Greta and Felicity on either side.

Greta raised her mug in a toast. "Here's to finding long-lost relatives."

Greta and Alice clinked mugs but Felicity left hers on the table.

"Come on, Mum." Greta looked at her expectantly. Beside her Alice's look was one of apprehension. "We're not a big family. A new aunty is rather cool, I think."

Felicity turned to Alice. "Are you truly Hazel's sister?"

Alice gave her an indulgent look then lifted the lid from the box. Almost reverently she took out several old photos, some in frames. She handed the first to Greta. "This is Hazel on her wedding day."

"Oh!" Greta squeaked. "This is Nan and Grandad." She looked up, her face glowing with excitement, and passed it to Felicity. "Nan has the same photo on her dresser."

Felicity glanced down. Her much younger mother smiled back at her from beneath a short veil that fluffed around her head and stopped at her shoulders. She wore an empire line fitted gown which sat just above her shoes and beside her Franklyn cut a dashing figure in black tails and grey pinstriped trousers. She stared at him, his features set in a proud smile, and anger swept over her. She tossed the photo back on the table.

"They could only afford a couple of official photos but I was there. I was Hazel's bridesmaid." Alice lifted a small black-and-white framed photo from the box. "I wore a cerise-pink empire line dress that fell in pleats to my shoes, which were painted the same shade of pink. Hazel's flatmate took this after we were dressed." Alice paused over the photo. "I felt like a princess," she whispered.

"You look so young."

"I was fifteen."

Felicity looked at the photo and even though there was a difference in their ages she could see a likeness between the siblings.

Alice lifted another photo from the box.

"That looks like Nan and Grandad." Greta passed it on to Felicity.

It was of the same era but in colour this time. Hazel wore a loose top that flowed out around her hips. Franklyn had one arm around his wife and the other extended along the roof of a gold-coloured Holden station wagon. "That was their first family car. Mum would have been pregnant with June." She looked up at Alice. "I've never seen this photo before."

Alice took another framed photo from the box, stared at it a moment then offered it to Felicity.

This photo was of two young women smiling brightly for the camera. Felicity recognised her mother. She looked slightly younger than in her wedding photo and had her arm around a much younger woman. Felicity glanced up at Alice. There was a strong resemblance. "This is you and Hazel."

"Yes." Alice took the photo back. "It was taken only about a month after the fires that claimed our parents and our home. Our parents were migrants. They came to Australia as ten-pound poms in the fifties. Hazel and I knew little about our English relatives. Our dad had an older sister. I was just short of my fourteenth birthday when our parents died and I could have been sent to live with the English aunt but Hazel assured the authorities she could look after me."

"You really are Hazel's sister – my aunt?"

Alice nodded, a tentative smile on her lips.

"It's just that I wasn't sure I could believe it," Felicity said. "After all the other recent revelations."

"You can believe it." Alice's smile widened. "I am your aunt."

Felicity felt a sense of calm from the certainty in Alice's voice. Even though it didn't change the fact that she was adopted, it gave her a feeling of security she'd lost since her father's letter and Ian's leaving, as if the scattering of her belief about who she was had been partly knitted back together.

*

Hazel stood at the head of the stairs. She gripped the rail with one hand, her body stiff. She'd heard voices when she came out of the shower and thought it was Alice and Greta. Felicity's door was shut so she'd assumed she was still inside but clearly that wasn't the case.

Hazel could hear the warmth in Alice's voice and she felt bad for what she was about to do but to save her family it had to be done. She stepped carefully down the stairs, her feet barely making a sound on the wooden steps.

"Why would Hazel have said you'd died in the fire with your parents?" Felicity asked.

Hazel took the last step onto the floor. "I said she'd died because…in effect she was dead to me."

"Nan!" Greta gasped.

Hazel ignored the others and kept her gaze firmly locked on Alice. "And nothing has changed," she said forcefully.

"Hazel." The name slipped from Alice's lips in a shocked whisper.

The hurt in her sister's eyes made Hazel falter. She glanced at her girls, Felicity then Greta. She'd lost her parents and then, in every practical sense, her sister – she wasn't going to lose her girls too.

Alice stood. "It's time for the truth, Hazel."

"There's no purpose." The truth would destroy the only family she had left.

"What truth?" Felicity and Greta spoke at once.

"We don't want dirty laundry aired, do we, Alice?"

"Ooh, Nan. I can't believe you'd have any." Greta was trying to lighten the mood. "You've got to tell us now."

Hazel had no choice. She had to bury Alice properly this time so she'd never come back. "What you did was despicable." Hazel swallowed, blinked tears into her eyes, dug out a hanky. "After all Franklyn and I did for you…" Her voice wobbled.

Greta rushed to her. "Don't upset yourself, Nan."

"What did she do?" Felicity asked. "What are you talking about, Hazel?"

"I did nothing." Alice's voice was little more than a whisper.

"Surely you don't want me to tell them your sordid details," Hazel snapped.

Alice sat back, and Hazel faltered at the resolve she saw on her face. She'd thought Alice would back down, that they'd pack up and leave, say goodbye to her for good, but it had been too much to hope for.

"Sordid details!" Alice snapped. "I had a child out of marriage. I didn't steal, I didn't murder. No-one bothers about unmarried mothers these days."

"It was only part of your immoral behaviour."

Alice gasped. Felicity's eyebrows shot up behind her glasses. Greta looked as if she'd rather be anywhere than here. Hazel had to finish this and get them to leave.

"Not only did your long-lost aunt have a baby out of wedlock but she was so wanton she tried to force herself on my husband."

Felicity and Greta both turned to Alice, whose face had gone pale.

"I think it's time we ended this so-called holiday and went on our way." Hazel could see her barbs had struck home. She turned back to the stairs. "Come on, girls. We should get our bags."

There was no sound behind her. She paused, one foot a step above the other.

"Stop, Hazel," Alice said. "You can't do this to me again."

Hazel spun back. Her hands clenched at her sides. Neither Felicity nor Greta had moved but Alice was standing halfway across the room in front of her. "What do you mean 'again'? Everything you did, you did to yourself. I haven't done anything to you."

"You left me," Alice croaked. "You promised me after our parents died that you'd look after me and you'd always be there for me but...you left me."

"I stayed with you until—"

"Not when I was having the baby."

"They wouldn't let me in. You know what it was like back then. They didn't let anyone but staff in on a birth."

"But afterwards."

"I had to be with June. You know what a sickly child she was. But I was only at Aunt Isabelle's. I fully intended to visit you after you'd had the baby. Franklyn went to see you as soon as we heard...well...he came back and said you wouldn't see anyone, that your baby...your baby had died and you wouldn't forgive us."

"I told him that, yes, but it was Franklyn I wouldn't forgive, not you. He'd all but excommunicated me after he found out I was pregnant. He told me I was such a terrible person I deserved for my baby to die."

Both Felicity and Greta gasped.

"I needed you, Hazel, and you didn't come."

"I was having some bad times with June – she was teething and I was awake more than I slept. By the time I slipped out and got to the home they said you'd run away. I begged Franklyn to look for you but he had no luck. We went back to Melbourne then. I was so miserable Franklyn said he'd go back to Torquay for one last look." Hazel drew herself up steeling herself for the final hurt. "He said he'd found you at Isabelle's and...he told me what you tried to do."

Alice threw her hands wide. "What had I tried to do?"

"He said you tried to get him to leave me and go with you," Hazel hissed.

"I think we should all calm down," Greta said but they both ignored her.

"That's ridiculous," Alice scoffed.

"Isabelle backed up his story."

"What story?"

"That you were topless and you threw yourself at him. Told him you were more desirable than me and that he should leave me and run away with you. How could you do that to your own sister?"

The room was silent then. Hazel glared at Alice's pale face. She'd asked for it and they'd all heard it, the whole sordid story.

"I did see him at Isabelle's," Alice whispered. "But it wasn't how he said."

"Isabelle saw you."

Alice shook her head slowly and sagged onto a chair. "I went bush after I left the hospital."

"Ran away."

"Yes, I ran away. You'd left me, I'd had a long torturous labour, my baby had died, and I never saw it."

"How awful," Felicity said.

"I got no sympathy from the staff. They wouldn't even tell me if I'd had a boy or a girl. Can you imagine how I felt, Hazel? After two nights of sleeping rough I was desperate. I managed to get to Isabelle's place and I snuck in for some food. She caught me, said I could stay for a while. I should have known there was something odd about her offer but I was so grateful for her small kindness.

"Isabelle fed me and offered her bathroom and some clean clothes." Alice shivered. "I was dressing in the spare bedroom when Franklyn burst in. Isabelle must have called him. I hadn't put my blouse on and he backed me in to a corner. My only modesty was to clutch my blouse to my chest. After all I went through having the baby and then for him to see me half naked...I was mortified. He seemed oblivious to my lack of decency. He ranted at me, accusing me of sullying his family, of trying to turn you against him, of being a slut. He said so many horrible things. In the end I couldn't take any more and I slapped him. He grabbed me, my shirt fell to the floor and I screamed. That's when Isabelle came in. When she asked what was going on he said I'd thrown myself at him. Isabelle ordered him out and me to get dressed and leave."

Hazel couldn't...no...*didn't* want to believe it. "When he came back he was so ashamed for your behaviour but he said we could see no more of you. He didn't want you infecting our home with your immoral conduct."

Alice shook her head. "He was lying to you, Hazel. Just like he lied to me."

"You would say that. He's dead now, so he can't—"

"Thank God," Alice snapped.

Greta gasped but neither she nor Felicity moved.

"Do you want to know what he told me about you?" Alice said.

"It makes no difference." Hazel pursed her lips.

"Nan!" Greta said. "You should give Alice a chance."

"To poison my family?"

"Franklyn did that a long time ago," Alice said.

Hazel felt a chill prickle in the back of her neck and then begin to creep down her back. "He told me you didn't want to see me. That you were disgusted by me. That you blamed me for the baby...for losing the baby."

Alice shook her head. "I didn't."

"You ran away."

"I was a sixteen-year-old, Hazel, with no-one to turn to. When Isabelle sent me packing she gave me some money and told me never to come near the family again."

Hazel scrambled to remember those terrible days. How hurt she'd felt thinking Alice hated her, blamed her for what had happened.

"Where was the father of the baby?" Greta asked. "How come he didn't help you?"

"Franklyn threatened him as soon as my pregnancy was discovered. Remember I begged you not to tell him, Hazel?"

"I had to. How could I keep it a secret?"

"Franklyn told him I would be looked after as long as he disappeared. We were so young..."

"Where did you go after you left Isabelle's?" Greta asked.

"A farming family took me in. I barely remember them except that they were kind to me but all I wanted was you, Hazel. I thought if I could just see you, I could convince you to...to love me again."

This time there were gasps from Greta and Felicity.

Hazel felt the air shift around her. She shot out a hand to grab the stair rail.

"Nan!" Greta rushed to her but Alice reached her first. A strong arm wrapped around her and guided her to a chair. Alice sat beside her and put a glass of water in front of her. Hazel took a sip, aware they were all watching her – Greta standing at her feet and Felicity a little further away, arms folded across her chest. Hazel knew the tenuous cocoon she'd formed around her family was beginning to unravel and there was nothing she could do to stop it. She reached for Alice's hand, felt the warmth of it in her own.

"I never stopped loving you, Alice."

Suddenly Alice's arms were around her, both of them crying. Hazel was aware of movement. A box of tissues was placed on the table beside them and Greta's hand gently patted her shoulder. Finally they let go of each other, sat back, their knees still touching.

"Franklyn drove us apart with his lies, Hazel. We've got so much time to make up."

Nausea still churned in the pit of Hazel's stomach. Trouble was, she'd knowingly gone along with part of the lie. She took another sip of water.

"I'm so glad you've found each other again," Greta said. "I'll put the kettle on. I think everyone needs a cup of tea."

"Well, it's nice for you all to play happy families." Felicity was still standing to one side, her face drawn up in a scowl. "I'm the second-hand member who doesn't belong."

"Mum, please."

Felicity turned to her daughter. "Technically, Greta, you and I have no connection to these two."

Silence settled briefly, then Greta lifted her chin and stared directly at Felicity. "Nan has been there for me all my life. Nothing can change that and I hope Alice will be happy to be a part of my future."

The kettle boiled. Felicity huffed out a breath and marched to the kitchen.

thirty-five

It had been the strangest of days, full of emotion, happy and sad, and yet, Alice thought, the happy had far outweighed the sad in so many ways. They'd moved from the dining table to the sitting area and she'd convinced Felicity no-one could see in if she put up the block-out blinds and left the sheer screening blinds down. The view across the road to the sea was beautiful and it was such a lovely autumn day outside. Felicity sat with her back to the windows, her coffee mug gripped in her hands like a totem, but at least she'd stayed with them rather than returning to her room.

Alice and Hazel had tentatively begun to fill in the gaps in their lives, talking about more recent times. Hazel had admitted she'd become housebound in the last years of Franklyn's life and Alice had talked about losing Roy.

Greta picked up one of the photos from the box that sat on the low table in front of them. "Who's the other woman in this photo?"

Alice took the small square of paper and smiled. "That's Caroline."

"My flatmate." Hazel smiled too. "She was such good fun."

"What happened to her?" Alice asked.

"I've no idea. After I married we…we lost touch."

Greta took out another photo. "You look very glam here, Alice."

"I was going to the school dance. Your nan made me that dress."

"I did, and I remember having to talk you into going."

"I wasn't much of a dancer back then and I was awkward with boys. As the dance got closer all the girls in my class talked of nothing else."

"What changed your mind?" Greta asked.

"A young man." Alice smiled. "He was as nervous as I was."

"So he was your first boyfriend?" Greta said.

Alice nodded. One dance and she'd fallen head over heels in love with him and he with her.

Alice felt Hazel stiffen beside her. "I'm sorry, Alice."

"What for?"

"That I didn't chaperone you better."

Alice swallowed, took a deep breath. "It's ancient history."

"This is all very well," Felicity said. "But how did the pair of you let Franklyn drive you apart?"

"I'd not been well after June," Hazel said. "I know it sounds weak but I relied on Franklyn for so much. Once we realised Alice was pregnant the only thing we could think of was the home for unmarried mothers at Geelong."

"I've heard stories about those places," Greta said. "What was it like?"

"Clean, comfortable," Alice said. "I made friends with some of the other mothers. The staff were pleasant but remote except for a couple of young nurses. I was terrified of matron and very homesick."

"I visited as often as I could."

"Until I had the baby."

Hazel flinched. Silence settled around them.

"It's amazing to think you both ended up relatively close to each other in South Australia and didn't know," Greta said brightly.

Alice nodded. "I tried to find Hazel." She paused, studying her sister, wondering how much more of the truth to tell. "Franklyn visited me one more time."

"Did he?" Hazel said.

"He came to the farm where I was working, said he'd support me, give me money as long as I had nothing to do with you."

Hazel's eyes widened but her lips remained firmly clamped together.

"This is the man you married, Hazel," Felicity said. "Great choice."

"He wasn't always like that."

"Deceitful, you mean," Felicity snapped. "How would you know? He had shares, cars, a bank balance you didn't know about, and he was supporting Alice. How do we know there's not some other family he's been keeping as well?"

"He didn't support me for long," Alice said. "After a couple of weeks, the money stopped. I found a job with Roy's family at Colac. The Pollards were dairy farmers and Mrs Pollard had died the year before. There was Roy, his three older brothers and their dad as well as Roy's oldest brother's wife. She'd just had twins and the family needed someone to help keep house and cook for them. I had some basic cooking skills thanks to Hazel so I got the job. On my first free day I caught the bus to Melbourne and went to your place, Hazel." Alice closed her eyes a moment. She could see herself walking back down that street as if it was yesterday. When she opened her eyes three other sets were trained on her. She swallowed her sorrow. There was no room for it now.

"What happened?" Greta said gently.

"It was a Friday and I took the risk that Franklyn would be at work but when I got there new people were moving in. They knew nothing of Hazel." She looked at her sister. "Your old neighbour told me you'd been gone two weeks and she didn't know where."

"We moved to Adelaide the week after you disappeared."

"After Franklyn got rid of her," Felicity said.

"Stop sniping at me, Felicity," Hazel said. "I'd lost my little sister. I agree now that Franklyn lied about what happened but I didn't know that then."

Felicity sniffed.

"It's easy for you to look down your nose at me. Times have changed. I was young, without an income and had two young children to care for. Franklyn was a considerate and loving husband to me and I was totally dependent on him."

Felicity pursed her lips.

"Franklyn got a job with the council at Salisbury," Hazel said. "I had to pack up a house and move. I hardly remember the first year in Adelaide except that I missed Alice terribly and I was exhausted all the time. I had two babies under one, a new house and garden to establish. I only left the house to do shopping and go to church."

"So when Alice came to Franklyn's funeral why didn't you accept her then?" Felicity asked. "He couldn't stop you any more."

"It was a shock." Hazel's cheeks flushed. She reached for the tea she'd been drinking and took a sip. "It was all so complicated." She turned to Alice. "How did you end up here?"

"I married Roy when I was twenty-one. By that time his other two brothers had also married and the dairy farm couldn't support us all. Roy saw a working man's job advertised on a property in South Australia. It was remote but came with a house. Walter Harvey was our employer. He was single, in his seventies and a tough task master. Roy worked beside him outdoors and I did too, when I wasn't milking cows, feeding hens, cooking and keeping house, not only our small cottage but Walter's large farmhouse. The work was hard but we were young and we threw ourselves into it."

"Is this your little boy?" Greta had been sifting through the photos and held one up now of Alice nursing her son.

"Yes. That's Toby."

"How did he die?" Greta's look was tentative. "If it's not too tough a question?"

"We didn't know until after he died he had cystic fibrosis."

"What's that?" Greta asked.

"It's a genetic condition that affects the lungs and digestive system. His older brother Brett died soon after birth but in hindsight my doctor thought that might have been the reason. Babies are tested for it at birth these days but not back when my boys were born."

"There was a girl I went to school with who had CF," Felicity said. "Do you remember, Hazel?"

"Vaguely."

"She was often unwell. I think she was about eight or nine before they found out why. She married around the same time as Ian and..." Felicity sniffed. "Anyway, she's running a small business from home making the most amazing upcycled jewellery. I've got a couple of pairs of her earrings. She's doing so well."

"It can affect people in different ways," Alice said. "And these days with regular treatment people with CF have a much better life expectancy but back when Roy and I had our babies it was a different story. We decided on no more children and focused on the work we did for Walter and our local community. Then, eight years after Toby died, Walter caught pneumonia."

"Gosh, you've had some sorrow in your life, Alice," Greta said.

Alice nodded. "Walter was always saying what didn't kill you made you stronger. He was right." She smiled, remembering fondly the old man who'd been such a tyrant in some ways and so stubborn. She'd been a bit frightened of him at first but soon discovered behind the gruff exterior there'd been a kind heart, especially when her sons had died. "He was a tough man. He refused to stay in hospital. I did my best to look after him but he went downhill so quickly. Roy and I were so sad to lose him – he'd become a friend as well as an employer. Then of course we were worried about what we'd do next. We were shocked and amazed to discover he'd left us his property." She smiled. "And we made a good go of it, as Roy liked to say."

"So you and Nan both ended up in South Australia but didn't know it." Greta blew out a breath and pushed her arms out in a long stretch.

Alice felt there'd been enough reminiscing for the moment. "We should go for a walk along the jetty before lunch," she said. "Get some fresh air and blow out the cobwebs."

"Great idea." Greta was instantly on her feet.

"I'd like that," Hazel said.

"I'm not leaving the house," Felicity said and put her feet up on the rest in front of her.

"While we're out you could do the dishes then," Hazel said.

Felicity gave her mother a sharp look but made no reply. Alice thought Hazel's tone was one you would use for children rather than an adult daughter but maybe Felicity needed that.

"Perhaps tomorrow you'll come with us," Alice said. "I'd like to take you for a drive through the national park. There's some beautiful scenery there."

Felicity screwed up her nose and shrugged her shoulders.

Alice smiled. At least it hadn't been a straight out no.

★

Greta was the first one back to the house after their walk. Hazel and Alice were strolling at a slower pace, chatting about things they had in common. At the moment it was cooking and they were discussing the ins and outs of how to make a decent jelly cake. Greta thought Alice won that prize but she wasn't brave enough to say it. She'd walked on ahead when they'd stopped to admire a bush in the front garden a couple of houses back. She'd realised as they were walking she hadn't been in touch with Joe to let him know they'd arrived safely. Last night it had been too late and this morning had been so full of drama she hadn't given it a thought until now. She didn't even know where her phone was.

"We're back," she said as she stepped inside.

"Nice walk?" Felicity was sitting in the same chair leafing through a magazine but Greta was pleased to see the table had been cleared and there was a neat stack of clean dishes on the kitchen bench.

"It was lovely. There are people fishing all along the jetty and we saw a massive stingray swim underneath. I can't believe I forgot my phone. I didn't get any pictures." Hazel and Alice came in the door behind her and Greta continued on up the stairs. "I'm going to ring Joe."

She went into her room and opened the blind, which gave her a spectacular view of the bay and the jetty she'd just walked along. She pulled up the quilt to make the bed and found her bag underneath. Her phone was inside and there was a missed call and a message from Joe. His reassuring voice, giving her a quick update on the reno and asking how the reunion was going, was a welcome normality in her current situation. She rang him and got his voicemail. No doubt he was up a ladder. She left a quick message and said she'd ring again tonight.

At the top of the stairs she could hear another phone. She recognised Felicity's ringtone. It stopped before she could reach it. Ian's name was just fading from the screen. She took the phone with her and headed back down the stairs.

"Dad just tried to ring you." She handed over Felicity's phone and it immediately began to ring again.

Felicity glanced at it then tossed it aside. "I don't want to talk to him."

Greta felt the tug of being piggy in the middle again. The phone stopped ringing and immediately Greta's started.

"Now he's trying me."

A flash of guilt crossed Felicity's face. "Don't answer it."

"Why?" Greta stared at her mum.

"He's probably ringing about the real estate agent's visit. That was this afternoon. I don't want to know about it."

Greta's phone pinged with a voice message and when she listened to it, Ian's voice was loud in her ear demanding she tell Felicity the house would be sold no matter how much she tried to sabotage it.

"What have you done?"

Hazel and Alice both stopped the food preparation they'd been doing together in the kitchen.

"Nothing." Felicity shifted in her chair and pulled her shirt lower.

"Dad used the word sabotage."

"Pffffh! He said he wanted sheets and towels for his new flat. I've just replaced our sheets and towels and he can jolly well get his own. I stripped the beds and emptied the linen press and locked everything in the boot of my car." Felicity sniffed. "He said he didn't like them anyway."

"That's it?"

"He said he was coming to collect his clothes so I stacked the remainder in the lounge."

"Stacked?" Greta fixed her mum with a stare and Felicity looked away.

"Perhaps tossed is a better word."

"Felicity!" Hazel had come to join them.

"What? I've been the one looking after the place since Ian left. Why should I have it looking immaculate for a real estate agent when I don't even want it to be sold?"

"What else did you do?" Hazel asked.

Once more Felicity looked sheepish.

"Mum?" Greta was horrified to think there could be more.

"I'd stripped the bed to pack away the sheets and I left the doona off. Ian didn't like the way the place was furnished so I stacked all the cushions on the bed in your room. I thought the wet areas needed cleaning and I started, then ran out of time." She tapped a finger to her chin. "I think I probably left cleaning products and cloths scattered about."

"You think?" Greta couldn't believe what she was hearing. Her mum was usually so houseproud.

Hazel made a soft strangled sound. Greta looked at her in alarm but Hazel had her hand over her mouth covering a grin.

"Nan, I can't believe you'd condone this."

"It does sound amusing."

Felicity sat forward in her chair. "And I didn't get Melody to feed Dolly."

"What?" Greta was appalled. "Poor Dolly."

"She'll be fine. I lined up three litter trays for her in the laundry and several bowls of food and water in the kitchen." Felicity put a finger in the air. "Oh, and when you came I hadn't had time to do the dishes."

Greta had a terrible sinking feeling in her stomach.

Hazel laughed. "You'll have a mess to clean up when you go home but I'm sure it will have been worth it."

"Exactly," Felicity said and laughed too.

All Greta could do was look from one to the other.

"Lunch is ready." Alice waved them to the table she'd set with a quiche and salad.

Greta was still shaking her head when she sat down.

Hazel had only taken one mouthful when she placed her fork back on the plate. "I did my own bit of sabotage before I left home." She looked at Alice. "Franklyn left our house to June, and she's taken to letting herself in whenever she feels like it, even if I'm not there. It's still my home and it feels like an invasion of privacy even though she's my daughter."

Greta sighed. "What did you do?"

"Nothing much. I just locked the screen doors. I never used to keep them locked so she doesn't have a key."

"Hah!" Felicity said. "I had a fiddle with locks too. I know he's your dad, Greta, but I got sick of Ian walking in whenever he felt like it."

"Don't tell me you changed the locks?" Hazel said.

"No. That would cost too much. I just put a security chain on the front door so that he'd have to go through the side gate and round to the laundry to get in."

Hazel and Felicity both began to laugh and Alice looked at them with what Greta thought was a shocked expression.

"Well, Alice," Greta said. "You might want to change your mind about being a part of this family." Then, to her surprise, Alice began to laugh too.

thirty-six

Alice drew the blinds on the darkening sky, straightened a cushion and adjusted the pile of magazines Felicity had been reading. After Felicity and Hazel had admitted the sabotage they'd conducted at their homes everyone had relaxed, even Greta who'd tried so hard to look disapproving. They'd lingered over lunch, then, when they'd cleared everything away, Alice had removed the tablecloth to reveal the partly done jigsaw underneath, which Greta had taken to, declaring she hadn't done one since she was a kid. Later they'd all played cards before Hazel had announced she would cook dinner and Felicity opened a bottle of wine. Alice had offered a bottle but Felicity had brought an esky full of leftovers from her birthday and had insisted they use hers.

It had been one of the best afternoons Alice could remember in a long time. Not that she didn't do that kind of thing with other people but these women were her family and it was a totally new experience. The funny ways they spoke to each other, occasionally sharp, often tender; the way they sometimes finished each other's sentences; their gentle teasing and casual laughter. Even though there were still small tensions between Hazel and Felicity, it had been so enjoyable to be included.

"Come and sit down," Hazel patted the seat beside her on the couch. "It's awkward letting other people take over your kitchen, isn't it?"

Alice sat beside her sister. Greta and Felicity were busy washing dishes and tidying up after the meal Hazel had cooked. "You're right," Alice said. "I think of it as my domain."

"So do I but I wanted to cook to say thank you for having us. It's the least I could do." Hazel glanced across the room. "You have a very well set-out kitchen."

"I helped plan it when we built the house. I do a lot of cooking."

"You don't find the house too big for one?"

"I don't use the upstairs unless I have visitors. I have families in need of respite here for short holidays from time to time. It's nice to have the space then."

"I had hoped to sell mine. I like the idea of a smaller place in one of those residential villages but turns out the house isn't mine to sell."

Alice pondered her next words carefully, knowing Hazel was a proud woman. "Greta told me you've been left in a difficult situation."

Hazel stiffened.

"I'm not poking my nose into your business," Alice said quickly. "But if you ever needed anything, any help financially ..."

"That won't be necessary."

"You did so much for me after our parents died. It couldn't have been easy. I just wanted—"

Tears brimmed in Hazel's eyes and she scrabbled for a hanky.

"I'm sorry. I didn't mean to upset you."

"You didn't." Hazel dabbed at her eyes. "Today has been such a mix of emotions and I find it hard to...you're being so generous after everything that's happened...all I did to you."

Anger came so quickly it took Alice by surprise. She had to take a breath before she spoke. "We were both vulnerable and deceived by Franklyn. I don't blame you, Hazel."

"But you should. Franklyn used the insurance money from our parents' house to buy the house in Adelaide. Half of that money should have been yours...and now...I've no way to pay you back."

Alice was aware that Felicity and Greta had finished in the kitchen and had moved closer, listening to their conversation.

"You don't need to pay me back, Hazel." Once more Alice swallowed the emotion that threatened to engulf her. "I live a simple existence and want for nothing. I've been left in a very comfortable position financially and I would be happy to help you if you needed."

Hazel dabbed harder at her eyes. Greta sat on her other side and took her hand. "Nan, I really think you should get another opinion about Grandad's will."

"He was financially astute," Felicity said. She hadn't sat but stood in front of the couch, arms folded. "He ripped off Hazel and Alice's insurance money and somehow built up a small fortune. He'd have it all locked up, don't you worry, grumpy old bugger."

"Felicity," Hazel said sternly. "He may have been difficult but he was your father and a good provider."

"There's more to family than that," Felicity snapped.

Hazel lurched forward. "It must have been Isabelle's money," she said.

"What was, Nan?"

"Since Franklyn died and we've realised he had so much money, I've wondered how he could have accumulated it but it must have started with Isabelle. Her house in Torquay was quite run-down when she died but the land was worth a fortune, I remember that much, and that Franklyn used some of the money from the sale to invest in other real estate. I've not really thought about it since." She glanced towards Greta. "It must seem so ridiculous to you but I never knew much about our financial affairs. There was never any need. Franklyn always provided for me and I always managed well."

"I'm not judging you," Greta said.

"Huh!" Felicity folded her arms. "He was very well-off, which makes what he did to you even meaner."

"He was my husband, for better or for worse."

"Well, you got the worst of it." Felicity snapped.

Alice was appalled to realise how much her sister appeared to have suffered in her marriage. And that Franklyn was overshadowing their lives still. "Would anyone like a cup of tea? I have some burnt butter biscuits you haven't tried yet."

Greta groaned and held her stomach. "I think I'm going to bust. Between you and Nan it's been non-stop food. I know it's early but would you all forgive me if I went to bed? I've hit the wall all of a sudden and I want to ring Joe before I fall asleep." She yawned, which set Felicity off too.

"You probably all need an early night," Alice said. "I thought tomorrow we'd go for a drive through the national park."

Felicity gave a slight shake of her head.

"See how you feel in the morning but I'd love to take you to one of my favourite little beaches. There're a few tourists about but it won't be busy there. We could have a picnic lunch."

"Sounds lovely." Greta linked her arm with Felicity's. "Come on, Mum, a good night's sleep and you'll be ready to go."

As their steps faded up the stairs, Hazel and Alice stayed put, all the things left unsaid pressing in on them.

Alice opened her mouth but Hazel cut in first. "I think they're right about an early night. The offer of the drive tomorrow sounds lovely. I'll see you in the morning."

Alice had hoped they could talk longer. Without the other two, there was more she wanted to say.

"Are you sure you wouldn't like a tea before you turn in? I have chamomile."

"No, thank you." Hazel gave a brief smile and headed up the stairs.

Alice swallowed her disappointment. "Good night," she said.

thirty-seven

The next day a beautiful blue sky scattered with wisps of white cloud greeted Alice when she opened the blinds and only a soft breeze stirred the bushes in the front garden. Perfect conditions for their sightseeing.

When the others came downstairs it was only Greta who showed enthusiasm for their outing. Hazel was quiet and Felicity declared she wasn't going. Greta finally talked her around and she agreed to go but only after she'd swathed her head in a large scarf and topped it with a big floppy hat Alice had spare.

Innes National Park had spectacular views but each time Alice stopped at a lookout only Greta and Hazel got out to take in the rugged coastline and sandy beaches. At one beach they'd seen a pod of dolphins surfing the waves. Greta and Hazel had both been enthusiastic in telling Felicity what she'd missed. Her scarf had slid a little then.

Alice noticed the hat had come off and the scarf had slipped right down after they'd pulled over to watch an emu stroll across in front of the car with a mob of stripy babies behind him. At the next stop, there were no other sightseers and Felicity got out of the car, although she didn't move far from it. By the time they reached Alice's favourite little beach the mood in the car was much lighter. All four of them were chatting and laughing, well, perhaps three of them with the odd interjection from Felicity.

Alice was glad to see there were no other vehicles in the carpark. They might get lucky and have the place to themselves. It was warm trudging along the track through the sandhills. The final stretch was uphill and hard work but there was nothing but enthusiastic comments when they reached the top and looked out over the small secluded bay. It was as picturesque as always with its white sand and aquamarine water merging to a darker blue as it got deeper.

"It's so bright," Felicity moaned and wrapped her scarf around her face again.

They took the worn stairs to the bottom and set up a small camp, tucking the esky in the shade of Alice's ageing beach shelter. Hazel watched them swim then helped Alice get out the picnic she'd prepared.

"What's beyond those rocks?" Greta asked as they packed everything up again.

Alice looked to the north where she was pointing. "Another beach, but before you get to it there are some large rock pools. People swim in them when the tide's right." She glanced down the beach. "Which it probably is now."

"I like the sound of rock pools," Greta said.

"It's a bit of a hike over rocks and soft sand."

"I think I'll paddle here," Hazel said.

To everyone's surprise Felicity jumped up. "I'll come with you."

Alice was torn between wanting to be with them when they found the pools, and staying with Hazel. The chance to be with her sister alone won.

"I'll stay here," she said.

Greta and Felicity set off. Greta was wearing a hat and a loose shirt over her bathers, Felicity's face was swathed in the scarf again under her hat. She wore a long-sleeved shirt and drawstring pants, her towel was around her shoulders while Greta's was wrapped around her waist like a sarong.

"At least she won't get sunburned," Hazel said.

Alice smiled and began to walk towards the water. "It's lovely in."

"I haven't swum for years. I don't even own bathers any more."

"You should have said. I could've lent you some."

They stopped at the water's edge, allowing their bodies time to adjust to the crisp cold against their sun-warmed skin.

"Have you been happy, Alice?" Hazel asked.

Alice paused, then gave a quick nod of her head. "Yes, mostly. I was lucky with Roy. It wasn't always an easy life together but it was a good one. Roy taught me how to laugh again, to enjoy life. This beach has so many happy memories."

"How did he die?" Hazel asked softly.

Alice looked out to sea. "It was an accident. He was replacing the hay shed roof and fell. He broke his neck."

"Oh, I'm so sorry."

"I wasn't home that day but they said it would have been instant. There wouldn't have been anything anyone could have done." Alice steeled herself against the pain that still gripped her when she thought of the way he died. "Our neighbour, John, found him, poor man. They'd been working on the shed together. They'd taken a lunch break and John had gone back to his place to get something they needed. When he came back he found Roy spreadeagled across a pile of wood on the ground." Alice braced herself for the anger that always followed the pain. "Roy was in a hurry to get the roof done. We had a rule, no ladder work unless someone else was there but...bloody men, think they're invincible."

"I'm sorry," Hazel said again.

"And I'm sorry your marriage didn't work out so well."

"It wasn't all bad. I did love Franklyn to begin with and I felt loved in return but as time went by he became more and more..."

"Controlling?"

"Yes, you could use that word."

They started walking along the edge of the beach, gentle waves rolling around their ankles.

"These days they call it abuse, Hazel."

"You don't think of it that way when you're living it. It just becomes the norm. I learned to deal with it and I allowed him to get his way."

"You did what you must to survive." Alice knew that well enough.

"You're right." Hazel bent to pick up a large white shell washed to the edge of the beach. "I learned strategies to defuse some of the tense times. I'm ashamed to say one that worked well was acting light-headed, as if I was going to faint." She grimaced. "I did it the first time when the girls were about seven and eight. We were driving back from a visit to Isabelle. Franklyn was cross. Isabelle was as stubborn as Franklyn and there'd been an argument. We stayed the night in a motel and set off for home early the next morning. June had been carsick on the way over so he made her sit in the front and me in the back with Felicity.

"It was January and no air-conditioned cars in those days. It was so hot and he refused to stop, said we could wait until we needed petrol. When the girls complained he roared at them to be quiet. Franklyn rarely raised his voice, he usually showed his anger in other ways. The girls were terrified. I wasn't feeling the best either and I wondered what he would do if I fainted. So in the end, as we neared a small town, I pretended I did."

"What happened?" Alice felt cold even though the sun was warm on her shoulders.

"He stopped immediately. I hadn't passed out, of course, so I just acted woozy. There was a picnic area. He got us all out of the car and we sat in the shade while Franklyn poured cups of water for us from the container in the boot. It was warm but at least it was wet." Hazel shook her head. "I know I should have stood up to him but acting weak worked so well. By the time everyone fussed around me the subject was changed and we all went on. I didn't do it all the time. Mostly to shield the girls. I guess that made me as manipulative as Franklyn."

"But you were being protective, not causing anyone harm."

"I couldn't protect you."

"I've thought back on it so many times, those days after Franklyn came into our lives. He was jealous of our relationship."

Hazel had a strange look on her face. Was it disbelief?

Alice pressed on. "In Franklyn's eyes there was only room for you in his life. You and I were so happy together and he couldn't stand it. Do you remember that day we decided to make lamingtons?"

"I do. I was pregnant with June and it was the first time I'd felt like cooking in months." Hazel smiled. "We found three different recipes including Mum's and baked them all to see if there was any difference. The kitchen was splattered in chocolate and sprinkled with coconut."

"Time got away from us. Franklyn came home and we were laughing together, having so much fun. He was angry."

"He got cross because of the mess and dinner wasn't started."

"I saw him before you did. The way he looked from me to you then back at me with such loathing." Alice shivered at the memory. "Back then I thought he was just angry but as time's gone by I realised it was the look of a green-eyed monster. He didn't want me to make you happy, he wanted you all for himself."

"I know." The words were so soft Alice barely heard them.

"You do?"

"Now." Hazel shook her head. "But at the time I didn't see it."

"There's something else that happened between me and Franklyn...after June was born and you were still in hospital."

They both stopped moving forward, their feet sinking in the soft sand. Hazel looked at Alice, her face creased with worry.

"We were all so anxious for you and the baby. I did my best at home to keep the house and cook the meals. Franklyn and I hardly saw each other between me being at school and him at work and visiting you. I only got a couple of opportunities to see you and the last time was when you were so much better and said you'd be coming home."

"I remember. The sister had just told me June was gaining weight and breathing well on her own and that the doctor thought we could go home soon. I couldn't believe how happy it made me. We danced around my hospital bed." Hazel smiled with the recollection.

"I caught the bus home and made a special effort with dinner so that I could share the good news with Franklyn like you'd asked. It was his late night at work so you weren't expecting him to visit you that evening." Alice closed her eyes and took a breath to steady herself. When she opened them Hazel's gaze was locked on hers and Alice faltered. Was she doing the right thing, digging up the past again? "I thought it was my fault for a long time."

"What was?"

"When Franklyn came home that night his eyes were already bright. I didn't realise at the time but I think he'd had a few drinks."

Hazel frowned. "He wasn't one for going to the pub."

"No, but that was also the day he got that promotion."

"Oh yes, June and I turning a corner overshadowed all that."

"When I told him your news he was so excited. I'd never seen him act so...so uninhibited. He got out a bottle of port and poured himself a glass to have with dinner and then he poured one for me."

"Goodness, he must have been in a good mood."

"The whole time we ate he talked animatedly about the future with you and June and his new job and even me. He said perhaps I might like to go to secretarial college when I finished school because there were lots of jobs going at his work for women with those skills. I was mesmerised by him paying me some attention at last."

"You see, back then he was a different man," Hazel said.

Alice braced herself. The next part of her story was still as clear in her mind as if it had happened yesterday.

"When I stood to tidy the table I felt giddy. The only alcohol I'd ever had was a sip of champagne at your wedding and I'd drunk a whole glass of port. Franklyn jumped up to help me and I wobbled against him and before I knew it he...he pressed his lips to mine."

Hazel gasped. "He must have been drunk."

"It didn't stop there." Alice had come this far, she had to tell it all. "He forced me against the wall and kissed me again. I was terrified. I tried to push him away but he slapped my face and said I'd been parading myself in front of him all these months and he could have a kiss if he wanted one."

Hazel paled in spite of the warm day.

Alice swallowed the bitter taste in her mouth at the memory. "I got away from him and ran outside. I hid in the park down the street for hours until the dark and the cold drove me home again. The house was in darkness and the doors all locked. I spent the rest of the night in the garden shed. The next morning after he went to work the back door was unlocked so I could get in to the house. You came home that day and he hardly spoke to me again."

"Is that…is that why you always kept the chair jammed behind your door at night?"

Alice nodded, a huge sense of relief replacing her fear.

"I thought it was a teenage thing. Wanting privacy."

"I tried to keep out of the way when Franklyn was at home. I was terrified he might do it again."

"And a few months later we discovered you were pregnant—" Hazel's hand went to her mouth again. "Dear, God it wasn't… Franklyn didn't…"

"No." Alice shook her head. "It was the boy from the formal. He was working by then, had a job locally so I saw him…he delivered our milk. Sometimes, in the early morning I'd sneak out to wait for him and we'd talk. He was so kind to me. We were in love and I found ways to be with him. Then I got sick," Alice said. "It was you who saw the signs of pregnancy. I had no idea."

"And you wouldn't tell me who the father was."

"We were going to run away together."

"You were sixteen."

"I know but I was also terrified of what Franklyn would do once he found out."

"I'm so sorry." Hazel reached for her. "I had no choice, I had to tell him."

"I know." Alice nodded. "Once he knew, he caught me outside one day when you were resting with June. He called me every horrible name, said I'd have to live in the gutter, no man would ever want me except as a whore. I felt so ashamed. He ranted for ages and then, as if he was being some kind of benevolent benefactor, he said he'd make sure I was taken care of. It was like a lifeline but there was a condition for his support. I had to tell him who the father was."

"And you did?"

Alice nodded. "The only other person beside you who loved me in the world was sent away. We were both too young to have managed, I know that now but…it was devastating for the young girl that I was."

Hazel said nothing, the emotions playing across her face as she took in what Alice had told her. Once more she reached out, laying a hand on Alice's arm. "I'm so sorry. All this time I've felt guilty because I wasn't there to guide you when it came to boyfriends and I should have been protecting you from Franklyn. My poor sweet Alice." Hazel gripped her arm tighter. "I was too focused on June and my own recovery to be of much help to you."

"It wasn't all miserable," Alice said. "My time at the home, before I had the baby, was mostly happy and there was no Franklyn. And I remember your visits. You'd collect me on Sundays and we'd take June for walks in the pram, talk about the future. I still held the hope I might go to secretarial school. My secret dream was that Franklyn would drop dead and you and I would raise June and my baby together. You even said not long before I had the baby that perhaps you'd ask Franklyn if you could raise it as your own."

Hazel's hand pulled away. "It was stupid of me to give you that hope."

Alice didn't want to give up those last happy memories. "We thought up names for the baby, remember? I wanted a name that would suit either a boy or a girl and you suggested our mother's maiden name – Morgan." Alice had tried so many times over the years that followed to remember the birth. She hadn't forgotten the long drawn-out labour, but by the time they'd told her to push she'd been groggy from drugs and all she could remember was feeling like she was being torn in two. "I never did know if that baby was a boy or a girl so in my heart it was always Morgan."

"It was a terrible thing Franklyn did." Hazel's gaze was off somewhere in the distance. "To both of us."

"He didn't ever hurt you *physically,* did he?"

Hazel blinked. "After June...once we finally resumed intimacy, he was different. Sex wasn't always...comfortable for me. I assumed it was because my body had changed and I did have some scarring but...let's just say you didn't say no to Franklyn."

Alice looked steadily at her sister. "That's rape, Hazel."

Hazel wiped the tears that trickled from under her sunglasses. "Franklyn got prostate cancer in his sixties." She sniffed. "After the treatment he...we were no longer intimate. I didn't miss it but I'm sure it affected him mentally. He began to withdraw until in his final years he rarely left the house unless it was a family thing. I became confined too. His demands were no longer of an intimate nature but I was at his beck and call for everything else and, gradually, I let go many of the things I'd enjoyed beyond our home. My only escape was my daily walk. He even resented me doing that but I had to get out of the house, even if it was just half an hour." She grimaced.

"He's gone now, Hazel."

She groaned and staggered to one side.

Alice wrapped her in her arms and pulled her close. Hazel's arms came around her and they stood in the ankle-deep water, clinging to each other like two women trying to save themselves from drowning. Gradually Hazel's shuddering sobs eased, the intensity of Alice's sorrow lessened, their arms relaxed and they edged apart but still held each other's hands, not wanting to let go.

"I thought…" Hazel sniffed. "I thought when he died that I could live a different life but he still haunts me."

"We're here and he's not," Alice said. "We can't let him spoil what's left of our lives. I overcame Franklyn. You can too."

Hazel dabbed at her eyes one more time and pushed her hanky back into her pocket.

"There's so much we can do to make up for the past even if we don't live close. We can talk every day on the phone, wish each other happy birthday and Merry Christmas, get together for celebrations or just to catch up for no reason at all, take holidays together…do you still dance?" Alice was so overwhelmed by the possibilities she barely acknowledged Hazel's slight shake of her head. "It's been such a joy to get to know Felicity and Greta. And then there's the rest of your family."

Hazel's shoulders straightened and she took a step back.

Alice sensed some kind of shutter had just closed inside her sister. "Are you worried about June and your house?"

A flash of something crossed Hazel's face. Alice couldn't tell if it was relief or surprise.

"Not worried," she said. "More annoyed, I suppose. June used to call in once a week before Franklyn died. Now she's checking on me all the time and she comes into the house as if…" Hazel sighed. "Well, I suppose it is hers but I still think of it as mine."

"Do you think she'll take something while you're away?"

Hazel looked puzzled.

"You said you locked the screens so she couldn't get in."

"Oh…yes." Hazel pressed her fingers to her lips. "She's determined, like Franklyn."

"Or perhaps like you?"

"Hmm. Perhaps." Hazel smiled. "I can just picture her face when she tries to get in."

Alice smiled too and it felt so good. And then they were both laughing hard, almost hysterically, then, when they'd composed themselves, she gave Hazel another brief hug.

"Hello!" Greta's voice echoed along the beach. She and Felicity were heading back.

Alice and Hazel both lifted hands in a wave. Their time alone was over for now.

Alice got cold drinks from the esky while Greta and Felicity told them about their rock pool experience.

"I can't believe we've got this beautiful place to ourselves," Felicity said as she sprawled out along her towel wearing only her bathers now and the scarf over her face to keep the sun from her eyes.

Greta went for another swim and Alice and Hazel talked of happier things with only the odd muffled interjection from Felicity. Alice talked about cooking for the local shop and babysitting Bec's girls and Hazel about her return to sewing and they discovered their mutual enjoyment of their weekly card games. When Greta came back they packed up and made the trek back to the car.

Alice was tired on the way home but happy. Hazel was quiet in the front seat beside her but Greta and Felicity were full of chat in the back. Alice replayed every bit of her conversation with Hazel, from Franklyn's ill-treatment of her to the happy sharing of their daily lives now. Somewhere between the beach and her home a gentle peace settled over her. Finally, she'd unburdened herself. The woman for whom it mattered most knew the truth, and she'd rediscovered the joy of having her sister back in her life. Alice felt at last that the past could be truly left behind.

*

Hazel stared out the window at the passing scenery but she wasn't really taking it in. Her head still spun with everything Alice had told her. Alice seemed to have overcome it, gone on to live a happy life, but Hazel couldn't forgive her own failure to protect her little sister and then to have gone along with Franklyn's deceitful scheme to keep her out of their lives…it was unforgivable.

For a short time today, she'd believed that she could continue the charade of welcoming Alice back into her life but now she knew she couldn't. If Hazel's deceit was revealed now, there'd be no forgiveness and her family would be ripped apart.

thirty-eight

Greta opened the blind and looked out across the bay. The sun glinted off the calm water and there were already people on the jetty. It was going to be another beautiful day even though a slight chill nipped at her bare arms and legs now. She hopped back into bed, propped herself up with the pillows so she could still see the view and picked up her phone. Last night's conversation with Joe had been brief. They'd both been exhausted – Joe had been at his sister's all day Friday helping to get the house ready and then all day yesterday painting.

For Greta, the previous day had been filled with an odd mixture of emotions. Alice had cooked them breakfast but both Felicity and Hazel had been silent, only picking at the delicious omelettes, and it had been up to Greta to fill the gaps. Then it had taken all her efforts to convince Felicity to go with them to the national park.

By the time they'd reached the second lookout stop Greta had been annoyed by her mother's indifference to the wild beauty around them. At least Hazel had been enthusiastic. Then when they got to Alice's special beach the day had changed completely.

Everyone had enjoyed themselves but both Alice and Hazel had been quiet on the drive home. Greta wondered what they'd talked about while she and her mum were at the rock pools. When they got back to Marion Bay, Felicity had joined Alice and Greta in a game of cards after dinner but Hazel had retired early.

Greta wasn't sure what was going through her grandmother's mind but she hoped a good night's sleep would put her in a better mood today. The previous night Greta had told Joe about Marion Bay and the national park but nothing about Alice and Hazel reconciling and now she was keen to fill him in.

The phone rang a long time and she thought it was going to his voicemail when he finally answered, his voice groggy.

"Were you still asleep?" she asked. "It's after eight. I thought you'd be ready to head off painting."

"I got my second wind after I spoke to you last night and I stayed up. How are things going there?"

"Okay." She filled him in on Hazel and Alice and then started on Alice's life story.

"So Alice has money?" Joe asked, when she'd told him about the farm and the beach house.

"I guess so."

"Maybe she could help Hazel out and we could keep Franklyn's generous donation to our future."

Greta felt a jab of annoyance. Her mind was full of empathy for Hazel and Alice and all he could think about was money. "I'm not keeping the money if there's a way for Nan to have it," she snapped.

"Okay, okay. Keep your shirt on. I was joking."

Greta pushed back into the pillows. It didn't seem like a joke to her. "When are you going to your sister's?"

"I should be on my way now. Lucky you woke me. It's going to be a long day. I think I'll camp at their place tonight. They've set up the beds in the garage till the painting's finished."

"Alice has another short tour planned for today. Some different beaches."

"And to think you could have been here painting instead."

"Mmm."

"It's got great bones, the old house. I've been thinking we should expand our search to include places that might need a bit of work."

"We've talked about this. You know I hate renovating."

"It might be a cheaper option and we could get married sooner."

"We could stay where we are and get married now."

"What?"

"Lots of people don't own their own place."

"This is probably the wrong time to be talking about it."

"Probably."

"I've got to get going. We can talk when you get back."

Greta sighed. She hated conversations like these over the phone. "Okay."

"Bye."

"Love you," she said, but he'd ended the call.

Feeling unsettled, she got up and dressed, pulled up the doona, tidied her possessions and opened her door. Across the hall the other two bedroom doors were shut and there wasn't any sound from the kitchen or delicious smells wafting up to greet her.

She moved silently down the stairs and was surprised to see Alice sitting at the table reading a magazine. She looked up as Greta came down the final step, pushed a pair of glasses more firmly onto her face and smiled.

"Good morning. I was going to cook bacon and eggs but I thought there was no point until you all came down."

"I'd be happy with toast and coffee," Greta said.

Alice got up from her chair.

"I can get it," Greta said, waving a hand at her, but Alice wouldn't be put off.

"You're my guest," she said.

Greta relaxed into a chair. Alice's home, and Alice herself, had become an extension of the family that she was enjoying and feeling more comfortable with all the time.

Alice glanced towards the stairs. "Are the others stirring?"

"I didn't hear a peep as I came down. I think they're both tired."

"A lot has happened in the last few days. We all need time to digest it."

Greta wanted to ask Alice how she was feeling but Felicity's legs appeared on the stairs and then the rest of her.

"I need coffee," she groaned.

"Didn't you sleep well?" Alice asked.

"Like a log and now I feel like one." Felicity groaned and went to the coffee machine.

Greta picked up the magazine Alice had left on the table and began to flick through it as Alice and Felicity chatted in the kitchen.

"Do you plan to search for your birth mother?" Alice asked as she followed Felicity to the table.

"I don't know. Evidently my original birth certificate was sealed."

"Surely the rules have changed about that these days." Alice sat a tray with the toast on the table.

"I'm not sure if it applies to babies born in nineteen seventy. I'm still coming to terms with being adopted I haven't checked into it."

"When's your birthday?"

Felicity plucked up a piece of toast. "I was supposedly born on the seventh of March – Felicity Morgan Gifford. That's if Hazel's to be believed."

There were sounds of footsteps coming down the stairs but Greta was distracted by Alice who'd flopped heavily onto the chair beside her.

"Good morning," Hazel said stiffly. Her face lacked its usual colour and there were shadows under her eyes.

"Come and join us." Felicity waved at an empty chair. "Alice has just been asking me about my birth. I told her the version you gave me but maybe it's changed again."

"Mum!" Greta had hoped this weekend would help mend the rift between Felicity and Hazel but for every step forward there were two back.

Hazel ignored Felicity and looked to Greta. "I know it's a big ask, Greta dear, but I'm really not feeling all that well and I was wondering if you might take me home?"

"Today?"

"Here we go."

Greta and Felicity spoke at once.

"Are you feeling faint, Hazel?"

Greta was surprised by the sharpness in Alice's tone and the strange look that passed between her and Hazel. "What's going on?" she asked.

"Your grandmother has become a master at deflecting difficult situations by feigning dizziness," Alice said, not shifting her gaze from Hazel.

"Hah!" Felicity said. "At last someone else has worked it out."

"What are you trying to distract us from, Hazel?" Alice said.

Hazel's lip wobbled and her already pale face drained the last of its colour. Greta jumped to her feet.

"Leave her, Greta," Felicity said. "She's not going to fall over, are you, Hazel?"

But Hazel did look shaky. Greta reached out and gripped her shoulders, guiding her to a chair, then she looked around. Alice was staring at Felicity like a hungry cat looked at a bird.

"Alice?" Greta said.

Alice's glance swept over Greta and fixed directly on Hazel. "Hazel, what have you done?"

Greta felt the shudder in Hazel's shoulders.

Felicity took a bite of toast. "Well, this is all going to hell in a handbasket, isn't it?" she muttered.

"Hazel?" Alice said again. "Felicity's just told me her birthdate—" Alice sucked in a breath. "And that her second name is Morgan."

"It was our mother's maiden name," Hazel croaked.

"And the name I chose for my baby. The baby that was born on the seventh of March, nineteen seventy. The baby I was told had *died*."

Felicity stopped eating her toast and looked from Alice to Hazel, who shivered again under Greta's hands.

"Did my baby die, Hazel?" Alice's voice was barely a whisper.

Felicity let out a strangled scream. "Are you saying..." She leaned across the table to Hazel. "Is Alice my mother?"

Hazel gave the slightest nod of her head, there was a shift in the air as if the earth had tilted slightly and then there was a blur of yells and screams and hugging and tears between Alice and Felicity. Greta felt like a bystander watching someone else's family rather than her own and all the time the woman she'd believed to be her nan sat silent on the chair, just the odd shiver trembling through her.

*

This time Hazel wasn't pretending to feel dizzy. Spots danced before her eyes and she was having trouble getting air. Felicity would truly hate her now, and Alice, and even Greta. Hazel was grateful her granddaughter had stood by her and for the strength flowing from Greta's hands to her shoulders, but they'd all want answers and the truth would rip these women from her. She'd be left with June and Derek, if they'd have her. Perhaps it was what she deserved.

Felicity and Alice drew apart from their embrace and looked at each other. Alice raised one hand, cupped Felicity's cheek and tenderly brushed her other hand over Felicity's hair, drinking her in with her gaze.

Hazel had always loved Felicity a little more than June, although she'd tried not to show it. Perhaps it was part of the guilt she felt that Felicity wasn't hers, but as they'd grown older June had taken after her father and Felicity after her mother, her birth mother. Her features were softer and she had a loving nature, even though it had been stretched to breaking point.

Alice was wearing glasses this morning, Hazel realised, and it made the similarity with Felicity striking. They turned towards her and she braced herself against their scrutiny – Alice's eyes full of despair and Felicity's disgust.

"I'm sure you have an explanation, Hazel," Alice said softly. "I'd like to hear it."

"This'll be good." Felicity folded her arms. "Not that we'll believe a word you say."

"We have to give her a chance," Alice said. "Nothing is ever black and white."

Hazel tried to speak but her lips were so dry they stuck together. "I need water," she croaked.

"Oh please!" Felicity said.

Greta shuffled around to Hazel's side and passed a glass of water from the table. Hazel took a sip and then a big swallow. Greta removed the glass from her trembling hands then sat down beside her and gripped one hand tightly. "Can you tell us now, Nan?"

Dear Greta. Hazel felt the squeeze of her hand and began. "It was Franklyn's idea—"

"Of course it was." Felicity's voice dripped with sarcasm.

"Let her tell the story," Alice said.

Hazel turned to Alice. "I did ask him if we could raise your baby. I didn't want to have more children after what I'd gone through with June and I thought it the perfect opportunity. You would be there to see your baby grow and to the world you'd be a doting aunt and Franklyn and I could grant the social correctness, but he'd have none of it. He just laughed at me. I was so upset and I didn't know how to tell you."

"How did you change his mind?" Alice asked.

"I reminded him of the insurance money and that half of it was yours. Franklyn was motivated by money, as we've come to know. I said if you lived with us we wouldn't have to split the money but it would go towards keeping a roof over yours and the baby's heads. He'd won the job in Adelaide and we were preparing to move. He wanted the money badly to buy us the house in Adelaide, I said no-one would know us there. The only people who would know the truth were the three of us."

"And Isabelle," Felicity said.

"We had to tell Isabelle." Hazel kept her gaze on Alice. "She knew I wasn't pregnant and you were."

"So Isabelle was part of the conspiracy," Felicity said. "I never did like her."

"But what happened when the baby...when Mum was born?" Greta asked.

"It took me a long time to recover after June's birth. Franklyn agreed I could stay with Isabelle and he would visit us on weekends. I jumped at the chance because it meant you and I would still be close, Alice. It wasn't an easy arrangement but I was beginning to feel stronger – even though June was still not sleeping well, she was feeding easily. The Sunday before Felicity was born, you and I had that terrible row and I was a mess. Franklyn arrived and was disappointed with me, he said I wasn't trying hard enough to get better. Isabelle had words with him when she heard him tell me I should pull myself together."

"I'm sorry we fought the last time we saw each other, Hazel."

"What did you fight about?" Greta asked.

"It was silly," Alice said quickly. "I was feeling fat and fed up, as you do nearing the end of a pregnancy, I'd had a run in with matron about keeping my space tidy and I was feeling anxious. The only birth I knew about had been June's and that hadn't gone well for mother or baby. I couldn't wait to meet up with Hazel and get out for a while. When she came she said she was tired and wanted to cut our visit short. I accused her of not caring. She called me thoughtless, blamed me for getting pregnant and causing all this stress. We said some horrible things to each other."

"I didn't mean what I said," Hazel whispered.

"I know that. Neither did I. We were both exhausted."

"It was that afternoon Franklyn arrived and found me in a state. He got a telling off from Isabelle—"

Felicity scoffed.

"She'd been a mother to him. He listened to her. He came to me almost grovelling with remorse. Told me he wanted another child but he could see how badly childbirth had affected me physically and emotionally. He was so gentle with me that night. The next morning he went back to Melbourne to work and the following Friday you went into labour, Alice. When he returned that weekend he told me he'd agree to us raising the baby. Perhaps he saw adopting Felicity as a way of having his cake and eating it too. I would be well and happy, we'd have our two children… whatever the reason, the day you went into labour, Alice, he told me we could keep your baby." Hazel didn't let her gaze falter from Alice. "There were conditions though."

"Of course there were," Felicity snarled.

Hazel didn't look away from Alice. "He wouldn't let me tell you, it had to be him and I had to stay away. I was prepared to do whatever it took to keep the baby. Then…after she…after Felicity was born…he said that he'd been to see you and that you were angry with me, you didn't want to see me and I wasn't to visit you. A day later he told me you'd run away."

"And you believed him," Felicity said.

"The last time I'd seen Alice she *had* been angry with me." Hazel dragged her gaze from Alice to Felicity. "He was very good at rearranging the truth."

"You were both good at that," Felicity snapped.

Alice reached for Felicity's hand. "He was a clever man who used his cleverness to deceive. He had me totally convinced that I was worthless and Hazel didn't want a bar of me. And because of our silly argument I accepted what he said."

Felicity shook her head.

Alice turned back to Hazel with such disappointment in her look that Hazel shrivelled inside.

"I understand what it must have been like for you, Hazel, but even with all that happened…how could you let me believe my baby had died?"

Hazel sagged in her chair. The little bits of oxygen she was managing to drag into her lungs were barely enough to keep her upright.

"The only way Franklyn would agree to the adoption was... that I break all ties with you and that..." Hazel shifted her gaze to Felicity who was staring at her with something akin to loathing in her eyes. "And that you never be told that you were adopted."

"But how could he just take a baby?" Greta said. "Surely there were staff who knew, forms to fill out."

"The forms were filled out," Hazel said. "I signed as the mother but it was all done after...when I thought Alice had run away. The midwife came to Isabelle's and brought Felicity with her. I watched Franklyn walk her to the car and he gave her something. It looked like an envelope which I'd assumed was part of the paperwork but...it was probably money."

"The doctor wasn't present when I had the baby," Alice said. "He'd gone home, said I was still a long way from delivering. It was that dreadful midwife who delivered Felicity. She was one of a few staff who treated me as if I was a sinful hussy, most of the others were aloof but caring."

"I can only assume Franklyn managed to manipulate the midwife as well," Hazel said.

"I don't know if it was better or worse believing my baby had died," Alice said. "But I still don't understand how you could have given up on *me*, Hazel."

"I didn't know you'd been told your baby died. Not until you said the other night. Franklyn went to the home the day after Felicity was born. He returned to tell me you'd run off and as we were next of kin he'd organised for us to adopt the baby. He convinced me that you...well, you were changed and no longer wanted to be my sister. You've got to believe me – I truly thought it was better for us to adopt your baby than strangers. I was still breastfeeding June so it was no problem for me to take on Felicity. He even let me choose the name. I'd had no say in June's. I'd always loved the name Felicity and…Morgan was for you."

"It's a beautiful name." Alice held Hazel's gaze, her voice little more than a whisper.

"It's easy to blame Franklyn for everything now," Felicity snapped. "But you've had fifty years to try to find Alice, to tell me the truth."

Hazel had no answer for that. How weak she'd been. Why hadn't she asked more questions, stood up to Franklyn? She'd been barely able to look after herself and the children. Franklyn had organised everything and she'd let him. Moving to Adelaide had nearly been her undoing but he'd taken care of her, even helped with meals and washing in those early days, and taken the babies for a walk around the block to give her a few minutes' rest. She'd been helpless without him.

"Life was different then," Alice said gently. "Your mother was dependant on Franklyn, it wasn't easy for her."

"How can you defend her?" Felicity said.

Hazel was surprised too. She'd thought Alice would reject her completely once she knew the truth.

Alice looked at her now, her face softened by sorrow and compassion. "Because I know what Franklyn was capable of," she whispered.

There was a collective drawing in of breath.

"I'm sorry to say it, especially in front of Greta," Alice said. "But Franklyn was a manipulative, arrogant and abusive man."

"Oh, no, Nan." Greta gripped Hazel's hand tighter. "Did he hit you?"

"No. He never did that. He was demanding and made sure he got his own way by making life miserable in other ways if he didn't."

"Like not coming to school plays and sports days," Felicity said.

"It was usually me he was cross with, not you," Hazel said. "He knew the way to manipulate me was through you girls."

"I can't believe all this." Greta looked as if she were going to cry but her eyes remained dry. "So, Alice is really Mum's mother and you are her aunt and that makes Alice my nan and you my great-aunt?"

Hazel nodded.

"And I have a living child." Alice turned to Felicity. "I never got to see you but a small part of me hoped they were lying, that my baby hadn't died. Then when I lost my two boys I thought it must have been true and I never thought to look for you again. I'm so sorry."

"You weren't to blame," Felicity mumbled.

Alice held her arms wide and Felicity stepped into them. "I get to hold my firstborn at last."

Felicity began to sob then and Alice as well. Greta finally gave in to her tears and threw her arms around the other two women. Hazel was the only one dry-eyed, sitting all alone, a table between them and a wall of misery surrounding her.

★

Alice's heart was on supercharge. There was an electric zing inside her she hadn't felt for a long time. It was a mix of happiness and hope. Happiness because she'd found the child she'd thought she'd never see and hope because at last she had her own family again. She eased herself from Felicity's embrace then out from under

Greta's arm, looking at them both with a maternal eye rather than an aunt's.

Then she looked over and her new-found joy was tempered by Hazel sitting stiffly across from her, so small and frail. It was difficult to know how to move forward from here but Alice knew she had to find it in her heart to forgive her sister if they were all to have any future together.

"Thank you, Hazel," she said.

Hazel lifted her gaze from her hands, despair etched on her face. "What for?"

"You did a fine job of raising Felicity in difficult circumstances and I know from how much Greta loves you that you've been an integral part of her life too."

"Of course she has." Greta rushed to Hazel and bobbed down beside her.

"We can't change what's done but I hope we can find a way forward...together," Alice said.

"Truly?" Hazel pressed her fingers to her trembling lips.

"This has all been a shock but I still love you, Nan." Greta turned back to Alice. "But if you're my nan too I can't call you both that."

Alice chuckled, releasing the tension inside her. "Alice will do just fine."

"Well, isn't that wonderful." Felicity leaped to her feet. "You might be ready to play happy families but I'm bloody well not." She swiped up a piece of toast and marched to the door, letting herself outside and shutting it firmly behind her.

The three women who were left behind watched dumbfounded as she passed the side window and marched out the front gate.

★

Felicity pushed her back against the base of the straggly she-oak she'd taken refuge under. Her eyes were squeezed shut against the glare of the cloudless morning sky and her glasses on the sand beside her. She'd been so angry at them all back at the house she'd marched outside and several metres along the road before she'd crossed paths with a man walking three big dogs and realised what she'd done. He'd smiled and said hello. Her mouth had gone dry and her breath came in short gasps. She'd known that wasn't good. She'd dashed across the road, startling a kid on a pushbike, and found herself this hidey-hole among the vegetation above the beach. And she'd been sitting here ever since, taking long slow breaths and steadying the galloping horses in her chest back to a trot. She didn't even have a hat or sunglasses to hide behind.

Inside her head was a mess of thoughts and in her heart a quagmire of emotion. It had been a shock to discover she was adopted. Then for Ian to leave her and want to sell the house had been what she'd thought was the final blow but they just kept coming. She had almost made up with Hazel but hadn't quite been able to go the final step to forgive her.

Now to find she'd been keeping such a huge secret – that Alice was Felicity's true mother – had been a bombshell that had blasted away the fragments of reconciliation between them. To top it off, Felicity had been stunned by Alice's easy forgiveness of Hazel. And then for Greta, Felicity's true flesh and blood, to also accept Hazel's duplicity had been more than she could stand.

Now here she was, stuck outside under a bush, unable to go back to Alice's but with nowhere else to hide. She groaned and gripped her head in her hands.

"Felicity?"

She hunched her shoulders over, pressed her face to her knees and held her breath. She didn't want to talk to Hazel right now – in fact she couldn't imagine ever wanting to talk to her again.

"There you are."

Felicity squinted one eye open. She saw Alice's shoes. When she'd called out she'd sounded so much like Hazel.

"Are you all right?" Alice asked.

Felicity put her head back on her knees. "Yes," she muttered.

"Do you mind if I sit?"

Felicity shook her head, bumping her nose on her knees. "Oww!" She rubbed her nose, felt for her glasses and slid them back on.

"It's such a bore to always have to wear glasses or contacts, isn't it?" Alice said. "Better than having no sight at all though, I suppose, so I shouldn't complain."

"Your glasses suit you," Felicity said. "I often have trouble with mine. I leave them in places where they get misplaced or broken on a regular basis."

"I used to be like that," Alice said. "Getting contacts has helped."

"I guess I inherited my short-sightedness from you."

"I hope that's all."

When Felicity looked at Alice she was staring out at the sea. "Are you thinking of the CF thing?"

"Yes. It makes no difference to you now." Alice grinned at her. "I'm assuming you're not planning on more babies, but if you carry the gene then you may have passed it on to Greta."

Felicity's heart skipped, remembering Alice's other children had died. "She could have a child with cystic fibrosis?"

"Only if both she and her partner carry the gene and then it's a one in four chance. It can be passed down for generations doing no harm until two parents, both carriers, have children. I know of a family where only one of the children has CF and another where all of the offspring have it."

"How would Greta find out?"

"She would have been tested at birth as part of the heel prick test they do these days, but there are variations, and now that there's a definite family history it might be worth seeing a GP for another test, to be sure. Forewarned is forearmed and the more information researchers can gather the better for CF carriers in the future."

Felicity stared out to sea then. When Greta was little she'd had lots of ear infections and Felicity had worried her hearing would be affected. She'd been so relieved when her preschool check had declared she had perfect hearing. Then she'd worried she'd need glasses like Felicity but her eyesight was also perfect, like Ian's. There'd been other things to be anxious about over the years, a broken arm, a terrible bout of flu and a ruptured appendix, but Greta had made it to adulthood in excellent health. Now there was this faulty gene thing to worry about for future grandchildren.

"That creased brow makes me think you might be a worrier like me."

Felicity turned back from the view to find Alice studying her.

"Greta and Hazel have decided to go home this afternoon."

"Today?" Felicity could think of nothing worse than spending hours in the car with Hazel.

"I wondered if you'd like to stay on here for a few more days," Alice said. "I can drive you back to Adelaide whenever you're ready but...it would be nice to have some time, just the two of us...or perhaps you'd prefer to go?"

The warm feeling rose inside Felicity again, the sense of security that she'd felt when Alice had announced she was her aunt and then later her mother. The tightness in her chest eased and she blew out a slow breath. "I'd like that."

Alice placed a tentative arm across her shoulders. "Things will sort themselves out, you know," she said.

Felicity leaned her head on Alice's shoulder and felt a small flutter of hope that she could be right.

thirty-nine

It was late afternoon when Greta pulled into the driveway of her parents' house. She'd promised her mum she'd check on Dolly and feed her each day until Felicity came home. She let her hands fall to her sides, pressed her head back against the rest and took a long slow breath. She'd had no idea when she'd planned the Easter holiday what a blow-up and ensuing fallout it would create.

There'd been an emotional scene as Greta and Hazel had prepared to leave with much hugging and promises of more catchups, except for Felicity who had hugged Greta goodbye but ignored Hazel. The drive back to Adelaide had been a long one. She'd tried to convince Hazel that Felicity would come around eventually, but Hazel hadn't said much and Greta knew she was miserable. It had been difficult to leave her when they'd arrived at Hazel's house. Greta had gone inside with her and had a cup of tea but Hazel had packed her off soon after.

Greta dragged herself from the car and down the side of the house, unlocked the gate and then the laundry door. The smell hit her as soon as she entered. Dolly's litter trays had been well used.

She covered her nose and mouth with one hand but still gagged as she dragged each one outside, her feet crunching on the crystals that were scattered over the floor. Dolly mewed loudly at her, wanting attention. She picked the cat up. "Poor Dolly, you don't like a smelly litter tray, do you?"

In the kitchen the smell wasn't so bad but the air was stale. There was still dry food in some of the bowls. Greta opened a can of cat food and Dolly devoured the contents immediately.

She opened up the back doors across the deck for some air flow and surveyed the house. She couldn't believe the mess Felicity had left in each room. Only the front lounge was reasonably tidy where her mum had said Ian's clothes had been. He must have taken them with him.

Back in the kitchen Dolly had eaten her fill and strolled outside. Greta cleaned up the empty food bowls, leaving only one with dry food. She'd come each day to make sure Dolly was okay. She washed the bowls and the other dishes her mother had left in the sink then went to tackle the litter trays.

Finally there was a small semblance of order in the laundry and kitchen at least, and Dolly was back inside cleaning herself on the couch. Greta gave her one last cuddle, promised to return the next day, locked up and left.

Thirty minutes later she was pulling up in her own driveway, relieved to get out of the car after a long day of driving and keen to see Joe. The decision to return to Adelaide early had meant a quick pack up and farewell and she hadn't rung him to let him know she was coming. It was almost dark and there were no lights on inside so she assumed he was still at his sister's. Greta would have to spoil the surprise and ring him in case he was planning to stay another night there. At least they'd have food. Alice had sent her home with a container of chicken curry and another full of pink jelly cakes.

Inside the townhouse the air was stale. It wasn't as bad as Dolly's litter trays but her enthusiasm at returning home dwindled as she took in the mess. There were dishes and pans scattered across kitchen benches, discarded clothes on the living room floor and a pizza box and empty beer bottles on the coffee table. A pile of Xbox games had toppled and spread across the floor in front of the TV. In the bedroom there were more clothes scattered and the doona and sheets and pillows were a jumbled mess across the bed.

Greta could so easily have dropped to the floor and cried. She wasn't a clean freak but the house had been tidy when she'd left, and after the weekend she'd had, this was the worst kind of homecoming. Given Joe wasn't expecting her he may have tried to clean up tomorrow but she doubted it. She flung everything off the bed ready to remake it. Then, as she bent to pick up the doona, she stopped. What the hell was she doing? Was this what life with Joe was always going to be like? Did it mean she'd fluctuate from feelings of adoration to feelings of animosity that he couldn't do a simple clean up after himself?

She went back to the kitchen, made herself a cup of coffee and with two jelly cakes in hand she pushed everything off the coffee table, set down her supper and settled on the couch in front of the TV. After a fruitless channel flick she went in search of her favourite DVD. Amelia Earhart's story always inspired her. She'd brought a few of her favourite movies with her when she'd moved in with Joe. She put it in the player, pressed play, but nothing happened. Even a polish with the corner of her shirt wasn't enough for it to play. It was simply worn out.

Disappointed, she sank back on her heels and surveyed the mess around her. No way was she going to clean it up. Instead she rummaged for another of her favourite movies, *The Guernsey Literary and Potato Peel Pie Society*. She needed some inspiration right now.

★

Hazel was at home, wandering aimlessly from room to room. Her place seemed cheerless compared to Alice's comfortable house by the beach or perhaps it was that she was alone once again. She wondered what Alice and Felicity would be doing now. At this hour Felicity would no doubt have her usual bottle of wine open. She pictured them sitting on Alice's couch, catching up on fifty years of missing memories.

Hazel wished she was there but Felicity was unlikely to ever speak to Hazel again so there had been little point in staying.

There was some relief in revealing a secret she'd kept for so long but it was countered by the guilt she felt at Alice's revelation. How could Hazel have not known what had happened under her roof? The sorrow of it clawed at her, making her question everything she'd known.

From somewhere in the bedroom she heard a faint noise then realised it was her phone, probably still in the bottom of her handbag. She walked slowly towards the sound. If it was June she wouldn't answer, but what if it was Alice or Felicity? It wasn't until she'd got back to Adelaide that she'd realised she didn't have Alice's number, and she didn't think Felicity would respond to a text to say they'd arrived safely but she'd sent it anyway. By the time she found her phone it had stopped ringing. Jack was at the top of her missed call list.

At least there was someone who wanted to talk to her. She pressed re-call. Five minutes later Hazel was in a state she could only describe as being in a tizz. Jack had come back a few days early from his blokes' trip in the north. One of the men had got sick and they'd decided it best to return home. He had some news for her and when she told him she was home too he'd asked if he could come to her house. Of course she'd said yes.

Now she was moving around her home with new purpose. Franklyn had been a miserable man. His final vengeance had been to destroy her relationship with her precious daughter but she wasn't going to be a victim any longer. She was seventy-six and for most of her life she'd been hiding in the shade, living at only half pace. She had to make the best of whatever time was left to her and purging herself of anything to do with Franklyn was the beginning.

She picked up any photos on display that included Franklyn and put them aside. The last was in pride of place on the large dresser beside the dining table. It had been taken two years earlier on their golden anniversary. They'd had a special family dinner together and everyone had been there: June, Derek and the boys; Felicity, Ian, Greta and Joe. Hazel studied her own face, her lips turned up in a smile. How many times over the years had she smiled for a photo when she was cringing inside but that night *had* been a happy one. Franklyn had been in a good mood and had paid for everything, drinks and dinner. She'd been surprised because it had been such an expensive restaurant.

She studied his face now, could almost smell the peppermint that would have been on his breath. His wide lips were turned up in the smallest of smiles, his eyes with a hint of spark and his dark hair neatly arranged so as not to show the thinning patches on his scalp. She leaned in and found the little smudge of colour that hadn't washed away from his temple. He didn't ever want her to let on to anyone that she dyed his hair but it must have been obvious. After his cancer treatment his hair had thinned and he'd gone grey. He'd ordered her to buy him some hair colour and put it in for him and she'd been doing it till the day he died.

"You didn't break me, Franklyn," she said. "And you didn't break Alice, you bastard."

She dropped the ornate gold frame, a gift from June and Derek, face down on the pile with the other photos and then just as quickly picked it up again. She turned it over, slid the little gold catches over the red velvet backing and lifted the cover. There was a second photo slipped in behind. It was a better photo and her favourite but she hadn't displayed it because Franklyn was missing from it. Now she slid the front photo out to reveal the group shot behind. It had been taken by a waitress at the restaurant who'd snapped the happy family shot while they'd waited for Franklyn to come back from the bathroom. June, Derek, Lachlan and Joshua stood over Hazel's right shoulder all smiling at the camera and Hazel was looking up at Felicity who'd leaned in and said something to make her laugh. Ian, Greta and Joe were laughing too.

She was sorry about Ian and Felicity. She'd always thought him a good man but people did change. She knew that as well as anyone. She put the cover back on the photo and returned the frame to its place on the dresser, then she tossed all the photos she'd gathered into one of the boxes she'd got to put Franklyn's books in. She wasn't up to packing the books tonight but first thing tomorrow she'd start and June could have the bloody things – as long as they were gone from the house.

Hazel opened drawers and cupboards, searching out anything that might have been Franklyn's, from old pens to keyrings, to an ancient camera and long-forgotten name badges trapped in corners of drawers and more opened mint packets – it all went in the bin.

By the time there was a knock on her front door she'd managed to eradicate nearly every link with Franklyn, and any last vestiges of physical and visual connections to her life with him had been firmly swept away.

★

Felicity closed the blind against the dark night sky. She'd been shocked by the black expanse beyond the glass when she'd switched on the bedroom light. Her foray outside and across to the beach earlier in the day had been as far as she was prepared to stretch herself for the moment. She turned back to take another look at the queen bed. At Alice's insistence she'd moved into the room Greta had vacated. Alice had said it was by far the better room, bigger with an en suite and a beautiful view.

Felicity shivered in the chilly air. The days had been warm but once the sun went down the temperature dropped quickly. Her dressing gown lay across the end of the bed. She dragged it on then trailed her fingers over the pretty pastel colours of the quilt cover, switched on the bedside lamp and turned off the main light. Her book sat there beneath the lamp but she wasn't in the mood to read now. Nor was she tired enough to sleep, but she'd told Alice she was, so she couldn't go back downstairs now.

She sat on the edge of the bed. She could hear the TV softly through the door. Alice would be sitting down there alone, watching a movie. The woman who had birthed her and yet had never held her until now. And there'd been no mention of her father. Had he been Alice's sweetheart? What happened to him? Did she have photos? Suddenly Felicity was filled with questions and the only person who could give her the answers was just one floor below her.

The wild horses were struggling against her chest and she was terrified of going back downstairs in case they escaped.

*

Alice settled on the couch with a cup of chamomile tea, drew a soft alpaca blanket over her knees and pressed play on the movie she'd selected from her stash. She'd chosen *Mission Impossible*, hoping the action wouldn't be too hard to follow and yet be enough of a distraction but she kept glancing up at the ceiling. Beyond it was the room where Felicity was sleeping.

Alice had been so happy she'd wanted to stay, but once they'd been on their own, conversation had been stilted. Felicity hadn't wanted to go outside again so Alice had taken her on a tour of the back part of the house where her bedroom was. They'd looked at her veggie patch and chickens through the window, placed a few more pieces in the jigsaw, talked about sport. Alice had been a keen tennis player when she and Roy had moved to the district. Felicity had said how she'd played as a kid and then kept up social tennis with a group of friends. They'd talked about decorating their respective new homes but Felicity had looked more and more dejected until, in the late afternoon, she'd opened a bottle of wine and they'd watched a travel show on TV, hardly talking at all.

Just before dinner there'd been a text message from Greta to say they'd arrived home safely. Felicity's phone had pinged at the same time but she hadn't looked at it. A bit later there'd been another ping and that time Felicity had shoved her phone into her pocket and taken a big gulp of wine.

Alice's heart ached for her. So much had happened in Felicity's life in the last month, she was acting like a woman who didn't know which way was up. Alice felt it herself and wished Felicity felt comfortable enough to talk to her. That there was some kind of peace she could offer her daughter. She was only a floor above but there might as well have been an ocean between them.

*

Greta woke as the credits of the movie rolled up. She'd barely made it through the first half before her eyes had grown heavy and she'd dozed off. Now she twisted her neck from side to side to shift the kinks caused by the awkward position she'd been sleeping in. It was eight o'clock and when she flicked off the TV there wasn't a sound but something had woken her. She felt around for her phone, finding it between the cushions on the couch. There was a message from her cousin in New Zealand. She smiled as she read it. It was the last piece of information she needed to put her plan into place. She sent a quick reply and then rang Joe.

"Hi, my lovely," he said. His voice had that warm buzzy sound he took on when he'd had a few drinks.

"I'm home early," she said.

"Oh no, you should have let me know."

"Where are you?"

"Still painting. Although it's only Dad who's actually working now, finishing off some door frames. The rest of us have been tucking into Mum's chicken wings and we've had a few beers." He groaned. "I've probably had one too many to drive yet."

Greta was disappointed.

"Hey, why don't you come over here? I've only got a mattress on the floor but we could share."

Greta wanted to see Joe but she wasn't up for a night on the garage floor. "How much more painting is there to do?"

"Only a couple of ceilings. We'll do them first thing then move most of the furniture back in."

"I'll come over tomorrow afternoon then. See the finished product and maybe I can help move stuff."

"Okay. How come you came back early? Didn't things work out?"

"It's complicated. I'll tell you all about it later."

"Okay. Call me when you're on your way tomorrow."

Greta ended the call. She sat for a moment taking in the mess that surrounded her again. Then she opened her phone and selected another number.

"Hi Nan," she said as soon as it was answered. "Is it too late for me to come over?"

*

Hazel opened the door to Greta and gave her a hug. "I didn't expect to be seeing you again so soon."

"You're sure I'm not interrupting?"

"Of course not. I'm glad you're here." Hazel's family relationships were so fractured and patched that she prayed her bond with Greta would remain strong even after tonight's news. She shut the door on the cool night and led Greta back to the warm kitchen. "I'd like you to meet Jack."

Jack rose to his feet as soon as they entered. "Hello. You must be the delightful Greta I've heard so much about."

They shook hands and Greta gave him one of her bright cheeky smiles in return. "And you're the mysterious Jack I've heard nothing about."

"That's not true, Greta." Hazel waved her to a chair. "I've told you Jack and I go to lunch and a movie each week."

"She didn't tell me you were so young and good looking."

Jack laughed. "She's a charmer this one."

"Have you eaten, Greta?" Hazel asked. "There's plenty of Alice's hotpot left."

Greta groaned and gripped her stomach. "That'd be great. Joe's not home and all I've had is cake."

"Hazel said you've got some good news for her," Jack said.

"Yes." Greta's eyes shone as Hazel came back to the table with a bowl of the hotpot.

"It's the night for it," Hazel said. "Jack's brought good news too."

"Well, let's not get too excited yet," Jack said.

"What's this about?" Greta swallowed a mouthful of food, glancing from one to the other.

"Jack has a granddaughter who's a lawyer." Hazel sat beside Greta. "And she thinks…" Hazel took a breath. Much of her life had been lived on lies, that Felicity was her real daughter, that her marriage was happy. Tonight, before Jack had rung, she'd determined there'd be no more.

Jack reached out and squeezed her hand. "Your nan should never have been advised by Kurt Blanchard. He's your granddad's lawyer."

Hazel felt strength flow from his hand to hers. She cleared her throat. "Jack's granddaughter thinks I've got a good case to contest Franklyn's will."

There was a pause as Greta took in what she'd said and then her delighted "Yes," took Hazel by surprise.

"You're not disappointed? It might mean you don't get your inheritance."

"That's what I wanted to talk to you about."

"Your inheritance?"

"Yes. I don't want the money." Greta grimaced. "Well, that sounds wrong – of course it would be nice but not to your detriment. Anyway, I've talked to a lawyer too and then to Lach and Josh and they both agree. We want you to have the money, Nan, not us."

"You're entitled to it."

"No, we're not. If anyone's entitled to anything it's you and the boys agree with me."

"I think we should be drinking a toast," Jack said. "Do you have any alcohol, Hazel?"

"Only brandy. Or there's some Irish cream left from Christmas."

"That'll do."

Greta only had one nip but Hazel and Jack had two and then Hazel had had a third. By the time Greta offered to drive Jack home and Hazel was waving them off she was in such high spirits she wasn't really sure if it was the possibility of being in charge of her own finances that was making her feel so light-headed or if she was perhaps just a teeny bit tipsy.

forty

It was mid-morning before Alice heard footsteps on the stairs. She'd been working quietly around the house and outside in the garden but hadn't been able to settle to anything, all the time thinking about Felicity and there she was at last.

"Good morning," Alice said.

Felicity's smile was brief. She moved straight to the coffee machine and inserted a pod. "Sorry I'm so late down. It took me a while to settle last night and then I must have gone into a deep sleep. I only woke up a while ago."

"You probably needed a good rest. There's been a lot to take in." Alice got up from the couch where she'd been flicking through magazines, not really concentrating on any of the contents. "Can I get you something to eat?"

"No, thank you. Coffee's fine for now."

Alice paused, not sure what to do.

Felicity made her coffee and took it to the chair in the corner of the lounge with its back to the view. It had become her favourite.

Alice's phone vibrated in her pocket. She snatched it out. "Hello, Elaine. How's Hugh?"

Elaine had sent several updates about her son's progress and now it seemed she was coming home the next day and bringing him with her.

"That's lovely news. I've been keeping an eye on your place and everything's fine. Nothing much happening here." Alice glanced at Felicity who was staring into her cup. "Shall I bring you round something for dinner?"

Elaine had sounded relieved at the prospect and had asked Alice if she could also bring any sweets she might have in her freezer. Evidently Hugh's appetite was returning.

"I'll see you tomorrow afternoon." Alice ended the call and slid her phone back into her pocket. "That was my friend Elaine. She has a son in Adelaide, lives with his dad but he's broken his leg and she's bringing him back to convalesce at her place for a while."

"Have you told her about me?"

"I haven't told anyone."

"It might shock your friends."

"I'm not worried about my friends." Alice conjured up the few names she'd call real friends: Betty, who lived an hour away, Elaine, Bec, the other women at cards, perhaps Errol now, but none of them knew her that well. Roy had been the only friend she'd needed. "They have to take me as I am. My concern is for you, for Hazel and Greta."

Felicity's fingernails tapped a sharp tune on the side of her cup. "How can you be such a saint, Alice? So forgiving after all the terrible things that have happened in your life?"

"I'm not a saint. I wished Franklyn dead for a long time. I even wanted to die myself after I lost you and Hazel didn't want anything to do with me—"

"I don't understand how she could do that to you." Felicity put the cup on the small table beside her and stood, her arms rigid at her sides. "June and I don't see eye to eye on a lot of things but I can't imagine cutting her out of my life forever."

"Not even if something happened that caused the emotions between you that you're feeling for Hazel right now?"

"It's not the same. How could she have raised me as hers and kept you, her own sister, a secret?"

"I believe her when she says that was the only way Franklyn would let her keep you."

"The only father I knew was a monster."

Alice couldn't say otherwise. She'd lived with that knowledge most of her life. "That doesn't make you one."

Felicity stared into her cup. "Since I found out I was adopted I've been thinking about who my parents might be. I've imagined so many scenarios. Then when I found out you were my mother it was a surprise but a relief that it was someone as nice as you."

"Would it help if I told you about your real father?"

"Your childhood sweetheart?"

Alice nodded. "We've been so focused on everyone else we—"

"Was he a good person?"

"He was." Alice smiled but stumbled over how to begin. She was suddenly shy about her early love life. It didn't feel right to just blurt out the circumstance of Felicity's conception. "Let's go to the beach."

"What?" Felicity blinked at her.

Alice pushed back from the table and went to Felicity. "The beach we visited the other day. It's a special place for me and...we can talk and relax and...I'd like to take you there again."

"Now?" Felicity cowered as if someone was going to attack her.

"You can do it. It's Easter Monday, probably won't be many people about."

Felicity's shoulders lowered.

"Just us together," Alice urged. "And with any luck we'll have the beach to ourselves again and we can talk. I can tell you all about your father...your biological father."

"I don't know if I can."

"You managed last time." Alice held out a hand. "You're stronger than you think."

Even after Felicity finally agreed, it took time for her to get ready and for Alice to throw together a picnic lunch. Everything was loaded in the car and they got as far as the door before Felicity put on the brakes.

"I don't have any sunglasses. I could barely see last time, it was so bright."

Not to be foiled at the last, Alice found a pair of sunglasses she wore when she had her contacts in and bundled Felicity into the car.

★

Greta sat at one of her favourite coffee spots in the busy cafe area at Harbour Town. A combination of Easter and school holidays and another sunny day had brought out the crowds. In spite of the busyness she was always happy here where she had a good view of the planes as they took off or landed. She and her dad had come here many times during her childhood or made the shorter trip to Parafield Airport. She waved at him now as he wove through the people towards her.

"It's good to see you, Grets." He wrapped her in a squeezy hug.

She closed her eyes and hugged him back, allowing herself a brief moment to forget all that had happened over the last few weeks. To imagine her mum was at home as normal and that her dad had just popped out to meet her for a bit of plane-spotting and a coffee.

"I got you a coffee." Greta waved at the two cups on the table as they sat down.

"Thanks. I wasn't expecting you to be home."

"Nan and I came back early but Mum decided to stay on for a while." She didn't have the energy to explain all the ins and outs of what had happened. "I was coming over this way anyway. I told Mum I'd feed Dolly."

He looked up quickly from his coffee. "Have you been to the house?"

"Yes."

"Then you've seen the mess."

"I've cleaned up the worst of it. Poor Dolly."

"I'm sorry. I would have done something but I thought your mum was coming back today and it would have served her right to be met by that stink. The real estate agent was gagging, poor guy."

Greta couldn't help but smile at the thought and then her dad chuckled. "She's good at making a point, your mum."

"She's hurting badly, Dad. Not only did you leave her but you did it on the day she found out she was adopted."

"I didn't know then. Hazel told me the day she and I met on the doorstep. I felt even worse about leaving. I'd been trying to do it for months. Would I have delayed if I'd known?" He shrugged. "There was always some family event or crisis. I couldn't keep putting it off."

"I guess not."

They were distracted by the sight of a Qantas plane roaring down the runway towards them to take off over the sea.

"Boeing 737," they both said at once.

Ian smiled. "How are you, Grets? And Joe. I feel as if I haven't seen him in ages."

Greta thought about the mess she still hadn't tidied at her place and her promise to go and help Joe's family move furniture this afternoon and another invite she'd got from Ivan that morning to go flying again.

"We're okay," she said.

"That sounds a bit noncommittal."

"I'm tired, that's all."

"What's up?" He wouldn't be put off.

"You and Mum. How do I know it's not going to happen to me and Joe?"

"Oh Grets, I'm so sorry. I didn't make this decision easily and part of that was because I didn't want to hurt you or your mum. I've changed and I guess there was no way of predicting that was going to happen but if you and Joe love each other and keep talking things through, you've got as good a chance as any at a long, happy marriage. Look at my parents at your nan and grandad, they have, had, happy—"

Greta let out a sob then clapped her hand to her mouth as the person on the next table looked at her.

"Greta, what is it? Has Joe done something?"

"It's more that he's done nothing," she snapped, the anger drying up her tears.

"What's that mean?"

Her dad's look was so compassionate she started talking about the mess she'd found at her place and then she was blathering out her annoyance at Joe for doing so little to help at home, how he was so fixated on buying a house and maybe one that would need renovating, that he didn't want her to fly even though it was her dream. Tears brimmed then and she stopped to dig a tissue from her bag.

He waited while she blew her nose. "Joe's a good bloke. Your mum and I thought he was a keeper from the start. We agreed on that. You need to talk to him."

"Then I sound like a nag." She blew her nose hard.

"Not when you're angry. I mean you need to plan it, sit down and talk to him. Tell him what bothers you and why. Ask him to tell you the same."

"Do you think that'd work?"

"If you truly love Joe it's worth a try." He shrugged. "Maybe if I'd done that with your mum…"

Another plane thundered along the runway but neither of them looked this time, they simply sat and waited as the noise faded away.

"Couldn't you still?" Greta said.

"I did try but not hard enough and time went by and…it's too late now."

"You don't love Mum…just a little bit?"

"I did truly love her but not now. I'll always have wonderful memories. And you're the best thing of all. Nothing can change that, Grets."

She smiled through her tears, wiped her eyes and blew her nose again. "Thanks, Dad. I guess you'll always be my number one dad too."

"I'm sorry I couldn't help with your flying dream. I didn't realise how much you wanted it. And now all my money's tied up with—"

"I never expected you to pay for that. You put me through uni, kept a roof over my head. It wasn't until I got this job I'm in that I realised how much I wanted to be the one flying the planes instead of helping manage them from the ground."

"You could still do it. You're only twenty-four."

"But Joe wants a house, and a wedding and babies."

"That's his dream, Grets, but if it's not yours you need to talk to him."

"I know." Her mind strayed to the conversation she'd had with Alice, the day they'd met at the airstrip. Since Alice had opened the door to the possibility of earning an income from flying she'd pondered it again and again.

They both sipped their coffees and when Ian set his back on the saucer, he fiddled with the handle. "It's early days..." He took a breath. "But I have actually met someone else."

Greta felt a stab of discomfort. She couldn't imagine her dad with anyone but her mum.

"I'd like you to meet her."

She put up her hand. "It's too soon, Dad."

His shoulders slumped but he maintained his smile. "Okay."

Another plane rumbled overhead. Greta looked around as the Jetstar flight touched down.

"Airbus 320," she said a second before her dad.

*

Jack thanked Hazel again for the ride as he got out of the car. "I'm happy to use public transport," he said, "but it's not so easy on public holidays."

"And I'm happy to pick you up. My car doesn't get much of a run these days," she said.

Jack had rung first thing to see if Hazel had time to meet his granddaughter. She'd said yes, of course, and had offered lunch and a movie at her house to follow, which had included an offer to pick him up. It wasn't until Greta was going to drive him home the previous night that Hazel had realised he didn't have a car and had taken a taxi to her place.

"It was lovely to meet Erin. What a clever woman she is." They'd spent the last hour with the young lawyer who'd very kindly gone through what could be done about Franklyn's will. Hazel almost floated back into her house, she felt so buoyed by Erin's enthusiasm.

"She's a good lass. Checks in on me from time to time. The only one of my wife's family who's kept in touch."

Hazel's jubilation was temporarily marred as she recalled Jack had lost the roof over his head. "It's a pity she couldn't help you."

"Erin was still at school when all that happened. I did get legal advice but there was little I could do. Anyway, that's all done now. We've other fish to fry. Doesn't this look flash." Jack had stopped beside the dining table she'd set with her white tablecloth and best silver cutlery and glassware.

"More things that don't get used much these days." Hazel went into the kitchen. "Please sit down. Would you like a glass of this wine you brought?"

"Put it in the fridge for now, unless you'd like one."

"I'll wait for lunch." She bent down to switch on the oven. "There's a selection of DVDs there." Hazel pointed to the stack she'd put at the end of the table.

She served up as he looked through the pile. They'd just finished and were on their second glass of wine when Hazel's doorbell rang.

"Bother," she said. They'd been having such an enjoyable time. Jack had been telling her about his weekend with the blokes and he'd had her in stitches at some of their antics. She'd barely had time to get out of her chair when the bell rang again.

Her good humour evaporated when she opened the door to reveal June beyond the screen.

"It's so annoying you keeping the screens locked," June said as Hazel let her in. June bent to kiss her. "Gosh, your cheeks look red. Are you okay?"

"I'm fine."

June strode ahead of Hazel towards the family room. "Is your phone flat? I couldn't get you. I rang Greta and she said you were home."

Hazel almost ran into the back of her daughter as she stopped abruptly. Hazel stepped around her as Jack rose to his feet.

June looked him up and down, cast her eye over the table then back at Jack. "Who are you?"

"June, that sounds rude," Hazel said. "This is my friend, I told you about Jack."

"Hello, June." Jack held out his hand and June gave it a brief shake.

"You're Mum's lunch-and-movie boy."

Hazel hoped Jack wouldn't take offence at June's manner. "It's good you've come over," she said. "I need to chat with you. Would you like a glass of wine?"

Once June was settled at the table, Hazel began to fill her in on all that Erin had told her. For once June remained silent and listened while Hazel explained the possibilities of a thing called a deed of family arrangement, and that the house should be Hazel's so that if the time came perhaps one day where she might need a nursing home she could pay her own way. "It's expensive to go into a home and I can't expect you to pay for me," Hazel concluded.

June's full lips turned up in a pout. "Felicity and I would both help when the time comes for that."

"Felicity doesn't have much money and she got nothing from your father's estate. It would be up to you and Derek to fund me."

"Oh...well." June was doing her goldfish impression again. "I'll have to talk to Derek."

"Yes, you do that." Hazel smiled as she played her last card. "My lawyer says Kurt should never have given me that advice. He was out of line. Being your father's lawyer, he should have insisted I get separate legal advice."

"I see." June's face was flushing bright pink.

"And my three darling grandchildren have generously declared they want me to have the money your father left them."

"Joshua and Lachlan haven't discussed that with us."

"I think they've been communicating with Greta."

"I hope Greta hasn't given them the wrong advice, perhaps Derek—"

"They've had their own legal advice."

"I see," June said again and downed the last of her wine. "I hope you haven't thrown out dad's books with all this meddling."

Hazel pursed her lips then forced them up in a smile. "Of course not. I just haven't decided what to do with them yet."

"If you do want to get rid of any let us know first. Derek was very keen on the full set of Biggles books." June turned to Jack. "You seem very involved in my mother's affairs. I hope your intentions are honourable."

Hazel's jaw dropped but Jack maintained a straight face. He'd be good at cards.

"Like you, I've her best interests at heart," he said, then gave her one of his warm smiles. "Now that we've got all the official business done, how about we finish the bottle of wine?"

"I'll leave you to it." June stood. "I've got a lot to do at home. I'll ring you tomorrow." Jack pursed his lips and Hazel rolled her eyes as June strode from the room and let herself out.

forty-one

Felicity had been quiet in the car and Alice had been glad. She wanted to tell her daughter the story of how her life had begun on the beach, not cooped up inside.

And so a good hour and a half from when the suggestion had first been made, Alice stopped the car in the beach carpark again. Once more it was empty but for them.

"I don't think anyone else is here," Alice called from the boot as she lifted out the small esky. "I've packed wine," she said, feeling a little guilty that she was using alcohol as a carrot to make sure Felicity would actually get out of the car.

The passenger door opened and Felicity climbed out. With the floaty white shirt, broad-brimmed hat swathed with her scarf and the dark glasses over her clear pair, she looked like an old-time film star going incognito.

At the cliff top they paused to gaze out over the pretty little bay again. The sight eased the tension that had built inside her. She hoped it would work its magic on Felicity too.

"Here we are," Alice said.

Felicity's chin lifted a little. "Here we are."

Alice led the way down the stairs to the beach where they ploughed their way through soft sand before finally reaching firmer footing. She put down her things. Felicity sat on the esky with her back to Alice, staring out to sea.

Alice didn't mind her silence, it was enough that they were together in this place that had been full of healing and happy memories for her. She studied Felicity, her gaze firmly fixed on the ocean in front of her. Alice prayed this place would help her begin to heal too.

"Would you like to go for a swim?" Alice asked.

"Not this time."

"What about a paddle in the water before we eat our lunch?" Alice stood in front of Felicity, forcing her to look up. "I'll put the esky in the shade and we can dip our feet in. If the tide's right I'll show you a funny little sideways wave that sometimes happens here. It's quite unusual. It runs perpendicular to the beach."

Felicity didn't respond.

"Then we can have our lunch, open the bottle of wine."

"Is that a bribe, Alice?"

"If you like."

Felicity sniffed.

"Come on." Alice offered her hand and Felicity took it.

They walked slowly to the water's edge. Felicity stopped to roll up her trousers and then they sucked in simultaneous breaths as the first wash of water swept over their feet. Alice started walking and Felicity followed. They kept to the edge of the waves.

"Roy and I used to come here a lot. When we were younger, and Walter gave us a day off, we'd camp overnight and go home as the sun rose next morning. We had a track across the paddocks from our place, so we didn't have to take the long loop road through the park. We'd swim and fish, explore the rock pools, and like today we were often the only two here. And at the end of the day we'd watch the sunset, cuddled together by a small campfire." She kept the skinny-dipping and the love-making on the beach to herself. Some things were her memories alone.

"I wish I could have met him."

"So do I. You two would have got along well. Roy was a gentleman. He could be kind and tender but he had no time for dwelling on what might have been. He thought deeply about things and he laughed easily. Your laugh reminds me of him, actually, and he was forthright like you are."

"Humph! I think others might describe that as blunt."

"You're at a low ebb now but I suspect you've an inner strength like he had."

Felicity stopped walking and looked at Alice, her eyes staring through the two sets of glasses. "You said you'd brought me here to tell me about my father."

Alice held her breath, nodded.

Felicity grabbed Alice's arm. "It's Roy, isn't it? Roy was...he was my father."

Alice nodded again, her lungs screaming for air. She gulped in a breath.

"How wonderful. You and Roy were childhood sweethearts."

Felicity let go of Alice's arm and spun in a circle, wobbling to a stop as the sand and water sucked at her feet.

"How did you...well, how did I..."

An internal heat added to the sun's warmth on Alice's cheeks. She began to walk again and Felicity followed.

"Roy was a country boy but he lived with his cousins in Melbourne so he could attend high school. He was good looking and shy. I'd noticed him but it wasn't until he asked me to the end-of-year dance that I knew he'd even registered I was alive. By the end of the night we were in love. I know some people say it's not possible to understand love at that age but we thought we knew." Alice closed her eyes and felt the warmth of her hand in Roy's hand, his other on her back as he taught her to dance, the scent of Lux soap when she rested her head against his shoulder. The first kiss at the end of the night before Franklyn picked her up. She stumbled in the water, opened her eyes.

"We saw little of each other, of course. You know how difficult it was for me to see friends, and once school finished Roy returned to the farm. The next year I went back to school but he started work, delivering milk. One morning the delivery was late and I'd been watching for it. I was amazed to see Roy walk up the front path with our bottles of milk in his hands.

"After that we met when we could, between the hours he worked and me keeping our catch-ups a secret from Franklyn… and to do that I also had to keep them a secret from Hazel. It was difficult. But Roy became my friend and confidant.

"He was a bit of a lost child too. He was the youngest and his mum had recently died. He felt her loss terribly. His dad thought sending him away to work would help. And I lived under the controlling hand of Franklyn.

"When Roy and I were together we were so happy and… friends became lovers and then…well, you know the rest."

Felicity stopped. Her brow crinkled as she peered at Alice again. "But if he was such a good man why didn't he stay and look out for you?"

"You've got to remember it was a different time. We were both sixteen. He was only a few months older than me. To be parents at that age and unmarried with no family support…"

"What about Roy's family?"

"His dad was very strict. Roy knew we'd get no help there. Anyway, after Hazel discovered I was pregnant I only saw Roy once more before Franklyn sent him away."

"How did you get back together?"

"Roy promised me he'd come back. Franklyn had threatened he would only support me if Roy stayed away but I managed to get word to him before he left that I was going to the home in Geelong. Roy kept his ear open through the milkie network. When he discovered Franklyn had left Melbourne he was distraught, thinking I'd gone too and no-one knew where.

"Roy's cousins still delivered our milk in Melbourne. It was through friends of his cousins that he found out I was living near Geelong. His family were looking for a housekeeper and I got the job. Roy and I kept our love a secret until he turned eighteen. I had no family to look out for me and his dad, who I got on well with by then, allowed us to become engaged and...you know the rest."

"I'm so sorry Roy died before I could meet him."

Alice looked out across the bay. "We loved this beach." It was here she'd come one day on her own, a year after he'd died, to scatter his ashes on the ocean. Another memory she'd decided was hers alone. "I feel close to him here."

They walked on a little further and reached the end of the beach where the land jutted out in a rocky point so they turned back. Their bodies were used to the water now and they ventured out deeper, letting it slide up past their calves.

"I can't make up for all we didn't have together. Roy would scoff at even trying." Alice waved a hand at the beach curving away in front of them. "But perhaps I can give you the gift of this beach."

Felicity glanced at her. A crease formed across her brow, the only part of her face Alice could see.

"I want you to be happy here," Alice said.

"I am trying."

"I know. Today is about you and me making new memories. Good ones. Let go all of the sad and hurtful things and just enjoy the beauty here. Then, wherever you are you can bring your mind back to this moment, this place. It's called visualisation."

"My doctor tried to talk me through that."

"It takes practice. Roy was the one who taught me to visualise. Losing our babies was a terrible time for both of us and this was the one place we both felt at peace. He'd done some reading about grief and he wanted us to focus on our special beach. It worked for us. It would be my gift if you could make it work for you."

They'd stopped walking, the waves washing against their legs. Then the breeze tugged at Felicity's scarf and it drifted away from her face. Alice was relieved to see a smile on her lips.

"I'd like to try," Felicity said.

Alice tucked her arm through Felicity's and they began to walk forward again. A ripple in the water caught her eye.

"Look," she pointed. "There it is."

They stopped and watched as a wave swept over the sand and then followed with a mini wave rolling sideways towards them, perpendicular to the beach.

"How amazing," Felicity said. "I didn't notice it last time."

"The tide wasn't right."

"What causes it?"

"I'm sure there's an explanation but I've no idea."

They stood, arms linked watching for the next wave to wobble towards them rather than onto the beach.

"It's so strange. Perhaps we can google it."

"Maybe," Alice said. "But I like the mystery of it. It's another reason this beach is remarkable. This funny little wave is like life, don't you think?"

Felicity tipped her head to one side, a puzzled look on her face.

"You said it was amazing and strange, I've added remarkable, and that's life. Always throwing us something to be excited by, in awe of." She was using Roy's words. He'd said something similar to her once.

Felicity shook her head and then she laughed.

Alice closed her eyes and heard Roy laughing too. *Our firstborn survived, Roy – and she's wonderful.*

"Look!"

Alice opened her eyes.

"Here comes another one. Amazing."

Felicity laughed again and Alice hugged her close as yet another strange wave rippled around them.

forty-two

Greta had taken her time at her mum's, refilling Dolly's bowls and giving her a cuddle, then she'd done a bit more tidying up, dug out some of the linen from the boot of Felicity's car and remade her parents' bed and her own. She'd been tempted to climb into it but instead she piled the stack of cushions that had covered it back on top and locked up the house. She couldn't put off going home and then on to Joe's sister's forever. With any luck, most of the work would be done before she got there.

By the time she turned into her street, planning to pick up the chicken curry and the rest of the jelly cakes on the way, it was almost two o'clock. She was about to slide her key into the front door when it was flung open. Joe stood there, hair dripping wet and wearing only a towel wrapped around his waist.

"I saw you pull in as I came out of the bathroom."

"I thought you'd still be at Hannah's. I was —" She didn't get time to finish as he dragged her inside, pushed his lovely warm lips to hers and took her in his arms.

"I got sent home," he said once they'd come up for air.

"Sent?"

432

"Hannah said I'd done enough and I should spend some time with you."

He pulled her into a hug again.

"I've missed you too," she said.

"I'm sorry we haven't had a lot of us time lately. I shouldn't have said I'd spend all weekend at Hannah's and I plan to make it up to you."

"How?"

His other hand slid under her t-shirt. "I can think of several ways, starting right now." He kissed her again and then trailed his lips down her neck.

Greta gave a brief thought to the state she'd left their bed in but to hell with it. They were only going to mess it up anyway.

It wasn't until much later, when Joe went out to the kitchen to get them some sparkling wine and insisted she stay put, that she realised she was lying on clean sheets and the only things discarded in the room were the doona, Joe's towel and the clothes she'd been wearing when she came in.

She smiled as he came back with a bottle, two glasses and a plate of cakes. "You found Alice's jelly cakes."

"I did."

Greta feasted her eyes on him as he worked the top from the bottle. The tight curl of hair that formed in the nape of his neck, the curve of his well-formed muscles, the scar below the elbow of his right arm, a childhood accident, the way his boxers hugged the curves of his butt. He poured the sparkling wine and climbed back in beside her. They tapped glasses and Greta smiled at the sensation of the bubbles tickling her nose as she sipped and that of Joe's hand on her bare thigh under the sheet. How she'd missed him.

"This is a lovely homecoming," she said. "And you changed the sheets."

"Yeah." He looked a bit hangdog then.

"What?"

"Hannah needed some things from the shop this morning and we came this way to that little supermarket a few streets over that opens early. They had some good meat specials so I bought some and asked her to stop off here so I could put the meat in the fridge. We were going to pick you up to save having two cars her way but then I got your message to say you were going for coffee with your dad. Anyway, Hannah came inside."

"Oh no." Greta groaned at the thought of the state their place had been in when she'd left that morning. She'd still been so annoyed and she hadn't done a thing but pull the doona over the bed and wash her own dishes.

"Hannah went ballistic at me. She said you wouldn't be happy coming home to a pigsty."

"Did she clean up?" Greta was mortified by the thought.

"Nooo," he moaned. "But she told me I'd better. That's why I came home early."

"So the rest of the place—?"

"Spotless."

Greta doubted that but it was a start.

"I'm sorry, Greta."

"For cleaning the house?"

"For leaving most of the work to you. Mum's one of those people who's always done everything around the house. Hannah told me she had to teach herself some life skills when she left home and she thought if I wanted you to hang around I'd better learn some too."

Go Hannah, Greta thought, but she didn't interrupt him. Besides, she liked the way his hand was tracing circles on her leg while he was talking.

"I think we should make a housework list, like they have at the gym, behind the door in the toilets."

Greta lurched up. "You want me to write the time and date each time I clean the toilet?" She wasn't so keen on housework she wanted it formalised.

"No. I mean we make a list of all the jobs that need doing, put aside a night a week and when we do each job we put the date and our initials, so it's fair." He beamed at her.

"Spoken like a true project manager," she said.

"But you have to accept the standard I complete the task at."

"Is that a cop out?"

"No, but I know you don't think I clean things as well as you do."

"That's not true."

He raised his eyebrows and she slunk back against the pillows.

"I'll get better at it," he said.

She tapped her glass against his. "I'll hold you to that."

"There's something else."

Greta wasn't sure if she was ready for something else.

"I've been thinking about what you said about us getting married before we buy a house."

"I was annoyed when I said that."

"Let's do it."

"Get married?"

"Yes."

"We will once we get the house...won't we?"

"Why wait?" Joe was studying her closely.

"Are you serious?"

"I'd suggest eloping but I think we'd have a few parents and grandparents who'd be upset by that but...would you be happy with a small wedding?"

Greta was speechless. This morning she'd felt so mixed up about Joe and their future she couldn't see it and he'd somehow read her thoughts.

"You don't like the idea?" he said.

"I do but…are you sure? You were so keen on the idea of having a house first. And I haven't had the chance to tell you – Lach and Josh and I aren't accepting Grandad's money."

He sat back, his grin fading. "Greta, you are more important to me than anything. I know I'm keen for us to get our own place but it's for us and our life together. I've wanted to be with you since the first day I met you. I love you for who you are, not your grandad's money."

"It was only because of you he left me the money in the first place."

"Me?"

"Yep. Grandad's stipulation was that I marry you or I didn't get the money."

"For real? Why?"

"He liked you, otherwise I don't think he would have left me anything."

Joe looked thoughtful. "So you didn't want to be a kept woman?"

She lurched up. "No, I did not!"

"Take it easy, tiger." He grinned and poked her. "I can't believe he did that."

Greta sighed and settled back again. "The money would have set us up."

"We don't need it, Greta. I'm not saying it wouldn't have been great to have it but you're doing the right thing. Your generosity is one of the reasons I love you." He kissed her.

Greta took a breath. "Joe, I need to talk to you about something. It involves finding more money."

"I know your parents are going through a tough time but I'm sure they'd help a bit with the wedding and my parents have offered to—"

"It's not about the wedding, Joe. I'd like to look into the possibility of taking flying lessons, getting my licence and...maybe getting work as a pilot."

"Woah! Steady up. It's a big step going from the odd flight with Ivan to being a pilot yourself."

"I know."

He sat back, staring into his glass.

"I'd recoup the money once I was flying full-time."

"You're serious?"

She nodded.

"You've never mentioned working as a pilot before."

"I've given it a lot of thought lately. I know it's my dream, not yours, and we've a wedding and a house deposit to pay for but—"

"This is a surprise. Can I have time to think about it?"

"Of course."

He took a sip from his glass.

"I love you, Joe. Flying is my dream and I'm prepared to wait till we get ourselves sorted."

"Do you still want a wedding, a house?"

She slipped her hand into his. "I do."

"So we're still going ahead."

"Definitely."

"Okay! So what do you reckon? Wedding or house first?"

"Wedding. I don't want anything fancy. I'd have married you in our shorts and t-shirts the day you proposed." That day he'd taken her for lunch and a swim at Glenelg then gone down on one knee in the sand. They'd both been shaking with emotion and she'd been terrified they'd lose the perfect solitaire diamond ring he'd bought her.

He leaned in again but she put a hand on his chest as she remembered the other thing she needed to talk to him about. "What about babies?"

"I thought you wanted to take flying lessons?"

"I do. That will put babies on hold for a while." She'd told Joe on the phone that Alice was Felicity's mother but hadn't mentioned the cystic fibrosis. They needed to look into that as well and talk about the implications.

"Fair enough. We're going to need two wages for quite a while yet anyway."

"It's more than that, though. I need to tell you about—"

Joe pressed his lips to hers. "We'll talk more later. I've missed you," he murmured and then one of his hands was taking her glass and setting it down while the other was trailing upwards over her stomach, then it stopped suddenly.

"Hang on, there was something else I needed to tell you too. About your grandad's books. That's part of the reason the place was such a mess, I've been spending my time at home searching and those books of Franklyn's are worth money."

"Really?" That was great for her nan but she wanted his hands to keep moving.

"Quite a lot of money—"

This time it was Greta who covered his lips with her hand and ran her other down his taut chest. "Stop talking, Joe," she whispered.

forty-three

Felicity unlocked her side gate and then the laundry door. She got ready to hold her breath but was surprised to see only one litter box and it didn't look disturbed, let alone smell. She went through to the kitchen, which was tidy except for Dolly's bowls. The cat jumped from her spot on the couch and wandered towards her with blinking eyes.

"Hello, Dolly, back in a minute." Felicity put down her handbag and went through the house. Nearly everything was back as it was before she'd created her sabotage, even her bed was made although there was no throw or cushions. She unlatched the security chain and walked quickly to Alice's car. It was broad daylight and sunny and she was outside but she kept her gaze locked on Alice and walked steadily forward, taking long slow breaths.

After several days together at Alice's with regular calls from Greta and then a desperate call from Tony to say that his record-keeping had finally let him down and begging for her help, Felicity had decided it was time to go home. Alice had offered to drive her as she'd promised and had agreed to stay a few days. One of Alice's provisos had been that Felicity must start her appointments with the counsellor. They'd rung before they left and there'd been an appointment free that afternoon so they'd driven straight there. Alice had agreed to go with her for the first visit. She'd sat beside her and held her hand while she'd told the counsellor her sorry tale. The counsellor had seemed to think she was suffering from the fear of having a panic attack and had been impressed with the progress Felicity was already making. She'd given her some breathing exercises to try and suggested she check out a great YouTube yoga instructor before they met next.

"It's okay, you can come in," she said as Alice opened her car door.

Felicity grabbed the rest of her things from the backseat and hurried inside. Alice followed her in.

"This looks lovely," she said as she put her small case down inside the front door. Felicity went to shut the door but Alice stopped her. "I'll bring in what's left and lock my car."

Felicity peered out at the street. She'd made such improvement while she'd been at Alice's place and the slow breathing had helped but now that she was home again...

"Stay here," Alice said. "I can manage the rest."

Felicity picked up Alice's bag, so grateful they'd come together. They'd done a lot of talking over the last few days and kept it up in the car all the way back from Marion Bay. They'd talked about their family history, the possibilities of being a CF carrier and Felicity's failed marriage, and they'd made small talk as well, swapping recipes, looking at photos, sharing funny anecdotes of their lives. Alice had sat beside her when she'd called Pam to say she'd be missing tennis again and then went on to tell her about the separation. It had been difficult listening to Pam's stunned and then sympathetic reactions but Alice had squeezed her hand tightly and she'd got through it.

Felicity put Alice's case in Greta's room where the bed was also made but covered in every cushion from the main bedroom and the lounge. She'd forgotten that's where she'd put them all. She took armfuls and reinstated them around the house.

Back in the kitchen she opened the blinds to reveal the deck and the backyard. Dolly wound around her feet. She picked up the cat and cuddled her while she checked the fridge to make sure she'd left wine in it. The last few nights she hadn't opened a bottle until she and Alice were preparing their evening meal.

"Here we are." Alice put Felicity's esky down beside the fridge. She'd packed it with containers of food and the remains of the milk and fresh veg from her fridge. "Sorry I took so long. I had a call from Elaine."

"She's good fun, your friend. I enjoyed meeting her."

They'd had a meal and another couple of visits to Elaine's over the last few days. Felicity had really liked her. She brought out another side to Alice, a brighter, sparklier woman than Felicity had first known.

"I'm looking forward to meeting your friends too. Pam sounds like a kind woman and I hope I can meet Suzie. Her photos have been very entertaining."

Felicity felt the familiar wave of panic but it wasn't so bad now. Its power over her lessening every day, and her visualisation technique was improving. It wouldn't be easy telling her story to Suzie but she felt stronger, especially with Alice by her side.

Alice scratched Dolly under the chin. "And this is the lovely Dolly you've been telling me about. What a pretty face she has." The cat lifted her head, basking in the admiration.

Felicity deposited her back on the floor and together she and Alice unpacked the esky. Then she took Alice on a guided tour of the house, explaining as she went the changes that had been made.

"It's a credit to you," Alice said.

"And only looking so tidy because of my daughter, I suspect," Felicity said. Greta hadn't mentioned the state of the house in any of her calls but Felicity was pretty sure it wouldn't have been Ian who'd cleaned up and put things back straight. They hadn't communicated since his angry call to her over Easter.

"Such a lot of work has gone into the place I can see why you love it so much."

"I do," Felicity looked around. "Wait a minute!" She strode to the kitchen and came to a stop by the bench that led to the butler's pantry. "The coffee machine's gone."

"Stolen, you mean?"

"Yes and I bet I damn well know who by…bloody Ian!"

"Oh."

"How dare he come in here and take stuff." Felicity stormed into the pantry, checking the shelves to see if anything else was gone. When she came out Alice was waiting for her.

"Could I buy you another one?"

Felicity frowned. "No! At least…thanks, Alice but no. It was such a hassle to make coffee with that machine. I didn't really like it."

Alice raised her eyebrows.

"I know I'm being perverse but he could have asked first."

"And how would you have replied?"

Felicity was saved from answering by her phone ringing. She was relieved it was Tony's name on the screen. Alice left her alone and returned as she ended the call.

"That was my builder friend, Tony. I hope you don't mind but I've invited him to join us for dinner."

"Not at all. As I said, I'm keen to meet your friends."

"He only wanted a quick word but I think he eats a lot of takeaway."

"I've brought the makings of a chicken and veg pie with me."

They'd just put the pie in the oven when Tony arrived bearing flowers, chocolates and sparkling wine. Once Felicity had done the introductions he explained the gifts.

"My offer's been accepted on the building that will become my office and showroom, so the bubbles are to celebrate. The flowers and chocolate are a direct bribe." He passed them over then got down on his knees and gripped his hands together.

"Please work for me, Felicity."

"Oh, you blockhead." Felicity waved a hand at him. "Get up, for goodness sake."

He got back to his feet. "My latest BAS is a mess and I haven't got long to get it in. I'm desperate for someone to do my financials, pay accounts, take calls and maintain that terrific photo gallery you started."

Alice smiled. "Sounds like a job made for you, Felicity." She looked back at Tony. "How much would it pay?"

"Alice!"

Tony smiled. "We'd have to work out the hours but award rates, of course."

"Hang on." The horses were stirring in Felicity's chest. She took a slow breath. "There's no way your new office will be ready for ages. Where would I work?"

"You've got a perfectly good office," Alice said. "Couldn't you work from here until the new place is ready?"

"I suppose," Felicity said. "But it wouldn't be big enough to sit down with clients."

"What about your front lounge?" Alice said. "Plenty of room there and you don't need the space."

"Sounds perfect," Tony said.

Felicity felt the stirrings of anticipation then just as quickly they were dashed. "But Ian wants to sell this place. I don't know how much longer I'll have it for."

"Why don't you worry about that when it happens?" Alice said.

Felicity glanced from Alice's expectant look to Tony's face, taut with desperation.

He understood her struggles with Ian's desertion. She recalled the day she'd spent putting the photo gallery together for Tony, how she'd dressed as if she was going out to work, sat at the desk in the study with the lovely view across the garden and how much she'd enjoyed it.

She tried not to think that it might not be her view for much longer, that her mother wasn't her mother but her aunt, that her husband had left her, instead she focused on the warm smile of the woman who stood beside her, her real mother. Alice had suffered some terrible times and yet here she was – loving, kind and wise and wanting to support Felicity.

She glanced from Alice to Tony. "I'll do it," she said.

"Yes!" Tony held up a hand to high five her. "Let's open the sparkling and drink a toast to new beginnings."

Felicity produced the glasses as he popped the top and bubbles fizzed out. They were all laughing, truly laughing, and for the first time since the terrible night of her fiftieth birthday party Felicity felt as if the marbles that had been skittering under her feet, sending her tumbling, were disappearing, and that she was back on firmer ground.

forty-four

Alice walked around Felicity's dining table, straightened a napkin, tucked a chair closer then glanced up at the large silver clock on the wall again. Only a few minutes and their guests would be arriving. The previous night had gone so well with Tony there for dinner that when Greta had rung to say she had news to share, Alice had asked Felicity if they could invite the young couple for dinner. She was keen to see Greta again and meet Joe.

Felicity had agreed readily but when Greta had said she wanted to bring Hazel as well, there'd been a moment when Alice had thought Felicity would call it off. After a pause she'd agreed.

They'd needed some grocery items for dinner so earlier in the afternoon Felicity had taken Alice to a small supermarket a few suburbs away. Once they had their items, which had included some blocks of chocolate, Felicity had directed them to a checkout instead of the twelve items or less queue, even though it was all but empty. They'd had to wait while the person in front had unpacked a trolley full of groceries. When it had finally been their turn, Felicity had beamed at the young man serving.

"Hello, Milo," she'd said. "Remember me?"

The young man had nodded and returned her smile, then when they'd paid for everything, Felicity had withdrawn one of the chocolates from the bag and given it to Milo along with a note.

"Thank you," she'd said.

"What was in the note?" Alice had asked as they'd walked away.

"Tony's details. Milo told me once he'd rather be outside working with tools. He may as well try out for the apprenticeship Tony's offering."

On the drive home she'd told Alice the story of not having money at the supermarket and how kind the lad had been to her. Alice's heart had swelled with joy at how far Felicity had come and what a delight it was to think she was her daughter.

Once they'd arrived home they'd worked together to get ready for dinner but Alice could see Felicity becoming more and more tense by the minute.

"Is it Hazel coming that's worrying you?" she asked.

"I don't know how I can face her again."

"You told me you didn't know how you'd be able to go back to that supermarket and face Milo again but you did."

"That's a totally different thing."

Alice put down the potato she'd been peeling. "I can't bear to be the reason you're not talking to your mother."

"She's not my mother."

"She is. I gave birth to you but she's the one who raised you and whether you like it or not everything she did was to give you as good a life as she could."

"How could she stay with him?"

"Franklyn could be charming. He loved your mother and your early family life was relatively happy for all of you, I gather. Hazel was his wife—"

"His chattel!"

"He was controlling but that kind of one-sided relationship doesn't always start out as well defined. Hazel needed Franklyn to be the strong one in the early days of their relationship and he took over her life but I suspect it happened in a gradual way until she didn't even notice. She didn't know all of Franklyn's deceits."

"So she says."

Alice sighed. "I know the kind of man he was and I believe her. Times were different. I'm not saying it was right but she did what she did to protect you and June and to survive. And when you look back on your life, was it truly so bad?"

Felicity put her hand to her head. "It's such a mess."

"Blaming Hazel, hating her, will only cause you so much more misery and will drive a wedge between you and the rest of your family. You said you haven't seen June since the will reading."

Felicity snorted.

"What about Greta and how torn she is? It's enough her parents are separated. Look at it from her point of view. It's hard for her tiptoeing between family. Worrying about who she might upset. You could end up driving away your own daughter."

Felicity pressed her fingers to her lips.

Alice went on. "Do you remember the day you stormed out of my place when, apart from that beach trip, you'd hardly set foot outside in daylight for weeks?"

Felicity gave the slightest of nods.

"Your anger that day was greater than your fear and it propelled you forward. Make your love greater than your hate. Forgive Hazel and let her back in your life."

Felicity had wiped her hands down her apron and without another word had left Alice alone in the kitchen.

Now she wondered if Felicity would come out when the others arrived.

Alice checked the dinner and, satisfied with its progress, wandered past the bench and around to the dining area. Felicity had set the table with round woven place mats and sleek silver cutlery, and in the centre she'd placed a blue-and-white china vase filled with deep blue hydrangeas. It looked a picture. In fact her whole house looked like something out of a home magazine, yet not as austere as they sometimes appeared. Alice hadn't seen any family photos on display except here on the sideboard where there were a couple of Felicity and Greta together. They were nestled beneath the vase of beautiful flowers Tony had brought. She'd meant to ask Felicity if she could have copies.

She leaned closer to study them. Two smiling faces so like hers. It was still such a new feeling for her – to realise she had family, not only a sister but a daughter and a granddaughter and a niece and great nephews. Another turning point in her life that she prayed would bring her great happiness.

There was a knock on the door. Alice started towards the hall but before she reached the front door, Felicity emerged from her bedroom, smiled at Alice, and let in her guests.

*

Hazel was the last to step inside Felicity's house. Ahead of her Greta was introducing Joe to Alice. And there were hugs all around. Hazel was surprised to receive a brief squeeze from Felicity.

"It's lovely to meet you at last, Joe," Alice said and reached up to kiss his cheek. "You're so tall."

"And handsome?" he smirked.

"Just ask him." Greta linked her arm through his and they followed Felicity back down the hall.

Alice took Hazel's arm. "How are you?" she asked.

"Glad to be here but a little nervous."

They'd talked on the phone since Alice had been in Adelaide and had filled each other in on what had happened since the weekend but this was their first get-together.

"How's Felicity going?" Hazel asked.

"I think she's feeling much better in general."

"She's always been able to get through the tough times, come out stronger...but with all this happening at once...I was worried..."

"She'll be okay, Hazel. She's got both of us to lean on when she needs."

Before they moved on to the family room Felicity came back.

"Can we have a quick chat, Hazel?" she said.

Hazel tensed.

Alice gave her arm a squeeze and slipped away.

"We can go in here." Felicity led the way to her lounge, flicked on the light and sat on one of her plush chairs.

Hazel folded herself slowly onto one opposite, straightening her skirt and finally looking up.

Felicity's hands were gripped tightly in her lap. "I want..." she began. "There are some things..." She lifted her face and looked Hazel directly in the eye. "I want to know the truth."

"You know it all now."

"What I don't know, don't understand, is why you didn't tell me I was adopted. If I'd only known...if I'd grown up with the knowledge it might have been easier."

"It might but we'll never know the answer to that. You said you want the truth and I'm telling you. Keeping your parentage from you was Franklyn's stipulation."

Felicity shook her head.

Hazel slid forward on her seat. "I wanted to tell you. Even Isabelle thought you should be told, but it was the one thing Franklyn wouldn't give in to, even for her. He said if he was to adopt you, no-one was to know. You have to understand, Felicity. I had no choice. Agreeing was the only way I could keep you, my sister's daughter. I'd lost everyone else, my parents, my sister, I didn't want to lose you too." Hazel's hands shook and she clasped them together, reliving the terror she'd felt whenever she thought about losing Felicity. "If I'd told you he would have driven you from me like he did Alice."

"Why was it so important to him?"

"I always thought it was to protect you."

"*Protect me!*"

"So that you wouldn't feel different."

"Well, I can tell you that failed."

Hazel felt Felicity's pain as sharply as her own. She hadn't been able to protect her from Franklyn but she'd done her best. And in the early years she'd been successful. They'd been a family in every way until the day Felicity started school. June's first year at school had been a struggle. She'd had trouble learning her sounds, was slow to pick up on words and number facts. Hazel spent a lot of time coaching her at home with Felicity by her side. When they dropped June at school Felicity wanted to stay, wailing her disapproval when she couldn't.

So when it was her turn to start she'd been ready for months. On her first day she was up and dressed before Franklyn left for work. He'd kissed her goodbye, told her he looked forward to hearing all about her day. The girls were fed and bathed waiting for him when he came home. He sat both of them on his knee. Felicity was full of news of her day but he made her stop and wait while he asked June to read to him first. Reading to Franklyn had always made June nervous and she began to stumble over the words. Felicity was eager to help her sister and to please Franklyn. She took the book from June and began to read fluently. Franklyn snatched it from her hands and reprimanded her for taking her sister's book and being a show-off. Hazel had tried to explain Felicity was trying to help her sister but he would have none of it. After that his attention was always directed at June first. He still showed some interest in Felicity's achievements but enthusiasm was rare. Hazel had done her best to make up for it but Franklyn was always watching for any opportunity to berate her for favouring Felicity over June. The changeling, he sometimes called her, but only when they were alone. He could be so cruel.

"Hazel?"

She became aware of Felicity's voice and then her face close to her.

"Sorry."

Felicity sat back in her chair. "I thought you really had gone off on one of your woozy moments then. Where were you?"

"It was pride."

Felicity gave her a strange look. "What was?"

"I thought he kept your adoption a secret to protect you but it was all about Franklyn's pride. He didn't want people to know he hadn't fathered both of our children."

"If it was pride, why did he reveal it now?"

Hazel swallowed the lump that had formed in her throat. Finally, she understood. "Because in the end his hatred of me was greater than his pride."

"I don't understand."

"He was always jealous of my relationships. First with Alice, then with you. June was safe because she was his daughter. I didn't ever have close friends. If I enjoyed something too much outside of my life with him, Franklyn found a way to spoil it."

"Oh, Mum." Felicity slid to her knees in front of Hazel and gripped her hands. "Why did you stay with him?"

"I had nowhere else to go." The lump was too hard to swallow now, the pain of it radiated down to her chest. "He made sure I could never leave him."

Felicity's arms went around her, one cheek pressed to hers. "He's gone now, Mum. Alice was right. We need each other and he can't...no...we won't let him hurt us any more."

They clung to each other for a while then the distant sound of laughter broke the silence. Felicity sat back. "Are you up to facing the others?"

Hazel nodded. There was comfort in them all being together.

"Alice will have Greta and Joe barricaded in the family room." Felicity tugged Hazel by the hands. "We'd better tidy ourselves up first or we'll scare them. I bet my mascara's smudged."

Hazel allowed her daughter to help her from the chair and lead the way to her bathroom. Her legs were like jelly but holding Felicity's hand in her own gave her strength. She looked at her daughter's reflection in the brightly lit mirror. "I'm sorry, Felicity. I truly did believe I was doing what was best for you."

"I'm sorry I'm such an ungrateful bitch. I am going to try to do better."

"You're not a bitch."

"Maybe just ungrateful."

They both managed a small smile.

"Try this colour." Felicity handed over a lipstick.

They patted at wet eyes, fluffed up their hair, turned from side to side.

"We could be sisters," Felicity said.

"Now you're pushing it." Hazel chuckled.

"Come on." Felicity slipped her arm through Hazel's. "They've been bailed up for long enough and I have news."

*

Alice felt the tension leave her body as soon as Felicity and Hazel walked into the room arm in arm.

Felicity halted and looked around. No-one spoke. "What's going on? Why haven't you opened the champagne?" She slipped away from Hazel and strode to the island bench.

Hazel met Alice's questioning look with a smile.

A cork popped and Felicity and Joe passed around glasses of champagne.

Felicity raised hers. "I'd like to propose a toast." She looked from Alice to Hazel. "To me—"

Greta groaned.

Felicity glared at her. "Let me start that again. To me, to my daughter and to my two wonderful mothers." She smiled a wobbly smile. "To happy days and good health."

They lifted their glasses and echoed her words. "To happy days and good health."

Joe whistled and Greta cheered. Hazel and Alice both dabbed their eyes with tissues.

"Selfie," Greta called and the four women huddled in for a shot.

"What about Joe?" Alice smiled at the young man who seemed to be taking the room full of emotional women in his stride.

They'd been having an in-depth discussion on how to make jelly cakes when Felicity and Hazel had returned.

"Come on, Joe." Greta beckoned him in and after more rearranging another lot of photos were snapped.

"Sorry, I left you out of the toast," Felicity said and raised her glass again. "Here's to Joe."

"To Joe," they all chorused and Greta kissed him.

"Alice is going to teach Greta and me to make her jelly cakes," he announced proudly.

"Hang on," Greta said. "I think that was you and you've never done much baking so we won't get too excited."

He looked at Alice. "There's a recipe, isn't there?"

"In my head, but I can write it down."

"There, you see, Greta. It's as simple as following a process."

"Hmm?" Greta smiled indulgently and kissed him again.

Felicity raised her glass once more. "And back to me."

"Mum!" Greta groaned.

"I've got a job."

There were more cheers and Felicity filled them in on Tony's offer. Alice swept her gaze from one family member to the other, trying to imprint this new way of life permanently in her mind. She couldn't imagine feeling any happier than she did right now.

"We've got news too," Greta said. "We want to be married before the end of the year."

"Oh, that's wonderful." Felicity hugged her daughter and Joe. Then Hazel and Alice took turns.

Felicity gave her daughter a closer look. "Is there a reason for your haste?"

"Whoa!" Joe held up his hand. "Only that we don't want to put the house before the wedding."

"We are already living together," Greta said. "You do realise we share the same bed, Mum."

"La, la la," Felicity said, putting a hand to her ear and everyone laughed.

"When and where were you planning to be married?" Hazel asked.

"That's the tricky bit," Joe said.

"We want it to be outside so it needs to be when the weather warms up," Greta said. "We've looked at several venues but they're already booked."

"There must be plenty of places, surely," Hazel said.

Felicity frowned. "Wedding venues can be booked years ahead, Mum."

"We're paying for it ourselves," Joe said.

"And we want low key and inexpensive," Greta added.

"What about a Friday or a Sunday?" Felicity said.

"Tried that."

"How many people?" Hazel asked.

Joe said forty at the same time as Greta said sixty.

Hazel and Felicity both looked perplexed.

Alice cleared her throat. "I've got a suggestion," she said.

forty-five

It was the perfect morning for a beach wedding. November could be so unpredictable, especially for an outside event, but the breeze was little more than a puff of air and the temperature had risen just enough to keep the ladies in short sleeves warm but not so hot that the men in their jackets and ties were uncomfortable.

Felicity paused between chatting to guests and took it all in. The last party she'd organised had been her fiftieth so she'd been nervous when Greta had asked her to plan her wedding. Added to her anxiety had been that the wedding was to be out in the open at Alice's special beach quite a distance into the national park, followed by a finger food lunch at Alice's house, all of which was a four-hour drive from Adelaide. But this event had been planned in detail and with help. She'd learned to delegate, which had made her job so much easier.

The pretty white wooden structure that the bride and groom would stand in front of had been made by Tony. He was to one side of it chatting to Hazel and Jack. She'd been nervous about Ian attending the wedding with his new partner and she'd asked Tony if he'd be her plus one. She had to admit he looked very suave in his black suit, white shirt and tie. She'd never seen him dressed up before. He'd even asked her what colour she was wearing and had chosen his floral tie with tones to match the soft blue of her dress.

The sheer white fabric that draped the frame had been added by Hazel, and Alice had sourced the flowers that adorned the top. Joe's family had been in charge of chairs for the grandparents and any others who might prefer to sit, along with the small rustic table they would use to sign the official documents. Joe and his sister were in charge of music and currently 'Wouldn't It be Nice' by the Beach Boys jingled from the speakers.

There were baskets of dried rose petals ready to throw over the newlyweds, courtesy of Hazel's card friends who'd been drying them since the first spring blooms had opened, and Alice had been around to all her friends' gardens to collect the fresh ones that Joe's niece would sprinkle as she walked ahead of the bride when she arrived.

The wedding cake had been a family affair. Hazel, Alice and Felicity had got together on several occasions to test run some recipes but Joe had vetoed them all and come up with a suggestion they'd all agreed to. It was a six-layered pink lamington cake, made by Alice, joined with lashings of vanilla cream whipped up by Hazel, and decorated by Felicity with fresh raspberries. Everyone had contributed to the catering including Joe's mum and sister, and Ian and Joe's dad had got together to organise the drinks. Jack had been there first thing this morning to help set Alice's deck and living area with tables and chairs and decorations and her neighbour, Bec, was there keeping an eye on things while they were at the beach.

"Time for the mother of the bride to be seated." Tony stood beside her, his elbow crooked out. She slipped her arm through his and together they walked to the front of the group and sat.

Working for Tony had been the challenge she'd needed to help her out of the anxious state she'd been in. It had given her a reason to get up each day, to get dressed and face the world. She still felt small bouts of panic in new situations but she was learning strategies to cope and it had been a while since she'd felt even one hoof beat let alone a stampede. Tony had said going out to dinner together once a week to somewhere new was a good strategy and they'd been testing his theory.

He squeezed her hand and winked at her and Felicity felt a tingle of pleasure. They'd become very good friends and the previous week when he'd dropped her home after dinner he'd kissed her softly on the lips. It had awakened sensations she hadn't felt in a long time and she'd kissed him back, no longer concerned at their few years' age difference. Now she felt ready to see where her new feelings for him might lead.

Alice and Hazel came to sit on her other side and then Jack. Felicity had come to realise how lucky she was. Instead of feeling second-hand, now she thought of herself as double value. Some people no longer had mothers and she'd been blessed with two. And not only that, because of them she still had her house. Between them they'd given her the money she'd needed to buy Ian out. They'd both insisted they'd rather she had the money when she needed it than her have to wait till they were dead to get it. She sincerely hoped that was a long while away. She wanted more time to get to know Alice and to explore her new relationship with Hazel.

The past few months hadn't been easy but Alice's gift of the special memories they'd made on their trip together to this beach had helped Felicity. She used those images when she needed a focus to help her relax. It had underpinned her moving on to enjoying life again.

From the corner of her eye she saw Joe straighten up and look beyond the gathering of people. A new piece of music played and the volume was turned up. Tony slipped his hand into hers and they stood. Felicity turned and blinked back tears at the vision before her. Her daughter looked so beautiful on Ian's arm, looking confidently ahead and smiling at the man she loved. To be here with her family on this special day was all any mother could ask.

Greta

Greta gripped Ian's arm tightly as she made her way down the wooden steps to the beach below where everyone she loved in the world waited. Her dad was nervous and she had been when she'd woken up that morning, but now the nerves had been replaced by a buzz of excitement and the man she was walking towards was totally responsible. Not only was Joe the man she loved and was planning to spend the rest of her life with but that morning he'd given her the most treasured gift. She hadn't actually seen him – her mum and two nans had been horrified at the suggestion the groom should see the bride before the wedding. Hannah had been given the task of delivering the small parcel. Greta had taken it to her room so she could open it in private. She'd smiled at the message he'd written. *You're my friend, you're my love, and today my wife, can't wait to fly into our new life.*

Ivan had flown over to meet them at the Yorketown airstrip first thing that morning and later, after the wedding feast – there was no other word for the food that had been prepared – he'd fly them back to Adelaide where they were catching a commercial flight to Melbourne and then on to Hobart. Neither of them had been to Tasmania and as they only had a week off work, a leisurely self-drive holiday had appealed to them both. She'd been amazed that it had been Joe who'd come up with the suggestion of the flight from Yorke Peninsula to Adelaide.

She slid the pink ribbon from the plain brown parcel and almost cried. It was a brand-new copy of the Amelia Earhart movie. There was another small envelope stuck to it and when she opened it and read the contents, her breath left her and she sagged to the bed. In her trembling fingers she held a voucher for flying lessons.

Two weeks ago they'd seen a house they both loved and while it wasn't brand new it wouldn't take much to spruce it up. Their offer had been accepted and once settlement was done, Greta had agreed to be in charge of refreshments the weekend Joe's family descended to do the painting. Her mum had offered to help with colour schemes and decorating ideas.

Now, as Greta reached the guests, the vibrant voices of Jason Mraz and Colbie Caillat singing 'Lucky' resonated from the speaker and she locked eyes with Joe. Her dad placed her hand in Joe's and before the celebrant had a chance to speak, she flung her arms around Joe's neck and kissed him.

The celebrant chuckled and cleared his throat into the mic. "Well, the bride's eager."

Behind them the guests laughed and there were a few cheers and wolf whistles.

Joe eased his lips from hers and tears brimmed in his eyes.

"Lucky to be in love with my best friend," he murmured as he let her go.

"Lucky." She smiled and turned to the celebrant.

Alice
Alice pressed a hanky to the corners of her eyes as Greta and Joe spoke their vows of love to each other. She hoped Roy was watching.

She trusted today's celebration would mean this beach would see many more happy family times together, whether it was just a couple of them or a large group. Greta had made it clear that it would be a while before they had children, but Alice secretly hoped they wouldn't leave it too long. She was glad Felicity and Greta had both had the genetic testing for CF. Felicity was a carrier but Greta wasn't. It was a relief to know that was one family inheritance her granddaughter had missed out on. The life-threatening condition would no longer be passed on through her direct family at least.

Alice smiled as the celebrant announced the newly wedded couple and they were chorused with cheers, the rose petals were tossed and music played. She moved forward to kiss the bride and groom. Then she stepped back as others took their turn.

The sea breeze had strengthened just a little. It stirred the sheer fabric around the frame and ruffled the bell sleeves of Alice's dress. She imagined it was Roy's gentle caress. Life had dealt her some terrible blows but she'd also been loved and today was another reason not to wallow in the hurts of the past but to rejoice in the moment. She was learning the joys of being a part of this beautiful new family she could call her own.

"Alice," Greta called. "Come and be in a photo."

Alice moved closer and smiled for the photographer. She would soon have plenty more happy photos to add to her collection.

Hazel

Hazel had been nervous when Greta had asked if she'd make her wedding gown but when she'd seen the simple pattern her granddaughter had chosen, she'd agreed. Now Hazel's heart swelled with pride both at the final results of her sewing and Greta's beauty. The dress had a V-shaped neckline and delicately pleated bodice with an empire waistline and slim skirt which flowed over

Greta's curves to a sweeping fuller train of fabric at the back. It was perfect for her.

"Well done, Mum." Felicity moved up beside her. "The dress is simple but elegant and so suited to Greta."

Hazel smiled, not so much from the praise but at the word mum. It had taken lots of talks and walks for Felicity and Hazel to be on good terms again but one of the outcomes had been her decision to call her mum and stick with Alice for Alice. But often, when they were all together, and Felicity said "Mum" both Hazel and Alice would respond.

"They're so happy," Felicity said. "I suppose I'd better go and speak to Emma."

"It's Gemma," Hazel whispered as she looked over at the woman on Ian's arm.

"Yes, Gemma, right." Felicity set off.

Hazel watched her give Ian a kiss on the cheek and then do the same to Gemma, who Hazel thought looked very much like Felicity. She wondered if anyone else had noticed that.

"Thanks for getting that money through so quickly, Hazel." Joe bent to give her a hug.

"You're very welcome and I see from Greta's entrance that your surprise was well received."

"Yes."

"You're a special man, Joe." She put a hand to his cheek. "It's not always easy to let people you love go enough to follow their dreams."

"Joe!" his sister called. "Family photo time."

Hazel stood back as the photographer tried to get Joe's family into a workable pose. She was glad the book money had been put to good use. When Joe had confided in her that he wanted to give Greta flying lessons as a wedding present, it had been easy to offer him the money from the sale of the book collection. He'd done all the work: researching, setting up an eBay account to sell them and posting them off. She'd kept only the full set of Biggles books and given them to June and Derek and couldn't help the smug feeling she got from knowing Franklyn hadn't mentioned them in his will.

She glanced across to where June and Derek stood talking to Felicity's good friend Suzie and her husband. June looked lovely in the dress she'd let Hazel help her select. It was made from sheer patterned fabric in muted sea greens and blues and fell from an empire line to just below the knee at the front with a hem that dipped into a flowing curve at the back. It softened June's angular features. They'd had a mother and daughter day out to select it, the day after the last details of Franklyn's paperwork had been settled.

They'd all been surprised by the final figure and Hazel had given both June and Felicity some of the money. With the house and the bulk of Franklyn's wealth now hers, Hazel had more than enough.

With no thanks to you, Frank! She smiled. Her husband's horrid plan to leave her with little money, no house and a broken family hadn't worked.

In two weeks she was going with Alice on a cruise to celebrate her friend Elaine's birthday. Hazel had been so excited when Alice had asked her and thankful she didn't have to accept Alice's offer to pay for her. The cruise would be another opportunity for them to make up for lost time.

"Nan!" Greta was walking towards her but before she reached Hazel, Felicity slipped an arm through Greta's and then Alice stepped up on her other side. They advanced on Hazel and Felicity offered her other arm. Elaine had been madly snapping pictures and turned and saw them with their arms linked together. Hazel felt strength flow through them. Four women across three generations, two of them sisters, but all connected by the tangle of often tenuous threads that made up their family and a past that had threatened but hadn't destroyed them.

"Stop right there," Elaine said, advancing on them as she lined up her phone. "Ready?"

"Ready!" They all chorused back.

"Oh, that looks lovely." Elaine squinted at her screen. "But let me take another just in case. Smile, girls."

"Girls!" Hazel chuckled then they all started. With arms gripped tightly around each other they laughed from sheer joy and Elaine looked happily at her screen again.

"Just perfect!" she declared.

acknowledgements

I found the process of editing this book a strange experience, quite different to any of my previous books. The edits for *The Family Inheritance* took place as the world was facing the COVID-19 challenge. For a writer, working from home is the norm, but as events unfolded it hit me that the story I was editing was possibly the last that would be untouched by the ramifications of this virus. Suddenly I saw everything my characters did through a different lens and I found myself saying well, that wouldn't happen, no shaking hands and hugging, no parties or large funerals, no planning cruise holidays, and the one that made me laugh out loud – Felicity forgetting the toilet paper and leaving it on the supermarket counter – definitely wouldn't have happened. I do hope by the time you are reading these notes that daily life has returned, not perhaps as we knew it, but in brighter and better ways.

The first seeds of this story were sewn several years ago. I was on tour with a different book and my tour guide and bookseller was Margie Arnold from Meg's Bookshop. On the road together 24/7 we had lots of chats! When the ideas for *The Family Inheritance*

465

were finally in place, I realised I'd need help with the legal aspects so once again I turned to friend and lawyer Kylie Mildwaters. I took my bare bones of an idea and we brainstormed scenarios. I went on to write the story and as you know writers never let the facts get in the way of a plot point so any variations on actual inheritance laws are my mistakes and not Kylie's.

There are many forms of inheritance and one of them is via genetics. In 1992 our family welcomed a new baby, my great-nephew, and through the heel prick test done at birth it was discovered this beautiful baby boy had cystic fibrosis. He looked perfect, still does, but this disease takes its toll on health as it affects the lungs and digestive system. From birth a person with CF undergoes constant medical treatment and physiotherapy. It's a stealthy disease, skipping generations until two parents who carry the gene have children and then it's a one in four chance that their offspring will have CF. I take my hat off to my nephew and the many people who live with CF. One in particular, Kerrie Taylor, has a cameo appearance in this book. Kerrie runs a fabulous upcycled jewellery business called Breathless Jewellery. You can find her shopfront on social media. If you'd like to know more about CF visit www.cysticfibrosis.org.au.

One quarter of Australians will experience an anxiety condition in their lifetime and I am sure the current pandemic and social isolation have increased that statistic dramatically. When I was writing Felicity's story I drew on my own experiences of extreme anxiety. At the time of my first attack I was in such pain I thought I was going to die. I am most grateful to those who helped me when I found it difficult to help myself. Everyone experiences anxiety from time to time but if that feeling doesn't go away the important thing to remember is you are not alone. Talk to someone you trust, seek professional help. It is possible to manage anxiety and live a normal (whatever that is) healthy, happy life. If you'd like more information beyondblue.org.au is a good place to start.

For help with some of the aviation elements in the book I turned to two friends, Scott Snodgrass and Tim Millard, one working in the industry and the other flying small planes. Thank you for casting your eye over some of the aviation elements in the story. You both know I like to change things up so while I appreciate your input I may have winged it in a few places.

Other writers are important bolsters and I am so lucky to be in touch with many who share their wisdom and support. I particularly want to thank Meredith Appleyard, Rachael Johns and Victoria Purman. It always helps to talk stories and writing life through with a fellow writer.

What a fabulous combined powerhouse make up the teams at Harlequin/HarperCollins who bring my books to you! My publisher, Jo Mackay, never ceases to encourage and extend my writing. In the case of this book I'm especially indebted to Jo – for the title! Most often the title of a story comes to me before I've written it but this time nothing was quite right. Jo came up with *The Family Inheritance,* which immediately seemed perfect. Thank you, Jo.

I love the editing process and am most grateful to my talented editor, Annabel Blay, for challenging and stretching me to make this story the best it could be. And for the laughs along the way, thank you. Thanks also to Laurie Ormond for casting your proofing eye over everything.

Big hurrah to Mark Campbell and the design team, Adam van Rooijen and the marketing team, Darren Kelly and the sales team, and to Sue Brockhoff, Natika Palka, Sarana Behan, Johanna Baker, Eloise Plant and the rest of the gang – you are all fabulous.

Thank you for making book number thirteen an extra special one.

Reading is one of life's greatest pleasures and I want to send a big thank you to all the sales reps, booksellers and librarians who have continued to ensure books reach the hands of readers. Even in the most difficult of times you've persevered, been even more innovative in spreading the word, created magic and kept morale high. The world is a better place because of your efforts.

And to you my dear readers, thank you for continuing to buy, borrow and share my books and for keeping in touch. I love to hear from you and particularly during this time of social isolating your emails and messages have been very much appreciated. There is another book well underway for you.

This book is dedicated to my niece Nerrilee. We're an eclectic mix, as I suspect most families are, and we don't all catch up often but when we do ... what fun it is. I also want to make a special mention of my dear Aunty Barbara who died this year at the grand age of almost ninety-five. One of my biggest supporters to the end who will live on in our hearts and through the legacy of her famous pink jelly cakes. I spend a lot of time alone but family are never far from my thoughts. In particular my husband, Daryl, and our brood, Kelly, Steven, Harry, Archie, Dylan, Sian, Jared and Alexandra, are always ready to help, support and encourage, doing their bit to keep me motivated and grounded. You're *my* team and I love you to the beach and back.

Turn over for a sneak peek.

birds *of a* feather

by

TRICIA STRINGER

Available October 2021

one

Eve Monk would never forget where she was and what she was doing the day she got the call to say her husband had been killed. She'd been packing the car, the bright orange Torana she and Rex had bought just after they were married. It was sixteen years old and Rex had bought several cars since but she loved the Torana. All that morning she'd been loading it with as many of the boys' things as she could fit, along with a few items of her own. She'd gone back inside to get the washing basket from the laundry. It was full of dirty clothes but they were mostly school uniforms and the boys would need them.

The phone was ringing at the other end of the house. She hesitated, not wanting to answer, but she always worried it would be the school. There'd been plenty of calls from both her sons' teachers over the last two years. No doubt after today they'd pick up in frequency again but it couldn't be helped.

"Eve!" A voice bellowed at her down the line.

"Spiro?" Her heart skipped a beat at the sound of her friend and business partner's voice. The trawlers had only gone out the previous night for the first fish of the season. She wasn't expecting them back for a few days. She glanced at the sky through the big kitchen window. There was no sign of bad weather.

"What's up?" She tried to keep the panic from her voice. She wasn't ready to face Rex. She'd hoped to have time to talk to the boys, explain why they were leaving their father and settle them in to their alternate accommodation before he returned.

"Eve," Spiro said again, this time more a moan followed by a shuddering sob. "Eve, I'm so sorry."

"Why? What's happened?"

"There's been an accident."

"Are you all right?"

"Yes."

"The boat?"

"It's fine. It's … Eve, it's Rex."

"Rex?" But Rex was invincible, always escaping harm although often creating it for others.

"We had some trouble with the winch and it fell. Eve, I'm so sorry. Rex was under it. The full force hit him on the head. There was nothing we could do."

Eve sagged to the stool beside the kitchen bench. "Are you telling me …"

"He's dead, Eve."

"Rex is dead?" The anger that had fuelled her mad packing spree all morning trickled from her as if she were a sieve full of holes, leaving behind tiny grains of sorrow bumping against the numbness inside her.

"We're over the other side of the gulf. The police are coming."

Spiro's voice went on and on but Eve could only hear the loud rushing sound in her head. Then Spiro was saying her name again.

"Eve? They're here. I have to go. I'll call you back soon."

"Okay."

"Should I phone Pam? You shouldn't be alone."

"I'll be okay." She ended the call and hung the phone back on the hook. Then reached for it again. She'd have to call Rex's parents. Their only son, their pride and joy … they'd be inconsolable. She put the phone back. Not yet. She had to give herself a moment.

Today she'd finally made up her mind to leave her duplicitous husband but instead he'd left her. A strange sensation burbled deep inside her and rose up. She clapped a hand to her mouth but the force of it was too strong, squeezing between her fingers and erupting – a crazy cackling noise. She took a deep breath and forced herself to be calm.

Spiro had said something about a winch falling. Had he given her more detail? She hadn't heard everything. Once more she reached for the phone and once more she stopped. She had no idea where Spiro had been calling from.

She looked around the kitchen. The old navy jumper Rex wore around home was draped over the back of his chair and a packet of his cigarettes lay on the desk among piles of papers and envelopes. A bottle of rakija sat on the bench. A sticky ring remained beside it. He'd overfilled her glass and she'd had to lean down and suck up the first mouthful. Little signs of Rex were everywhere. Before Spiro's phone call she'd been stoically ignoring them, avoiding Rex's things and grabbing as much of hers and the boys as she could. She'd wanted to be gone, well before he returned.

She hadn't been moving far away, just to a friend's beach shack, a temporary stopgap until she could sort things out with Rex. It was the washing that had finally done it. After the boys had gone to school she'd begun the mountain of washing that had been languishing around the house. She'd do anything needed if it related to their prawn fishing business but housework bored her. When she'd come to the pile of shorts and jeans she'd carefully emptied pockets. Arlo often had paper folded in his, covered in his scribbled diagrams and workings out, and Zac had his usual assortment of string, empty lolly wrappers and a plastic fishing float.

It was what she'd found in Rex's pockets that had sent her head spinning and her heart thudding. In one was a crumpled receipt from a motel in a town further up the coast. The date was from two nights earlier. The night he'd said he was spending on the trawler, getting it ready for the start of the season. He'd paid cash. And in the other pocket was a set of earrings wrapped in a scrap of paper. They were gold loop earrings for pierced ears. Eve didn't have pierced ears. There was a phone number scrawled across the paper. She dialled the number. A woman answered. Eve gasped.

"Hello?" The woman said again.

"Who is this?" Eve asked but in her heart she already knew.

"Eve?" The voice was little more than a whisper now.

Eve dropped the phone back on its cradle. Bile rose in her throat as she ripped the paper to tiny shreds.

Then she'd gone to their bedroom and started pulling things out of his drawers. Tucked at the back of one she found a box of condoms, open, with several missing. Eve had had her tubes tied a few years after Zac was born. They never used condoms.

All of the horror of two years prior had come rushing back.

The discovery that Rex had had an affair then had nearly destroyed her. The town had buzzed with gossip. The woman had been the wife of a local businessman, and friendships and families had been blown apart as everyone took a side. Rex had sworn it was a mistake and he'd never do it again. He'd begged Eve to take him back. Spiro had stood by them both, not taking sides but making it clear to Rex what a fool he was and to Eve that he would support whatever decision she made. The woman had left town and in the end Eve had stayed with Rex. They had two sons and a business together. She wasn't giving it up easily.

Time had eased her pain and she'd almost felt like they were a proper family again. Three nights ago they'd toasted the success of the new prawn season with two glasses of rakija. Rex's enthusiasm for the fishing season ahead had been infectious – his fervent mood had warmed her as much as the alcohol. They'd talked and laughed together and taken to their bed like young lovers. And the next night he'd been with someone else.

Discovering fresh signs of deception, realising he'd been with another woman, and who knew how often – it was too much. Eve felt old beyond her thirty-seven years. Already she was building another wall around her heart, cocooning herself from the hurt of his betrayal. It came easily, probably because deep down she'd never truly forgiven him.

But none of it mattered now, she realised. Rex was gone, and with any luck this latest treachery would be buried with him. Eve thought of Arlo and Zac and her heart ached. She had to protect them. It was bad enough they'd lost their father – at least they wouldn't know about this latest affair. They had good friends to see them through. Her best friends, Pam and Eric Paterson and Gert and Tom Belling, had stood by her last time and would help her again. Their children were all friends. Pam's two, Heath and Julia, and Eve's boys were especially close. She knew Heath looked out for Arlo and Julia did her best to stop Zac spending too much time alone.

Eve rose from the stool and quickly sank back to it as her legs refused to support her. Her heart thudded in her chest. She sucked in a breath and then another as her lungs screamed for more. Her fingers gripped the edge of the stool and she forced herself to take deep, slow breaths. She'd felt like this after Rex's first affair too, but she couldn't afford to panic now.

The desk caught her attention and she focused on it like a lost traveller would a light in the dark. Built into a nook off the kitchen, it was their office. Beside it was the filing cabinet, one drawer half open and a pile of files stacked on top of it. Rex had a life insurance policy. She slapped her hand over her mouth as the realisation hit – Rex was dead and suddenly her financial situation was stronger than if she'd left him.

Between the insurance and the fishing she could continue to support her family financially. Eve did the books, the cooking for the crew, mended nets and generally filled any role needed. That could continue. They'd have to employ someone to take Rex's place. The measured deep breaths had succeeded in slowing her racing heart. Panic was useless. She had to think of her boys and their future.

She dragged herself from the stool and went back to her bedroom. She paused at the door, seeing the jumble she'd created – first from digging through Rex's things, and then the chaos she'd left as she'd wrenched her own clothes from the cupboards. Her lips trembled at the sight of his belongings strewn around. She'd been so angry, yet a small part of her had hoped if she left him he'd come to his senses, want her back, work harder to make them a family again. Now that could never happen. Rex was never coming home. Tears brimmed in her eyes. She stiffened and batted them away. What good were tears? She'd cried enough of them over Rex. She had to be strong now, for her boys and for the business that was their future.

Eve swallowed the lump in her throat and lifted her chin. She strode forward, tidied the mess and tossed the condoms in the bin. Then she unpacked the car, put everything back where it had been and, instead of preparing to tell her sons they were leaving their father, she prepared to tell them he was dead.

two

Present day

Every Thursday morning Eve drove her Holden Torana coupe into Wallaby Bay. She parked it in the shade of the massive pines on the edge of the supermarket carpark and walked the length of the street to do her jobs. Because she did it at the same time each week, she knew who she would and wouldn't meet. She always called at the post office first, to check her mailbox and pay bills, and the supermarket last, so that her dairy and meat items would remain cool in the esky for the ten-minute journey home. Not that the temperature was a worry today. The first week of June had been cold, a sudden prelude to the winter that was to come.

In between the post office and the supermarket, Eve stopped at the newsagency to buy the local paper. Terry, who only worked behind the counter on Thursdays and was a Holden buff, asked her if she wanted to sell her car, as always.

She popped in at the hairdresser to say hello – her tight curls were trimmed every six weeks on a Tuesday so it was purely a social call. Moira was halfway through an intricate updo for a young woman Eve didn't know. Eve asked, but there was no special occasion, the woman said, and then Moira had given her a quick rundown on the previous evening's local business meeting. Apparently there was a stalemate on what kind of plants should be put in the new garden boxes the council had installed along the street. Half the meeting wanted shrubs that would only need water and the odd prune, the rest wanted colourful annuals to brighten up the street. A decision hadn't been reached.

She stepped quickly past the op shop, keeping her gaze strictly ahead. There'd been a time when she'd loved to search through, looking for the treasures that could be found among someone else's cast-offs, but not now. She just had time to visit the fruit and veg shop before the she met Gert. She loved the way Franco nestled her apples and pears gently into her basket as if they were eggs being placed in a nest. Her last stop on the main street would be the cafe to get a takeaway coffee.

Once a year she visited her husband's grave on his birthday but that wasn't today. Today she was meeting Gert at their mutual friend Pam Paterson's graveside. It was the anniversary of Pam's death and Gert and Eve always met at the grave on this date, and again on Pam's birthday, to fill their friend in on local goings-on.

Eve was running behind schedule when she whipped into the Cinnamon Bark Cafe at the end of the main street. She had a quick chat to Dale and Brent who ran the cafe, more planter box discussions – they were on the side of colourful annuals. They made her coffee to take away and as she turned to go two women entered. They both paused, looked from Eve to each other.

Eve drew herself up, annoyed at the sudden race of her heart. "Audrey, Norma," she said with a nod as she strode towards the door.

Audrey stepped into Eve's path. Her finely plucked and pencilled eyebrows shot up to meet her lacquered fringe. "What are you doing here?"

"Buying a coffee. I believe anyone can."

"Well! There's no need for that tone," Norma muttered.

Audrey put a hand on Norma's arm and turned her sharp gaze back to Eve. "Haven't seen you about in a long time."

"I'm still here."

"Not coming back to help at the museum again?"

"Not likely."

"We won't hold you up then."

Eve stood her ground. She wasn't about to be dismissed by Audrey Owens. "What's happening with the prawn industry display?"

"No agreement has been reached about that."

"I wonder why?"

Audrey's look turned hawk-like. "Withdrawing your donation has slowed things, but others will come on board."

"No-one else in the industry will make a donation unless a proper plan is developed."

"Unless you allow them to, you mean."

"Each business is their own master, Audrey."

Norma sniffed her displeasure but Audrey's lips turned up in a cat-that-got-the-cream smile.

"That's so true," she said. "I suppose you've heard about Chrissie's engagement."

"No." Eve swallowed the why-would-she-care retort that sprung to her lips. She felt sorry for whoever was going to get

Audrey as a mother-in-law. Rumour had it that her other two sons-in-law danced to her tune. But of course Eve wasn't one to listen to gossip.

"Nicholas Colston." Audrey was beaming now and Eve could understand why. The Colstons were based in Port Lincoln. Ralph Colston was another pioneer of the local prawn industry. Three generations of the family helped manage their extensive fishing business. Audrey's youngest daughter was marrying into fishing royalty.

"Please give them my congratulations."

"Oh, the queen is giving her blessing, is she?" Sarcasm dripped from Audrey's tongue, her smile gone. "You've had your say for too long, Eve Monk. Your influence is on the way out."

Eve's cheeks warmed and her heart picked up speed again. She was aware that the tinkle-clink of cutlery on crockery and the mumbled conversations around them had stopped.

"Is everything all right here?" Dale had left the counter to stand beside them.

The cafe was almost silent and Eve felt the collective gaze of those seated around her press close, an invisible wall of condemnation. A horrible feeling of deja vu swept over her.

"It's fine," she said and strode outside.

She could hear Norma's complaining voice start up before the door even closed behind her.

"That was unfortunate," Eve muttered.

A young bloke gave her a strange look as he passed. She forced a smile to her lips.

Damn! Eve hurried across the road. Of all people to run into. It wasn't Audrey so much as the people observing that bothered her. She blew out a breath, adjusted her grip on her coffee and made her way back to her car. The adrenaline that had charged round her body was ebbing, leaving her hand shaky as she searched for her keys.

It hadn't always been like that with Audrey. While they weren't friends, Wallaby Bay was a small town and over the years they'd managed to move in different circles. Eve's volunteering had been devoted to the school council, the women's and children's hospital auxiliary, the hockey club and Meals on Wheels, while Audrey, with three daughters, had spent her time at netball and callisthenics. They had different friends and interest groups. And on the rare occasions they found themselves in the same place they had tolerated each other.

That was up until the previous year when Audrey had joined the local museum committee, a committee that Eve had held various positions on for over twenty years. Audrey's presence and interference had been difficult enough but then there'd been Audrey's unfortunate accident. Time might patch old hurts but in Eve's case they had never truly healed.

She reached the cemetery, determined to put today's confrontation with Audrey from her mind. There were better people to devote her time to. She drove right in and parked at the end of the row. Gert was already there. Eve took out her small folding chair and sat it next to her friend.

Gert had a few years on Eve's seventy but they and Pam had all arrived in the district in the late sixties, new teachers at their first postings or, in Gert's case, second. The three of them had married local men, seen each other through life's highs and lows. They were all widowed now; Pam and Eve both years ago and Gert only last year.

"You're early." Eve said as soon as she was settled. "Or am I late?"

"I visited Tom first," Gert said.

"How is he?"

"Much the same." Gert managed a smile that almost broke Eve's heart. Grief had taken its toll on her friend.

"No more suffering," Eve said softly.

"No more suffering," Gert echoed.

They both looked down at the headstone in front of them.

"We're here for a chat, Pam." Eve rested her flowers next to a small bunch of Gert's home-grown chrysanthemums.

Gert lifted her coffee in the air. Hers was in a proper china mug she'd poured from the thermos at her feet. Eve tapped her cardboard takeaway cup against it.

"Cheers." They both took sips then settled back in their chairs and chatted as old friends do, about family and mutual acquaintances and the last prawn run for the season, and ended up discussing the flower boxes in the main street.

"I wish they'd put a few out here," Gert said. The wind-swept expanse of the cemetery was barren of colour except for whatever people put on the graves, which often blew away, sometimes arriving back at the cemetery gate before the person who'd delivered them. At the moment, though, the breeze was gentle.

"It is a bit bleak." Eve looked across at the monolith marking Rex's grave. His parents had wanted it and now they were buried in equally grand fashion beside him. "I want my ashes to be scattered at sea."

"But then there's nowhere for your friends and family to visit."

"My family aren't here and I don't imagine anyone but you would visit me. By the time I go you'll be too doddery to come out here."

Gert huffed. "I visit Tom every week."

"He was a good man." Eve said. She'd certainly not wasted her life visiting her husband's grave every week. Her friends Gert and Pam had drawn the long straws with the men they'd married.

They sat in silence for a moment. Eve had thought to tell her story of running into Audrey – a hurt shared with an old friend would ease it – but Gert spoke first.

"I need to head off." She stood. "I've got a hair appointment in twenty minutes."

"No need to rush then." The cemetery was a five-minute drive from Moira's.

"I've changed hairdressers."

"Really?" Moira had been their hairdresser since she'd opened her salon at least twenty years ago.

"Don't give me that face, Evelyn."

"I'm not making a face." Eve's tone had risen a notch. Gert only called her Evelyn when she was taking her to task and that was becoming more common lately.

"Moira doesn't listen to what I say. I'm trying someone new and I don't want to be late."

Gert's fine silver hair had thinned in the last few years and the previous month Moira had suggested a pixie cut. Eve had thought it looked great, very Judi Dench–like, to which Gert had retorted she wasn't that old yet. Eve glanced at her friend. Her hair had a bit more growing to do if she wanted a different style.

"I'll call in tomorrow and see how you got on." Eve smiled.

"I'm going to Adelaide first thing."

"Are you?"

"It's the baby's first birthday. There's a big party planned." Gert said. "I'm sure I told you."

"Maybe."

Gert's two sons and their families lived in Adelaide. Between them they'd produced five children who ranged in age from the baby turning one to ten-year-old twins. Eve had always envied their proximity. She had one son in Darwin and the other in Singapore. They were good at keeping in touch but for all the information she got via the video calls with her teenage grandchildren, she may as well have been talking in a foreign language. She sighed. Perhaps she was.

"How about early next week?" Eve said.

"I'm not sure which day I'll be back."

"Coffee on Thursday then?"

"Yes."

"We'll meet at the Cutty Sark. Let's write it down."

Gert sniffed. "I don't need to write it down."

Eve drew her phone from her bag. "I record every appointment on here these days. It even sends me reminders."

"There's nothing wrong with my memory." Gert pinned Eve with a glare that dared her to say otherwise.

"I'll see you next week then." Eve's smile was a forced response to Gert's sharp nod. "Say hello to the family," she called as Gert strode towards her car. Never mind Judi Dench – with Gert dressed in a knee-length coat and sensible walking shoes, her chair in one hand and a large handbag in the other, she only needed a scarf on her head or a corgi at her side and she could have been a younger Queen Elizabeth.

Eve turned back to Pam's grave as Gert drove away. "Wish you were still here, dear friend. We're getting old, Gert and I. Perhaps I'd feel less ancient with you beside me." A little barb of sorrow jabbed inside her. She didn't miss her husband but there was still an empty space in her heart for Pam. And even though she'd been gone for years, recently the space had become bigger. She longed for Pam's gung-ho attitude and wise counsel.

"I'm worried about Gert. I know she's lost Tom but it's more than that. Something's not right and I can't put my finger on it. Oh, and I ran into Audrey and Norma on my way here. Still no change on the museum committee and Audrey's ridiculous ideas. That despicable woman continues to thwart me."

Two vehicles pulled up outside the cemetery. Doors banged and voices carried as a group of people made their way through the gates. Eve packed up her things. There were already enough stories about her without adding talking to dead friends.

On the short drive back to the shops and all the way around the supermarket, Eve tested the tiny festering hurt that Gert's abruptness had caused. Had she always been that way and Eve hadn't noticed it, or was it a change brought on by the weight of being a full-time carer and then losing her husband?

Eve couldn't pinpoint when the changes had begun but she did remember the first time Gert had snapped at her. It was when Tom hadn't long been housebound. One of their sons had come up from Adelaide to spend a few days doing maintenance jobs around the house and keep his dad company. Eve had suggested she and Gert go out for lunch and a movie. She couldn't remember what they'd seen but she did remember shouting Gert lunch at the pub and then Gert being annoyed because she'd been served the wrong dish. She'd insisted she'd wanted chicken with bechamel sauce. Eve had been surprised when Gert had changed her mind and agreed to the special the waitress had recited. That had been chicken schnitzel with parmigiana sauce and the added extra of pulled pork, caramelised onion, cheese and BBQ sauce. They'd both groaned at the sight of it piled high on the plate.

"What is that?" Gert had exclaimed.

"The chicken special."

"It's not what the girl said." The young waitress had spent a lot of time explaining the menu items before the two women had settled on what they wanted and Eve had gone to the bar to order it.

"Yes it was."

Gert had drawn herself up and glared at Eve. "I know what she said and this is not chicken bechamel. You ordered the wrong thing."

Eve had felt terrible. In all their years of friendship they'd hardly had a cross word let alone berated each other so sharply. Eve had apologised, although she hadn't felt she'd needed to. After all, she'd bought the lunch Gert had asked for. Gert had pursed her lips and eyed the mountain of food. "It's too much," she'd groaned.

Eve had suggested cutting the meal in half and sliding it onto another plate. Gert's good humour had returned and the rest of the day had gone smoothly.

By the time Eve pulled into her driveway she was stewing over the several times recently that Gert had berated her over something small that had escalated to something big. The knot inside her made her feel as if she'd rather not meet Gert for coffee, but it was a whole week away, and a silly misunderstanding was not something to dispel fifty years of friendship.

The wind that often came up the hill from the bay had strengthened and was tossing the bushes in her garden as she walked the path from the garage to her home, shopping bags dragging at both her arms. Eve looked up at the weathervane at the top of the post in the middle of the yard. In the shape of a snapper, it pointed steadily south-west. She followed the direction of its snout, over the shrubs of her side garden, to the bay where white caps ruffled the deep blue water. The two prawn trawlers she and Spiro owned were safely moored at a pontoon in the marina so the wind wouldn't bother them.

Her gaze swept on along the shoreline. White sand edged the shallow water, which was a pretty turquoise colour today, and then beyond where the houses clung to the curve until the groin of the marina, the higher structures of the silos and then the wharf that pointed its long arm out into the bay. She never tired of this view.

The old house had been run-down when Rex had insisted they buy it. She'd wanted to live in town but he'd been in love with the property and she'd soon come to his way of thinking. Their business had done well enough for them to renovate, keeping the wonderful bones of the original building but with a more practical internal layout that made better use of the view.

Eve adjusted her handbag on her shoulder and moved on until she was protected from the breeze on the vast iron-roofed verandah. She reached for the screen door. As she gripped the handle and tugged the bag full of food swung forward. The bottom of the door usually caught on the wooden doorstep but today it leaped open, her arm flung wide with it, and the combined weight of her bag and the shopping propelled her arm backwards. She gasped as a sharp pain jagged her shoulder.

"Damn!"

She dropped the shopping bag and clasped her shoulder until the pain eased. Taking a deep breath, she went inside with the first load and then back for the bag by the door.

"Should have made two trips from the car," she muttered and avoided using her right arm as she unpacked her shopping.

She turned her thoughts to the dinner she was planning for tomorrow night. She'd bought some herb-and-camembert-stuffed chicken rolls. Spiro and Mary were bringing a prawn dish for entree and Eve had also bought the ingredients to make a cheese-cake for dessert. She managed very well on her own, but it was always good to have something to look forward to.

By the time she'd put everything away, the pain in her shoulder was only a dull ache. She glanced at the bottle of rakija on the bench then at the clock. It was a little early for her nightly glass.

"Wine!" She clapped a hand to her forehead. She'd meant to buy wine while she was in town. She swept her keys from the bench and grimaced as her shoulder complained at the movement. She gave it a rub and headed for the door. More than anything she hated the waste of time and fuel in making two trips to town but it was better she went back today. She wanted to leave tomorrow free to prepare for her dinner guests. She always had stocks of rakija, the fruity brandy she had learned to enjoy when she had first met Rex. Spiro had introduced the potent drink to him and they'd delighted in initiating Eve but Mary had never liked it and preferred a light red wine. Something told Eve her dinner guests weren't coming purely for a social outing and she wanted to be on the front foot.

 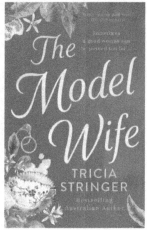

BESTSELLING AUSTRALIAN AUTHOR

TRICIA STRINGER

*Warm-hearted rural romance
from the voice of Australian storytelling.*

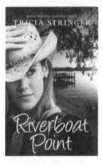

talk about it

Let's talk about books.

Join the conversation:

 facebook.com/harlequinaustralia

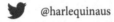 @harlequinaus

 @harlequinaus

harpercollins.com.au/hq

If you love reading and want to know about our
authors and titles, then let's talk about it.